THE LEGEND OF SLEEPY HOLLOW

& OTHER MACABRE TALES

THE LEGEND OF SLEEPY HOLLOW & OTHER MACABRE TALES

WASHINGTON IRVING

FALL RIVER PRESS

This 2010 edition published by Fall River Press.

Book design by Michele Trombley

Fall River Press
122 Fifth Avenue
New York, NY 10011

ISBN: 978-1-4351-2505-6

Printed and bound in the United States of America

1 3 5 7 9 10 8 6 4 2

CONTENTS

Introduction   VI

Rip Van Winkle   1

The Spectre Bridegroom   20

The Legend of Sleepy Hollow   38

Strange Stories by a Nervous Gentleman   73

    THE HUNTING DINNER   75

    THE ADVENTURE OF MY UNCLE   80

    THE ADVENTURE OF MY AUNT   93

    THE BOLD DRAGOON   99

    THE ADVENTURE OF THE GERMAN STUDENT   109

    THE ADVENTURE OF THE MYSTERIOUS PICTURE 116

    THE ADVENTURE OF THE MYSTERIOUS STRANGER 125

    THE STORY OF THE YOUNG ITALIAN   134

The Devil and Tom Walker   165

Wolfert Webber or, Golden Dreams   180

    THE ADVENTURE OF THE BLACK FISHERMAN   205

Guests from Gibbet Island   239

Legend of the Two Discreet Statues   253

The Grand Prior of Minorca   272

Don Juan: A Spectral Research   289

Legend of the Engulphed Convent   300

The Enchanted Island   306

    THE ADELANTADO OF THE SEVEN CITIES   309

INTRODUCTION

The stories of Washington Irving have been entertaining readers for nearly two centuries and several are standards in the American literary canon. Yet for every reader who is familiar with his fantasy classics "Rip Van Winkle" and "The Legend of Sleepy Hollow," scores are unaware that Irving wrote enough fantastic tales to fill a full volume. Fewer still are aware of the significance these stories have in the history of American literature. Not only was Irving one of the earliest American writers of fiction, he was a pioneer of the short story as a literary form. Many of his fantasy tales—which represent about half of his short fiction output—feature American settings, and were instrumental for establishing the history and folklore of the newly formed United States as raw materials with the same creative potential as their European counterparts.

Irving was born in 1783, five days before the end of the Revolutionary War. He showed an aptitude for writing early in his life, but initially fit it around work experience as a lawyer, a soldier, and a businessman. His first two published works of note, the satirical *Salmagundi* papers and *A History of New York*, both of which appeared under the pseudonym Diedrich Knickerbocker, established his reputation as a humorist. With *The Sketch Book*, which was published in parts between 1819 and 1820 before being collected as a single volume, Irving earned renown as a writer with a fine eye for the local color of his native land, particular the Hudson River Valley of New York state.

The stories in this volume are selected from four primary collections of Irving's work. *The Sketch Book*, whose contents were attributed to yet another Irving pseudonym, Geoffrey Crayon, originated "Rip Van Winkle," "The Legend of Sleepy Hollow," and "The Spectre Bridegroom." The latter, like "The Adventure of the German Student," from *Tales of a Traveller* (1824), is an example of the European Gothic tradition from which Irving strove to distance his work. Both "Rip Van Winkle" and "The Legend of Sleepy Hollow" took their inspiration from German folktales, but Irving made them quintessentially American stories by rooting them in colonial settings shaped by the history and superstitions of New York's Dutch settlers. Furthermore, he softened their supernaturalism with his trademark humor so that they read more like tall tales than serious evocations of the uncanny.

In *Tales of a Traveller*, Irving grouped stories into four cycles whose individual components build on one another. The first of these, "Strange Stories of a Nervous Gentleman," were written as counterpoint to "The Stout Gentleman," a fanciful sketch narrated by the same "nervous gentleman" in Irving's miscellany *Bracebridge Hall* (1822). The stories present a mélange of motifs and themes common to tales told by the fireside, and it is not surprising that the two best known, "The Adventure of the German Student" and The Bold Dragoon," are the most overtly supernatural. The book's fourth and concluding cycle, "The Money Diggers," includes "The Devil and Tom Walker," a story that provides the template for many deal-with-the-devil stories written by other authors since, and "Wolfert Webber or, Golden Dreams." Like "Guests from Gibbet Island," selected from *Chronicles of Wolfert's Roost and Other Papers*

(1855), these stories are among the earliest to weave American folk legends around the larger-than-life exploits of the notorious pirate Captain Kidd and the hunt for his treasure.

Irving had lived in Spain between 1826 and 1829, and briefly resided in the Moorish palace known as the Alhambra. His volume *The Alhambra* (1832), represented here by "Legend of the Two Discreet Statues," collected a number of Spanish folktales he had uncovered during his residence and re-told in the tradition of *The Arabian Nights*. Like the continental tales that dominate *Chronicles of Wolfert's Roost*—in particular the story-within-a-story, "The Adelantado of the Seven Cities," and its variation on the theme of "Rip Van Winkle"—they can be read as Irving's reimagining of classic continental legends. Filtered through a fancy that did not discriminate between European or American sources, they transcend their national origins to stand, like all the stories in this volume, as extraordinary contributions to world literature.

—Michael Kelahan
New York, 2010

RIP VAN WINKLE

By Woden, God of Saxons,
From whence comes Wensday, that is Wodensday,
Truth is a thing that ever I will keep
Unto thylke day in which I creep into
My sepulchre—

CARTWRIGHT

Whoever has made a voyage up the Hudson must remember the Kaatskill mountains. They are a dismembered branch of the great Appalachian family, and are seen away to the west of the river, swelling up to a noble height, and lording it over the surrounding country. Every change of season, every change of weather, indeed, every hour of the day produces some change in the magical hues and shapes of these mountains; and they are regarded by all the good wives, far and near, as perfect barometers. When the weather is fair and settled, they are clothed in blue and purple, and print their bold outlines on the clear evening sky; but sometimes, when the rest of the landscape is cloudless, they will gather a hood of gray vapors about their summits, which, in the last rays of the setting sun, will glow and light up like a crown of glory.

At the foot of these fairy mountains, the voyager may have descried the light smoke curling up from a village, whose shingle roofs gleam among the trees, just where the blue tints of the upland melt away into the fresh green of the nearer landscape. It is a little village of great antiquity, having been founded by some of the Dutch colonists, in the early times of the province, just about the beginning of the government of the good Peter Stuyvesant (may he rest in peace!), and there were some of the houses of the original settlers standing within a few years, built of small yellow bricks, brought from Holland, having latticed windows and gable fronts, surmounted with weathercocks.

In that same village, and in one of these very houses (which, to tell the precise truth, was sadly time-worn and weather-beaten) there lived many years since, while the country was yet a province of Great Britain, a simple, good natured fellow of the name of Rip Van Winkle. He was a descendant of the Van Winkles who figured so gallantly in the chivalrous days of Peter Stuyvesant, and accompanied him to the siege of Fort Christina. He inherited, however, but little of the martial character of his ancestors. I have observed that he was a simple good natured man; he was moreover a kind neighbour, and an obedient henpecked husband. Indeed, to the latter circumstance might be owing that meekness of spirit which gained him such universal popularity; for those men are apt to be obsequious and conciliating abroad, who are under the discipline of shrews at home. Their tempers doubtless are rendered pliant and malleable in the fiery furnace of domestic tribulation, and a curtain lecture is worth all the sermons in the world for teaching the virtues of patience and long-suffering. A termagant wife may, therefore, in some respects, be considered a tolerable blessing—and if so, Rip Van Winkle was thrice blessed.

Certain it is, that he was a great favourite among all the good wives of the village, who as usual with the amiable sex, took his part in all family squabbles, and never failed, whenever they talked those matters over in their evening gossippings, to lay all the blame on Dame Van Winkle. The children of the village too would shout with joy whenever he approached. He assisted at their sports, made their play things, taught them to fly kites and shoot marbles, and told them long stories of ghosts, witches, and Indians. Whenever he went dodging about the village he was surrounded by a troop of them hanging on his skirts, clambering on his back, and playing a thousand tricks on him with impunity; and not a dog would bark at him throughout the neighbourhood.

The great error in Rip's composition was an insuperable aversion to all kinds of profitable labour. It could not be for want of assiduity or perseverance; for he would sit on a wet rock, with a rod as long and heavy as a Tartar's lance, and fish all day without a murmur, even though he should not be encouraged by a single nibble. He would carry a fowling piece on his shoulder for hours together, trudging through woods and swamps, and up hill and down dale, to shoot a few squirrels or wild pigeons. He would never refuse to assist a neighbour even in the roughest toil, and was a foremost man in all country frolicks for husking Indian corn, or building stone fences; the women of the village too used to employ him to run their errands and to do such little odd jobs as their less obliging husbands would not do for them—in a word Rip was ready to attend to anybody's business but his own; but as to doing family duty, and keeping his farm in order, he found it impossible.

In fact he declared it was of no use to work on his farm; it was the most pestilent little piece of ground in the whole country; every thing about it went wrong, in spite of him. His fences were continually falling to pieces; his cow would either go astray, or get among the cabbages, weeds were sure to grow quicker in his fields than any where else, the rain always made a point of setting in just as he had some out-door work to do. So that though his patrimonial estate had dwindled away under his management, acre by acre until there was little more left than a mere patch of Indian corn and potatoes, yet it was the worst-conditioned farm in the neighbourhood.

His children too were as ragged and wild as if they belonged to nobody. His son Rip, an urchin begotten in his own likeness, promised to inherit the habits with the old clothes of his father. He was generally seen trooping like a colt at his mother's heels, equipped in a pair of his father's cast off galligaskins, which he had much ado to hold up with one hand, as a fine lady does her train in bad weather.

Rip Van Winkle, however, was one of those happy mortals, of foolish, well oiled dispositions, who take the world easy, eat white bread or brown, whichever can be got with least thought or trouble, and would rather starve on a penny than work for a pound. If left to himself, he would have whistled life away in perfect contentment, but his wife kept continually dinning in his ears about his idleness, his carelessness and the ruin he was bringing on his family. Morning noon and night her tongue was incessantly going, and every thing he said or did was sure to produce a torrent of household eloquence. Rip had but one way of replying to all lectures of the kind, and that by frequent use had grown into a habit. He shrugged his shoulders, shook his head, cast up his eyes, but said nothing. This, however, always provoked a fresh volley from his wife, so that he was fain to draw off his forces and take to the outside of the house—the only side which, in truth, belongs to a henpecked husband.

Rip's sole domestic adherent was his dog Wolf who was as much henpecked as his master, for Dame Van Winkle regarded them as companions in idleness, and even looked upon Wolf with an evil eye as the cause of his master's going so often astray. True it is, in all points of spirit befitting in honourable dog, he was as courageous an animal as ever scoured the woods—but what courage can withstand the evil-doing and all-besetting terrors of a woman's tongue? The moment Wolf entered the house his crest fell, his tail drooped to the ground or curled between his legs, he sneaked about with a gallows air, casting many a sidelong glance at Dame Van Winkle, and at the least flourish of a broomstick or ladle, he would fly to the door with yelping precipitation.

Times grew worse and worse with Rip Van Winkle as years of matrimony rolled on; a tart temper never mellows with age, and a sharp tongue is the only edged tool that grows keener with constant use. For a long while he used to console himself when driven from home, by frequenting a kind of perpetual club of the sages, philosophers, and other idle personages of the village, which held its sessions on a bench before a small inn, designated by a rubicund portrait of his majesty George the Third. Here they used to sit in the shade through a long lazy summer's day, talking listlessly over village gossip, or telling endless sleepy stories about nothing. But it would have been worth any statesman's money to have heard the profound discussions which sometimes took place, when by chance an old newspaper fell into their hands from some passing traveller. How solemnly they would listen to the contents as drawled out by Derrick Van Bummel the schoolmaster, a dapper, learned little man, who was not to be daunted by the most gigantic word in the dictionary; and how sagely they would deliberate upon public events some months after they had taken place.

The opinions of this junto were completely controlled by Nicholaus Vedder, a patriarch of the village, and landlord of the inn, at the door of which he took his seat from morning till night, just moving sufficiently to avoid the sun and keep in the shade of a large tree;

so that the neighbours could tell the hour by his movements as accurately as by a sun dial. It is true he was rarely heard to speak, but smoked his pipe incessantly. His adherents, however (for every great man has his adherents), perfectly understood him and knew how to gather his opinions. When any thing that was read or related displeased him, he was observed to smoke his pipe vehemently, and to send forth short, frequent, and angry puffs; but when pleased he would inhale the smoke slowly and tranquilly and emit it in light and placid clouds, and sometimes taking the pipe from his mouth and letting the fragrant vapor curl about his nose, would gravely nod his head in token of perfect approbation.

From even this strong hold the unlucky Rip was at length routed by his termagant wife, who would suddenly break in upon the tranquillity of the assemblage, and call the members all to naught; nor was that august personage Nicholaus Vedder himself, sacred from the daring tongue of this terrible virago, who charged him outright with encouraging her husband in habits of idleness.

Poor Rip was at last reduced almost to despair; and his only alternative, to escape from the labour of the farm and the clamour of his wife, was to take gun in hand, and stroll away into the woods. Here he would sometimes seat himself at the foot of a tree and share the contents of his wallet with Wolf, with whom he sympathized as a fellow sufferer in persecution. "Poor Wolf," he would say, "thy mistress leads thee a dog's life of it; but never mind my lad, whilst I live thou shalt never want a friend to stand by thee!" Wolf would wag his tail, look wistfully in his master's face, and if dogs can feel pity, I verily believe he reciprocated the sentiment with all his heart.

In a long ramble of the kind, on a fine autumnal day, Rip had unconsciously scrambled to one of the highest parts of the Kaatskill mountains. He was after his favourite sport of squirrel shooting and the still solitudes had echoed and re-echoed with the reports of his gun. Panting and fatigued he threw himself, late in the afternoon, on a green knoll, covered with mountain herbage, that crowned the brow of a precipice. From an opening between the trees he could overlook all the lower country for many a mile of rich woodland. He saw at a distance the lordly Hudson, far, far below him, moving on its silent but majestic course, with the reflection of a purple cloud, or the sail of a lagging bark here and there sleeping on its glassy bosom and at last losing itself in the blue highlands.

On the other side he looked down into a deep mountain glen, wild, lonely, and shagged, the bottom filled with fragments from the impending cliffs, and scarcely lighted by the reflected rays of the setting sun. For some time Rip lay musing on this scene, evening was gradually advancing, the mountains began to throw their long blue shadows over the valleys, he saw that it would be dark long before he could reach the village, and he heaved a heavy sigh when he thought of encountering the terrors of Dame Van Winkle.

As he was about to descend he heard a voice from a distance hallooing: "Rip Van Winkle! Rip Van Winkle!" He looked around, but could see nothing but a crow winging its solitary flight across the mountain. He thought his fancy must have deceived him and turned again to descend, when he heard the same cry ring through the still evening air: "Rip Van Winkle! Rip Van Winkle!"—at the same time Wolf bristled up his back and giving a low growl, skulked to his master's side, looking fearfully down into the glen. Rip now felt a vague apprehension stealing over him; he looked anxiously in the same direction and perceived a strange figure slowly toiling up the rocks and bending under the weight of something he carried on his back. He was surprised to see any human being in this lonely and unfrequented place, but supposing it to be some one of the neighbourhood in need of his assistance he hastened down to yield it.

On nearer approach he was still more surprised at the singularity of the stranger's appearance. He was a short, square built old fellow, with thick bushy hair and a grizzled beard. His dress was of the antique Dutch fashion, a cloth jerkin strapped round the waist, several pairs of breeches, the outer one of ample volume decorated with rows of buttons down the sides and bunches at the knees. He bore on his shoulders a stout keg that seemed full of liquor, and made signs for Rip to approach and assist him with the load. Though rather shy and distrustful of this new acquaintance Rip complied with his usual alacrity, and mutually relieving each other, they clambered up a narrow gully, apparently the dry bed of a mountain torrent. As they ascended, Rip every now and then heard long rolling peals like distant thunder, that seemed to issue out of a deep ravine or rather cleft between lofty rocks, toward which their rugged path conducted. He paused for an instant, but supposing it to be the muttering of one of those transient thunder showers which often take place in the mountain heights, he proceeded. Passing through the ravine, they came to a hollow like a small amphitheatre, surrounded by perpendicular precipices, over the brinks of which impending trees shot their branches, so that you only caught glimpses of the azure sky, and the bright evening cloud. During the whole time Rip and his companion had laboured on in silence, for though the former marvelled greatly what could be the object of carrying a keg of liquor up this wild mountain, yet there was something strange and incomprehensible about the unknown, that inspired awe and checked familiarity.

On entering the amphitheatre new objects of wonder presented themselves. On a level spot in the centre was a company of odd-looking personages playing at ninepins. They were dressed in quaint outlandish fashion—some wore short doublets, others jerkins with long knives in their belts, and most of them had enormous breeches of similar style with that of the guide's. Their visages too were peculiar. One had a large head, broad face and small piggish eyes. The face of another seemed to consist entirely of nose, and was surmounted by a white sugarloaf hat, set off with a little red cock's tail. They all had beards, of various shapes and colours. There was one who seemed to be the Commander. He was a stout old gentleman, with a weatherbeaten countenance. He wore a laced doublet, broad belt and hanger, high-crowned hat and feather, red stockings, and high-heel'd shoes with roses in them. The whole group reminded Rip of the figures in an old Flemish painting, in the parlour of Dominie Van Schaick the village parson, and which had been brought over from Holland at the time of the settlement.

What seemed particularly odd to Rip was, that though these folks were evidently amusing themselves, yet they maintained the gravest faces, the most mysterious silence, and were, withal, the most melancholy party of pleasure he had ever witnessed. Nothing interrupted the stillness of the scene, but the noise of the balls, which, whenever they were rolled, echoed along the mountains like rumbling peals of thunder.

As Rip and his companion approached them they suddenly desisted from their play and stared at him with such a fixed statue-like gaze, and such strange uncouth, lack lustre countenances, that his heart turned within him, and his knees smote together. His companion now emptied the contents of the keg into large flagons and made signs to him to wait upon the company. He obeyed with fear and trembling; they quaffed the liquor in profound silence, and then returned to their game.

By degrees Rip's awe and apprehension subsided. He even ventured, when no eye was fixed upon him, to taste the beverage which he found had much of the flavour of excellent hollands. He was naturally a thirsty soul and was soon tempted to repeat the draught. One taste provoked another, and he reiterated his visits to the flagon so often that at length his senses were overpowered, his eyes swam in his head—his head gradually declined, and he fell into a deep sleep.

On waking, he found himself on the green knoll whence he had first seen the old man of the glen. He rubbed his eyes—it was a bright, sunny morning. The birds were hopping and twittering among the bushes, and the eagle was wheeling aloft and breasting the pure mountain breeze. "Surely," thought Rip, "I have not slept here all night." He recalled the occurrences before he fell asleep. The strange man with the keg of liquor—the mountain ravine—the wild retreat among the rocks—the woe begone party at nine-pins—the flagon—"ah! that flagon! that wicked flagon!" thought Rip—"what excuse shall I make to Dame Van Winkle?"

He looked round for his gun, but in place of the clean well oiled fowling piece, he found an old firelock lying by him, the barrel encrusted with rust; the lock falling off and the stock wormeaten. He now suspected that the grave roysterers of the mountains had put a trick upon him, and having dosed him with liquor, had robbed him of his gun. Wolf too had disappeared, but he might have strayed away after a squirrel or partridge. He whistled after him and shouted his name—but all in vain; the echoes repeated his whistle and shout, but no dog was to be seen.

He determined to revisit the scene of the last evening's gambol, and if he met with any of the party, to demand his dog and gun. As he rose to walk, he found himself stiff in the joints, and wanting in his usual activity. "These mountain beds do not agree with me," thought Rip, "and if this frolick should lay me up with a fit of the rheumatism, I shall have a blessed time with Dame Van Winkle." With some difficulty he got down into the glen: he found the gully up which he and his companion had ascended the preceding evening, but to his astonishment a mountain stream was now foaming down it; leaping from rock to rock, and filling the glen with babbling murmurs. He, however, made shift to scramble up its sides, working his toilsome way through thickets of birch, sassafras, and witch-hazel, and sometimes tripped up or entangled by the wild grape vines that twisted their coils and tendrils from tree to tree, and spread a kind of net work in his path.

At length he reached to where the ravine had opened through the cliffs, to the amphitheatre—but no traces of such opening remained. The rocks presented a high impenetrable wall, over which the torrent came tumbling in a sheet of feathery foam, and fell into a broad deep basin, black from the shadows of the surrounding forest. Here, then, poor Rip was brought to a stand. He again called and whistled after his dog—he was only answered by the cawing of a flock of idle crows, sporting high in the air about a dry tree that overhung a sunny precipice; and who, secure in their elevation seemed to look down and scoff at the poor man's perplexities.

What was to be done? The morning was passing away and Rip felt famished for want of his breakfast. He grieved to give up his dog and gun; he dreaded to meet his wife; but it would not do to starve among the mountains. He shook his head, shouldered the rusty fire lock and with a heart full of trouble and anxiety, turned his steps homeward.

As he approached the village, he met a number of people, but none whom he new, which somewhat surprised him, for he had thought himself acquainted with every one in the country round. Their dress too was of a different fashion from that to which he was accustomed. They all stared at him with equal marks of surprise, and whenever they cast eyes upon him, invariably stroked their chins. The constant recurrence of this gesture induced Rip, involuntarily to do, the same, when to his astonishment he found his beard had grown a foot long!

He had now entered the skirts of the village. A troop of strange children ran at his heels, hooting after him, and pointing at his grey beard. The dogs, too, not one of which he recognized for an old acquaintance, barked at him as he passed. The very village was altered—it was larger and more populous. There were rows of houses which he had never seen before, and those which had been his familiar haunts had disappeared. Strange names were over the doors—strange faces at the windows—every thing was strange. His mind now misgave him; he began to doubt whether both he and the world around him were not bewitched. Surely this was his native village, which he had left but a day before. There stood the Kaatskill mountains—there ran the silver Hudson at a distance—there was every hill and dale precisely as it had always been—Rip was sorely perplexed—"That flagon last night," thought he, "has addled my poor head sadly!"

It was with some difficulty that he found the way to his own house, which he approached with silent awe, expecting every moment to hear the shrill voice of Dame Van Winkle. He found the house gone to decay—the roof had fallen in, the windows shattered, and the doors off the hinges. A half starved dog that looked like Wolf was skulking about it. Rip called him by name but the cur snarled, shewed his teeth, and passed on. This was an unkind cut indeed.—"My very dog," sighed poor Rip, "has forgotten me!"

He entered the house, which, to tell the truth, Dame Van Winkle had always kept in neat order. It was empty, forlorn, and apparently abandoned. This desolateness overcame all his connubial fears—he called loudly for his wife and children—the lonely chambers rang for a moment with his voice, and then all again was silence.

He now hurried forth and hastened to his old resort, the village inn—but it too was gone. A large rickety wooden building stood in its place, with great gaping windows, some of them broken, and mended with old hats and petticoats, and over the door was painted, "The Union Hotel, by Jonathan Doolittle." Instead of the great tree, that used to shelter the quiet little Dutch inn of yore, there now was reared a tall naked pole with something on the top that looked like a red nightcap, and from it was fluttering a flag, on which was a singular assemblage of stars and stripes—all this was strange and incomprehensible. He recognized on the sign, however, the ruby face of King George, under which he had smoked so many a peaceful pipe, but even this was singularly metamorphosed. The red coat was changed for one of blue and buff; a sword was held in the hand instead of a sceptre; the head was decorated with a cocked hat, and underneath was painted in large characters GENERAL WASHINGTON.

There was as usual a crowd of folk about the door; but none that Rip recollected. The very character of the people seemed changed. There was a busy, bustling, disputatious tone about it, instead of the accustomed phlegm and drowsy tranquility. He looked in vain for the sage Nicholaus Vedder, with his broad face, double chin, and fair long pipe, uttering clouds of tobacco smoke instead of idle speeches. Or Van Bummel the schoolmaster doling forth the contents of an ancient newspaper. In place of these a lean bilious looking fellow with his pockets full of hand bills, was haranguing, vehemently about rights of citizens—elections—members of Congress—liberty—Bunker's hill—heroes of seventy-six—and other words, which were a perfect babylonish jargon to the bewildered Van Winkle.

The appearance of Rip with his long grizzled beard, his rusty fowling piece, his uncouth dress and the army of women and children at his heels, soon attracted the attention of the tavern politicians. They crowded round him eying him from head to foot, with great curiosity. The orator bustled up to him, and drawing him partly aside, enquired "on which side he voted?"—Rip stared in vacant stupidity. Another short but busy little fellow, pulled him by the arm and rising on tiptoe, enquired in his ear "whether he was Federal or Democrat?"—Rip was equally at a loss to comprehend the question; when a knowing, self important old gentleman, in a sharp cocked hat, made his way through the crowd, putting them to the right and left with his elbows as he passed, and planting himself before Van Winkle, with one arm akimbo, the other resting on his cane, his keen eyes and sharp hat penetrating as it were, into his very soul, demanded in an austere tone—"what brought him to the election with a gun on his shoulder, and a mob at his heels; and whether he meant to breed a riot in the village?"—"Alas gentlemen," cried Rip, somewhat dismayed, "I am a poor, quiet man, a native of the place, and a loyal subject of the King, God bless him!"

Here a general shout burst from the bystanders—"A tory! a tory! a spy! a Refugee! hustle him! away with him!"—It was with great difficulty that the self-important man in the cocked hat restored order; and having assumed a tenfold austerity of brow, demanded again of the unknown culprit, what he came there for and whom he was seeking. The poor man humbly assured him that he meant no harm but merely came there in search of some of his neighbours, who used to keep about the tavern.

"—Well—who are they?—name them."

Rip bethought himself a moment and enquired, "Where's Nicholaus Vedder?"

There was a silence for a little while, when an old man replied, in a thin, piping voice, "Nicholaus Vedder? why, he is dead and gone these eighteen years! There was a wooden tombstone in the churchyard that used to tell all about him, but that's rotted and gone too."

"Where's Brom Dutcher?"

"Oh, he went off to the army in the beginning of the war; some say he was killed at the storming of Stoney Point—others say he was drowned in a squall at the foot of Antony's Nose—I don't know—he never came back again."

"Where's Van Bummel, the schoolmaster?"

"He went off to the wars too—was a great militia general, and is now in Congress."

Rip's heart died away at hearing of these sad changes in his home and friends, and finding himself thus alone in the world—Every answer puzzled him too, by treating of such enormous lapses of time and of matters which he could not understand—war—Congress, Stoney Point;—he had no courage to ask after any more friends, but cried out in despair, "Does nobody here know Rip Van Winkle?"

"Oh, Rip Van Winkle!" exclaimed two or three. "Oh, to be sure! that's Rip Van Winkle—yonder—leaning against the tree."

Rip looked and beheld a precise counterpart of himself as he went up the mountain: apparently as lazy and certainly as ragged! The poor fellow was now completely confounded. He doubted his own identity, and whether he was himself or another man. In the midst of his bewilderment, the man in the cocked hat demanded who he was,—and what was his name?

"God knows!" exclaimed he at his wit's end; "I'm not myself.—I'm somebody else—that's me yonder-no—that's somebody else, got into my shoes—I was myself last night, but I fell asleep on the mountain—and they've changed my gun, and everything's changed—and I'm changed—and I can't tell what's my name, or who I am!"

The byestanders began now to look at each other, nod, wink significantly, and tap their fingers against their foreheads. There was a whisper also about securing the gun, and keeping the old fellow from doing mischief—at the very suggestion of which, the self-important man with the cocked hat retired with some precipitation. At this critical moment a fresh likely looking woman pressed through the throng to get a peep at the greybearded man. She had a chubby child in her arms, which frightened at his looks began to cry. "Hush Rip," cried she, "hush you little fool; the old man won't hurt you." The name of the child, the air of the mother, the tone of her voice, all awakened a train of recollections in his mind. "What is your name, my good woman?" asked he.

"Judith Gardenier."

"And your father's name?"

"Ah, poor man, Rip Van Winkle was his name, but it's twenty years since he went away from home with his gun, and never has been heard of since—his dog came home without him—but whether he shot himself, or was carried away by the Indians, nobody can tell. I was then but a little girl."

Rip had but one more question to ask; but he put it with a faltering voice—

"Where's your mother?"—

Oh, she too had died but a short time since—she broke a blood vessel in a fit of passion at a New England pedlar.—

There was a drop of comfort, at least, in this intelligence. The honest man could contain himself no longer—he caught his daughter and her child in his arms.—"I am your father!" cried he—"Young

Rip Van Winkle once—old Rip Van Winkle now!—does nobody know poor Rip Van Winkle!"

All stood amazed, until an old woman, tottering out from among the crowd, put her hand to her brow, and peering under it in his face for a moment exclaimed—"Sure enough!—it is Rip Van Winkle—it is himself—welcome home again, old neighbour—why, where have you been these twenty long years?"

Rip's story was soon told, for the whole twenty years had been to him but as one night. The neighbours stared when they heard it; some were seen to wink at each other and put their tongues in their cheeks, and the self important man in the cocked hat, who when the alarm was over had returned to the field, screwed down the corners of his mouth, and shook his head—upon which there was a general shaking of the head throughout the assemblage.

It was determined, however, to take the opinion of old Peter Vanderdonk, who was seen slowly advancing up the road. He was a descendant of the historian of that name, who wrote one of the earliest accounts of the province. Peter was the most ancient inhabitant of the village, and well versed in all the wonderful events and traditions of the neighbourhood. He recollected Rip at once, and corroborated his story in the most satisfactory manner. He assured the company that it was a fact handed down from his ancestor the historian, that the Kaatskill mountains had always been haunted by strange beings. That it was affirmed that the great Hendrick Hudson, the first discoverer of the river and country, kept a kind of vigil there every twenty years, with his crew of the Half Moon—being permitted in this way to revisit the scenes of his enterprize, and keep a guardian eye upon the river and the great city called by his name. That his father had once seen them in their old Dutch dresses playing at nine-pins in the hollow of the mountain; and that he himself had heard, one summer afternoon the sound of their balls, like distant peals of thunder.

To make a long story short—the company broke up, and returned to the more important concerns of the election. Rip's daughter took him home to live with her; she had a snug, well furnished house, and a stout cheery farmer for a husband whom Rip recollected for one of the urchins that used to climb upon his back. As to Rip's son and heir, who was the ditto of himself seen leaning against the tree; he was employed to work on the farm; but evinced an hereditary disposition to attend to any thing else but his business.

Rip now resumed his old walks and habits; he soon found many of his former cronies, though all rather the worse for the wear and tear of time; and preferred making friends among the rising generation, with whom he soon grew into great favour. Having nothing to do at home, and being arrived at that happy age when a man can be idle, with impunity, he took his place once more on the bench at the inn door and was reverenced as one of the patriarchs of the village, and a chronicle of the old times "before the war." It was some time before he could get into the regular track of gossip, or could be made to comprehend the strange events that had taken place during his torpor. How that there had been a revolutionary war—that the country had thrown off the yoke of Old England and that instead of being a subject to his majesty George the Third, he was now a free citizen of the United States. Rip in fact was no politician; the changes of states and empires made but little impression on him; but there was one species of despotism under which he had long groaned and that was petticoat government. Happily that was at an end—he had got his neck out of the yoke of matrimony, and could go in and out whenever he pleased without dreading the tyranny of Dame Van Winkle. Whenever her name was mentioned, however, he shook his head, shrugged his shoulders, and cast up his eyes; which might pass either for an expression of resignation to his fate, or joy at his deliverance.

He used to tell his story to every stranger that arrived at Mr. Doolittle's hotel. He was observed, at first, to vary on some points every time he told it, which was, doubtless, owing to his having so recently awaked. It at last settled down precisely to the tale I have related, and not a man woman or child in the neighbourhood, but knew it by heart. Some always pretended to doubt the reality of it, and insisted that Rip had been out of his head, and that this was one point on which he always remained flighty. The old Dutch inhabitants, however, almost universally gave it full credit—Even to this day, they never hear a thunder-storm of a summer afternoon about the Kaatskill, but they say Hendrick Hudson and his crew are at their game of ninepins; and it is a common wish of all henpecked husbands in the neighbourhood, when life hangs heavy on their hands, that they might have a quieting draught out of Rip Van Winkle's flagon.

THE SPECTRE BRIDEGROOM*

He that supper for is dight,
He lyes full cold, I trow, this night!
Yestreen to chamber I him led,
This night Gray-steel has made his bed!

SIR EGER, SIR GRAHAME,
AND SIR GRAY-STEEL

On the summit of one of the heights of the Odenwald, a wild and romantic tract of Upper Germany that lies not far from the confluence of the Main and the Rhine, there stood many, many years since, the castle of the Baron Von Landshort. It is now quite fallen to decay, and almost buried among beech trees and dark firs, above which, however, its old watch-tower may still be seen struggling, like the former possessor I have mentioned, to carry a high head, and look down upon the neighbouring country.

The Baron was a dry branch of the great family of Katzenellenbogen,+ and inherited the reliques of the property, and all the pride of his

---

*The erudite reader, well versed in good for nothing lore, will perceive that the above tale must have been suggested to the old Swiss by a little French anecdote, a circumstance said to have taken place in Paris.

+ i.e., CATSELBOW—the name of a family of those parts, and very powerful in former times. The appellation, we are told, was given in compliment to a peerless dame of the family, celebrated for a fine arm.

ancestors. Though the warlike disposition of his predecessors had much impaired the family possessions, yet the Baron still endeavored to keep up some show of former state. The times were peaceable, and the German nobles, in general, had abandoned their inconvenient old castles, perched like eagles' nests among the mountains, and had built more convenient residences in the valleys: still, the Baron remained proudly drawn up in his little fortress, cherishing with hereditary inveteracy, all the old family feuds, so that he was on ill terms with some of his nearest neighbours, on account of disputes that had happened between their great great grandfathers.

The Baron had but one child, a daughter, but nature, when she grants but one child, always compensates by making it a prodigy; and so it was with the daughter of the Baron. All the nurses, gossips, and country cousins assured her father that she had not her equal for beauty in all Germany; and who should know better than they. She had, moreover, been brought up with great care under the superintendence of two maiden aunts, who had spent some years of their early life at one of the little German courts, and were skilled in all branches of knowledge necessary to the education of a fine lady. Under their instructions she became a miracle of accomplishments. By the time she was eighteen she could embroider to admiration, and had worked whole histories of the saints in tapestry with such strength of expression in their countenances, that they looked like so many souls in purgatory. She could read without great difficulty, and had spelled her way through several Church legends and almost all the chivalric wonders of the Heldenbuch. She had even made considerable proficiency in writing, could sign her own name without missing a letter, and so legibly that her aunts could read it without spectacles. She excelled in making little elegant good for nothing, lady like nick nacks of all kinds; was versed in the most abstruse dancing of the day; played a number of airs on the harp and guitar; and knew all the tender ballads of the Minnelieders by heart.

Her aunts, too, having been great flirts and coquettes in their younger days, were admirably calculated to be vigilant guardians and strict censors of the conduct of their niece; for there is no duenna so rigidly prudent and inexorably decorous as a superannuated coquette. She was rarely suffered out of their sight; never went beyond the domains of the castle, unless well attended, or rather, well watched; had continual lectures read to her about strict decorum and implicit obedience; and, as to the men—pah!— she was taught to hold them at such a distance and in such absolute distrust, that unless properly authorized, she would not have cast a glance upon the handsomest cavalier in the world—no, not if he were even dying at her feet!

The good effects of this system were wonderfully apparent. The young lady was a pattern of docility and correctness. While others were wasting their sweetness in the glare of the world, and liable to be plucked and thrown aside by every hand, she was coyly blooming into fresh and lovely womanhood under the protection of those immaculate spinsters, like a rosebud blushing forth among guardian thorns. Her aunts looked upon her with pride and exultation, and vaunted that, though all the other young ladies in the world might go astray, yet thank Heaven, nothing of the kind could happen to the heiress of Katzenellenbogen.

But, however scantily the Baron Von Landshort might be provided with children, his household was by no means a small one, for providence had enriched him with abundance of poor relations. They, one and all, possessed the affectionate disposition common to humble relatives: were wonderfully attached to the Baron, and took every possible occasion to come in swarms and enliven the castle. All family festivals were commemorated by these good people at the Baron's expense; and when they were filled with good cheer they would declare that there was nothing on earth so delightful as these family meetings, these jubilees of the heart.

The Baron, though a small man, had a large soul, and it swelled with satisfaction at the consciousness of being the greatest man in the little world about him. He loved to tell long stories about the stark old warriors whose portraits looked grimly down from the walls around, and he found no listeners equal to those who fed at his expense. He was much given to the marvellous, and a firm believer in all those supernatural tales with which every mountain and valley in Germany abounds. The faith of his guests exceeded even his own: they listened to every tale of wonder with open eyes and mouth, and never failed to be astonished, even though repeated for the hundredth time. Thus lived the Baron Von Landshort, the oracle of his table, the absolute monarch of his little territory, and happy, above all things, in the persuasion that he was the wisest man of the age.

At the time of which my story treats there was a great family gathering at the Castle, on an affair of the utmost importance. It was to receive the destined bridegroom of the Baron's daughter. A negotiation had been carried on between the father, and an old nobleman of Bavaria, to unite the dignity of their houses by the marriage of their children. The preliminaries had been conducted with proper punctilio. The young people were betrothed without seeing each other, and the time was appointed for the marriage ceremony. The young Count Von Altenburg had been recalled from the army for the purpose, and was actually on his way to the Baron's to receive his bride. Missives had even been received from him, from

Wurtzburg, where he was accidentally detained, mentioning the day and hour when he might be expected to arrive.

The castle was in a tumult of preparation to give him a suitable welcome. The fair bride had been decked out with uncommon care. The two aunts had superintended her toilet, and quarrelled the whole morning about every article of her dress. The young lady had taken advantage of their contest to follow the bent of her own taste; and fortunately it was a good one. She looked as lovely as youthful bridegroom could desire; and the flutter of expectation heightened the lustre of her charms.

The suffusions that mantled her face and neck, the gentle heaving of the bosom, the eye now and then lost in reverie, all betrayed the soft tumult that was going on in her little heart. The aunts were continually hovering around her; for maiden aunts are apt to take great interest in affairs of this nature. They were giving her a world of staid counsel how to deport herself, what to say, and in what manner to receive the expected lover.

The Baron was no less busied in preparations. He had, in truth, nothing exactly to do; but he was naturally a fuming, bustling little man, and could not remain passive when all the world was in a hurry. He worried from top to bottom of the castle with an air of infinite anxiety; he continually called the servants from their work to exhort them to be diligent; and buzzed about every hall and chamber, as idly restless and importunate as a blue bottle fly on a warm summer's day.

In the mean time, the fatted calf had been killed; the forests had rung with the clamor of the huntsmen; the kitchen was crowded with good cheer; the cellars had yielded up whole oceans of *Rhein-wein* and *Ferne-wein*, and even the great Heidelberg tun had been laid under contribution. Everything was ready to receive the distinguished guest with *Saus und Braus* in the true spirit of German hospitality—but the guest delayed to make his appearance. Hour rolled after hour. The sun that had poured his downward rays upon the rich forest of the Odenwald, now just gleamed along the summits of the mountains. The Baron mounted the highest tower, and strained his eyes in hopes of catching a distant sight of the count and his attendants. Once he thought he beheld them; the sound of horns came floating from the valley, prolonged by the mountain echoes. A number of horsemen were seen far below slowly advancing along the road; but when they had nearly reached the foot of the mountain, they suddenly struck off in a different direction. The last ray of sunshine departed—the bats began to flit by in the twilight—the road grew dimmer and dimmer to the view, and nothing appeared stirring in it, but now and then a peasant lagging homeward from his labour.

While the old castle of Landshort was in this state of perplexity, a very interesting scene was transacting in a different part of the Odenwald.

The young Count Von Altenburg was tranquilly pursuing his route in that sober jog trot way in which a man travels toward matrimony, when his friends have taken all the trouble and uncertainty of courtship off his hands and a bride is waiting for him as—certainly as a dinner, at the end of his journey. He had encountered, at Wurtzburg, a youthful companion in arms with whom he had seen some service on the frontiers; Herman Von Starkenfaust, one of the stoutest hands, and worthiest hearts of German chivalry, who was now returning from the army. His father's castle was not far distant from the old fortress of Landshort, although an hereditary feud rendered the families hostile and strangers to each other.

In the warm hearted moment of recognition the young friends related all their past adventures and fortunes, and the count gave the whole history of his intended nuptials with a young lady whom he had never seen, but of whose charms he had received the most enrapturing descriptions.

As the route of the friends lay in the same direction, they agreed to perform the rest of their journey together, and that they might do it the more leisurely, set off from Wurtzburg at an early hour, the count having given directions for his retinue to follow and overtake him.

They beguiled their wayfaring with recollections of their military scenes and adventures; but the count was apt to be a little tedious now and then about the reputed charms of his bride, and the felicity that awaited him.

In this way they had entered among the mountains of the Odenwald, and were traversing one of its most lonely and thickly wooded passes. It is well known that the forests of Germany have always been as much infested by robbers as its castles by spectres; and, at this time, the former were particularly numerous, from the hordes of disbanded soldiers wandering about the country. It will not appear extraordinary, therefore, that the cavaliers were attacked by a gang of these stragglers, in the midst of the forest. They defended themselves with bravery, but were nearly overpowered when the count's retinue arrived to their assistance. At sight of them the robbers fled, but not until the count had received a mortal wound. He was slowly and carefully conveyed back to the city of Wurtzburg, and a friar summoned from a neighbouring convent, who was famous for his skill in administering to both soul and body. But half of his skill was superfluous; the moments of the unfortunate count were numbered.

With his dying breath he entreated his friend to repair instantly to the castle of Landshort and explain the fatal cause of his not keeping his appointment with his bride. Though not the most ardent of lovers, he was one of the most punctilious of men, and appeared earnestly solicitous that his mission should be speedily and courteously executed. "Unless this is done," said he, "I shall not sleep quietly in my grave!" He repeated these last words with peculiar solemnity. A request, at a moment so impressive, admitted no hesitation. Starkenfaust endeavored to soothe him to calmness, promised faithfully to execute his wish, and gave him his hand in solemn pledge. The dying man pressed it in acknowledgment, but soon lapsed into delirium—raved about his bride—his engagements—his plighted word; ordered his horse, that he might ride to the castle of Landshort, and expired in the fancied act of vaulting into the saddle.

Starkenfaust bestowed a sigh, and a soldier's tear, on the untimely fate of his comrade; and then pondered on the awkward mission he had undertaken. His heart was heavy, and his head perplexed; for he was to present himself an unbidden guest among hostile people, and to damp their festivity with tidings fatal to their hopes. Still there were certain whisperings of curiosity in his bosom to see this far-famed beauty of Katzenellenbogen, so cautiously shut up from the world; for he was a passionate admirer of the sex, and there was a dash of eccentricity and enterprise in his character that made him fond of all singular adventure.

Previous to his departure he made all due arrangements with the holy fraternity of the convent for the funeral solemnities of his friend, who was to be buried in the cathedral of Wurtzburg, near some of his illustrious relatives, and the mourning retinue of the count took charge of his remains.

It is now high time that we should return to the ancient family of Katzenellenbogen, who were impatient for their guest, and still more for their dinner, and to the worthy little Baron, whom we left airing himself on the watch tower.

Night closed in, but still no guest arrived. The Baron descended from the tower in despair. The banquet, which had been delayed from hour to hour could no longer be postponed. The meats were already overdone; the cook in an agony; and the whole household had the look of a garrison, that had been reduced by famine. The Baron was obliged reluctantly to give orders for the feast without the presence of the guest. All were seated at table, and just on the point of commencing, when the sound of a horn from without the gate gave notice of the approach of a stranger. Another long blast filled the old courts of the castle with its echoes, and was answered by the warder from the walls. The Baron hastened to receive his future son in law.

The drawbridge had been let down, and the stranger was before the gate. He was a tall gallant cavalier, mounted on a black steed. His countenance was pale, but he had a beaming, romantic eye and an air of stately melancholy. The Baron was a little mortified that he should have come in this simple, solitary style. His dignity for a moment was ruffled, and he felt disposed to consider it a want of proper respect for the important occasion and the important family with which he was to be connected. He, however, pacified himself with the conclusion that it must have been youthful impatience which had induced him thus to spur on sooner than his attendants.

"I am sorry," said the stranger, "to break in upon you thus unseasonably—"

Here the Baron interrupted him with a world of compliments and greetings; for, to tell the truth, he prided himself upon his courtesy and eloquence. The stranger attempted once or twice to stem the torrent of words, but in vain, so he bowed his head and suffered it to flow on. By the time the Baron had come to a pause they had reached the inner court of the castle; and the stranger was again about to speak, when he was once more interrupted by the appearance of the female part of the family, leading forth the shrinking and blushing bride. He gazed on her for a moment as one entranced; it seemed as if his whole soul beamed forth in the gaze, and rested upon that lovely form. One of the maiden aunts whispered something in her ear; she made an effort to speak; her moist blue eye was timidly raised, gave a shy glance of inquiry on the stranger, and was cast again to the ground. The words died away; but there was a sweet smile playing about her lips, and a soft dimpling of the cheek that showed her glance had not been unsatisfactory. It was impossible for a girl of the fond age of eighteen, highly predisposed for love and matrimony, not to be pleased with so gallant a cavalier.

The late hour at which the guest had arrived, left no time for parley. The Baron was peremptory, and deferred all particular conversation until the morning, and led the way to the untasted banquet.

It was served up in the great hall of the castle. Around the walls hung the hard favoured portraits of the heroes of the house of Katzenellenbogen, and the trophies which they had gained in the field and in the chase. Hacked corselets; splintered jousting spears, and tattered banners, were mingled with the spoils of sylvan warfare: the jaws of the wolf and the tusks of the boar grinned horribly among crossbows and battle axes, and a huge pair of antlers branched immediately over the head of the youthful bridegroom.

The cavalier took but little notice of the company, or the entertainment. He scarcely tasted the banquet, but seemed absorbed in admiration of his bride. He conversed in a low tone that could not be overheard—for the language of love is never loud; but where is the female ear so dull that it cannot catch the softest whisper of the lover? There was a mingled tenderness and gravity in his manner, that appeared to have a powerful effect upon the young lady. Her colour came and went as she listened with deep attention. Now and then she made some blushing reply, and when his eye was turned away she would steal a side long glance at his romantic countenance, and heave a gentle sigh of tender happiness. It was evident that the young couple were completely enamoured. The aunts, who were deeply versed in the mysteries of the heart, declared that they had fallen in love with each other at first sight.

The feast went on merrily, or at least noisily, for the guests were all blessed with those keen appetites that attend upon light purses and mountain air. The Baron told his best and longest stories, and never had he told them so well or with such great effect. If there was anything marvellous, his auditors were lost in astonishment; and if anything facetious, they were sure to laugh exactly in the right place. The Baron, it is true, like most great men, was too dignified to utter any joke but a dull one; it was always enforced, however, by a bumper of excellent Hochheimer; and even a dull joke at one's own table, served up with jolly old wine, is irresistible. Many good things were said by poorer and keener wits that would not bear repeating, except on similar occasions; many sly speeches whispered in ladies' ears that almost convulsed them with suppressed laughter; and a song or two roared out by a poor, but merry and broad faced cousin of the Baron, that absolutely made the maiden aunts hold up their fans.

Amidst all this revelry, the stranger guest maintained a most singular and unseasonable gravity. His countenance assumed a deeper cast of dejection as the evening advanced, and, strange as it may appear, even the Baron's jokes seemed only to render him the more melancholy. At times he was lost in thought, and at times there was a perturbed and restless wandering of the eye that bespoke a mind but ill at ease. His conversations with the bride became more and more earnest and mysterious. Lowering clouds began to steal over the fair serenity of her brow, and tremors to run through her tender frame.

All this could not escape the notice of the company. Their gayety was chilled by the unaccountable gloom of the bridegroom; their spirits were infected; whispers and glances were interchanged, accompanied by shrugs and dubious shakes of the head. The song and the laugh grew less and less frequent: there were dreary pauses in the conversation, which were at length succeeded by wild tales, and supernatural legends. One dismal story produced another still more dismal, and the Baron nearly frightened some of the ladies into hysterics with the history of the goblin horseman that carried away the fair Leonora; a dreadful, but true story, which has since been put into excellent verse, and is read and believed by all the world.

The bridegroom listened to this tale with profound attention. He kept his eyes steadily fixed on the Baron, and as the story drew to a close, began gradually to rise from his seat, growing taller and taller, until in the Baron's entranced eye he seemed almost to tower into a giant. The moment the tale was finished he heaved a deep sigh, and took a solemn farewell of the company. They were all amazement. The Baron was perfectly thunderstruck.

"What! going to leave the castle at midnight? why, every thing was prepared for his reception; a chamber was ready for him if he wished to retire."

The stranger shook his head mournfully and mysteriously: "I must lay my head in a different chamber tonight."

There was something in this reply, and the tone in which it was uttered, that made the Baron's heart misgive him; but he rallied his forces and repeated his hospitable entreaties.

The stranger shook his head silently, but positively, at every offer, and, waving his farewell to the company, stalked slowly out of the hall. The maiden aunts were absolutely petrified—the bride hung her head, and a tear stole to her eye.

The Baron followed the stranger to the great court of the castle, where the black charger stood pawing the earth and snorting with impatience. When they had reached the portal, whose deep archway was dimly lighted by a cresset, the stranger paused, and addressed the Baron in a hollow tone of voice, which the vaulted roof rendered still more sepulchral.

"Now that we are alone," said he, "I will impart to you the reason of my going. I have a solemn, an indispensable engagement—"

"Why," said the Baron, "cannot you send some one in your place?"

"It admits of no substitute—I must attend it in person—I must away to Wurtzburg cathedral—"

"Aye," said the Baron, plucking up spirit, "but not until tomorrow—tomorrow you shall take your bride there."

"No! no!" replied the stranger, with tenfold solemnity, "my engagement is with no bride—the worms! the worms expect me! I am a dead man—I have been slain by robbers—my body lies at Wurtzburg—at midnight I am to be buried—the grave is waiting for me—I must keep my appointment!"

He sprang on his black charger, dashed over the drawbridge, and the clattering of his horse's hoofs was lost in the whistling of the night blast.

The Baron returned to the hall in the utmost consternation, and related what had passed. Two ladies fainted outright, others sickened at the idea of having banqueted with a spectre. It was the opinion of some that this might be the wild huntsman, famous in German legend. Some talked of mountain-sprites, of wood-demons, and of other supernatural beings with which the good people of Germany have been so grievously harassed since time immemorial. One of the poor relations ventured to suggest that it might be some sportive evasion of the young cavalier, and that the very gloominess of the caprice seemed to accord with so melancholy a personage. This, however, drew on him, the indignation of the whole company, and especially of the Baron, who looked upon him as little better than an infidel; so that he was fain to abjure his heresy as speedily as possible and come into the faith of the true believers.

But, whatever may have been the doubts entertained, they were completely put to an end by the arrival next day of regular missives confirming the intelligence of the young count's murder and his interment in Wurtzburg cathedral.

The dismay at the castle may well be imagined. The Baron shut himself up in his chamber. The guests, who had come to rejoice with him, could not think of abandoning him in his distress. They wandered about the courts or collected in groups in the hall, shaking their heads and shrugging their shoulders, at the troubles of so good a man, and sat longer than ever at table, and ate and drank more stoutly than ever, by way of keeping up their spirits. But the situation of the widowed bride was the most pitiable. To have lost a husband before she had even embraced him—and such a husband! If the very spectre could be so gracious and noble, what must have been the living man? She filled the house with lamentations.

On the night of the second day of her widowhood she had retired to her chamber, accompanied by one of her aunts, who insisted on sleeping with her. The aunt, who was one of the best tellers of ghost-stories in all Germany, had just been recounting one of her longest, and had fallen asleep in the very midst of it. The chamber was remote and overlooked a small garden. The niece lay pensively gazing at the beams of the rising moon as they trembled on the leaves of an aspen tree before the lattice. The castle clock had just tolled midnight when a soft strain of music stole up from the garden. She rose hastily from her bed and stepped lightly to the window. A tall figure stood among the shadows of the trees. As it raised its head a beam of moonlight fell upon the countenance. Heaven and earth! she beheld the Spectre Bridegroom! A loud shriek at that moment burst upon her ear, and her aunt, who had been awakened by the music and had followed her silently to the window, fell into her arms. When she looked again the spectre had disappeared.

Of the two females, the aunt now required the most soothing, for she was perfectly beside herself with terror. As to the young lady, there was something even in the spectre of her lover that seemed endearing. There was still the semblance of manly beauty; and, though the shadow of a man is but little calculated to satisfy the affections of a lovesick girl, yet, where the substance is not to be had even that is consoling. The aunt declared she would never sleep in that chamber again; the niece, for once, was refractory, and declared as strongly that she would sleep in no other in the castle: the consequence was, that she had to sleep in it alone; but she drew a promise from her aunt not to relate the story of the spectre, lest she should be denied the only melancholy pleasure left her on earth— that of inhabiting the chamber over which the guardian shade of her lover kept its nightly vigils.

How long the good old lady would have observed this promise is uncertain, for she dearly loved to talk of the marvellous, and there is a triumph in being the first to tell a frightful story; it is, however, still quoted in the neighbourhood, as a memorable instance of female secrecy that she kept it to herself for a whole week, when she was suddenly absolved from all further restraint by intelligence brought to the breakfast-table one morning that the young lady was not to be found. Her room was empty—the bed had not been slept in—the window was open and the bird had flown!

The astonishment and concern with which the intelligence was received can only be imagined by those who have witnessed the agitation which the mishaps of a great man cause among his friends. Even the poor relations paused for a moment from the indefatigable labours of the trencher, when the aunt, who had at first been struck speechless, wrung her hands and shrieked out, "the goblin, the goblin! she's carried away by the goblin!"

In a few words, she related the fearful scene of the garden, and concluded that the spectre must have carried off his bride. Two of the domestics corroborated the opinion, for they had heard the clattering of a horse's hoofs down the mountain about midnight, and had no doubt that it was the spectre on his black charger bearing her away to the tomb. All present were struck with the direful probability for events of the kind are extremely common in Germany, as many well authenticated histories bear witness.

What a lamentable situation was that of the poor Baron! What a heartrending dilemma for a fond father and a member of the great family of Katzenellenbogen! His only daughter had either been rapt away to the grave, or he was to have some wood-demon for a son in law, and perchance a troop of goblin grand children. As usual, he was completely bewildered, and all the castle in an uproar. The men were ordered to take horse and scour every road and path and glen of the Odenwald. The Baron himself had just drawn on his jack-boots, girded on his sword, and was about to mount his steed to sally forth on the doubtful quest, when he was brought to a pause by a new apparition. A lady was seen approaching the castle, mounted on a palfrey, attended by a cavalier on horseback. She galloped up to the gate, sprang from her horse, and, falling at the Baron's feet, embraced his knees. It was his lost daughter, and her companion—the Spectre Bridegroom! The Baron was astounded. He looked at his daughter, then at the spectre, and almost doubted the evidence of his senses. The latter, too, was wonderfully improved in his appearance since his visit to the world of spirits. His dress was splendid, and set off a noble figure of manly symmetry. He was no longer pale and melancholy. His fine countenance was flushed with the glow of youth, and joy rioted in his large dark eye.

The mystery was soon cleared up. The cavalier (for in truth, as you must have known all the while, he was no goblin) announced himself as Sir Herman Von Starkenfaust. He related his adventure with the young Count. He told how he had hastened to the castle to deliver the unwelcome tidings, but that the eloquence of the Baron had interrupted him in every attempt to tell his tale. How the sight of the bride had completely captivated him and that to pass a few hours near her he had tacitly suffered the mistake to continue. How he had been sorely perplexed in what way to make a decent retreat, until the Baron's goblin stories had suggested his eccentric exit. How, fearing the feudal hostility of the family, he had repeated his visits by stealth—had haunted the garden beneath the young lady's window—had wooed—had won—had borne away in triumph—and, in a word, had wedded the fair.

Under any other circumstances the Baron would have been inflexible, for he was tenacious of paternal authority and devoutly obstinate in all family feuds; but he loved his daughter; he had lamented her as lost; he rejoiced to find her still alive; and, though her husband was of a hostile house, yet, thank heaven! he was not a goblin. There was something, it must be acknowledged, that did not exactly accord with his notions of strict veracity, in the joke the knight had passed upon him of his being a dead man; but several old friends present, who had served in the wars, assured him that every stratagem was excusable in love, and that the cavalier was entitled to especial privilege, having lately served as a trooper.

Matters, therefore, were happily arranged. The Baron pardoned the young couple on the spot. The revels at the castle were resumed. The poor relations overwhelmed this new member of the family with loving-kindness; he was so gallant, so generous, and so rich. The aunts, it is true, were somewhat scandalized that their system of strict seclusion, and passive obedience should be so badly exemplified, but attributed it all to their negligence, in not having the windows grated. One of them was particularly mortified at having her marvellous story marred, and that the only spectre she had ever seen should turn out a counterfeit; but the niece seemed perfectly happy at having found him substantial flesh and blood—and so the story ends.

THE LEGEND OF SLEEPY HOLLOW

A pleasing land of drowsy-head it was,
Of dreams that wave before the half-shut eye;
And of gay castles in the clouds that pass,
For ever flushing round a summer sky.

CASTLE OF INDOLENCE

In the bosom of one of those spacious coves which indent the eastern shore of the Hudson, at that broad expansion of the river denominated by the ancient Dutch navigators the Tappan Zee, and where they always prudently shortened sail and implored the protection of St. Nicholas when they crossed, there lies a small market town or rural port which by some is called Greensburgh, but which is more generally and properly known by the name of Tarry Town. This name was given, we are told, in former days by the good housewives of the adjacent country from the inveterate propensity of their husbands to linger about the village tavern on market days. Be that as it may, I do not vouch for the fact, but merely advert to it for the sake of being precise and authentic. Not far from this village, perhaps about two miles, there is a little valley, or rather lap of land, among high hills, which is one of the quietest places in the whole world. A small brook glides through it, with just murmur enough to lull one to repose, and the occasional whistle of a quail or tapping of a woodpecker is almost the only sound that ever breaks in upon the uniform tranquillity.

I recollect that when a stripling my first exploit in squirrel-shooting was in a grove of tall walnut trees that shades one side of the valley. I had wandered into it at noontime, when all Nature is peculiarly quiet, and was startled by the roar of my own gun as it broke the Sabbath stillness around and was prolonged and reverberated by the angry echoes. If ever I should wish for a retreat whither I might steal from the world and its distractions and dream quietly away the remnant of a troubled life, I know of none more promising than this little valley.

From the listless repose of the place and the peculiar character of its inhabitants, who are descendants from the original Dutch settlers, this sequestered glen has long been known by the name of SLEEPY HOLLOW, and its rustic lads are called the Sleepy Hollow Boys throughout all the neighbouring country. A drowsy, dreamy influence seems to hang over the land and to pervade the very atmosphere. Some say that the place was bewitched by a High German doctor during the early days of the settlement; others, that an old Indian chief, the prophet or wizard of his tribe, held his powwows there before the country was discovered by Master Hendrick Hudson. Certain it is, the place still continues under the sway of some witching power that holds a spell over the minds of the good people, causing them to walk in a continual reverie. They are given to all kinds of marvellous beliefs, are subject to trances and visions, and frequently see strange sights and hear music and voices in the air. The whole neighbourhood abounds with local tales, haunted spots, and twilight superstitions; stars shoot and meteors glare oftener across the valley than in any other part of the country, and the night mare, with her whole ninefold, seems to make it the favorite scene of her gambols.

The dominant spirit, however, that haunts this enchanted region, and seems to be commander in chief of all the powers of the air, is the apparition of a figure on horseback without a head. It is said by some to be the ghost of a Hessian trooper, whose head had been carried away by a cannonball in some nameless battle during the Revolutionary War, and who is ever and anon seen by the country-folk hurrying along in the gloom of night as if on the wings of the wind. His haunts are not confined to the valley, but extend at times to the adjacent roads, and especially to the vicinity of a church at no great distance. Indeed, certain of the most authentic historians of those parts, who have been careful in collecting and collating the floating facts concerning this spectre, allege that the body of the trooper, having been buried in the churchyard, the ghost rides forth to the scene of battle in nightly quest of his head, and that the rushing speed with which he sometimes passes along the Hollow, like a midnight blast, is owing to his being belated and in a hurry to get back to the churchyard before day Break.

Such is the general purport of this legendary superstition, which has furnished materials for many a wild story in that region of shadows; and the spectre is known, at all the country firesides, by the name of the Headless Horseman of Sleepy Hollow.

It is remarkable, that the visionary propensity I have mentioned is not confined to the native inhabitants of the valley, but is unconsciously imbibed by every one who resides there for a time. However wide awake they may have been before they entered that sleepy region, they are sure in a little time to inhale the witching influence of the air and begin to grow imaginative—to dream dreams, and see apparitions.

I mention this peaceful spot with all possible laud, for it is in such little retired Dutch valleys, found here and there embosomed in the great State of New York, that population, manners, and customs, remain fixed, while the great torrent of migration and improvement, which is making such incessant changes in other parts of this restless country, sweeps by them unobserved. They are like those little nooks of still water, which border a rapid stream where we may see the straw and bubble riding quietly at anchor, or slowly revolving in their mimic harbor, undisturbed by the rush of the passing current. Though many years have elapsed since I trod the drowsy shades of Sleepy Hollow, yet I question whether I should not still find the same trees and the same families vegetating in its sheltered bosom.

In this byplace of Nature there abode, in a remote period of American history, that is to say, some thirty years since, a worthy wight of the name of Ichabod Crane, who sojourned, or, as he expressed it, "tarried," in Sleepy Hollow for the purpose of instructing the children of the vicinity. He was a native of Connecticut, a State which supplies the Union with pioneers for the mind as well as for the forest, and sends forth yearly its legions of frontier woodmen and country schoolmasters. The cognomen of Crane was not inapplicable to his person. He was tall, but exceedingly lank, with narrow shoulders, long arms and legs, hands that dangled a mile out of his sleeves, feet that might have served for shovels, and his whole frame most loosely hung together. His head was small, and flat at top, with huge ears, large green glassy eyes, and a long snip nose, so that it looked like a weathercock perched upon his spindle neck to tell which way the wind blew. To see him striding along the profile of a hill on a windy day, with his clothes bagging and fluttering about him, one might have mistaken him for the genius of

Famine descending upon the earth or some scarecrow eloped from a cornfield.

His school house was a low building of one large room, rudely constructed of logs; the windows partly glazed and partly patched with leaves of old copy books. It was most ingeniously secured at vacant hours by a withe twisted in the handle of the door, and stakes set against the window shutters; so that, though a thief might get in with perfect ease, he would find some embarrassment in getting out; an idea most probably borrowed by the architect, Yost Van Houten, from the mystery of an eelpot. The school house stood in a rather lonely but pleasant situation, just at the foot of a woody hill, with a brook running close by and a formidable birch tree growing at one end of it. From hence the low murmur of his pupils' voices, conning over their lessons, might be heard in a drowsy summer's day like the hum of a bee hive, interrupted now and then by the authoritative voice of the master in the tone of menace or command, or peradventure, by the appalling sound of the birch as he urged some tardy loiterer along the flowery path of knowledge. Truth to say, he was a conscientious man, and ever bore in mind the golden maxim, "spare the rod and spoil the child."—Ichabod Crane's scholars certainly were not spoiled.

I would not have it imagined, however, that he was one of those cruel potentates of the school who joy in the smart of their subjects; on the contrary, he administered justice with discrimination rather than severity; taking the burden off the backs of the weak, and laying it on those of the strong. Your mere puny stripling, that winced at the least flourish of the rod, was passed by with indulgence; but the claims of justice were satisfied by inflicting a double portion on some little tough, wrong-headed, broad-skirted Dutch urchin, who sulked and swelled and grew dogged and sullen beneath the birch. All this he called "doing his duty by their parents"; and he never inflicted a chastisement without following it by the assurance, so consolatory to the smarting urchin, that "he would remember it and thank him for it the longest day he had to live."

When school hours were over he was even the companion and playmate of the larger boys, and on holiday afternoons would convoy some of the smaller ones home who happened to have pretty sisters, or good housewives for mothers, noted for the comforts of the cupboard. Indeed, it behooved him to keep on good terms with his pupils. The revenue arising from his school was small, and would have been scarcely sufficient to furnish him with daily bread, for he was a huge feeder, and, though lank, had the dilating powers of an Anaconda; but to help out his maintenance he was, according to country custom in those parts, boarded and lodged at the houses of the farmers, whose children he instructed. With these he lived successively a week at a time, thus going the rounds of the neighbourhood with all his worldly effects tied up in a cotton handkerchief.

That all this might not be too onerous on the purses of his rustic patrons, who are apt to consider the costs of schooling a grievous burden and schoolmasters as mere drones, he had various ways of rendering himself both useful and agreeable. He assisted the farmers occasionally in the lighter labours of their farms, helped to make hay, mended the fences, took the horses to water, drove the cows from pasture, and cut wood for the winter fire. He laid aside, too, all the dominant dignity and absolute sway with which he lorded it in his little empire, the school, and became wonderfully gentle and ingratiating. He found favor in the eyes of the mothers by petting the children, particularly the youngest; and like the lion bold, which whilom so magnanimously the lamb did hold, he would sit with a child on one knee and rock a cradle with his foot for whole hours together.

In addition to his other vocations, he was the singing master of the neighbourhood and picked up many bright shillings by instructing the young folks in psalmody. It was a matter of no little vanity to him on Sundays to take his station in front of the church gallery with a band of chosen singers, where, in his own mind, he completely carried away the palm from the parson. Certain it is, his voice resounded far above all the rest of the congregation, and there are peculiar quavers still to be heard in that church, and which may even be heard half a mile off, quite to the opposite side of the mill pond on a still Sunday morning, which are said to be legitimately descended from the nose of Ichabod Crane. Thus, by divers little makeshifts in that ingenious way which is commonly denominated "by hook and by crook," the worthy pedagogue got on tolerably enough, and was thought, by all who understood nothing of the labour of headwork, to have a wonderfully easy life of it.

The schoolmaster is generally a man of some importance in the female circle of a rural neighbourhood, being considered a kind of idle, gentleman like personage of vastly superior taste and accomplishments to the rough country swains, and, indeed, inferior in learning only to the parson. His appearance, therefore, is apt to occasion some little stir at the tea table of a farm house and the addition of a supernumerary dish of cakes or sweetmeats, or peradventure, the parade of a silver tea pot. Our man of letters, therefore, was peculiarly happy in the smiles of all the country damsels. How he would figure among them in the churchyard between services on Sundays, gathering grapes for them from the wild vines that overrun the surrounding trees; reciting for their amusement all the epitaphs on the tombstones; or sauntering, with a whole bevy of them, along the banks of the adjacent mill pond, while the more bashful country bumpkins hung sheepishly back, envying his superior elegance and address.

From his half-itinerant life, also, he was a kind of travelling gazette, carrying the whole budget of local gossip from house to house so that his appearance was always greeted with satisfaction. He was, moreover, esteemed by the women as a man of great erudition, for he had read several books quite through, and was a perfect master of Cotton Mather's History of New England Witchcraft, in which, by the way, he most firmly and potently believed.

He was, in fact, an odd mixture of small shrewdness and simple credulity. His appetite for the marvellous, and his powers of digesting it, were equally extraordinary, and both had been increased by his residence in this spell bound region. No tale was too gross or monstrous for his capacious swallow. It was often his delight, after his school was dismissed in the afternoon, to stretch himself on the rich bed of clover bordering the little brook that whimpered by his school house, and there con over old Mather's direful tales until the gathering dusk of the evening made the printed page a mere mist before his eyes. Then, as he wended his way by swamp and stream and awful woodland to the farmhouse where he happened to be quartered, every sound of Nature at that witching hour fluttered his excited imagination—the moan of the whip-poor-will* from the hillside; the boding cry of the tree toad, that harbinger of storm; the dreary hooting of the screech owl; or the sudden rustling in the thicket of birds frightened from their roost. The fire flies, too, which sparkled most vividly in the darkest places, now and then startled him as one of uncommon brightness would stream across his path; and if, by chance, a huge blockhead of a beetle came winging his blundering flight against him, the poor varlet was ready to give up the ghost, with the idea that he was struck with a witch's

---

*The whip-poor-will is a bird which is only heard at night. It receives its name from its note, which is thought to resemble those words.

token. His only resource on such occasions, either to drown thought or drive away evil spirits, was to sing psalm tunes—and the good people of Sleepy Hollow, as they sat by their doors of an evening, were often filled with awe at hearing his nasal melody, "in linked sweetness long drawn out," floating from the distant hill or along the dusky road.

Another of his sources of fearful pleasure was to pass long winter evenings with the old Dutch wives as they sat spinning by the fire, with a row of apples roasting and spluttering along the hearth, and listen to their marvellous tales of ghosts and goblins, and haunted fields, and haunted brooks, and haunted bridges, and haunted houses, and particularly of the headless horseman, or Galloping Hessian of the Hollow, as they sometimes called him. He would delight them equally by his anecdotes of witchcraft and of the direful omens and portentous sights and sounds in the air, which prevailed in the earlier times of Connecticut; and would frighten them woefully with speculations upon comets and shooting stars, and with the alarming fact that the world did absolutely turn round and that they were half the time topsy-turvy!

But if there was a pleasure in all this while snugly cuddling in the chimney-corner of a chamber that was all of a ruddy glow from the crackling wood fire, and where, of course, no spectre dared to show its face, it was dearly purchased by the terrors of his subsequent walk homewards. What fearful shapes and shadows beset his path amidst the dim and ghastly glare of a snowy night!—With what wistful look did be eye every trembling ray of light streaming across the waste fields from some distant window!—How often was he appalled by some shrub covered with snow, which, like a sheeted spectre, beset his very path!—How often did he shrink with curdling awe at the sound of his own steps on the frosty crust beneath his feet, and dread to look over his shoulder, lest he should behold some uncouth being tramping close behind him!—and how often was he thrown into complete dismay by some rushing blast howling among the trees, in the idea that it was the Galloping Hessian on one of his nightly scourings!

All these, however, were mere terrors of the night, phantoms of the mind that walk in darkness; and though he had seen many spectres in his time, and been more than once beset by Satan in divers shapes in his lonely perambulations, yet daylight put an end to all these evils; and he would have passed a pleasant life of it, in despite of the devil and all his works, if his path had not been crossed by a being that causes more perplexity to mortal man than ghosts, goblins, and the whole race of witches put together, and that was—a woman.

Among the musical disciples who assembled, one evening in each week, to receive his instructions in psalmody, was Katrina Van Tassel, the daughter and only child of a substantial Dutch farmer. She was a blooming lass of fresh eighteen; plump as a partridge, ripe and melting and rosy-cheeked as one of her father's peaches, and universally famed, not merely for her beauty, but her vast expectations. She was withal a little of a coquette, as might be perceived even in her dress, which was a mixture of ancient and modern fashions, as most suited to set off her charms. She wore the ornaments of pure yellow gold which her great great grandmother had brought over from Saardam, the tempting stomacher of the olden time, and withal a provokingly short petticoat to display the prettiest foot and ankle in the country round.

Ichabod Crane had a soft and foolish heart towards the sex; and it is not to be wondered at, that so tempting a morsel soon found favor in his eyes, more especially after he had visited her in her paternal mansion. Old Baltus Van Tassel was a perfect picture of a thriving, contented, liberal-hearted farmer. He seldom, it is true, sent either his eyes or his thoughts beyond the boundaries of his own farm, but within those everything was snug, happy, and well-conditioned. He was satisfied with his wealth but not proud of it, and piqued himself upon the hearty abundance, rather than the style, in which he lived. His strong hold was situated on the banks of the Hudson, in one of those green, sheltered, fertile nooks in which the Dutch farmers are so fond of nestling. A great elm tree spread its broad branches over it, at the foot of which bubbled up a spring of the softest and sweetest water, in a little well, formed of a barrel, and then stole sparkling away through the grass to a neighbouring brook that bubbled along among alders and dwarf willows. Hard by the farm house was a vast barn, that might have served for a church; every window and crevice of which seemed bursting forth with the treasures of the farm; the flail was busily resounding within it from morning to night; swallows and martins skimmed twittering about the eaves; and rows of pigeons, some with one eye turned up, as if watching the weather, some with their heads under their wings or buried in their bosoms, and others, swelling, and cooing, and bowing about their dames, were enjoying the sunshine on the roof. Sleek, unwieldy porkers were grunting in the repose and abundance of their pens, whence sallied forth, now and then, troops of sucking pigs as if to snuff the air. A stately squadron of snowy geese were riding in an adjoining pond, convoying whole fleets of ducks; regiments of turkeys were gobbling through the farm yard, and guinea fowls fretting about it, like ill-tempered housewives, with their peevish, discontented cry. Before the barndoor strutted the gallant cock, that pattern of a husband, a warrior, and a fine gentleman, clapping his burnished wings and crowing in the pride and gladness of his heart—sometimes tearing up the earth with his feet, and then generously calling his ever-hungry family of wives and children to enjoy the rich morsel which he had discovered.

The pedagogue's mouth watered as he looked upon this sumptuous promise of luxurious winter fare. In his devouring mind's eye he pictured to himself every roasting-pig running about with a pudding in his belly and an apple in his mouth; the pigeons were snugly put to bed in a comfortable pie and tucked in with a coverlet of crust; the geese were swimming in their own gravy; and the ducks pairing cosily in dishes, like snug married couples, with a decent competency of onion sauce; in the porkers he saw carved out the future sleek side of bacon and juicy relishing ham; not a turkey but he beheld daintily trussed up, with its gizzard under its wing, and, peradventure, a necklace of savory sausages; and even bright Chanticleer himself lay sprawling on his back in a side-dish, with uplifted claws, as if craving that quarter which his chivalrous spirit disdained to ask while living.

As the enraptured Ichabod fancied all this, and as he rolled his great green eyes over the fat meadow-lands, the rich fields of wheat, of rye, of buckwheat, and Indian corn, and the orchards burdened with ruddy fruit, which surrounded the warm tenement of Van Tassel, his heart yearned after the damsel who was to inherit these domains, and his imagination expanded with the idea how they might be readily turned into cash and the money invested in immense tracts of wild land and shingle palaces in the wilderness. Nay, his busy fancy already realized his hopes, and presented to him the blooming Katrina, with a whole family of children, mounted on the top of a wagon loaded with household trumpery, with pots and kettles dangling beneath, and he beheld himself bestriding a pacing mare, with a colt at her heels, setting out for Kentucky, Tennessee, or the Lord knows where!

When he entered the house the conquest of his heart was complete. It was one of those spacious farmhouses with high ridged but lowly sloping roofs, built in the style handed down from the first Dutch settlers, the low projecting eaves forming a piazza along the front capable of being closed up in bad weather. Under this were hung flails, harness, various utensils of husbandry, and nets for fishing in the neighbouring river. Benches were built along the sides for summer use, and a great spinning-wheel at one end and a churn at the other showed the various uses to which this important porch might be devoted. From this piazza the wondering Ichabod entered the hall, which formed the centre of the mansion and the place of usual residence. Here rows of resplendent pewter, ranged on a long dresser, dazzled his eyes. In one corner stood a huge bag of wool ready to be spun; in another a quantity of linsey-woolsey just from the loom; ears of Indian corn and strings of dried apples and peaches hung in gay festoons along the walls, mingled with the gaud of red peppers; and a door left ajar gave him a peep into the best parlor, where the claw-footed chairs and dark mahogany tables shone like mirrors; andirons, with their accompanying shovel and tongs, glistened from their covert of asparagus tops; mock-oranges and conch-shells decorated the mantelpiece; strings of various-colored birds' eggs were suspended above it; a great ostrich egg was hung from the centre of the room, and a corner cupboard, knowingly left open, displayed immense treasures of old silver and well-mended china.

From the moment Ichabod laid his eyes upon these regions of delight, the peace of his mind was at an end, and his only study was how to gain the affections of the peerless daughter of Van Tassel. In this enterprize, however, he had more real difficulties than generally fell to the lot of a knight errant of yore, who seldom had any thing but giants, enchanters, fiery dragons, and such-like easily-conquered adversaries to contend with, and had to make his way merely through gates of iron and brass and walls of adamant to the castle keep, where the lady of his heart was confined; all which he achieved as easily as a man would carve his way to the centre of a Christmas pie, and then the lady gave him her hand as a matter of course. Ichabod, on the contrary, had to win his way to the heart of a country coquette beset with a labyrinth of whims and caprices, which were for ever presenting new difficulties and impediments, and he had to encounter a host of fearful adversaries of real flesh and blood, the numerous rustic admirers who beset every portal to her heart, keeping a watchful and angry eye upon each other, but ready to fly out in the common cause against any new competitor.

Among these the most formidable was a burly, roaring, roistering blade of the name of Abraham, or, according to the Dutch abbreviation, Brom Van Brunt, the hero of the country round, which rang with his feats of strength and hardihood. He was broad-shouldered and double-jointed, with short curly black hair and a bluff but not unpleasant countenance, having a mingled air of fun and arrogance. From his Herculean frame and great powers of limb, he had received the nickname of BROM BONES, by which he was universally known. He was famed for great knowledge and skill in horsemanship, being as dexterous on horseback as a Tartar. He was foremost at all races and cockfights, and, with the ascendancy which bodily strength acquires in rustic life, was the umpire in all disputes, setting his hat on one side and giving his decisions with an air and tone admitting of no gainsay or appeal. He was always ready for either a fight or a frolic, but had more mischief than ill will in his composition; and with all his overbearing roughness there was a strong dash of waggish good humour at bottom. He had three or four boon companions, who regarded him as their model, and at the head of whom he scoured the country, attending every scene of feud or merriment for miles around. In cold weather he was distinguished by a fur cap, surmounted with a flaunting fox's tail, and when the folks at a country gathering descried this well known crest at a distance, whisking about among a squad of hard riders, they always stood by for a squall. Sometimes his crew would be heard dashing along past the farm-houses at midnight with whoop and halloo, like a troop of Don Cossacks, and the old dames, startled out of their sleep, would listen for a moment till the hurry-scurry had clattered by, and then exclaim, "aye, there goes Brom Bones and his gang!" The neighbours looked upon him with a mixture of awe, admiration, and good-will, and when any madcap prank or rustic brawl occurred in the vicinity always shook their heads and warranted Brom Bones was at the bottom of it.

This rantipole hero had for some time singled out the blooming Katrina for the object of his uncouth gallantries, and, though his amorous toyings were something like the gentle caresses and endearments of a bear, yet it was whispered that she did not altogether discourage his hopes. Certain it is, his advances were signals for rival candidates to retire who felt no inclination to cross a line in his amours; insomuch, that when his horse was seen tied to Van Tassel's paling on a Sunday night (a sure sign that his master was courting or, as it is termed, "sparking," within), all other suitors passed by in despair and carried the war into other quarters.

Such was the formidable rival with whom Ichabod Crane had to contend, and, considering all things, a stouter man than he would have shrunk from the competition and a wiser man would have despaired. He had, however, a happy mixture of pliability and perseverance in his nature; he was in form and spirit like a supple jack—yielding, but tough; though he bent, he never broke and though he bowed beneath the slightest pressure, yet the moment it was away—jerk!—he was as erect and carried his head as high as ever.

To have taken the field openly against his rival would have been madness for he was not man to be thwarted in his amours, any more than that stormy lover, Achilles. Ichabod, therefore, made his advances in a quiet and gently insinuating manner. Under cover of his character of singing master, he made frequent visits at the farmhouse; not that he had anything to apprehend from the meddlesome interference of parents, which is so often a stumbling block in the path of lovers. Balt Van Tassel was an easy indulgent soul; he loved his daughter better even than his pipe, and, like a reasonable man and an excellent father, let her have her way in every thing. His notable little wife too, had enough to do to attend to her housekeeping and manage her poultry, for, as she sagely observed, ducks and geese are foolish things and must be looked after, but girls can take care of themselves. Thus while the busy dame bustled about the house, or plied her spinning-wheel at one end of the piazza, honest Balt would sit smoking his evening pipe at the other, watching the achievements of a little wooden warrior who, armed with a sword in each hand, was most valiantly fighting the wind on the pinnacle of the barn. In the mean time, Ichabod would carry on his suit with the daughter by the side of the spring under the great elm, or sauntering along in the twilight, that hour so favorable to the lover's eloquence.

I profess not to know how women's hearts are wooed and won. To me they have always been matters of riddle and admiration. Some seem to have but one vulnerable point, or door of access, while others have a thousand avenues and may be captured in a thousand different ways. It is a great triumph of skill to gain the former, but still greater proof of generalship to maintain possession of the latter, for the man must battle for his fortress at every door and window. He who wins a thousand common hearts is therefore entitled to some renown, but he who keeps undisputed sway over the heart of a coquette is indeed a hero. Certain it is, this was not the case with the redoubtable Brom Bones; and from the moment Ichabod Crane made his advances, the interests of the former evidently declined; his horse was no longer seen tied at the palings on Sunday nights, and a deadly feud gradually arose between him and the preceptor of Sleepy Hollow.

Brom, who had a degree of rough chivalry in his nature, would fain have carried matters to open warfare, and have settled their pretensions to the lady according to the mode of those most concise and simple reasoners, the knights errant of yore—by single combat; but Ichabod was too conscious of the superior might of his adversary to enter the lists against him: he had overheard a boast of Bones, that he would "double the schoolmaster up, and lay him on a shelf of his own school house"; and he was too wary to give him an opportunity. There was something extremely provoking in this obstinately pacific system; it left Brom no alternative but to draw upon the funds of rustic waggery in his disposition, and to play off boorish practical jokes upon his rival. Ichabod became the object of whimsical persecution to Bones, and his gang of rough riders. They harried his hitherto peaceful domains; smoked out his singing school, by stopping up the chimney; broke into the schoolhouse at night in spite of its formidable fastenings of withe and window stakes, and turned everything topsy-turvy; so that the poor schoolmaster began to think all the witches in the country held their meetings there. But what was still more annoying, Brom took all opportunities of turning him into ridicule in presence of his mistress, and had a scoundrel dog whom he taught to whine in the most ludicrous manner, and introduced as a rival of Ichabod's, to instruct her in psalmody.

In this way, matters went on for some time without producing any material effect on the relative situation of the contending powers. On a fine autumnal afternoon Ichabod, in pensive mood, sat enthroned on the lofty stool whence he usually watched all the concerns of his little literary realm. In his hand he swayed a ferule, that sceptre of despotic power; the birch of justice reposed on three nails behind the throne, a constant terror to evil doers; while on the desk before him might be seen sundry contraband articles and prohibited weapons detected upon the persons of idle urchins, such as half-munched apples, popguns, whirligigs, fly cages, and whole legions of rampant little paper gamecocks. Apparently there had been some appalling act of justice recently inflicted, for his scholars were all busily intent upon their books or slyly whispering behind them with one eye kept upon the master, and a kind of buzzing stillness reigned throughout the school room. It was suddenly interrupted by the appearance of a negro in tow cloth jacket and trowsers, a round crowned fragment of a hat like the cap of Mercury, and mounted on the back of a ragged, wild, half broken colt, which he managed with a rope by way of halter. He came clattering up to the school door with an invitation to Ichabod to attend a merry making or "quilting frolick," to be held that evening at Mynheer Van Tassel's; and, having delivered his message with that air of importance and effort at fine language which a negro is apt to display on petty embassies of the kind, he dashed over the brook, and was seen scampering away up the hollow, full of the importance and hurry of his mission.

All was now bustle and hubbub in the late quiet school room. The scholars were hurried through their lessons without stopping at trifles; those who were nimble skipped over half with impunity, and those who were tardy had a smart application now and then in the rear to quicken their speed or help them over a tall word. Books were flung aside without being put away on the shelves; inkstands were overturned, benches thrown down, and the whole school was turned loose an hour before the usual time, bursting forth like a legion of young imps, yelping and racketing about the green in joy at their early emancipation.

The gallant Ichabod now spent at least an extra half hour at his toilet, brushing and furbishing up his best, and indeed only, suit of rusty black, and arranging his locks by a bit of broken looking glass that hung up in the school house. That he might make his appearance before his mistress in the true style of a cavalier, he borrowed a horse from the farmer with whom he was domiciliated, a choleric old Dutchman of the name of Hans Van Ripper, and, thus gallantly mounted, issued forth like a knight errant in quest of adventures. But it is meet I should, in the true spirit of romantic story, give some account of the looks and equipments of my hero and his steed. The animal he bestrode was a broken down plough horse, that had outlived almost everything but his viciousness. He was gaunt and shagged, with a ewe neck and a head like a hammer; his rusty mane and tail were tangled and knotted with burrs; one eye had lost its pupil and was glaring and spectral, but the other had the gleam of a genuine devil in it. Still, he must have had fire and mettle in his day, if we may judge from the name he bore of Gunpowder. He had, in fact, been a favorite steed of his master's, the choleric Van Ripper, who was a furious rider, and had infused, very probably, some of his own spirit into the animal, for, old and broken down as he looked, there was more of the lurking devil in him than in any young filly in the country.

Ichabod was a suitable figure for such a steed. He rode with short stirrups, which brought his knees nearly up to the pommel of the saddle; his sharp elbows stuck out like grasshoppers'; he carried his whip perpendicularly in his hand like a sceptre; and as his horse jogged on the motion of his arms was not unlike the flapping of a pair of wings. A small wool hat rested on the top of his nose, for so his scanty strip of forehead might be called, and the skirts of his black coat fluttered out almost to his horse's tail. Such was the appearance of Ichabod and his steed as they shambled out of the gate of Hans Van Ripper, and it was altogether such an apparition as is seldom to be met with in broad day light.

It was, as I have said, a fine autumnal day, the sky was clear and serene, and Nature wore that rich and golden livery which we always associate with the idea of abundance. The forests had put on their sober brown and yellow, while some trees of the tenderer kind had been nipped by the frosts into brilliant dyes of orange, purple, and scarlet. Streaming files of wild ducks began to make their appearance high in the air; the bark of the squirrel might be heard from the groves of beech and hickory nuts, and the pensive whistle of the quail at intervals from the neighbouring stubble field.

The small birds were taking their farewell banquets. In the fullness of their revelry they fluttered, chirping and frolicking, from bush to bush and tree to tree, capricious from the very profusion and variety around them. There was the honest cock robin, the favorite game of stripling sportsmen, with its loud querulous note; and the twittering blackbirds, flying in sable clouds; and the golden winged woodpecker, with his crimson crest, his broad black gorget, and splendid plumage; and the cedar-bird, with its red-tipt wings and yellow-tipt tail and its little monteiro cap of feathers; and the blue jay, that noisy coxcomb, in his gay light-blue coat and white under clothes, screaming and chattering, bobbing and nodding and bowing, and pretending to be on good terms with every songster of the grove.

As Ichabod jogged slowly on his way his eye, ever open to every symptom of culinary abundance, ranged with delight over the treasures of jolly autumn. On all sides he beheld vast store of apples, some hanging in oppressive opulence on the trees, some gathered into baskets and barrels for the market, others heaped up in rich piles for the cider-press. Further on he beheld great fields of Indian corn, with its golden ears peeping from their leafy coverts and holding out the promise of cakes and hasty pudding; and the yellow pumpkins lying beneath them, turning up their fair round bellies to the sun, and giving ample prospects of the most luxurious of pies; and anon he passed the fragrant buckwheat fields, breathing the odor of the beehive, and as he beheld them soft anticipations stole over his mind of dainty slapjacks, well buttered and garnished with honey or treacle by the delicate little dimpled hand of Katrina Van Tassel.

Thus feeding his mind with many sweet thoughts and "sugared suppositions," he journeyed along the sides of a range of hills which look out upon some of the goodliest scenes of the mighty Hudson. The sun gradually wheeled his broad disk down into the west. The wide bosom of the Tappan Zee lay motionless and glassy, excepting that here and there a gentle undulation waved and prolonged the blue shadow of the distant mountain: a few amber clouds floated in the sky, without a breath of air to move them. The horizon was of a fine golden tint, changing gradually into a pure apple green, and from that into the deep blue of the mid-heaven. A slanting ray lingered on the woody crests of the precipices that overhung some parts of the river, giving greater depth to the dark grey and purple of their rocky sides. A sloop was loitering in the distance, dropping slowly down with the tide, her sail hanging uselessly against the mast, and as the reflection of the sky gleamed along the still water it seemed as if the vessel was suspended in the air.

It was toward evening that Ichabod arrived at the castle of the Heer Van Tassel, which he found thronged with the pride and flower of the adjacent country. Old farmers, a spare leathern faced race, in homespun coats and breeches, blue stockings, huge shoes, and magnificent pewter buckles. Their brisk withered little dames, in close crimped caps, long waisted short gowns, homespun petticoats, with scissors and pincushions, and gay calico pockets hanging on the outside. Buxom lasses, almost as antiquated as their mothers, excepting where a straw hat, a fine ribband, or perhaps a white frock, gave symptoms of city innovation. The sons, in short square-skirted coats with rows of stupendous brass buttons, and their hair generally queued in the fashion of the times, especially if they could procure an eel skin for the purpose, it being esteemed throughout the country as a potent nourisher and strengthener of the hair.

Brom Bones, however, was the hero of the scene, having come to the gathering on his favorite steed Daredevil, a creature, like himself full of metal and mischief, and which no one but himself could manage. He was, in fact, noted for preferring vicious animals, given to all kinds of tricks, which kept the rider in constant risk of his neck, for he held a tractable, well-broken horse as unworthy of a lad of spirit.

Fain would I pause to dwell upon the world of charms that burst upon the enraptured gaze of my hero, as he entered the state parlour of Van Tassel's mansion. Not those of the bevy of buxom lasses with their luxurious display of red and white, but the ample charms of a genuine Dutch country tea table in the sumptuous time of autumn. Such heaped up platters of cakes of various and almost indescribable kinds, known only to experienced Dutch housewives! There was the doughty doughnut, the tenderer oily koek, and the crisp and crumbling cruller; sweet cakes and short cakes, ginger cakes and honey cakes, and the whole family of cakes. And then there were apple pies and peach pies and pumpkin pies; besides slices of ham and smoked beef; and moreover delectable dishes of preserved plums and peaches and pears and quinces; not to mention broiled shad and roasted chickens; together with bowls of milk and cream, all mingled higgledy-piggledy, pretty much as I have enumerated them, with the motherly teapot sending up its clouds of vapor from the midst—Heaven bless the mark! I want breath and time to discuss this banquet as it deserves, and am too eager to get on with my story. Happily, Ichabod Crane was not in so great a hurry as his historian, but did ample justice to every dainty.

He was a kind and thankful creature, whose heart dilated in proportion as his skin was filled with good cheer, and whose spirits rose with eating as some men's do with drink. He could not help, too, rolling his large eyes round him as he ate, and chuckling with the possibility that he might one day be lord of all this scene of almost unimaginable luxury and splendour. Then, he thought, how soon he'd turn his back upon the old school house, snap his fingers in the face of Hans Van Ripper, and every other niggardly patron, and kick any itinerant pedagogue out of doors that should dare to call him comrade!

Old Baltus Van Tassel moved about among his guests with a face dilated with content and good-humor, round and jolly as the harvest moon. His hospitable attentions were brief, but expressive, being confined to a shake of the hand, a slap on the shoulder, a loud laugh, and a pressing invitation to "fall to and help themselves."

And now the sound of the music from the common room, or hall, summoned to the dance. The musician was an old grey headed negro who had been the itinerant orchestra of the neighbourhood for more than half a century. His instrument was as old and battered as himself. The greater part of the time he scraped on two or three strings, accompanying every movement of the bow with a motion of the head, bowing almost to the ground, and stamping with his foot whenever a fresh couple were to start.

Ichobod prided himself upon his dancing as much as upon his vocal powers. Not a limb, not a fibre about him was idle; and to have seen his loosely hung frame in full motion and clattering about the room you would have thought Saint Vitus himself, that blessed patron of the dance, was figuring before you in person. He was the admiration of all the negroes, who, having gathered, of all ages and sizes, from the farm and the neighbourhood, stood forming a pyramid of shining black faces at every door and window, gazing with delight at the scene, rolling their white eyeballs, and showing grinning rows of ivory from ear to ear. How could the flogger of urchins be otherwise than animated and joyous; the lady of his heart was his partner in the dance; and smiling graciously in reply to all his amorous oglings, while Brom Bones, sorely smitten with love and jealousy, sat brooding by himself in one corner.

When the dance was at an end Ichabod was attracted to a knot of the sager folks, who, with old Van Tassel, sat smoking at one end of the piazza gossiping over former times and drawing out long stories about the war.

This neighbourhood, at the time of which I am speaking, was one of those highly favored places which abound with chronicle and great men. The British and American line had run near it during the war; it had therefore been the scene of marauding and infested with refugees, cow boys, and all kinds of border chivalry. Just sufficient time had elapsed to enable each storyteller to dress up his tale with a little becoming fiction, and in the indistinctness of his recollection to make himself the hero of every exploit.

There was the story of Doffue Martling, a large blue-bearded Dutchman, who had nearly taken a British frigate with an old iron nine-pounder from a mud breastwork, only that his gun burst at the sixth discharge. And there was an old gentleman who shall be nameless, being too rich a mynheer to be lightly mentioned, who, in the battle of Whiteplains, being an excellent master of defence, parried a musket-ball with a small sword, insomuch that he absolutely felt it whiz round the blade, and glance off at the hilt: in proof of which he was ready at any time to show the sword, with the hilt a little bent. There were several more that had been equally great in the field, not one of whom but was persuaded that he had a considerable hand in bringing the war to a happy termination.

But all these were nothing to the tales of ghosts and apparitions that succeeded. The neighbourhood is rich in legendary treasures of the kind. Local tales and superstitions thrive best in these sheltered, long settled retreats but are trampled under foot by the shifting throng that forms the population of most of our country places. Besides, there is no encouragement for ghosts in most of our villages, for they have scarcely had time to finish their first nap and turn themselves in their graves before their surviving friends have travelled away from the neighbourhood; so that when they turn out at night to walk their rounds they have no acquaintance left to call upon. This is perhaps the reason why we so seldom hear of ghosts except in our long-established Dutch communities.

The immediate causes however, of the prevalence of supernatural stories in these parts, was doubtless owing to the vicinity of Sleepy Hollow. There was a contagion in the very air that blew from that haunted region; it breathed forth an atmosphere of dreams and fancies infecting all the land. Several of the Sleepy Hollow people were present at Van Tassel's, and, as usual, were doling out their wild and wonderful legends. Many dismal tales were told about funeral trains and mourning cries and wailings heard and seen about the great tree where the unfortunate Major André was taken, and which stood in the neighbourhood. Some mention was made also of the woman in white that haunted the dark glen at Raven Rock, and was often heard to shriek on winter nights before a storm, having perished there in the snow. The chief part of the stories, however, turned upon the favorite spectre of Sleepy Hollow, the headless horseman, who had been heard several times of late patroling the country; and, it was said, tethered his horse nightly among the graves in the churchyard.

The sequestered situation of this church seems always to have made it a favorite haunt of troubled spirits. It stands on a knoll surrounded by locust trees and lofty elms, from among which its decent whitewashed walls shine modestly forth, like Christian purity beaming through the shades of retirement. A gentle slope descends from it to a silver sheet of water bordered by high trees, between which peeps may be caught at the blue hills of the Hudson. To look upon its grass-grown yard, where the sunbeams seem to sleep so quietly, one would think that there at least the dead might rest in peace. On one side of the church extends a wide woody dell, along, which raves a large brook among broken rocks and trunks of fallen trees. Over a deep black part of the stream, not far from the church, was formerly thrown a wooden bridge; the road that led to it and the bridge itself were thickly shaded by overhanging trees, which cast a gloom about it even in the daytime, but occasioned a fearful darkness at night. Such was one of the favourite haunts of the headless horseman, and the place where he was most frequently encountered. The tale was told of old Brouwer, a most heretical disbeliever in ghosts, how he met the horseman returning from his foray into Sleepy Hollow, and was obliged to get up behind him; how they galloped over bush and brake, over hill and swamp, until they reached the bridge, when the horseman suddenly turned into a skeleton, threw old Brouwer into the brook, and sprang away over the tree tops with a clap of thunder.

This story was immediately matched by a thrice marvellous adventure of Brom Bones, who made light of the galloping Hessian as an arrant jockey. He affirmed that on returning one night from the neighbouring village of Sing-Sing, he had been over taken by this midnight trooper; that he had offered to race with him for a bowl of punch, and should have won it too, for Daredevil beat the goblin horse all hollow, but just as they came to the church bridge the Hessian bolted and vanished in a flash of fire.

All these tales, told in that drowsy undertone with which men talk in the dark, the countenances of the listeners only now and then receiving a casual gleam from the glare of a pipe, sank deep in the mind of Ichabod. He repaid them in kind with large extracts from his invaluable author, Cotton Mather, and added many marvellous events that had taken place in his native state of Connecticut and fearful sights which he had seen in his nightly walks about Sleepy Hollow.

The revel now gradually broke up. The old farmers gathered together their families in their wagons, and were heard for some time rattling along the hollow roads and over the distant hills. Some of the damsels mounted on pillions behind their favorite swains, and their light hearted laughter, mingling with the clatter of hoofs, echoed along the silent woodlands, sounding fainter and fainter until they gradually died away—and the late scene of noise and frolic was all silent and deserted. Ichabod only lingered behind, according to the custom of country lovers, to have a *tête-à-tête* with the heiress, fully convinced that he was now on the high road to success. What passed at this interview I will not pretend to say, for in fact I do not know. Something, however, I fear me, must have gone wrong, for he certainly sallied forth, after no very great interval, with an air quite desolate and chop fallen—Oh these women! these women! Could that girl have been playing off any of her coquettish tricks?—Was her encouragement of the poor pedagogue all a mere sham to secure her conquest of his rival?—Heaven only knows, not I!—Let it suffice to say, Ichabod stole forth with the air of one who had been sacking a hen-roost, rather than a fair lady's heart. Without looking to the right or left to notice the scene of rural wealth on which he had so often gloated, he went straight to the stable, and with several hearty cuffs and kicks roused his steed most uncourteously from the comfortable quarters in which he was soundly sleeping, dreaming of mountains of corn and oats and whole valleys of timothy and clover.

It was the very witching time of night that Ichabod, heavy hearted and crestfallen, pursued his travel homewards along the sides of the lofty hills which rise above Tarry Town, and which he had traversed so cheerily in the afternoon. The hour was as dismal as himself. Far below him the Tappan Zee spread its dusky and indistinct waste of waters, with here and there the tall mast of a sloop riding quietly at anchor under the land. In the dead hush of midnight he could even hear the barking of the watch dog from the opposite shore of the Hudson; but it was so vague and faint as only to give an idea of his distance from this faithful companion of man. Now and then, too, the long drawn crowing of a cock, accidentally awakened, would sound far, far off, from some farm house away among the hills; but it was like a dreaming sound in his ear. No signs of life occurred near him, but occasionally the melancholy chirp of a cricket, or perhaps the guttural twang of a bull frog from a neighbouring marsh, as if sleeping uncomfortably and turning suddenly in his bed.

All the stories of ghosts and goblins that he had heard in the afternoon, now came crowding upon his recollection. The night grew darker and darker; the stars seemed to sink deeper in the sky, and driving clouds occasionally had them from his sight. He had never felt so lonely and dismal. He was, moreover, approaching the very place where many of the scenes of the ghost-stories had been laid. In the centre of the road stood an enormous tulip tree which towered like a giant above all the other trees of the neighbourhood and formed a kind of landmark. Its limbs were gnarled and fantastic, large enough to form trunks for ordinary trees, twisting down almost to the earth and rising again into the air. It was connected with the tragical story of the unfortunate André, who had been taken prisoner hard by, and was universally known by the name of Major André's tree. The common people regarded it with a mixture of respect and superstition, partly out of sympathy for the fate of its ill-starred namesake, and partly from the tales of strange sights and doleful lamentations told concerning it.

As Ichabod approached this fearful tree he began to whistle: he thought his whistle was answered: it was but a blast sweeping sharply through the dry branches. As he approached a little nearer he thought he saw something white hanging in the midst of the tree: he paused and ceased whistling, but on looking more narrowly perceived that it was a place where the tree had been scathed by lightning and the white wood laid bare. Suddenly he heard a groan—his teeth chattered and his knees smote against the saddle: it was but the rubbing of one huge bough upon another as they were swayed about by the breeze. He passed the tree in safety, but new perils lay before him.

About two hundred yards from the tree a small brook crossed the road and ran into a marshy and thickly wooded glen known by the name of Wiley's Swamp. A few rough logs, laid side by side, served for a bridge over this stream. On that side of the road where the brook entered the wood a group of oaks and chestnuts, matted thick with wild grape vines, threw a cavernous gloom over it. To pass this bridge was the severest trial. It was at this identical spot that the unfortunate André was captured, and under the covert of those chestnuts and vines were the sturdy yeomen concealed who surprised him. This has ever since been considered a haunted stream, and fearful are the feelings of the schoolboy who has to pass it alone after dark.

As he approached the stream his heart began to thump; he summoned up, however, all his resolution, gave his horse half a score of kicks in the ribs, and attempted to dash briskly across the bridge; but instead of starting forward, the perverse old animal made a lateral movement and ran broadside against the fence. Ichabod, whose fears increased with the delay, jerked the reins on the other side and kicked lustily with the contrary foot: it was all in vain; his steed started, it is true, but it was only to plunge to the opposite side of the road into a thicket of brambles and alder bushes. The schoolmaster now bestowed both whip and heel upon the starveling ribs of old Gunpowder, who dashed forward, snuffing and snorting, but came to a stand just by the bridge with a suddenness that had nearly sent his rider sprawling over his head. Just at this moment a plashy tramp by the side of the bridge caught the sensitive ear of Ichabod. In the dark shadow of the grove on the margin of the brook he beheld something huge, misshapen, black, and towering. It stirred not, but seemed gathered up in the gloom, like some gigantic monster ready to spring upon the traveller.

The hair of the affrighted pedagogue rose upon his head with terror. What was to be done? To turn and fly was now too late; and besides, what chance was there of escaping ghost or goblin, if such it was, which could ride upon the wings of the wind? Summoning up, therefore, a show of courage, he demanded in stammering accents— "who are you?" He received no reply. He repeated his demand in a still more agitated voice.—Still there was no answer. Once more he cudgelled the sides of the inflexible Gunpowder, and, shutting his eyes, broke forth with involuntary fervor into a psalm tune. Just then the shadowy object of alarm put itself in motion, and with a scramble and a bound stood at once in the middle of the road. Though the night was dark and dismal, yet the form of the unknown might now in some degree be ascertained. He appeared to be a horseman of large dimensions and mounted on a black horse of powerful frame. He made no offer of molestation or sociability, but kept aloof on one side of the road, jogging along on the blind side of old Gunpowder, who had now got over his fright and waywardness.

Ichabod, who had no relish for this strange midnight companion, and bethought himself of the adventure of Brom Bones with the Galloping Hessian, now quickened his steed in hopes of leaving him behind. The stranger, however, quickened his horse to an equal pace; Ichabod pulled up, and fell into a walk, thinking to lag behind—the other did the same. His heart began to sink within him; he endeavored to resume his psalm tune, but his parched tongue clove to the roof of his mouth and he could not utter a stave. There was something in the moody and dogged silence of this pertinacious companion that was mysterious and appalling. It was soon fearfully accounted for. On mounting a rising ground, which brought the figure of his fellow-traveller in relief against the sky, gigantic in height and muffled in a cloak, Ichabod was horror struck on perceiving that he was headless! but his horror was still more increased on observing that the head, which should have rested on his shoulders, was carried before him on the pommel of the saddle. His terror rose to desperation, he rained a shower of kicks and blows upon Gunpowder, hoping by a sudden movement to give his companion the slip—but the spectre started full jump with him. Away, then, they dashed through thick and thin; stones flying and sparks flashing at every bound. Ichabod's flimsy garments fluttered in the air as he stretched his long lank body away over his horse's head in the eagerness of his flight.

They had now reached the road which turns off to Sleepy Hollow; but Gunpowder, who seemed possessed with a demon, instead of keeping up it, made an opposite turn and plunged headlong down hill to the left. This road leads through a sandy hollow shaded by trees for about a quarter of a mile, where it crosses the bridge famous in goblin story, and just beyond swells the green knoll on which stands the whitewashed church.

As yet the panic of the steed bad given his unskillful rider an apparent advantage in the chace; but just as he had got halfway through the hollow the girths of the saddle gave away and he felt it slipping from under him; he seized it by the pommel and endeavored to hold it firm, but in vain, and had just time to save himself by clasping old Gunpowder round the neck, when the saddle fell to the earth, and he heard it trampled under foot by his pursuer. For a moment the terror of Hans Van Ripper's wrath passed across his mind—for it was his Sunday saddle; but this was no time for petty fears: the goblin was hard on his haunches, and (unskilful rider that he was!) he had much ado to maintain his seat, sometimes slipping on one side, sometimes on another, and sometimes jolted on the high ridge of his horse's back-bone with a violence that he verily feared would cleave him asunder.

An opening in the trees now cheered him with the hopes that the church bridge was at hand. The wavering reflection of a silver star in the bosom of the brook told him that he was not mistaken. He saw the walls of the church dimly glaring under the trees beyond. He recollected the place where Brom Bones' ghostly competitor had disappeared. "If I can but reach that bridge," thought Ichabod, "I am safe." Just then he heard the black steed panting and blowing close behind him; he even fancied that he felt his hot breath. Another convulsive kick in the ribs, and old Gunpowder sprang upon the bridge; he thundered over the resounding planks; he gained the opposite side; and now Ichabod cast a look behind to see if his pursuer should vanish, according to rule, in a flash of fire and brimstone. Just then he saw the goblin rising in his stirrups, and in the very act of hurling his head at him. Ichabod endeavored to dodge the horrible missile, but too late. It encountered his cranium with a tremendous crash—he was tumbled headlong into the dust, and Gunpowder, the black steed, and the goblin rider passed by like a whirlwind.

The next morning the old horse was found, without his saddle and with he bridle under his feet, soberly cropping the grass at his master's gate. Ichabod did not make his appearance at breakfast—dinner hour came, but no Ichabod. The boys assembled at the school house and strolled idly about the banks of the brook; but no schoolmaster. Hans Van Ripper now began to feel some uneasiness about the fate of poor Ichabod and his saddle. An inquiry was set on foot, and after diligent investigation they came upon his traces. In one part of the road leading to the church was found the saddle trampled in the dirt; the tracks of horses' hoofs, deeply dented in the road and evidently at furious speed, were traced to the bridge, beyond which, on the bank of a broad part of the brook, where the water ran deep and black, was found the hat of the unfortunate Ichabod, and close beside it a spattered pumpkin.

The brook was searched, but the body of the schoolmaster was not to be discovered. Hans Van Ripper, as executor of his estate, examined the bundle which contained all his worldly effects. They consisted of two shirts and a half; two stocks for the neck; a pair or two of worsted stockings; an old pair of corduroy small-clothes; a rusty razor; a book of psalm tunes full of dog's ears; and a broken pitch pipe. As to the books and furniture of the schoolhouse, they belonged to the community, excepting Cotton Mather's History of Witchcraft, a New England Almanac, and a book of dreams and fortune telling; in which last was a sheet of foolscap much scribbled and blotted in several fruitless attempts to make a copy of verses in honor of the heiress of Van Tassel. These magic books and the poetic scrawl were forthwith consigned to the flames by Hans Van Ripper, who from that time forward determined to send his children no more to school, observing that he never knew any good come of this same reading and writing. Whatever money the schoolmaster possessed— and he had received his quarter's pay but a day or two before, he must have had about his person at the time of his disappearance.

The mysterious event caused much speculation at the church on the following Sunday. Knots of gazers and gossips were collected in the churchyard, at the bridge, and at the spot where the hat and pumpkin had been found. The stories of Brouwer, of Bones, and a whole budget of others were called to mind, and when they had diligently considered them all, and compared them with the symptoms of the present case, they shook their heads and came to the conclusion that Ichabod had been carried off by the galloping Hessian. As he was a bachelor and in nobody's debt, nobody troubled his head any more about him, the school was removed to a different quarter of the hollow and another pedagogue reigned in his stead.

It is true an old farmer, who had been down to New York on a visit several years after, and from whom this account of the ghostly adventure was received, brought home the intelligence that Ichabod Crane was still alive; that he had left the neighbourhood, partly through fear of the goblin and Hans Van Ripper, and partly in mortification at having been suddenly dismissed by the heiress; that he had changed his quarters to a distant part of the country; had kept school and studied law at the same time; had been admitted to the bar, turned politician electioneered, written for the newspapers, and finally had been made a justice of the Ten Pound Court. Brom Bones too, who shortly after his rival's disappearance conducted the blooming Katrina in triumph to the altar, was observed to look exceedingly knowing whenever the story of Ichabod was related, and always burst into a hearty laugh at the mention of the pumpkin; which led some to suspect that he knew more about the matter than he chose to tell.

The old country wives, however, who are the best judges of these matters, maintain to this day, that Ichabod was spirited away by supernatural means; and it is a favorite story often told about the neighbourhood round the interevening fire. The bridge became more than ever an object of superstitious awe, and that may be the reason why the road has been altered of late years, so as to approach the church by the border of the millpond. The schoolhouse, being deserted, soon fell to decay, and was reported to be haunted by the ghost of the unfortunate pedagogue; and the plough boy, loitering homeward of a still summer evening, has often fancied his voice at a distance, chanting a melancholy psalm tune among the tranquil solitudes of Sleepy Hollow.

STRANGE STORIES BY A NERVOUS GENTLEMAN

I'll tell you more; there was a fish taken,
A monstrous fish, with, a sword by's side, a long sword,
A pike in's neck, and a gun in's nose, a huge gun,
And letters of mart in's mouth, from the Duke of Florence.
  Cleanthes. *This is a monstrous lie.*
  Tony. *I do confess it.*
Do you think I'd tell you truths?

FLETCHER'S WIFE FOR A MONTH

The following adventures were related to me by the same nervous gentleman who told me the romantic tale of THE STOUT GENTLEMAN, published in *Bracebridge Hall.*
It is very singular, that although I expressly stated that story to have been told to me, and described the very person who told it, still it has been received as an adventure that happened to myself. Now, I protest I never met with any adventure of the kind. I should not have grieved at this, had it not been intimated by the author of Waverley, in an introduction to his romance of Peveril of the Peak, that he was himself

the Stout Gentleman alluded to. I have ever since been importuned by letters and questions from gentlemen, and particularly from ladies without number, touching what I had seen of the great unknown.

Now, all this is extremely tantalizing. It is like being congratulated on the high prize when one has drawn a blank; for I have just as great a desire as any one of the public to penetrate the mystery of that very singular personage, whose voice fills every corner of the world, without any one being able to tell from whence it comes.

My friend, the nervous gentleman, also, who is a man of very shy retired habits, complains that he has been excessively annoyed in consequence of its getting about in his neighbourhood that he is the fortunate personage. Insomuch, that he has become a character of considerable notoriety in two or three country towns; and has been repeatedly teased to exhibit himself at blue-stocking parties, for no other reason than that of being "the gentleman who has had a glimpse of the author of Waverley."

Indeed, the poor man has grown ten times as nervous as ever, since he has discovered, on such good authority, who the stout gentleman was; and will never forgive himself for not having made a more resolute effort to get a full sight of him. He has anxiously endeavored to call up a recollection of what he saw of that portly personage; and has ever since kept a curious eye on all gentlemen of more than ordinary dimensions, whom he has seen getting into stage coaches. All in vain! The features he had caught a glimpse of seem common to the whole race of stout gentlemen; and the great unknown remains as great an unknown as ever.

* * *

Having premised these circumstances, I will now let the nervous gentleman proceed with his stories.

THE HUNTING DINNER

I was once at a hunting dinner, given by a worthy fox-hunting old Baronet, who kept Bachelor's Hall in jovial style, in an ancient rook-haunted family mansion, in one of the middle counties. He had been a devoted admirer of the fair sex in his young days; but having travelled much, studied the sex in various countries with distinguished success, and returned home profoundly instructed, as he supposed, in the ways of woman, and a perfect master of the art of pleasing, he had the mortification of being jilted by a little boarding school girl, who was scarcely versed in the accidence of love.

The Baronet was completely overcome by such an incredible defeat; retired from the world in disgust, put himself under the government of his housekeeper, and took to fox-hunting like a perfect Nimrod. Whatever poets may say to the contrary, a man will grow out of love as he grows old; and a pack of fox hounds may chase out of his heart even the memory of a boarding-school goddess. The Baronet was when I saw him as merry and mellow an old bachelor as ever followed a hound; and the love he had once felt for one woman had spread itself over the whole sex; so that there was not a pretty face in the whole country round, but came in for a share.

The dinner was prolonged till a late hour; for our host having no ladies in his household to summon us to the drawing room, the bottle maintained its true bachelor sway, unrivalled by its potent enemy the tea kettle. The old hall in which we dined echoed to bursts of robustious fox hunting merriment, that made the ancient antlers shake on the walls. By degrees, however, the wine and wassail of mine host began to operate upon bodies already a little jaded by the chase. The choice spirits that flashed up at the beginning of the dinner, sparkled for a time, then gradually went out one after another, or only emitted now and then a faint gleam from the socket. Some of the briskest talkers, who had given tongue so bravely at the first burst, fell fast asleep; and none kept on their way but certain of those long winded prosers, who, like short legged hounds, worry on unnoticed at the bottom of conversation, but are sure to be in at the death. Even these at length subsided into silence; and scarcely any thing was heard but the nasal communications of two or three veteran masticators, who, having been silent while awake, were indemnifying the company in their sleep.

At length the announcement of tea and coffee in the cedar parlour roused all hands from this temporary torpor. Every one awoke marvellously renovated, and while sipping the refreshing beverage out of the Baronet's old fashioned hereditary china, began to think of departing for their several homes. But here a sudden difficulty arose. While we had been prolonging our repast, a heavy winter storm had set in, with snow, rain, and sleet, driven by such bitter blasts of wind, that they threatened to penetrate to the very bone.

"It's all in vain," said our hospitable host, "to think of putting one's head out of doors in such weather. So, gentlemen, I hold you my guests for this night at least, and will have your quarters prepared accordingly."

The unruly weather, which became more and more tempestuous, rendered The hospitable suggestion unanswerable. The only question was, whether such an unexpected accession of company, to an already crowded house, would not put the housekeeper to her trumps to accommodate them.

"Pshaw," cried mine host, "did you ever know of a Bachelor's Hall that was not elastic, and able to accommodate twice as many as it could hold?" So out of a good humoured pique the housekeeper was summoned to consultation before us all. The old lady appeared, in her gala suit of faded brocade, which rustled with flurry and agitation, for in spite of mine host's bravado, she was a little perplexed. But in a bachelor's house, and with bachelor guests, these matters are readily managed. There is no lady of the house to stand upon squeamish points about lodging guests in odd holes and corners, and exposing the shabby parts of the establishment. A bachelor's housekeeper is used to shifts and emergencies. After much worrying to and fro, and divers consultations about the red room, and the blue room, and the chintz room, and the damask room, and the little room with the bow window, the matter was finally arranged.

When all this was done, we were once more summoned to the standing Rural amusement of eating. The time that had been consumed in dozing after dinner, and in the refreshment and consultation of the cedar parlour, was sufficient, in the opinion of the rosy faced butler, to engender a reasonable appetite for supper. A slight repast had therefore been tricked up from the residue of dinner, consisting of cold sirloin of beef; hashed venison; a devilled leg of a turkey or so, and a few other of those light articles taken by country gentlemen to ensure sound sleep and heavy snoring.

The nap after dinner had brightened up every one's wit; and a great deal of excellent humor was expended upon the perplexities of mine host and his housekeeper, by certain married gentlemen of the company, who considered themselves privileged in joking with a bachelor's establishment. From this the banter turned as to what quarters each would find, on being thus suddenly billeted in so antiquated a mansion.

"By my soul," said an Irish captain of dragoons, one of the most merry and boisterous of the party—"by my soul, but I should not be surprised if some of those good-looking gentlefolks that hang along the walls, should walk about the rooms of this stormy night; or if I should find the ghost of one of these long waisted ladies turning into my bed in mistake for her grave in the church yard.

"Do you believe in ghosts, then?" said a thin, hatchet-faced gentleman, with projecting eyes like a lobster.

I had remarked this last personage throughout dinner time for one of those incessant questioners, who seem to have a craving, unhealthy appetite in conversation. He never seemed satisfied with the whole of a story; never laughed when others laughed; but always put the joke to the question. He could never enjoy the kernel of the nut, but pestered himself to get more out of the shell.

"Do you believe in ghosts, then?" said the inquisitive gentleman.

"Faith, but I do," replied the jovial Irishman; "I was brought up in the fear and belief of them; we had a Benshee in our own family, honey."

"A Benshee—and what's that?" cried the questioner.

"Why an old lady ghost that tends upon your real Milesian families, and wails at their window to let them know when some of them are to die."

"A mighty pleasant piece of information," cried an elderly gentleman, with a knowing look and a flexible nose, to which he could give a whimsical twist when he wished to be waggish.

"By my soul, but I'd have you know it's a piece of distinction to be waited upon by a Benshee. It's a proof that one has pure blood in one's veins. But, egad, now we're talking of ghosts, there never was a house or a night better fitted than the present for a ghost adventure. Pray, Sir John, haven't you such a thing as a haunted chamber to put a guest in?"

"Perhaps," said the Baronet smiling, "I might accommodate you even on that point."

"Oh, I should like it of all things, my jewel. Some dark oaken room, with ugly wobegone portraits that stare dismally at one, and about which the housekeeper has a power of delightful stories of love and murder. And then a dim lamp, a table with a rusty sword across it, and a spectre all in white to draw aside one's curtains at midnight—"

"In truth," said an old gentleman at one end of the table, "you put me in mind of an anecdote—"

"Oh, a ghost story! a ghost story!" was vociferated round the board, every one edging his chair a little nearer.

The attention of the whole company was now turned upon the speaker. He was an old gentleman, one side of whose face was no match for the other. The eyelid drooped and hung down like an unhinged window shutter. Indeed, the whole side of his head was dilapidated, and seemed like the wing of a house shut up and haunted. I'll warrant that side was well stuffed with ghost stories.

There was a universal demand for the tale.

"Nay," said the old gentleman, "it's a mere anecdote—and a very common-place one; but such as it is you shall have it. It is a story that I once heard my uncle tell as having happened to himself. He was a man very apt to meet with strange adventures. I have heard him tell of others much more singular."

"What kind of man was your uncle?" said the questioning gentleman.

"Why, he was rather a dry, shrewd kind of body; a great traveller, and fond of telling his adventures."

"Pray, how old might he have been when this happened?"

"When what happened?" cried the gentleman with the flexible nose, impatiently—"Egad, you have not given any thing a chance to happen—come, never mind our uncle's age; let us have his adventures."

The inquisitive gentleman being for the moment silenced, the old gentleman with the haunted head proceeded.

THE ADVENTURE OF MY UNCLE

Many years since, a long time before the French revolution, my uncle had passed several months at Paris. The English and French were on better terms, in those days, than at present, and mingled cordially together in society. The English went abroad to spend money then, and the French were always ready to help them: they go abroad to save money at present, and that they can do without French assistance. Perhaps the travelling English were fewer and choicer then, than at present, when the whole nation has broke loose, and inundated the continent. At any rate, they circulated more readily and currently in foreign society, and my uncle, during his residence in Paris, made many very intimate acquaintances among the French noblesse.

Some time afterwards, he was making a journey in the winter-time, in that part of Normandy called the Pays de Caux, when, as evening was closing in, he perceived the turrets of an ancient chateau rising out of the trees of its walled park, each turret with its high conical roof of gray slate, like a candle with an extinguisher on it.

"To whom does that chateau belong, friend?" cried my uncle to a meager, but fiery postillion, who, with tremendous jack boots and cocked hat, was floundering on before him.

"To Monseigneur the Marquis de——," said the postillion, touching his hat, partly out of respect to my uncle, and partly out of reverence to the noble name pronounced. My uncle recollected the Marquis for a particular friend in Paris, who had often expressed a wish to see him at his paternal chateau. My uncle was an old traveller, one that knew how to turn things to account. He revolved for a few moments in his mind how agreeable it would be to his friend the Marquis to be surprised in this sociable way by a pop visit; and how much more agreeable to himself to get into snug quarters in a chateau, and have a relish of the Marquis's well known kitchen, and a smack of his superior champagne and burgundy; rather than take up with the miserable lodgment, and miserable fare of a country inn. In a few minutes, therefore, the meager postillion was cracking his whip like a very devil, or like a true Frenchman, up the long straight avenue that led to the chateau.

You have no doubt all seen French chateaus, as every body travels in France nowadays. This was one of the oldest; standing naked and alone, in the midst of a desert of gravel walks and cold stone terraces; with a cold looking formal garden, cut into angles and rhomboids; and a cold leafless park, divided geometrically by straight alleys; and two or three noseless, cold-looking statues without any clothing; and fountains spouting cold water enough to make one's teeth chatter. At least, such was the feeling they imparted on the wintry day of my uncle's visit; though, in hot summer weather, I'll warrant there was glare enough to scorch one's eyes out.

The smacking of the postillion's whip, which grew more and more intense the nearer they approached, frightened a flight of pigeons out of the dove-cot, and rooks out of the roofs; and finally a crew of servants out of the chateau, with the Marquis at their head. He was enchanted to see my uncle; for his chateau, like the house of our worthy host, had not many more guests at the time than it could accommodate. So he kissed my uncle on each cheek, after the French fashion, and ushered him into the castle.

The Marquis did the honors of his house with the urbanity of his country. In fact, he was proud of his old family chateau; for part of it was extremely old. There was a tower and chapel that had been built almost before the memory of man; but the rest was more modern; the castle having been nearly demolished during the wars of the League. The Marquis dwelt upon this event with great satisfaction, and seemed really to entertain a grateful feeling towards Henry the Fourth, for having thought his paternal mansion worth battering down. He had many stories to tell of the prowess of his ancestors, and several skullcaps, helmets, and crossbows to show; and divers huge boots and buff jerkins, that had been worn by the Leaguers. Above all, there was a two-handled sword, which he could hardly wield; but which he displayed as a proof that there had been giants in his family.

In truth, he was but a small descendant from such great warriors. When you looked at their bluff visages and brawny limbs, as depicted in their portraits, and then at the little Marquis, with his spindle shanks; his sallow lanthern visage, flanked with a pair of powdered ear locks, or *ailes de pigeon,* that seemed ready to fly away with it; you would hardly believe him to be of the same race. But when you looked at the eyes that sparkled out like a beetle's from each side of his hooked nose, you saw at once that he inherited all the fiery spirit of his forefathers. In fact, a Frenchman's spirit never exhales, however his body may dwindle. It rather rarefies, and grows more inflammable, as the earthly particles diminish; and I have seen valor enough in a little fiery hearted French dwarf, to have furnished out a tolerable giant.

When once the Marquis, as he was wont, put on one of the old helmets that were stuck up in his hall; though his head no more filled it than a dry pea its pease cod; yet his eyes sparkled from the bottom of the iron cavern with the brilliancy of carbuncles, and when he poised the ponderous two handled sword of his ancestors, you would have thought you saw the doughty little David wielding the sword of Goliath, which was unto him like a weaver's beam.

However, gentlemen, I am dwelling too long on this description of the Marquis and his chateau; but you must excuse me; he was an old friend of my uncle's, and whenever my uncle told the story, he was always fond of talking a great deal about his host.—Poor little Marquis! He was one of that handful of gallant courtiers, who made such a devoted, but hopeless stand in the cause of their sovereign, in the chateau of the Tuilleries, against the irruption of the mob, on the sad tenth of August. He displayed the valour of a preux French chevalier to the last; flourished feebly his little court sword with a sa-sa! in face of a whole legion of *sans culottes*; but was pinned to the wall like a butterfly, by the pike of a poissarde, and his heroic soul was borne up to heaven on his *ailes de pigeon*.

But all this has nothing to do with my story; to the point then:— When the hour arrived for retiring for the night, my uncle was shown to his room, in a venerable old tower. It was the oldest part of the chateau, and had in ancient times been the Donjon or strong hold; of course the chamber was none of the best. The Marquis had put him there, however, because he knew him to be a traveller of taste, and fond of antiquities; and also because the better apartments were already occupied. Indeed, he perfectly reconciled my uncle to his quarters by mentioning the great personages who had once inhabited them, all of whom were in some way or other connected with the family. If you would take his word for it, John Baliol, or, as he called him, Jean de Bailleul, had died of chagrin in this very chamber on hearing of the success of his rival, Robert the Bruce, at the battle of Bannockburn; and when he added that the Duke de Guise had slept in it during the wars of the League, my uncle was fain to felicitate himself upon being honoured with such distinguished quarters.

The night was shrewd and windy, and the chamber none of the warmest. An old, long-faced, long-bodied servant in quaint livery, who attended upon my uncle, threw down an armful of wood beside the fire place, gave a queer look about the room, and then wished him *bon repos*, with a grimace and a shrug that would have been suspicious from any other than an old French servant. The chamber had indeed a wild, crazy look, enough to strike any one who had read romances with apprehension and foreboding. The windows were high and narrow, and had once been loop holes, but had been rudely enlarged, as well as the extreme thickness of the walls would permit; and the ill-fitted casements rattled to every breeze. You would have thought, on a windy night, some of the old Leaguers were tramping and clanking about the apartment in their huge boots and rattling spurs. A door which stood ajar, and like a true French door would stand ajar, in spite of every reason and effort to the contrary, opened upon a long, dark corridor, that led the Lord knows whither, and seemed just made for ghosts to air themselves in, when they turned out of their graves at midnight. The wind would spring up into a hoarse murmur through this passage, and creak the door to and fro, as if some dubious ghost were balancing in its mind whether to come in or not. In a word, it was precisely the kind of comfortless apartment that a ghost, if ghost there were in the chateau, would single out for its favourite lounge.

My uncle, however, though a man accustomed to meet with strange adventures, apprehended none at the time. He made several attempts to shut the door, but in vain. Not that he apprehended any thing, for he was too old a traveller to be daunted by a wild looking apartment; but the night, as I have said, was cold and gusty, something like the present, and the wind howled about the old turret, pretty much as it does round this old mansion at this moment; and the breeze from the long dark corridor came in as damp and chilly as if from a dungeon. My uncle, therefore, since he could not close the door, threw a quantity of wood on the fire, which soon sent up a flame in the great wide-mouthed chimney that illumined the whole chamber, and made the shadow of the tongs on the opposite wall, look like a long legged giant. My uncle now clambered on top of the half score of mattresses which form a French bed, and which stood in a deep recess; then tucking himself snugly in, and burying himself up to the chin in the bed clothes, he lay looking at the fire, and listening to the wind, and chuckling to think how knowingly he had come over his friend the Marquis for a night's lodgings: and so he fell asleep.

He had not taken above half of his first nap, when he was awakened by the clock of the chateau, in the turret over his chamber, which struck midnight. It was just such an old clock as ghosts are fond of. It had a deep, dismal tone, and struck so slowly and tediously that my uncle thought it would never have done. He counted and counted till he was confident he counted thirteen, and then it stopped.

The fire had burnt low, and the blaze of the last faggot was almost expiring, burning in small blue flames, which now and then lengthened up into little white gleams. My uncle lay with his eyes half closed, and his nightcap drawn almost down to his nose. His fancy was already wandering, and began to mingle up the present scene with the crater of Vesuvius, the French opera, the Coliseum at Rome, Dolly's chop house in London, and all the farrago of noted places with which the brain of a traveller is crammed—in a word, he was just falling asleep.

Suddenly he was aroused by the sound of foot-steps that appeared to be slowly pacing along the corridor. My uncle, as I have often heard him say himself, was a man not easily frightened; so he lay quiet, supposing that this might be some other guest; or some servant on his way to bed. The footsteps, however, approached the door; the door gently opened; whether of its own accord, or whether pushed open, my uncle could not distinguish:—a figure all in white glided in. It was a female, tall and stately in person, and of a most commanding air. Her dress was of an ancient fashion, ample in volume and sweeping the floor. She walked up to the fire place without regarding my uncle; who raised his nightcap with one hand, and stared earnestly at her. She remained for some time standing by the fire, which flashing up at intervals cast blue and white gleams of light that enabled my uncle to remark her appearance minutely.

Her face was ghastly pale, and perhaps rendered still more so by the blueish light of the fire. It possessed beauty, but its beauty was saddened by care and anxiety. There was the look of one accustomed to trouble, but of one whom trouble could not cast down nor subdue; for there was still the predominating air of proud, unconquerable resolution. Such, at least, was the opinion formed by my uncle, and he considered himself a great physiognomist.

The figure remained, as I said, for some time by the fire, putting out first one hand, then the other, then each foot, alternately, as if warming itself; for your ghosts, if ghost it really was, are apt to be cold. My uncle furthermore remarked that it wore high-heeled shoes, after an ancient fashion, with paste or diamond buckles, that sparkled as though they were alive. At length the figure turned gently round, casting a glassy look about the apartment, which, as it passed over my uncle, made his blood run cold, and chilled the very marrow in his bones. It then stretched its arms toward heaven, clasped its hands, and wringing them in a supplicating manner, glided slowly out of the room.

My uncle lay for some time meditating on this visitation, for (as he Remarked when he told me the story) though a man of firmness, he was also a man of reflection, and did not reject a thing because it was out of the regular course of events. However, being, as I have before said, a great traveller, and accustomed to strange adventures, he drew his nightcap resolutely over his eyes, turned his back to the door, hoisted the bedclothes high over his shoulders, and gradually fell asleep.

How long he slept he could not say, when he was awakened by the voice of some one at his bed side. He turned round and beheld the old French servant, with his ear locks in tight buckles on each side of a long, lanthorn face, on which habit had deeply wrinkled an everlasting smile. He made a thousand grimaces and asked a thousand pardons for disturbing Monsieur, but the morning was considerably advanced. While my uncle was dressing, he called vaguely to mind the visitor of the preceding night. He asked the ancient domestic what lady was in the habit of rambling about this part of the chateau at night. The old valet shrugged his shoulders as high as his head, laid one hand on his bosom, threw open the other with every finger extended; made a most whimsical grimace, which he meant to be complimentary, and replied, that it was not for him to know any thing of *les bonnes fortunes* of Monsieur.

My uncle saw there was nothing satisfactory to be learnt in this quarter. After breakfast he was walking with the Marquis through the modern apartments of the chateau; sliding over the well-waxed floors of silken saloons, amidst furniture rich in gilding and brocade; until they came to a long picture gallery, containing many portraits, some in oil and some in chalks.

Here was an ample field for the eloquence of his host, who had all the family pride of a nobleman of the *ancient regime*. There was not a grand name in Normandy, and hardly one in France, that was not, in some way or other, connected with his house. My uncle stood listening with inward impatience, resting sometimes on one leg, sometimes on the other, as the little Marquis descanted, with his usual fire and vivacity, on the achievements of his ancestors, whose portraits hung along the wall; from the martial deeds of the stern warriors in steel, to the gallantries and intrigues of the blue eyed gentlemen, with fair smiling faces, powdered ear locks, laced ruffles, and pink and blue silk coats and breeches; not forgetting the conquests of the lovely shepherdesses, with hoop petticoats and waists no thicker than an hour glass, who appeared ruling over their sheep and their swains with dainty crooks decorated with fluttering ribbands.

In the midst of his friend's discourse my uncle's eyes rested on a full-length portrait, which struck him as being the very counterpart of his visitor of the preceding night.

"Methinks," said he, pointing to it, "I have seen the original of this portrait."

"*Pardonnez moi*," replied the Marquis politely, "that can hardly be, as the lady has been dead more than a hundred years. That was the beautiful Duchess de Longueville, who figured during the minority of Louis the Fourteenth."

"And was there any thing remarkable in her history."

Never was question more unlucky. The little Marquis immediately threw himself into the attitude of a man about to tell a long story. In fact, my uncle had pulled upon himself the whole history of the civil war of the Fronde, in which the beautiful Duchess had played so distinguished a part. Turenne, Coligni, Mazarin, were called up from their graves to grace his narration; nor were the affairs of the Barricadoes, nor the chivalry of the Port Cocheres forgotten. My uncle began to wish himself a thousand leagues off from the Marquis and his merciless memory, when suddenly the little man's recollections took a more interesting turn. He was relating the imprisonment of the Duke de Longueville, with the Princes Condé and Conti, in the chateau of Vincennes, and the ineffectual efforts of the Duchess to rouse the sturdy Normans to their rescue. He had come to that part where she was invested by the royal forces in the chateau of Dieppe, and in imminent danger of falling into their hands.

"The spirit of the Duchess," proceeded the Marquis, "rose with her trials. It was astonishing to see so delicate and beautiful a being buffet so resolutely with hardships. She determined on a desperate means of escape. One dark unruly night, she issued secretly out of a small postern gate of the castle, which the enemy had neglected to guard. She was followed by her female attendants, a few domestics, and some gallant cavaliers who still remained faithful to her fortunes. Her object was to gain a small port about two leagues distant, where she had privately provided a vessel for her escape in case of emergency.

"The little band of fugitives were obliged to perform the distance on foot. When they arrived at the port the wind was high and stormy, the tide contrary, the vessel anchored far off in the road, and no means of getting on board, but by a fishing shallop that lay tossing like a cockle shell on the edge of the surf. The Duchess determined to risk the attempt. The seamen endeavored to dissuade her, but the imminence of her danger on shore, and the magnanimity of her spirit urged her on. She had to be borne to the shallop in the arms of a mariner. Such was the violence of the wind and waves, that he faltered, lost his foothold, and let his precious burden fall into the sea.

"The Duchess was nearly drowned; but partly through her own struggles, partly by the exertions of the seamen, she got to land. As soon as she had a little recovered strength, she insisted on renewing the attempt. The storm, however, had by this time become so violent as to set all efforts at defiance. To delay, was to be discovered and taken prisoner. As the only resource left, she procured horses; mounted with her female attendants *en croupe* behind the gallant gentlemen who accompanied her; and scoured the country to seek some temporary asylum.

"While the Duchess," continued the Marquis, laying his forefinger on my uncle's breast to arouse his flagging attention, "while the Duchess, poor lady, was wandering amid the tempest in this disconsolate manner, she arrived at this chateau. Her approach caused some uneasiness; for the clattering of a troop of horse, at dead of night, up the avenue of a lonely chateau, in those unsettled times, and in a troubled part of the country, was enough to occasion alarm.

"A tall, broad shouldered chasseur, armed to the teeth, galloped ahead, and announced the name of the visitor. All uneasiness was dispelled. The household turned out with flambeaux to receive her, and never did torches gleam on a more weather beaten, travel stained band than came tramping into the court. Such pale, care worn faces, such bedraggled dresses, as the poor Duchess and her females presented, each seated behind her cavalier; while half drenched, half drowsy pages and attendants seemed ready to fall from their horses with sleep and fatigue.

"The Duchess was received with a hearty welcome by my ancestors. She was ushered into the Hall of the chateau, and the fires soon crackled and blazed to cheer herself and her train; and every spit and stewpan was put in requisition to prepare ample refreshments for the wayfarers.

"She had a right to our hospitalities," continued the little Marquis, drawing himself up with a slight degree of stateliness, "for she was related to our family. I'll tell you how it was: Her father, Henry de Bourbon, Prince of Condé—"

"But did the Duchess pass the night in the chateau?" said my uncle rather abruptly, terrified at the idea of getting involved in one of the Marquis's genealogical discussions.

"Oh, as to the Duchess, she was put into the apartment you occupied last night; which, at that time, was a kind of state apartment. Her followers were quartered in the chambers opening upon the neighbouring corridor, and her favorite page slept in an adjoining closet. Up and down the corridor walked the great chasseur, who had announced her arrival, and who acted as a kind of sentinel or guard. He was a dark, stern, powerful looking fellow, and as the light of a lamp in the corridor fell upon his deeply marked face and sinewy form, he seemed capable of defending the castle with his single arm.

"It was a rough, rude night; about this time of the year.—*Apropos*—now I think of it, last night was the anniversary of her visit. I may well remember the precise date, for it was a night not to be forgotten by our house. There is a singular tradition concerning it in our family." Here the Marquis hesitated, and a cloud seemed to gather about his bushy eyebrows. "There is a tradition—that a strange occurrence took place that night—a strange, mysterious, inexplicable occurrence."

Here he checked himself and paused.

"Did it relate to that lady?" inquired my uncle, eagerly.

"It was past the hour of midnight," resumed the Marquis—"when the whole chateau—"

Here he paused again—my uncle made a movement of anxious curiosity.

"Excuse me," said the Marquis—a slight blush streaking his sullen visage. "There are some circumstances connected with our family history which I do not like to relate. That was a rude period. A time of great crimes among great men: for you know high blood, when it runs wrong, will not run tamely like blood of the *canaille*—poor lady!—But I have a little family pride, that—excuse me—we will change the subject if you please."—

My uncle's curiosity was piqued. The pompous and magnificent introduction had led him to expect something wonderful in the story to which it served as a kind of avenue. He had no idea of being cheated out of it by a sudden fit of unreasonable squeamishness. Besides, being a traveller, in quest of information, considered it his duty to inquire into every thing.

The Marquis, however, evaded every question.

"Well," said my uncle, a little petulantly, "whatever you may think of it, I saw that lady last night."

The Marquis stepped back and gazed at him with surprise.

"She paid me a visit in my bed chamber."

The Marquis pulled out his snuff-box with a shrug and a smile; taking it no doubt for an awkward piece of English pleasantry, which politeness required him to be charmed with. My uncle went on gravely, however, and related the whole circumstance. The Marquis heard him through with profound attention, holding his snuff-box unopened in his hand. When the story was finished he tapped on the lid of his box deliberately; took a long sonorous pinch of snuff—

"Bah!" said the Marquis, and walked toward the other end of the gallery.—

* * *

Here the narrator paused. The company waited for some time for him to resume his narrative; but he continued silent.

"Well," said the inquisitive gentleman, "and what did your uncle say then?"

"Nothing," replied the other.

"And what did the Marquis say farther?"

"Nothing."

"And is that all?"

"That is all," said the narrator, filling a glass of wine.

"I surmise," said the shrewd old gentleman with the waggish nose—"I surmise it was the old housekeeper walking her rounds to see that all was right."

"Bah!" said the narrator, "my uncle was too much accustomed to strange sights not to know a ghost from a housekeeper!"

There was a murmur round the table half of merriment, half of disappointment. I was inclined to think the old gentleman had really an afterpart of his story in reserve; but he sipped his wine and said nothing more; and there was an odd expression about his dilapidated countenance that left me in doubt whether he were in drollery or earnest.

"Egad," said the knowing gentleman with the flexible nose, "this story of your uncle puts me in mind of one that used to be told of an aunt of mine, by the mother's side; though I don't know that it will bear a comparison; as the good lady was not quite so prone to meet with strange adventures. But at any rate, you shall have it."

THE ADVENTURE OF MY AUNT

My aunt was a lady of large frame, strong mind, and great resolution; she was what might be termed a very manly woman. My uncle was a thin, puny little man, very meek and acquiescent, and no match for my aunt. It was observed that he dwindled and dwindled gradually away, from the day of his marriage. His wife's powerful mind was too much for him; it wore him out. My aunt, however, took all possible care of him, had half the doctors in town to prescribe for him, made him take all their prescriptions, and dosed him with physic enough to cure a whole hospital. All was in vain. My uncle grew worse and worse the more dosing and nursing he underwent, until in the end he added another to the long list of matrimonial victims, who have been killed with kindness.

"And was it his ghost that appeared to her?" asked the inquisitive gentleman, who had questioned the former story teller.

"You shall hear," replied the narrator:—My aunt took on mightily for the death of her poor dear husband! Perhaps she felt some compunction at having given him so much physic, and nursed him into his grave. At any rate, she did all that a widow could do to honor his memory. She spared no expense in either the quantity or quality of her mourning weeds; she wore a miniature of him about her neck, as large as a little sun dial; and she had a full length portrait of him always hanging in her bed chamber. All the world extolled her conduct to the skies; and it was determined, that a woman who behaved so well to the memory of one husband, deserved soon to get another.

It was not long after this that she went to take up her residence in an old country seat in Derbyshire, which had long been in the care of merely a steward and housekeeper. She took most of her servants with her, intending to make it her principal abode. The house stood in a lonely, wild part of the country among the gray Derbyshire hills; with a murderer hanging in chains on a bleak height in full view.

The servants from town were half frightened out of their wits, at the idea of living in such a dismal, pagan looking place; especially when they got together in the servants' hall in the evening, and compared notes on all the hobgoblin stories they had picked up in the course of the day. They were afraid to venture alone about the forlorn black-looking chambers. My ladies' maid, who was troubled with nerves, declared she could never sleep alone in such a "gashly, rummaging old building"; and the footman, who was a kind hearted young fellow, did all in his power to cheer her up.

My aunt, herself, seemed to be struck with the lonely appearance of the house. Before she went to bed, therefore, she examined well the fastenings of the doors and windows, locked up the plate with her own hands, and carried the keys, together with a little box of money and jewels, to her own room; for she was a notable woman, and always saw to all things herself. Having put the keys under her pillow, and dismissed her maid, she sat by her toilet arranging her hair; for, being, in spite of her grief for my uncle, rather a buxom widow, she was a little particular about her person. She sat for a little while looking at her face in the glass, first on one side, then on the other, as ladies are apt to do, when they would ascertain if they have been in good looks; for a roystering country squire of the neighbourhood, with whom she had flirted when a girl, had called that day to welcome her to the country.

All of a sudden she thought she heard something move behind her. She looked hastily round, but there was nothing to be seen. Nothing but the grimly painted portrait of her poor dear man, which had been hung against the wall. She gave a heavy sigh to his memory, as she was accustomed to do, whenever she spoke of him in company; and went on adjusting her nightdress. Her sigh was re-echoed; or answered by a long-drawn breath. She looked round again, but no one was to be seen. She ascribed these sounds to the wind, oozing through the rat holes of the old mansion; and proceeded leisurely to put her hair in papers, when, all at once, she thought she perceived one of the eyes of the portrait move.

"The back of her head being towards it!" said the story teller with the ruined head, giving a knowing wink on the sound side of his visage, "good!"

"Yes, sir!" replied drily the narrator, "her back being towards the portrait, but her eye fixed on its reflection in the glass."

Well, as I was saying, she perceived one of the eyes of the portrait move. So strange a circumstance, as you may well suppose, gave her a sudden shock. To assure herself cautiously of the fact, she put one hand to her forehead, as if rubbing it; peeped through her fingers, and moved the candle with the other hand. The light of the taper gleamed on the eye, and was reflected from it. She was sure it moved. Nay, more, it seemed to give her a wink, as she had sometimes known her husband to do when living! It struck a momentary chill to her heart; for she was a lone woman, and felt herself fearfully situated.

The chill was but transient. My aunt, who was almost as resolute a personage as your uncle, sir (turning to the old story teller), became instantly calm and collected. She went on adjusting her dress. She even hummed a favourite air, and did not make a single false note. She casually overturned a dressing box; took a candle and picked up the articles leisurely, one by one, from the floor; pursued a rolling pin cushion that was making the best of its way under the bed; then opened the door; looked for an instant into the corridor, as if in doubt whether to go; and then walked quietly out.

She hastened down stairs, ordered the servants to arm themselves with the first weapons that came to hand, placed herself at their head, and returned almost immediately.

Her hastily levied army presented a formidable force. The steward had a rusty blunderbuss; the coachman a loaded whip; the footman a pair of horse pistols; the cook a huge chopping knife, and the butler a bottle in each hand. My aunt led the van with a red hot poker; and, in my opinion, she was the most formidable of the party. The waiting maid brought up the rear, dreading to stay alone in the servants' hall, smelling to a broken bottle of volatile salts, and expressing her terror of the ghosteses.

"Ghosts!" said my aunt resolutely, "I'll singe their whiskers for them!"

They entered the chamber. All was still and undisturbed as when she left it. They approached the portrait of my uncle.

"Pull me down that picture!" cried my aunt.

A heavy groan, and a sound like the chattering of teeth, was heard from the portrait. The servants shrunk back. The maid uttered a faint shriek, and clung to the footman.

"Instantly!" added my aunt, with a stamp of the foot.

The picture was pulled down, and from a recess behind it, in which had formerly stood a clock, they hauled forth a round shouldered, black bearded varlet, with a knife as long as my arm, but trembling all over like an aspen leaf.

"Well, and who was he? No ghost, I suppose!" said the inquisitive gentleman.

"A Knight of the Post," replied the narrator, "who had been smitten with the worth of the wealthy widow; or rather a marauding Tarquin, who had stolen into her chamber to violate her purse and rifle her strong box when all the house should be asleep. In plain terms," continued he, "the vagabond was a loose idle fellow of the neighbourhood, who had once been a servant in the house, and had been employed to assist in arranging it for the reception of its mistress. He confessed that he had contrived his hiding place for his nefarious purposes, and had borrowed an eye from the portrait by way of a reconnoitering hole."

"And what did they do with him—did they hang him?" resumed the questioner.

"Hang him?—how could they?" exclaimed a beetle-browed barrister, with a hawk's nose—"the offence was not capital—no robbery nor assault had been committed—no forcible entry or breaking into the premises"—

"My aunt," said the narrator, "was a woman of spirit, and apt to take the law into her own hands. She had her own notions of cleanliness also. She ordered the fellow to be drawn through the horsepond to cleanse away all offences, and then to be well rubbed down with an oaken towel."

"And what became of him afterwards?" said the inquisitive gentleman.

"I do not exactly know—I believe he was sent on a voyage of improvement to Botany Bay."

"And your aunt"—said the inquisitive gentleman—"I'll warrant she took care to make her maid sleep in the room with her after that."

"No, sir, she did better—she gave her hand shortly after to the roystering squire; for she used to observe it was a dismal thing for a woman to sleep alone in the country."

"She was right," observed the inquisitive gentleman, nodding his head sagaciously—"but I am sorry they did not hang that fellow."

It was agreed on all hands that the last narrator had brought his tale to the most satisfactory conclusion; though a country clergyman present regretted that the uncle and aunt, who figured in the different stories, had not been married together. They certainly would have been well matched.

"But I don't see, after all," said the inquisitive gentleman, "that there was any ghost in this last story."

"Oh, if it's ghosts you want, honey," cried the Irish captain of dragoons, "if it's ghosts you want, you shall have a whole regiment of them. And since these gentlemen have been giving the adventures of their uncles and aunts, faith and I'll e'en give you a chapter too, out of my own family history."

THE BOLD DRAGOON, OR THE ADVENTURE OF MY GRANDFATHER

My grandfather was a bold dragoon, for it's a profession, d'ye see, that has run in the family. All my forefathers have been dragoons and died upon the field of honor except myself, and I hope my posterity may be able to say the same; however, I don't mean to be vainglorious. Well, my grandfather, as I said, was a bold dragoon, and had served in the Low Countries. In fact, he was one of that very army, which, according to my uncle Toby, "swore so terribly in Flanders." He could swear a good stick himself; and, moreover, was the very man that introduced the doctrine Corporal Trim mentions, of radical heat and radical moisture; or, in other words, the mode of keeping out the damps of ditch water by burnt brandy. Be that as it may, it's nothing to the purport of my story. I only tell it to show you that my grandfather was a man not easily to be humbugged. He had seen service; or, according to his own phrase, "he had seen the devil"—and that's saying every thing.

Well, gentlemen, my grandfather was on his way to England, for which he intended to embark at Ostend;—bad luck to the place for one where I was kept by storms and head winds for three long days, and the divil of a jolly companion or pretty face to comfort me. Well, as I was saying, my grandfather was on his way to England, or rather to

Ostend—no matter which, it's all the same. So one evening, towards nightfall, he rode jollily into Bruges. Very like you all know Bruges, gentlemen, a queer, old fashioned Flemish town, once they say a great place for trade and money-making, in old times, when the Mynheers were in their glory; but almost as large and as empty as an Irishman's pocket at the present day. Well, gentlemen, it was the time of the annual fair. All Bruges was crowded; and the canals swarmed with Dutch boats, and the streets swarmed with Dutch merchants; and there was hardly any getting along for goods, wares, and merchandises, and peasants in big breeches, and women in half a score of petticoats.

My grandfather rode jollily along in his easy, slashing way, for he was a saucy, sunshiny fellow—staring about him at the motley crowd, and the old houses with gable ends to the street and storks' nests on the chimneys; winking at the ya vrouws who showed their faces at the windows, and joking the women right and left in the street; all of whom laughed and took it in amazing good part; for though he did not know a word of their language, yet he always had a knack of making himself understood among the women.

Well, gentlemen, it being the time of the annual fair, all the town was crowded; every inn and tavern full, and my grandfather applied in vain from one to the other for admittance. At length he rode up to an old rackety inn that looked ready to fall to pieces, and which all the rats would have run away from, if they could have found room in any other house to put their heads. It was just such a queer building as you see in Dutch pictures, with a tall roof that reached up into the clouds; and as many garrets, one over the other, as the seven heavens of Mahomet. Nothing had saved it from tumbling down but a stork's nest on the chimney, which always brings good luck to a house in the Low Countries; and at the very time of my grandfather's arrival, there were two of these long-legged birds of grace, standing like ghosts on the chimney top. Faith, but they've kept the house on its legs to this very day; for you may see it any time you pass through Bruges, as it stands there yet; only it is turned into a brewery—a brewery of strong Flemish beer; at least it was so when I came that way after the battle of Waterloo.

My grandfather eyed the house curiously as he approached. It might not altogether have struck his fancy, had he not seen in large letters over the door,

HEER VERKOOPT MAN GOEDEN DRANK

My grandfather had learnt enough of the language to know that the sign promised good liquor. "This is the house for me," said he, stopping short before the door.

The sudden appearance of a dashing dragoon was an event in an old inn, frequented only by the peaceful sons of traffic. A rich burgher of Antwerp, a stately ample man, in a broad Flemish hat, and who was the great man and great patron of the establishment, sat smoking a clean long pipe on one side of the door; a fat little distiller of Geneva from Schiedam, sat smoking on the other, and the bottle-nosed host stood in the door, and the comely hostess, in crimped cap, beside him; and the hostess' daughter, a plump Flanders lass, with long gold pendants in her ears, was at a side window.

"Humph!" said the rich burgher of Antwerp, with a sulky glance at the stranger.

"Der duyvel!" said the fat little distiller of Schiedam.

The landlord saw with the quick glance of a publican that the new guest was not at all, at all, to the taste of the old ones; and to tell the truth, he did not himself like my grandfather's saucy eye.

He shook his head—"Not a garret in the house but was full."

"Not a garret!" echoed the landlady.

"Not a garret!" echoed the daughter.

The burgher of Antwerp and the little distiller of Schiedam continued to smoke their pipes sullenly, eyed the enemy askance from under their broad hats, but said nothing.

My grandfather was not a man to be browbeaten. He threw the reins on his horse's neck, cocked his hat on one side, stuck one arm akimbo—

"Faith and troth!" said he, "but I'll sleep in this house this very night!"

As he said this he gave a slap on his thigh, by way of emphasis—the slap went to the landlady's heart.

He followed up the vow by jumping off his horse, and making his way past the staring Mynheers into the public room. May be you've been in the barroom of an old Flemish inn—faith, but a handsome chamber it was as you'd wish to see; with a brick floor, a great fire-place, with the whole Bible history in glazed tiles; and then the mantel-piece, pitching itself head foremost out of the wall, with a whole regiment of cracked tea-pots and earthen jugs paraded on it; not to mention half a dozen great Delft platters hung about the room by way of pictures; and the little bar in one corner, and the bouncing bar-maid inside of it with a red calico cap and yellow ear-drops.

My grandfather snapped his fingers over his head, as he cast an eye round the room: "Faith, this is the very house I've been looking after," said he.

There was some farther show of resistance on the part of the garrison, but my grandfather was an old soldier, and an Irishman to boot, and not easily repulsed, especially after he had got into the fortress. So he blarney'd the landlord, kissed the landlord's wife, tickled the landlord's daughter, chucked the bar maid under the chin; and it was agreed on all hands that it would be a thousand pities, and a burning shame into the bargain, to turn such a bold dragoon into the streets. So they laid their heads together, that is to say, my grandfather and the landlady, and it was at length agreed to accommodate him with an old chamber that had for some time been shut up.

"Some say it's haunted!" whispered the landlord's daughter, "but you're a bold dragoon, and I dare say you don't fear ghosts."

"The divil a bit!" said my grandfather, pinching her plump cheek; "but if I should be troubled by ghosts, I've been to the Red Sea in my time, and have a pleasant way of laying them, my darling!"

And then he whispered something to the girl which made her laugh, and give him a good humoured box on the ear. In short, there was nobody knew better how to make his way among the petticoats than my grandfather.

In a little while, as was his usual way, he took complete possession of the house: swaggering all over it:—into the stable to look after his horse; into the kitchen to look after his supper. He had something to say or do with every one; smoked with the Dutchmen; drank with the Germans; slapped the landlord on the shoulder, romped with his daughter and the bar maid:—never since the days of Ally Croaker had such a rattling blade been seen. The landlord stared at him with astonishment; the landlord's daughter hung her head and giggled whenever he came near; and as he turned his back and swaggered along, his tight jacket setting off his broad shoulders and plump buckskins, and his long sword trailing by his side, the maids whispered to one another—"What a proper man!"

At supper my grandfather took command of the table d'hôte as though he had been at home; helped everybody, not forgetting himself; talked with every one, whether he understood their language or not; and made his way into the intimacy of the rich burgher of Antwerp, who had never been known to be sociable with any one during his life. In fact, he revolutionized the whole establishment, and gave it such a rouse, that the very house reeled with it. He outsat every one at table excepting the little fat distiller of Schiedam, who had sat soaking for a long time before he broke forth; but when he did, he was a very devil incarnate. He took a violent affection for my grandfather; so they sat drinking, and smoking, and telling stories, and singing Dutch and Irish songs, without understanding a word each other said, until the little Hollander was fairly swampt with his own gin and water, and carried off to bed, whooping and hiccuping, and trolling the burthen of a Low Dutch love song.

Well, gentlemen, my grandfather was shown to his quarters, up a huge staircase composed of loads of hewn timber; and through long rigmarole passages, hung with blackened paintings of fruit, and fish, and game, and country frollics, and huge kitchens, and portly burgomasters, such as you see about old-fashioned Flemish inns, till at length he arrived at his room.

An old-times chamber it was, sure enough, and crowded with all kinds of trumpery. It looked like an infirmary for decayed and superannuated furniture; where everything diseased and disabled was sent to nurse, or to be forgotten. Or rather, it might have been taken for a general congress of old legitimate moveables, where every kind and country had a representative. No two chairs were alike: such high backs and low backs, and leather bottoms and worsted bottoms, and straw bottoms, and no bottoms; and cracked marble tables with curiously carved legs, holding balls in their claws, as though they were going to play at nine pins.

My grandfather made a bow to the motley assemblage as he entered, and having undressed himself, placed his light in the fire place, asking pardon of the tongs, which seemed to be making love to the shovel in the chimney corner, and whispering soft nonsense in its ear.

The rest of the guests were by this time sound asleep; for your Mynheers are huge sleepers. The house maids, one by one, crept up yawning to their attics, and not a female head in the inn was laid on a pillow that night without dreaming of the Bold Dragoon.

My grandfather, for his part, got into bed, and drew over him one of those great bags of down, under which they smother a man in the Low Countries; and there he lay, melting between, two feather beds, like an anchovy sandwich between two slices of toast and butter. He was a warm complexioned man, and this smothering played the very deuce with him. So, sure enough, in a little while it seemed as if a legion of imps were twitching at him and all the blood in his veins was in fever heat.

He lay still, however, until all the house was quiet, excepting the snoring of the Mynheers from the different chambers; who answered one another in all kinds of tones and cadences, like so many bull-frogs in a swamp. The quieter the house became, the more unquiet became my grandfather. He waxed warmer and warmer, until at length the bed became too hot to hold him.

"May be the maid had warmed it too much?" said the curious gentleman, inquiringly.

"I rather think the contrary," replied the Irishman. "But be that as it may, it grew too hot for my grandfather."

"Faith there's no standing this any longer," says he; so he jumped out of bed and went strolling about the house.

"What for?" said the inquisitive gentleman.

"Why, to cool himself to be sure," replied the other, "or perhaps to find a more comfortable bed—or perhaps—but no matter what he went for—he never mentioned; and there's no use in taking up our time in conjecturing."

Well, my grandfather had been for some time absent from his room, and was returning, perfectly cool, when just as he reached the door he heard a strange noise within. He paused and listened. It seemed as if some one was trying to hum a tune in defiance of the asthma. He recollected the report of the room's being haunted; but he was no believer in ghosts. So he pushed the door gently ajar, and peeped in.

Egad, gentlemen, there was a gambol carrying on within enough to have astonished St. Anthony.

By the light of the fire he saw a pale weazen-faced fellow in a long flannel gown and a tall white nightcap with a tassel to it, who sat by the fire, with a bellows under his arm by way of bagpipe, from which he forced the asthmatical music that had bothered my grandfather. As he played, too, he kept twitching about with a thousand queer contortions; nodding his head and bobbing about his tasselled nightcap.

My grandfather thought this very odd, and mighty presumptuous, and was about to demand what business he had to play his wind instruments in another gentleman's quarters, when a new cause of astonishment met his eye. From the opposite side of the room a long backed, bandy legged chair, covered with leather, and studded all over in a coxcomical fashion with little brass nails, got suddenly into motion; thrust out first a claw foot, then a crooked arm, and at length, making a leg, slided gracefully up to an easy chair, of tarnished brocade, with a hole in its bottom, and led it gallantly out in a ghostly minuet about the floor.

The musician now played fiercer and fiercer, and bobbed his head and his nightcap about like mad. By degrees the dancing mania seemed to seize upon all the other pieces of furniture. The antique, long bodied chairs paired off in couples and led down a country dance;

a three legged stool danced a hornpipe, though horribly puzzled by its supernumerary limb; while the amorous tongs seized the shovel round the waist, and whirled it about the room in a German waltz. In short, all the moveables got in motion, capering about; pirouetting, hands across, right and left, like so many devils, all except a great clothes-press, which kept curtseying and curtseying, like a dowager, in one corner, in exquisite time to the music;—being either too corpulent to dance, or perhaps at a loss for a partner.

My grandfather concluded the latter to be the reason; so, being, like a true Irishman, devoted to the sex, and at all times ready for a frolick, he bounced into the room, calling to the musician to strike up "Paddy O'Rafferty," capered up to the clothes-press and seized upon two handles to lead her out:—When, whirr!—the whole revel was at an end. The chairs, tables, tongs, and shovel slunk in an instant as quietly into their places as if nothing had happened; and the musician vanished up the chimney, leaving the bellows behind him in his hurry. My grandfather found himself seated in the middle of the floor, with the clothes press sprawling before him, and the two handles jerked off and in his hands.

"Then after all, this was a mere dream!" said the inquisitive gentleman.

"The divil a bit of a dream!" replied the Irishman: "there never was a truer fact in this world. Faith, I should have liked to see any man tell my grandfather it was a dream."

Well, gentlemen, as the clothes press was a mighty heavy body, and my grandfather likewise, particularly in rear, you may easily suppose two such heavy bodies coming to the ground would make a bit of a noise. Faith, the old mansion shook as though it had mistaken it for an earthquake. The whole garrison was alarmed. The landlord, who slept just below, hurried up with a candle to inquire the cause, but with all his haste his daughter had hurried to the scene of uproar before him. The landlord was followed by the landlady, who was followed by the bouncing bar maid, who was followed by the simpering chambermaids all holding together, as well as they could, such garments as they had first lain hands on; but all in a terrible hurry to see what the devil was to pay in the chamber of the bold dragoon.

My grandfather related the marvellous scene he had witnessed, and the prostrate clothes press, and the broken handles, bore testimony to the fact. There was no contesting such evidence; particularly with a lad of my grandfather's complexion, who seemed able to make good every word either with sword or shillelah. So the landlord scratched his head and looked silly, as he was apt to do when puzzled. The landlady scratched—no, she did not scratch her head,—but she knit her brow, and did not seem half pleased with the explanation. But the landlady's daughter corroborated it by recollecting that the last person who had dwelt in that chamber was a famous juggler who had died of St. Vitus's dance, and no doubt had infected all the furniture.

This set all things to rights, particularly when the chambermaids declared that they had all witnessed strange carryings on in that room;—and as they declared this "upon their honors," there could not remain a doubt upon the subject.

"And did your grandfather go to bed again in that room?" said the inquisitive gentleman.

"That's more than I can tell. Where he passed the rest of the night was a secret he never disclosed. In fact, though he had seen much service, he was but indifferently acquainted with geography, and apt to make blunders in his travels about inns at night, that it would have puzzled him sadly to account for in the morning."

"Was he ever apt to walk in his sleep?" said the knowing old gentleman.

"Never that I heard of."

There was a little pause after this rigmarole Irish romance, when the old gentleman with the haunted head observed, that the stories hitherto related had rather a burlesque tendency. "I recollect an adventure, however," added he, "which I heard of during a residence at Paris, for the truth of which I can undertake to vouch, and which is of a very grave and singular nature."

THE ADVENTURE OF THE GERMAN STUDENT

On a stormy night, in the tempestuous times of the French Revolution, a young German was returning to his lodgings, at a late hour, across the old part of Paris. The lightning gleamed, and the loud claps of thunder rattled through the lofty narrow streets— but I should first tell you something about this young German.

Gottfried Wolfgang was a young man of good family. He had studied for some time at Gottingen, but being of a visionary and enthusiastic character, he had wandered into those wild and speculative doctrines which have so often bewildered German students. His secluded life, his intense application, and the singular nature of his studies, had an effect on both mind and body. His health was impaired; his imagination diseased. He had been indulging in fanciful speculations on spiritual essences, until, like Swedenborg, he had an ideal world of his own around him. He took up a notion, I do not know from what cause, that there was an evil influence hanging over him; an evil genius or spirit seeking to ensnare him and ensure his perdition. Such an idea working on his melancholy temperament produced the most gloomy effects. He became haggard and desponding. His friends discovered the mental malady preying upon him, and determined that the best cure was a change of scene; he was sent, therefore, to finish his studies amidst the splendors and gaieties of Paris.

Wolfgang arrived at Paris at the breaking out of the revolution. The popular delirium at first caught his enthusiastic mind, and he was captivated by the political and philosophical theories of the day: but the scenes of blood which followed shocked his sensitive nature, disgusted him with society and the world, and made him more than ever a recluse. He shut himself up in a solitary apartment in the *Pays Latin*, the quarter of students. There, in a gloomy street not far from the monastic walls of the Sorbonne, he pursued his favorite speculations. Sometimes he spend hours together in the great libraries of Paris, those catacombs of departed authors, rummaging among their hoards of dusty and obsolete works in quest of food for his unhealthy appetite. He was, in a manner, a literary goul, feeding in the charnel house of decayed literature.

Wolfgang, though solitary and recluse, was of an ardent temperament, but for a time it operated merely upon his imagination. He was too shy and ignorant of the world to make any advances to the fair, but he was a passionate admirer of female beauty, and in his lonely chamber would often lose himself in reveries on forms and faces which he had seen, and his fancy would deck out images of loveliness far surpassing the reality.

While his mind was in this excited and sublimated state, a dream produced an extraordinary effect upon him. It was of a female face of transcendent beauty. So strong was the impression made, that he dreamt of it again and again. It haunted his thoughts by day, his slumbers by night; in fine, he became passionately enamoured of this shadow of a dream. This lasted so long that it became one of those fixed ideas which haunt the minds of melancholy men, and are at times mistaken for madness.

Such was Gottfried Wolfgang, and such his situation at the time I mentioned. He was returning home late on stormy night, through some of the old and gloomy streets of the *Marais*, the ancient part of Paris. The loud claps of thunder rattled among the high houses of the narrow streets. He came to the Place de Grêve, the square, where public executions are performed. The lightning quivered about the pinnacles of the ancient Hôtel de Ville, and shed flickering gleams over the open space in front. As Wolfgang was crossing the square, he shrank back with horror at finding himself close by the guillotine. It was the height of the reign of terror, when this dreadful instrument of death stood ever ready, and its scaffold was continually running with the blood of the virtuous and the brave. It had that very day been actively employed in the work of carnage, and there it stood in grim array, amidst a silent and sleeping city, waiting for fresh victims.

Wolfgang's heart sickened within him, and he was turning shuddering from the horrible engine, when he beheld a shadowy form, cowering as it were at the foot of the steps which led up to the scaffold. A succession of vivid flashes of lightning revealed it more distinctly. It was a female figure, dressed in black. She was seated on one of the lower steps of the scaffold, leaning forward, her face hid in her lap; and her long dishevelled tresses hanging to the ground, streaming with the rain which fell in torrents. Wolfgang paused. There was something awful in this solitary monument of woe. The female had the appearance of being above the common order. He knew the times to be full of vicissitude, and that many a fair head, which had once been pillowed on down, now wandered houseless.

Perhaps this was some poor mourner whom the dreadful axe had rendered desolate, and who sat here heart-broken on the strand of existence, from which all that was dear to her had been launched into eternity.

He approached, and addressed her in the accents of sympathy. She raised her head and gazed wildly at him. What was his astonishment at beholding, by the bright glare of the lighting, the very face which had haunted him in his dreams. It was pale and disconsolate, but ravishingly beautiful.

Trembling with violent and conflicting emotions, Wolfgang again accosted her. He spoke something of her being exposed at such an hour of the night, and to the fury of such a storm, and offered to conduct her to her friends. She pointed to the guillotine with a gesture of dreadful signification.

"I have no friend on earth!" said she.

"But you have a home," said Wolfgang.

"Yes—in the grave!"

The heart of the student melted at the words.

"If a stranger dare make an offer," said he, "without danger of being misunderstood, I would offer my humble dwelling as a shelter; myself as a devoted friend. I am friendless myself in Paris, and a stranger in the land; but if my life could be of service, it is at your disposal, and should be sacrificed before harm or indignity should come to you."

There was an honest earnestness in the young man's manner that had its effect. His foreign accent, too, was in his favor; it showed him not to be a hackneyed inhabitant of Paris. Indeed, there is an eloquence in true enthusiasm that is not to be doubted. The homeless stranger confided herself implicitly to the protection of the student.

He supported her faltering steps across the Pont Neuf, and by the place where the statue of Henry the Fourth had been overthrown by the populace. The storm had abated, and the thunder rumbled at a distance. All Paris was quiet; that great volcano of human passion slumbered for a while, to gather fresh strength for the next day's eruption. The student conducted his charge through the ancient streets of the *Pays Latin,* and by the dusky walls of the Sorbonne, to the great dingy hotel which he inhabited. The old portress who admitted them stared with surprise at the unusual sight of the melancholy Wolfgang with a female companion.

On entering his apartment, the student, for the first time, blushed at the scantiness and indifference of his dwelling. He had but one chamber—an old-fashioned saloon—heavily carved, and fantastically furnished with the remains of former magnificence, for it was one of those hotels in the quarter of the Luxembourg palace which had once belonghed to nobility. It was lumbered with books and papers, and all the usual apparatus of a student, and his bed stood in a recess at one end.

When lights were brought, and Wolfgang had a better opportunity of contemplating the stranger, he was more than ever intoxicated by her beauty. Her face was pale, but of a dazzling fairness, set off by a profusion of raven hair that hung clustering about it. Her eyes were large and brilliant, with a singular expression approaching almost to wildness. As far as her black dress permitted her shape to be seen, it was of perfect symmetry. Her whole appearance was highly striking, though she was dressed in the simplest style. The only thing approaching to an ornament which she wore was a broad, black band round her neck, clasped by diamonds.

The perplexity now commenced with the student how to dispose of the helpless being thus thrown upon his protection. He thought of abandoning his chamber to her, and seeking shelter for himself elsewhere. Still he was so fascinate by her charms, there seemed to be such a spell upon his thoughts and senses, that he could not tear himself from her presence. Her manner, too, was singular and unaccountable. She spoke no more of the guillotine. Her grief had abated. The attentions of the student had first won her confidence, and then, apparently, her heart. She was evidently an enthusiast like himself, and enthusiasts soon understand each other.

In the infatuation of the moment, Wolfgang avowed his passion for her. He told her the story of his mysterious dream, and how she had possessed his heart before he had even seen her. She was strangely affected by his recital, and acknowledged to have felt an impulse towards him equally unaccountable. It was the time for wild theory and wild actions. Old prejudices and superstitions were done away; everything was under the sway of the "Goddess of Reason." Among other rubbish of the old times, the forms and ceremonies of marriage began to be considered superfluous bonds for honorable minds. Social compacts were the vogue. Wolfgang was too much of theorist not to be tainted by the liberal doctrines of the day.

"Why should we separate?" said he: "our hearts are united; in the eye of reason and honor we are as one. What need is there of sordid forms to bind high soul together?"

The stranger listened with emotion: she had evidently received illumination at the same school.

"You have no home nor family," continued he; "let me be everything to you, or rather let us be everything to one another. If form is necessary, form shall be observed—there is my hand. I pledge myself to you for ever."

"For ever?" said the stranger, solemnly.

"For ever!" repeated Wolfgang.

The stranger clasped the hand extended to her: "Then I am yours," murmured she, and sank upon his bosom.

The next morning the student left his bride sleeping, and sallied forth at an early hour to seek more spacious apartments suitable to the change in his situation. When he returned, he found the stranger lying with her head hanging over the bed, and one arm thrown over it. He spoke to her, but received no reply. He advanced to awaken her from her uneasy posture. On taking her hand, it was cold—there was no pulsation—her face was pallid and ghastly.—In a word she was a corpse.

Horrified and frantic, he alarmed the house. A scene of confusion ensued. The police was summoned. As the officer of police entered the room, he started back on beholding the corpse.

"Great heaven!" cried he, "how did this woman come here?"

"Do you know anything about her?" said Wolfgang eagerly.

"Do I?" exclaimed the officer: "she was guillotined yesterday!"

He stepped forward; undid the black collar round the neck of the corpse, and the head rolled on the floor!

The student burst into a frenzy. "The fiend! the fiend has gained possession of me!" shrieked he: "I am lost for ever."

They tried to soothe him, but in vain. He was possessed with the frightful belief that an evil spirit had re-animated the dead body to ensnare him. He went distracted, and died in a madhouse.

* * *

Here the old gentleman with the haunted head finished his narrative.

"And is this really a fact?" said the inquisitive gentleman.

"A fact not to be doubted," replied the other. "I had it from the best authority. The student told it me himself. I saw him in a madhouse in Paris."

THE ADVENTURE OF THE
MYSTERIOUS PICTURE

As one story of the kind produces another, and as all the company seemed fully engrossed by the topic, and disposed to bring their relatives and ancestors upon the scene, there is no knowing how many more ghost adventures we might have heard, had not a corpulent old fox hunter, who had slept soundly through the whole, now suddenly awakened, with a loud and long-drawn yawn. The sound broke the charm; the ghosts took to flight as though it had been cock-crowing, and there was a universal move for bed.

"And now for the haunted chamber," said the Irish captain, taking his candle.

"Aye, who's to be the hero of the night?" said the gentleman with the ruined head.

"That we shall see in the morning," said the old gentleman with the nose: "whoever looks pale and grizzly will have seen the ghost."

"Well, gentlemen," said the Baronet, "there's many a true thing said in jest. In fact, one of you will sleep in a room tonight"—

"What—a haunted room? a haunted room? I claim the adventure— and I—and I—and I," cried a dozen guests, talking and laughing at the same time.

"No—no," said mine host, "there is a secret about one of my rooms on which I feel disposed to try an experiment. So, gentlemen, none of you shall know who has the haunted chamber, until circumstances reveal it. I will not even know it myself, but will leave it to chance and the allotment of the housekeeper. At the same time, if it will be any satisfaction to you, I will observe, for the honor of my paternal mansion, that there's scarcely a chamber in it but is well worthy of being haunted."

We now separated for the night, and each went to his allotted room. Mine was in one wing of the building, and I could not but smile at its resemblance in style to those eventful apartments described in the tales of the supper table. It was spacious and gloomy, decorated with lamp black portraits, a bed of ancient damask, with a tester sufficiently lofty to grace a couch of state, and a number of massive pieces of old-fashioned furniture. I drew a great claw-footed arm chair before the wide fire place; stirred up the fire; sat looking into it, and musing upon the odd stories I had heard; until, partly overcome by the fatigue of the day's hunting, and partly by the wine and wassail of mine host, I fell asleep in my chair.

The uneasiness of my position made my slumber troubled, and laid me at the mercy of all kinds of wild and fearful dreams; now it was that my perfidious dinner and supper rose in rebellion against my peace. I was hag-ridden by a fat saddle of mutton; a plum pudding weighed like lead upon my conscience; the merry thought of a capon filled me with horrible suggestions; and a devilled leg of a turkey stalked in all kinds of diabolical shapes through my imagination. In short, I had a violent fit of the nightmare. Some strange indefinite evil seemed hanging over me that I could not avert; something terrible and loathsome oppressed me that I could not shake off. I was conscious of being asleep, and strove to rouse myself, but every effort redoubled the evil; until gasping, struggling, almost strangling, I suddenly sprang bolt upright in my chair, and awoke.

The light on the mantel piece had burnt low, and the wick was divided; there was a great winding sheet made by the dripping wax, on the side towards me. The disordered taper emitted a broad flaring flame, and threw a strong light on a painting over the fire place, which I had not hitherto observed.

It consisted merely of a head, or rather a face, that appeared to be staring full upon me, and with an expression that was startling. It was without a frame, and at the first glance I could hardly persuade myself that it was not a real face, thrusting itself out of the dark oaken pannel. I sat in my chair gazing at it, and the more I gazed the more it disquieted me. I had never before been affected in the same way by any painting. The emotions it caused were strange and indefinite. They were something like what I have heard ascribed to the eyes of the basilisk; or like that mysterious influence in reptiles termed fascination. I passed my hand over my eyes several times, as if seeking instinctively to brush away this allusion—in vain—they instantly reverted to the picture, and its chilling, creeping influence over my flesh was redoubled.

I looked around the room on other pictures, either to divert my attention, or to see whether the same effect would be produced by them. Some of them were grim enough to produce the effect, if the mere grimness of the painting produced it—no such thing. My eye passed over them all with perfect indifference, but the moment it reverted to this visage over the fire-place, it was as if an electric shock darted through me. The other pictures were dim and faded; but this one protruded from a plain black ground in the strongest relief, and with wonderful truth of coloring. The expression was that of agony—the agony of intense bodily pain; but a menace scowled upon the brow, and a few sprinklings of blood added to its ghastliness. Yet it was not all these characteristics—it was some horror of the mind, some inscrutable antipathy awakened by this picture, which harrowed up my feelings.

I tried to persuade myself that this was chimerical; that my brain was confused by the fumes of mine host's good cheer, and, in some measure, by the odd stories about paintings which had been told at supper. I determined to shake off these vapours of the mind; rose from my chair, and walked about the room; snapped my fingers; rallied myself; laughed aloud. It was a forced laugh, and the echo of it in the old chamber jarred upon my ear. I walked to the window; tried to discern the landscape through the glass. It was pitch darkness, and howling storm without; and as I heard the wind moan among the trees, I caught a reflection of this accursed visage in the pane of glass, as though it were staring through the window at me. Even the reflection of it was thrilling.

How was this vile nervous fit, for such I now persuaded myself it was, to be conquered? I determined to force myself not to look at the painting but to undress quickly and get into bed. I began to undress, but in spite of every effort I could not keep myself from stealing a glance every now and then at the picture; and a glance was now sufficient to distress me. Even when my back was turned to it, the idea of this strange face behind me, peering over my shoulder, was insufferable. I threw off my clothes and hurried into bed; but still this visage gazed upon me. I had a full view of it from my bed, and for some time could not take my eyes from it. I had grown nervous to a dismal degree.

I put out the light, and tried to force myself to sleep;—all in vain! The fire gleaming up a little, threw an uncertain light about the room, leaving, however, the region of the picture in deep shadow. What, thought I, if this be the chamber about which mine host spoke as having a mystery reigning over it?—I had taken his words merely as spoken in jest; might they have a real import? I looked around. The faintly lighted apartment had all the qualifications requisite for a haunted chamber. It began in my infected imagination to assume strange appearances. The old portraits turned paler and paler, and blacker and blacker; the streaks of light and shadow thrown among the quaint old articles of furniture, gave them singular shapes and characters. There was a huge dark clothes press of antique form, gorgeous in brass and lustrous with wax, that began to grow oppressive to me.

Am I then, thought I, indeed, the hero of the haunted room? Is there really a spell laid upon me, or is this all some contrivance of mine host, to raise a laugh at my expense? The idea of being hag-ridden by my own fancy all night, and then bantered on my haggard looks the next day was intolerable; but the very idea was sufficient to produce the effect, and to render me still more nervous. Pish, said I, it can be no such thing. How could my worthy host imagine that I, or any man would be so worried by a mere picture? It is my own diseased imagination that torments me. I turned in my bed, and shifted from side to side, to try to fall asleep; but all in vain. When one cannot get asleep by lying quiet, it is seldom that tossing about will effect the purpose. The fire gradually went out and left the room in darkness. Still I had the idea of this inexplicable countenance gazing and keeping watch upon me through the darkness. Nay, what was worse, the very darkness seemed to give it additional power, and to multiply its terrors. It was like having an unseen enemy hovering about one in the night. Instead of having one picture now to worry me, I had a hundred. I fancied it in every direction. There it is, thought I,—and there, and there,—with its horrible and mysterious expression, still gazing and gazing on me. No if I must suffer this strange and dismal influence, it were better face a single foe, than thus be haunted by a thousand images of it.

Whoever has been in such a state of nervous agitation must know that the longer it continues, the more uncontrollable it grows; the very air of the chamber seemed at length infected by the baleful presence of this picture. I fancied it hovering over me. I almost felt the fearful visage from the wall approaching my face,—it seemed breathing upon me. This is not to be borne, said I, at length, springing out of bed. I can stand this no longer. I shall only tumble and toss about here all night; make a very spectre of myself, and become the hero of the haunted chamber in good earnest. Whatever be the consequence. I'll quit this cursed room, and seek a night's rest elsewhere. They can but laugh at me at all events, and they'll be sure to have the laugh upon me if I pass a sleepless night and show them a haggard and wo-begone visage in the morning.

All this was half muttered to myself, as I hastily slipped on my clothes; which having done, I groped my way out of the room, and down-stairs to the drawing-room. Here, after tumbling over two or three pieces of furniture, I made out to reach a sofa, and stretching myself upon it determined to bivouack there for the night.

The moment I found myself out of the neighbourhood of that strange picture, it seemed as if the charm were broken. All its influence was at an end. I felt assured that it was confined to its own dreary chamber, for I had, with a sort of instinctive caution, turned the key when I closed the door. I soon calmed down, therefore, into a state of tranquillity; from that into a drowsiness, and finally into a deep sleep; out of which I did not awake, until the housemaid, with her besom and her matin song, came to put the room in order. She stared at finding me stretched upon the sofa; but I presume circumstances of the kind were not uncommon after hunting dinners, in her master's bachelor establishment; for she went on with her song and her work, and took no farther heed of me.

I had an unconquerable repugnance to return to my chamber; so I found my way to the butler's quarters, made my toilet in the best way circumstances would permit, and was among the first to appear at the breakfast table. Our breakfast was a substantial fox-hunter's repast, and the company were generally assembled at it. When ample justice had been done to the tea, coffee, cold meats, and humming ale, for all these were furnished in abundance, according to the tastes of the different guests, the conversation began to break out, with all the liveliness and freshness of morning mirth.

"But who is the hero of the haunted chamber?—Who has seen the ghost last night?" said the inquisitive gentleman, rolling his lobster eyes about the table.

The question set every tongue in motion; a vast deal of bantering; criticising of countenances; of mutual accusation and retort took place. Some had drunk deep, and some were unshaven, so that there were suspicious faces enough in the assembly. I alone could not enter with ease and vivacity into the joke. I felt tongue-tied—embarrassed. A recollection of what I had seen and felt the preceding night still haunted my mind.

It seemed as if the mysterious picture still held a thrall upon me. I thought also that our host's eye was turned on me with an air of curiosity. In short, I was conscious that I was the hero of the night, and felt as if every one might read it in my looks.

The joke, however, passed over, and no suspicion seemed to attach to me. I was just congratulating myself on my escape, when a servant came in, saying, that the gentleman who had slept on the sofa in the drawing room, had left his watch under one of the pillows. My repeater was in his hand.

"What!" said the inquisitive gentleman, "did any gentleman sleep on the sofa?"

"Soho! soho! a hare—a hare!" cried the old gentleman with the flexible nose.

I could not avoid acknowledging the watch, and was rising in great confusion, when a boisterous old squire who sat beside me, exclaimed, slapping me on the shoulder, "'Sblood, lad! thou'rt the man as has seen the ghost!"

The attention of the company was immediately turned to me; if my face had been pale the moment before, it now glowed almost to burning. I tried to laugh, but could only make a grimace; and found all the muscles of my face twitching at sixes and sevens, and totally out of all control.

It takes but little to raise a laugh among a set of fox-hunters. There was a world of merriment and joking at my expense; and as I never relished a joke overmuch when it was at my own expense, I began to feel a little nettled. I tried to look cool and calm and to restrain my pique; but the coolness and calmness of a man in a passion are confounded treacherous.

Gentlemen, said I, with a slight cocking of the chin, and a bad attempt at a smile, this is all very pleasant—ha! ha!—very pleasant— but I'd have you know I am as little superstitious as any of you—ha! ha!—and as to anything like timidity—you may smile, gentlemen— but I trust there is no one here means to insinuate that.—As to a room's being haunted, I repeat, gentlemen—(growing a little warm at seeing a cursed grin breaking out round me)—as to a room's being haunted, I have as little faith in such silly stories as any one. But, since you put the matter home to me, I will say that I have met with something in my room strange and inexplicable to me—(a shout of laughter). Gentlemen, I am serious—I know well what I am saying—I am calm, gentlemen (striking my flat upon the table)—by heaven I am calm. I am neither trifling, nor do I wish to be trifled with—(the laughter of the company suppressed with ludicrous attempts at gravity). There is a picture in the room in which I was put last night, that has had an effect upon me the most singular and incomprehensible.

"A picture!" said the old gentleman with the haunted head. "A picture!" cried the narrator with the waggish nose. "A picture! a picture!" echoed several voices. Here there was an ungovernable peal of laughter.

I could not contain myself. I started up from my seat—looked round on the company with fiery indignation—thrust both my hands into my pockets, and strode up to one of the windows, as though I would have walked through it. I stopped short; looked out upon the landscape without distinguishing a feature of it; and felt my gorge rising almost to suffocation.

Mine host saw it was time to interfere. He had maintained an air of Gravity through the whole of the scene, and now stepped forth as if to shelter me from the overwhelming merriment of my companions.

"Gentlemen," said he, "I dislike to spoil sport, but you have had your laugh, and the joke of the haunted chamber has been enjoyed. I must now take the part of my guest. I must not only vindicate him from your pleasantries, but I must reconcile him to himself, for I suspect he is a little out of humour with his own feelings; and above all, I must crave his pardon for having made him the subject of a kind of experiment.

"Yes, gentlemen, there is something strange and peculiar in the chamber to which our friend was shown last night. There is a picture which possesses a singular and mysterious influence; and with which there is connected a very curious story. It is a picture to which I attach a value from a variety of circumstances; and though I have often been tempted to destroy it from the odd and uncomfortable sensations it produces in every one that beholds it; yet I have never been able to prevail upon myself to make the sacrifice. It is a picture I never like to look upon myself; and which is held in awe by all my servants. I have, therefore, banished it to a room but rarely used; and should have had it covered last night, had not the nature of our conversation, and the whimsical talk about a haunted chamber tempted me to let it remain, by way of experiment, whether a stranger, totally unacquainted with its story, would be affected by it."

The words of the Baronet had turned every thought into a different channel; all were anxious to hear the story of the mysterious picture; and for myself, so strongly were my feelings interested, that I forgot to feel piqued at the experiment which my host had made upon my nerves, and joined eagerly in the general entreaty.

As the morning was stormy, and precluded all egress, my host was glad of any means of entertaining his company; so drawing his arm-chair beside the fire, he began—

THE ADVENTURE OF THE MYSTERIOUS STRANGER

Many years since, when I was a young man, and had just left Oxford, I was sent on the grand tour to finish my education. I believe my parents had tried in vain to inoculate me with wisdom; so they sent me to mingle with society, in hopes I might take it the natural way. Such, at least, appears to be the reason for which nine-tenths of our youngsters are sent abroad.

In the course of my tour I remained some time at Venice. The romantic character of the place delighted me; I was very much amused by the air of adventure and intrigue that prevailed in this region of masks and gondolas; and I was exceedingly smitten by a pair of languishing black eyes, that played upon my heart from under an Italian mantle. So I persuaded myself that I was lingering at Venice to study men and manners. At least I persuaded my friends so, and that answered all my purpose. Indeed, I was a little prone to be struck by peculiarities in character and conduct, and my imagination was so full of romantic associations with Italy, that I was always on the lookout for adventure.

Every thing chimed in with such a humour in this old mermaid of a city. My suite of apartments were in a proud, melancholy palace on the grand canal, formerly the residence of a Magnifico, and sumptuous with the traces of decayed grandeur. My gondolier was one of the shrewdest of his class, active, merry, intelligent, and, like his brethren, secret as the grave; that is to say, secret to all the world except his master. I had not had him a week before he put me behind all the curtains in Venice. I liked the silence and mystery of the place, and when I sometimes saw from my window a black gondola gliding mysteriously along in the dusk of the evening, with nothing visible but its little glimmering lantern, I would jump into my own zendaletta, and give a signal for pursuit. But I am running away from my subject with the recollection of youthful follies, said the Baronet, checking himself, "let us come to the point."

Among my familiar resorts was a Cassino under the Arcades on one side of the grand square of St. Mark. Here I used frequently to lounge and take my ice on those warm summer nights when in Italy every body lives abroad until morning. I was seated here one evening, when a group of Italians took seat at a table on the opposite side of the saloon. Their conversation was gay and animated, and carried on with Italian vivacity and gesticulation.

I remarked among them one young man, however, who appeared to take no share, and find no enjoyment in the conversation; though he seemed to force himself to attend to it. He was tall and slender, and of extremely prepossessing appearance. His features were fine, though emaciated. He had a profusion of black glossy hair that curled lightly about his head, and contrasted with the extreme paleness of his countenance. His brow was haggard; deep furrows seemed to have been ploughed into his visage by care, not by age, for he was evidently in the prime of youth. His eye was full of expression and fire, but wild and unsteady. He seemed to be tormented by some strange fancy or apprehension. In spite of every effort to fix his attention on the conversation of his companions, I noticed that every now and then he would turn his head slowly round, give a glance over his shoulder, and then withdraw it with a sudden jerk, as if something painful had met his eye. This was repeated at intervals of about a minute, and he appeared hardly to have got over one shock, before I saw him slowly preparing to encounter another.

After sitting some time in the Cassino, the party paid for the refreshments they had taken, and departed. The young man was the last to leave the saloon, and I remarked him glancing behind him in the same way, just as he passed out at the door. I could not resist the impulse to rise and follow him; for I was at an age when a romantic feeling of curiosity is easily awakened. The party walked slowly down the Arcades, talking and laughing as they went. They crossed the Piazzetta, but paused in the middle of it to enjoy the scene. It was one of those moonlight nights so brilliant and clear in the pure atmosphere of Italy. The moon beams streamed on the tall tower of St. Mark, and lighted up the magnificent front and swelling domes of the Cathedral. The party expressed their delight in animated terms. I kept my eye upon the young man. He alone seemed abstracted and self occupied. I noticed the same singular, and, as it were, furtive glance over the shoulder that had attracted my attention in the Cassino. The party moved on, and I followed; they passed along the walks called the Broglio; turned the corner of the Ducal palace, and getting into a gondola, glided swiftly away.

The countenance and conduct of this young man dwelt upon my mind. There was something in his appearance that interested me exceedingly. I met him a day or two after in a gallery of paintings. He was evidently a connoisseur, for he always singled out the most masterly productions, and the few remarks drawn from him by his companions showed an intimate acquaintance with the art. His own taste, however, ran on singular extremes. On Salvator Rosa in his most savage and solitary scenes; on Raphael, Titian, and Corregio in their softest delineations of female beauty. On these he would occasionally gaze with transient enthusiasm. But this seemed only a momentary forgetfullness. Still would recur that cautious glance behind, and always quickly withdrawn, as though something terrible had met his view.

I encountered him frequently afterwards. At the theatre, at balls, at concerts; at the promenades in the gardens of San Georgio; at the grotesque exhibitions in the square of St. Mark; among the throng of merchants on the Exchange by the Rialto. He seemed, in fact, to seek crowds; to hunt after bustle and amusement; yet never to take any interest in either the business or gayety of the scene. Ever an air of painful thought, of wretched abstraction; and ever that strange and recurring movement, of glancing fearfully over the shoulder. I did not know at first but this might be caused by apprehension of arrest; or perhaps from dread of assassination. But, if so, why should he go thus continually abroad; why expose himself at all times and in all places?

I became anxious to know this stranger. I was drawn to him by that Romantic sympathy that sometimes draws young men towards each other. His melancholy threw a charm about him in my eyes, which was no doubt heightened by the touching expression of his countenance, and the manly graces of his person; for manly beauty has its effect even upon man. I had an Englishman's habitual diffidence and awkwardness of address to contend with; but I subdued it, and from frequently meeting him in the Cassino, gradually edged myself into his acquaintance. I had no reserve on his part to contend with. He seemed on the contrary to court society; and in fact to seek anything rather than be alone.

When he found I really took an interest in him he threw himself entirely upon my friendship. He clung to me like a drowning man. He would walk with me for hours up and down the place of St. Mark—or he would sit until night was far advanced in my apartment; he took rooms under the same roof with me; and his constant request was, that I would permit him, when it did not incommode me, to sit by me in my saloon. It was not that he seemed to take a particular delight in my conversation; but rather that he craved the vicinity of a human being; and above all, of a being that sympathized with him. "I have often heard," said he, "of the sincerity of Englishmen—thank God I have one at length for a friend!"

Yet he never seemed disposed to avail himself of my sympathy other than by mere companionship. He never sought to unbosom himself to me; there appeared to be a settled corroding anguish in his bosom that neither could be soothed "by silence nor by speaking." A devouring melancholy preyed upon his heart, and seemed to be drying up the very blood in his veins. It was not a soft melancholy— the disease of the affections; but a parching, withering agony. I could see at times that his mouth was dry and feverish; he almost panted rather than breathed; his eyes were bloodshot; his cheeks pale and livid; with now and then faint streaks athwart them— baleful gleams of the fire that was consuming his heart. As my arm was within his, I felt him press it at times with a convulsive motion to his side; his hands would clinch themselves involuntarily, and a kind of shudder would run through his frame. I reasoned with him about his melancholy, and sought to draw from him the cause—he shrunk from all confiding. "Do not seek to know it," said he, "you could not relieve it if you knew it; you would not even seek to relieve it—on the contrary, I should lose your sympathy; and that," said he, pressing my hand convulsively, "that I feel has become too dear to me to risk."

I endeavoured to awaken hope within him. He was young; life had a thousand pleasures in store for him; there is a healthy reaction in the youthful heart; it medicines its own wounds—"Come, come," said I, "there is no grief so great that youth cannot outgrow it."— "No! no!" said he, clinching his teeth, and striking repeatedly, with the energy of despair, upon his bosom—"It is here—here—deep rooted; draining my heart's blood. It grows and grows, while my heart withers and withers! I have a dreadful monitor that gives me no repose—that follows me step by step; and will follow me step by step, until it pushes me into my grave!"

As he said this he gave involuntarily one of those fearful glances over his shoulder, and shrunk back with more than usual horror. I could not resist the temptation to allude to this movement, which I supposed to be some mere malady of the nerves. The moment I mentioned it his face became crimsoned and convulsed—he grasped me by both hands: "For God's sake," exclaimed he, with a piercing agony of voice—"never allude to that again; let us avoid this subject, my friend; you cannot relieve me, indeed you cannot relieve me; but you may add to the torments I suffer;—at some future day you shall know all."

I never resumed the subject; for however much my curiosity might be aroused, I felt too true compassion for his sufferings to increase them by my intrusion. I sought various ways to divert his mind, and to arouse him from the constant meditations in which he was plunged. He saw my efforts, and seconded them as far as in his power, for there was nothing moody or wayward in his nature; on the contrary, there was something frank, generous, unassuming, in his whole deportment. All the sentiments that he uttered were noble and lofty. He claimed no indulgence; he asked no toleration. He seemed content to carry his load of misery in silence, and only sought to carry it by my side. There was a mute beseeching manner about him, as if he craved companionship as a charitable boon; and a tacit thankfulness in his looks, as if he felt grateful to me for not repulsing him.

I felt this melancholy to be infectious. It stole over my spirits; Interfered with all my gay pursuits, and gradually saddened my life; yet I could not prevail upon myself to shake off a being who seemed to hang upon me for support. In truth, the generous traits of character that beamed through all this gloom had penetrated to my heart. His bounty was lavish and open handed. His charity melting and spontaneous. Not confined to mere donations, which often humiliate as much as they relieve. The tone of his voice, the beam of his eye, enhanced every gift, and surprised the poor suppliant with that rarest and sweetest of charities, the charity not merely of the hand, but of the heart. Indeed, his liberality seemed to have something in it of self abasement and expiation. He humbled himself, in a manner, before the mendicant. "What right have I to ease and affluence," would he murmur to himself, "when innocence wanders in misery and rags?"

The Carnival time arrived. I had hoped that the gay scenes which then Presented themselves might have some cheering effect. I mingled with him in the motley throng that crowded the place of St. Mark. We frequented operas, masquerades, balls. All in vain. The evil kept growing on him; he became more and more haggard and agitated. Often, after we had returned from one of these scenes of revelry,

I have entered his room, and found him lying on his face on the sofa: his hands clinched in his fine hair, and his whole countenance bearing traces of the convulsions of his mind.

The Carnival passed away; the season of Lent succeeded; Passion week arrived. We attended one evening a solemn service in one of the churches; in the course of which a grand piece of vocal and instrumental music was performed relating to the death of our Saviour.

I had remarked that he was always powerfully affected by music; on this occasion he was so in an extraordinary degree. As the peeling notes swelled through the lofty aisles, he seemed to kindle up with fervor. His eyes rolled upwards, until nothing but the whites were visible; his hands were clasped together, until the fingers were deeply imprinted in the flesh. When the music expressed the dying agony, his face gradually sunk upon his knees; and at the touching words resounding through the church, "*Jesu mori,*" sobs burst from him uncontrolled. I had never seen him weep before; his had always been agony rather than sorrow. I augured well from the circumstance. I let him weep on uninterrupted. When the service was ended we left the church. He hung on my arm as we walked homewards, with something of a softer and more subdued manner; instead of that nervous agitation I had been accustomed to witness. He alluded to the service we had heard. "Music," said he, "is indeed the voice of heaven; never before have I felt more impressed by the story of the atonement of our Saviour. Yes, my friend," said he, clasping his hands with a kind of transport, "I know that my Redeemer liveth."

We parted for the night. His room was not far from mine, and I heard him for some time busied in it. I fell asleep, but was awakened before daylight. The young man stood by my bed-side, dressed for travelling. He held a sealed packet and a large parcel in his hand, which he laid on the table. "Farewell, my friend," said he, "I am about to set forth on a long journey; but, before I go, I leave with you these remembrances. In this packet you will find the particulars of my story. When you read them, I shall be far away; do not remember me with aversion. You have been, indeed, a friend to me. You have poured oil into a broken heart,—but you could not heal it.—Farewell—let me kiss your hand—I am unworthy to embrace you." He sunk on his knees, seized my hand in despite of my efforts to the contrary, and covered it with kisses. I was so surprised by all this scene that I had not been able to say a word.

But we shall meet again, said I, hastily, as I saw him hurrying towards the door.

"Never—never in this world!" said he, solemnly. He sprang once more to my bed-side—seized my hand, pressed it to his heart and to his lips, and rushed out of the room.

Here the Baronet paused. He seemed lost in thought, and sat looking upon the floor and drumming with his fingers on the arm of his chair.

"And did this mysterious personage return?" said the inquisitive gentleman. "Never!" replied the Baronet, with a pensive shake of the head: "I never saw him again." "And pray what has all this to do with the picture?" inquired the old gentleman with the nose—"True!" said the questioner—"Is it the portrait of this crack-brained Italian?" "No!" said the Baronet drily, not half liking the appellation given to his hero; "but this picture was inclosed in the parcel he left with me. The sealed packet contained its explanation. There was a request on the outside that I would not open it until six months had elapsed. I kept my promise, in spite of my curiosity. I have a translation of it by me, and had meant to read it, by way of accounting for the mystery of the chamber, but I fear I have already detained the company too long."

Here there was a general wish expressed to have the manuscript read; particularly on the part of the inquisitive gentleman. So the worthy Baronet drew out a fairly written manuscript, and wiping his spectacles, read aloud the following story:—

THE STORY OF THE YOUNG ITALIAN

I was born at Naples. My parents, though of noble rank, were limited in fortune, or rather my father was ostentatious beyond his means, and expended so much in his palace, his equipage, and his retinue, that he was continually straitened in his pecuniary circumstances. I was a younger son, and looked upon with indifference by my father, who, from a principle of family pride, wished to leave all his property to my elder brother.

I showed, when quite a child, an extreme sensibility. Every thing affected me violently. While yet an infant in my mother's arms, and before I had learnt to talk, I could be wrought upon to a wonderful degree of anguish or delight by the power of music. As I grew older my feelings remained equally acute, and I was easily transported into paroxysms of pleasure or rage. It was the amusement of my relatives and of the domestics to play upon this irritable temperament. I was moved to tears, tickled to laughter, provoked to fury, for the entertainment of company, who were amused by such a tempest of mighty passion in a pigmy frame. They little thought, or perhaps little heeded the dangerous sensibilities they were fostering. I thus became a little creature of passion, before reason was developed. In a short time I grew too old to be a plaything, and then I became a torment. The tricks and passions I had been teased into became irksome, and I was disliked by my teachers for the very lessons they had taught me.

My mother died; and my power as a spoiled child was at an end. There was no longer any necessity to humor or tolerate me, for there was nothing to be gained by it, as I was no favorite of my father. I therefore experienced the fate of a spoiled child in such situation, and was neglected or noticed only to be crossed and contradicted. Such was the early treatment of a heart, which, if I am judge of it at all, was naturally disposed to the extremes of tenderness and affection.

My father, as I have already said, never liked me—in fact, he never understood me; he looked upon me as wilful and wayward, as deficient in natural affection:—it was the stateliness of his own manner; the loftiness and grandeur of his own look that had repelled me from his arms. I always pictured him to myself as I had seen him clad in his senatorial robes, rustling with pomp and pride. The magnificence of his person had daunted my strong imagination. I could never approach him with the confiding affection of a child.

My father's feelings were wrapped up in my elder brother. He was to be the inheritor of the family title and the family dignity, and every thing was sacrificed to him—I, as well as every thing else. It was determined to devote me to the church, that so my humors and myself might be removed out of the way, either of tasking my father's time and trouble, or interfering with the interests of my brother. At an early age, therefore, before my mind had dawned upon the world and its delights, or known any thing of it beyond the precincts of my father's palace, I was sent to a convent, the superior of which was my uncle, and was confided entirely to his care.

My uncle was a man totally estranged from the world; he had never relished, for he had never tasted its pleasures; and he deemed rigid self-denial as the great basis of Christian virtue. He considered every one's temperament like his own; or at least he made them conform to it. His character and habits had an influence over the fraternity of which he was superior. A more gloomy, saturnine set of beings were never assembled together. The convent, too, was calculated to awaken sad and solitary thoughts. It was situated in a gloomy gorge of those mountains away south of Vesuvius. All distant views were shut out by sterile volcanic heights. A mountain stream raved beneath its walls, and eagles screamed about its turrets.

I had been sent to this place at so tender an age as soon to lose all distinct recollection of the scenes I had left behind. As my mind expanded, therefore, it formed its idea of the world from the convent and its vicinity, and a dreary world it appeared to me. An early tinge of melancholy was thus infused into my character; and the dismal stories of the monks, about devils and evil spirits, with which they affrighted my young imagination, gave me a tendency to superstition, which I could never effectually shake off. They took the same delight to work upon my ardent feelings that had been so mischievously exercised by my father's household.

I can recollect the horrors with which they fed my heated fancy during an eruption of Vesuvius. We were distant from that volcano, with mountains between us; but its convulsive throes shook the solid foundations of nature. Earthquakes threatened to topple down our convent towers. A lurid, baleful light hung in the heavens at night, and showers of ashes, borne by the wind, fell in our narrow valley. The monks talked of the earth being honey-combed beneath us; of Streams of molten lava raging through its veins; of caverns of sulphurous flames roaring in the centre, the abodes of demons and the damned; of fiery gulfs ready to yawn beneath our feet. All these tales were told to the doleful accompaniment of the mountain's thunders, whose low bellowing made the walls of our convent vibrate.

One of the monks had been a painter, but had retired from the world, and embraced this dismal life in expiation of some crime. He was a

melancholy man, who pursued his art in the solitude of his cell, but
made it a source of penance to him. His employment was to portray,
either on canvas or in waxen models, the human face and human
form, in the agonies of death and in all the stages of dissolution and
decay. The fearful mysteries of the charnel house were unfolded in
his labours—the loathsome banquet of the beetle and the worm.—
I turn with shuddering even from the recollection of his works. Yet,
at that time, my strong, but ill-directed imagination seized with
ardour upon his instructions in his art. Any thing was a variety from
the dry studies and monotonous duties of the cloister. In a little while
I became expert with my pencil, and my gloomy productions were
thought worthy of decorating some of the altars of the chapel.

In this dismal way was a creature of feeling and fancy brought
up. Every thing genial and amiable in my nature was repressed and
nothing brought out but what was unprofitable and ungracious. I
was ardent in my temperament; quick, mercurial, impetuous, formed
to be a creature all love and adoration; but a leaden hand was laid
on all my finer qualities. I was taught nothing but fear and hatred.
I hated my uncle, I hated the monks, I hated the convent in which
I was immured. I hated the world, and I almost hated myself, for
being, as I supposed, so hating and hateful an animal.

When I had nearly attained the age of sixteen, I was suffered, on one
occasion, to accompany one of the brethren on a mission to a distant
part of the country. We soon left behind us the gloomy valley in which
I had been pent up for so many years, and after a short journey among
the mountains, emerged upon the voluptuous landscape that spreads
itself about the Bay of Naples. Heavens! How transported was I, when
I stretched my gaze over a vast reach of delicious sunny country, gay
with groves and vineyards; with Vesuvius rearing its forked summit
to my right; the blue Mediterranean to my left, with its enchanting

coast, studded with shining towns and sumptuous villas; and Naples, my native Naples, gleaming far, far in the distance.

Good God! was this the lovely world from which I had been excluded! I Had reached that age when the sensibilities are in all their bloom and freshness. Mine had been checked and chilled. They now burst forth with the suddenness of a retarded spring. My heart, hitherto unnaturally shrunk up, expanded into a riot of vague, but delicious emotions. The beauty of nature intoxicated, bewildered me. The song of the peasants; their cheerful looks; their happy avocations; the picturesque gayety of their dresses; their rustic music; their dances; all broke upon me like witchcraft. My soul responded to the music; my heart danced in my bosom. All the men appeared amiable, all the women lovely.

I returned to the convent, that is to say, my body returned but my heart and soul never entered there again. I could not forget this glimpse of a beautiful and a happy world; a world so suited to my natural character. I had felt so happy while in it; so different a being from what I felt myself while in the convent—that tomb of the living. I contrasted the countenances of the beings I had seen, full of fire and freshness and enjoyment, with the pallid, leaden, lack lustre visages of the monks; the music of the dance, with the droning chant of the chapel. I had before found the exercises of the cloister wearisome; they now became intolerable. The dull round of duties wore away my spirit; my nerves became irritated by the fretful tinkling of the convent bell; evermore dinging among the mountain echoes; evermore calling me from my repose at night, my pencil by day, to attend to some tedious and mechanical ceremony of devotion.

I was not of a nature to meditate long, without putting my thoughts into action. My spirit had been suddenly aroused, and was now all awake within me. I watched my opportunity, fled from the convent, and made my way on foot to Naples. As I entered its gay and crowded streets, and beheld the variety and stir of life around me, the luxury of palaces, the splendor of equipages, and the pantomimic animation of the motley populace, I seemed as if awakened to a world of enchantment, and solemnly vowed that nothing should force me back to the monotony of the cloister.

I had to inquire my way to my father's palace, for I had been so young on leaving it, that I knew not its situation. I found some difficulty in getting admitted to my father's presence, for the domestics scarcely knew that there was such a being as myself in existence, and my monastic dress did not operate in my favor. Even my father entertained no recollection of my person. I told him my name, threw myself at his feet, implored his forgiveness, and entreated that I might not be sent back to the convent.

He received me with the condescension of a patron rather than the kindness of a parent. He listened patiently, but coldly, to my tale of monastic grievances and disgusts, and promised to think what else could be done for me. This coldness blighted and drove back all the frank affection of my nature that was ready to spring forth at the least warmth of parental kindness. All my early feelings towards my father revived; I again looked up to him as the stately magnificent being that had daunted my childish imagination, and felt as if I had no pretensions to his sympathies. My brother engrossed all his care and love; he inherited his nature, and carried himself towards me with a protecting rather than a fraternal air. It wounded my pride, which was great. I could brook condescension from my father, for I looked up to him with awe as a superior being, but I could not brook patronage from a brother, who, I felt, was intellectually my inferior. The servants perceived that I was an unwelcome intruder in the paternal mansion, and, menial-like, they treated me with neglect.

Thus baffled at every point; my affections outraged wherever they would attach themselves, I became sullen, silent, and despondent. My feelings driven back upon myself, entered and preyed upon my own heart. I remained for some days an unwelcome guest rather than a restored son in my father's house. I was doomed never to be properly known there. I was made, by wrong treatment, strange even to myself; and they judged of me from my strangeness.

I was startled one day at the sight of one of the monks of my convent, gliding out of my father's room. He saw me, but pretended not to notice me; and this very hypocrisy made me suspect something. I had become sore and susceptible in my feelings; every thing inflicted a wound on them. In this state of mind I was treated with marked disrespect by a pampered minion, the favorite servant of my father. All the pride and passion of my nature rose in an instant, and I struck him to the earth.

My father was passing by; he stopped not to inquire the reason, nor indeed could he read the long course of mental sufferings which were the real cause. He rebuked me with anger and scorn; he summoned all the haughtiness of his nature, and grandeur of his look, to give weight to the contumely with which he treated me. I felt I had not deserved it—I felt that I was not appreciated— I felt that I had that within me which merited better treatment; my heart swelled against a father's injustice. I broke through my habitual awe of him. I replied to him with impatience; my hot spirit flushed in my cheek and kindled in my eye, but my sensitive heart swelled as quickly, and before I had half vented my passion I felt it suffocated and quenched in my tears. My father was astonished and incensed at this turning of the worm, and ordered me to my chamber. I retired in silence, choking with contending emotions.

I had not been long there when I overheard voices in an adjoining apartment. It was a consultation between my father and the monk, about the means of getting me back quietly to the convent. My resolution was taken. I had no longer a home nor a father. That very night I left the paternal roof. I got on board a vessel about making sail from the harbour, and abandoned myself to the wide world. No matter to what port she steered; any part of so beautiful a world was better than my convent. No matter where I was cast by fortune; any place would be more a home to me than the home I had left behind. The vessel was bound to Genoa. We arrived there after a voyage of a few days.

As I entered the harbour, between the moles which embrace it, and beheld the amphitheatre of palaces and churches and splendid gardens, rising one above another, I felt at once its title to the appellation of Genoa the Superb. I landed on the mole an utter stranger, without knowing what to do, or whither to direct my steps. No matter; I was released from the thraldom of the convent and the humiliations of home! When I traversed the Strada Balbi and the Strada Nuova, those streets of palaces, and gazed at the wonders of architecture around me; when I wandered at close of day, amid a gay throng of the brilliant and the beautiful, through the green alleys of the Aqua Verdi, or among the colonnades and terraces of the magnificent Doria Gardens, I thought it impossible to be ever otherwise than happy in Genoa.

A few days sufficed to show me my mistake. My scanty purse was exhausted, and for the first time in my life I experienced the sordid distress of penury. I had never known the want of money, and had never adverted to the possibility of such an evil. I was ignorant of the world and all its ways; and when first the idea of destitution came over my mind its effect was withering. I was wandering pensively through the streets which no longer delighted my eyes, when chance led my stops into the magnificent church of the Annunciata.

A celebrated painter of the day was at that moment superintending the placing of one of his pictures over an altar. The proficiency which I had acquired in his art during my residence in the convent had made me an enthusiastic amateur. I was struck, at the first glance, with the painting. It was the face of a Madonna. So innocent, so lovely, such a divine expression of maternal tenderness! I lost for the moment all recollection of myself in the enthusiasm of my art. I clasped my hands together, and uttered an ejaculation of delight. The painter perceived my emotion. He was flattered and gratified by it. My air and manner pleased him, and he accosted me. I felt too much the want of friendship to repel the advances of a stranger, and there was something in this one so benevolent and winning that in a moment he gained my confidence.

I told him my story and my situation, concealing only my name and rank. He appeared strongly interested by my recital; invited me to his house, and from that time I became his favorite pupil. He thought he perceived in me extraordinary talents for the art, and his encomiums awakened all my ardor. What a blissful period of my existence was it that I passed beneath his roof. Another being seemed created within me, or rather, all that was amiable and excellent was drawn out. I was as recluse as ever I had been at the convent, but how different was my seclusion. My time was spent in storing my mind with lofty and poetical ideas; in meditating on all that was striking and noble in history or fiction; in studying and tracing all that was sublime and beautiful in nature. I was always a visionary, imaginative being, but now my reveries and imaginings all elevated me to rapture.

I looked up to my master as to a benevolent genius that had opened to me a region of enchantment. I became devotedly attached to him.

He was not a native of Genoa, but had been drawn thither by the solicitation of several of the nobility, and had resided there but a few years, for the completion of certain works he had undertaken. His health was delicate, and he had to confide much of the filling up of his designs to the pencils of his scholars. He considered me as particularly happy in delineating the human countenance; in seizing upon characteristic, though fleeting expressions and fixing them powerfully upon my canvas. I was employed continually, therefore, in sketching faces, and often when some particular grace or beauty or expression was wanted in a countenance, it was entrusted to my pencil. My benefactor was fond of bringing me forward; and partly, perhaps, through my actual skill, and partly by his partial praises, I began to be noted for the expression of my countenances.

Among the various works which he had undertaken, was an historical piece for one of the palaces of Genoa, in which were to be introduced the likenesses of several of the family. Among these was one entrusted to my pencil. It was that of a young girl, who as yet was in a convent for her education. She came out for the purpose of sitting for the picture. I first saw her in an apartment of one of the sumptuous palaces of Genoa. She stood before a casement that looked out upon the bay, a stream of vernal sunshine fell upon her, and shed a kind of glory round her as it lit up the rich crimson chamber. She was but sixteen years of age—and oh, how lovely! The scene broke upon me like a mere vision of spring and youth and beauty. I could have fallen down and worshipped her. She was like one of those fictions of poets and painters, when they would express the *beau ideal* that haunts their minds with shapes of indescribable perfection.

I was permitted to sketch her countenance in various positions, and I fondly protracted the study that was undoing me. The more I gazed on her the more I became enamoured; there was something almost painful in my intense admiration. I was but nineteen years of age; shy, diffident, and inexperienced. I was treated with attention and encouragement, for my youth and my enthusiasm in my art had won favor for me; and I am inclined to think that there was something in my air and manner that inspired interest and respect. Still the kindness with which I was treated could not dispel the embarrassment into which my own imagination threw me when in presence of this lovely being. It elevated her into something almost more than mortal. She seemed too exquisite for earthly use; too delicate and exalted for human attainment. As I sat tracing her charms on my canvas, with my eyes occasionally riveted on her features, I drank in delicious poison that made me giddy. My heart alternately gushed with tenderness, and ached with despair. Now I became more than ever sensible of the violent fires that had lain dormant at the bottom of my soul. You who are born in a more temperate climate and under a cooler sky, have little idea of the violence of passion in our southern bosoms.

A few days finished my task; Bianca returned to her convent, but her image remained indelibly impressed upon my heart. It dwelt on my imagination; it became my pervading idea of beauty. It had an effect even upon my pencil; I became noted for my felicity in depicting female loveliness; it was but because I multiplied the image of Bianca. I soothed, and yet fed my fancy, by introducing her in all the productions of my master. I have stood with delight in one of the chapels of the Annunciata, and heard the crowd extol the seraphic beauty of a saint which I had painted; I have seen them bow down in adoration before the painting: they were bowing before the loveliness of Bianca.

I existed in this kind of dream, I might almost say delirium, for upwards of a year. Such is the tenacity of my imagination that the image which was formed in it continued in all its power and freshness. Indeed, I was a solitary, meditative being, much given to reverie, and apt to foster ideas which had once taken strong possession of me. I was roused from this fond, melancholy, delicious dream by the death of my worthy benefactor. I cannot describe the pangs his death occasioned me. It left me alone and almost broken hearted. He bequeathed to me his little property; which, from the liberality of his disposition and his expensive style of living, was indeed but small; and he most particularly recommended me, in dying, to the protection of a nobleman who had been his patron.

The latter was a man who passed for munificent. He was a lover and an encourager of the arts, and evidently wished to be thought so. He fancied he saw in me indications of future excellence; my pencil had already attracted attention; he took me at once under his protection; seeing that I was overwhelmed with grief, and incapable of exerting myself in the mansion of my late benefactor, he invited me to sojourn for a time in a villa which he possessed on the border of the sea, in the picturesque neighbourhood of Sestri de Ponenti.

I found at the villa the Count's only son Filippo: he was nearly of my age, prepossessing in his appearance, and fascinating in his manners; he attached himself to me, and seemed to court my good opinion. I thought there was something of profession in his kindness, and of caprice in his disposition; but I had nothing else near me to attach myself to, and my heart felt the need of something to repose itself upon. His education had been neglected; he looked upon me as his superior in mental powers and acquirements, and tacitly acknowledged my superiority. I felt that I was his equal in birth, and that gave an independence to my manner which had its effect. The caprice and tyranny I saw sometimes exercised on others, over whom he had power, were never manifested towards me. We became intimate friends, and frequent companions. Still I loved to be alone, and to indulge in the reveries of my own imagination, among the beautiful scenery by which I was surrounded.

The villa stood in the midst of ornamented grounds, finely decorated With statues and fountains, and laid out into groves and alleys and shady bowers. It commanded a wide view of the Mediterranean, and the picturesque Ligurian coast. Every thing was assembled here that could gratify the taste or agreeably occupy the mind. Soothed by the tranquillity of this elegant retreat, the turbulence of my feelings gradually subsided, and, blending with the romantic spell that still reigned over my imagination, produced a soft voluptuous melancholy.

I had not been long under the roof of the Count, when our solitude was enlivened by another inhabitant. It was a daughter of a relation of the Count, who had lately died in reduced circumstances, bequeathing this only child to his protection. I had heard much of her beauty from Filippo, but my fancy had become so engrossed by one idea of beauty as not to admit of any other. We were in the central saloon of the villa when she arrived. She was still in mourning, and approached, leaning on the Count's arm. As they ascended the marble portico, I was struck by the elegance of her figure and movement, by the grace with which the *mezzaro*, the bewitching veil of Genoa, was folded about her slender form. They entered. Heavens! what was my surprise when I beheld Bianca before me. It was herself; pale with grief; but still more matured in loveliness than when I had last beheld her. The time that had elapsed had developed the graces of her person; and the sorrow she had undergone had diffused over her countenance an irresistible tenderness.

She blushed and trembled at seeing me, and tears rushed into her eyes, for she remembered in whose company she had been accustomed to behold me. For my part, I cannot express what were my emotions. By degrees I overcame the extreme shyness that had formerly paralyzed me in her presence. We were drawn together by sympathy of situation. We had each lost our best friend in the world; we were each, in some measure thrown upon the kindness of others. When I came to know her intellectually, all my ideal picturings of her were confirmed. Her newness to the world, her delightful susceptibility to every thing beautiful and agreeable in nature, reminded me of my own emotions when first I escaped from the convent. Her rectitude of thinking delighted my judgment; the sweetness of her nature wrapped itself around my heart; and then her young and tender and budding loveliness, sent a delicious madness to my brain.

I gazed upon her with a kind of idolatry, as something more than mortal; and I felt humiliated at the idea of my comparative unworthiness. Yet she was mortal; and one of mortality's most susceptible and loving compounds; for she loved me!

How first I discovered the transporting truth I cannot recollect; I believe it stole upon me by degrees, as a wonder past hope or belief. We were both at such a tender and loving age; in constant intercourse with each other; mingling in the same elegant pursuits; for music, poetry, and painting were our mutual delights, and we were almost separated from society, among lovely and romantic scenery! Is it strange that two young hearts thus brought together should readily twine round each other?

Oh, gods! what a dream—a transient dream! of unalloyed delight then passed over my soul! Then it was that the world around me was indeed a paradise, for I had a woman—lovely, delicious woman, to share it with me. How often have I rambled over the picturesque shores of Sestri, or climbed its wild mountains, with the coast gemmed with villas, and the blue sea far below me, and the slender Pharo of Genoa on its romantic promontory in the distance; and as I sustained the faltering steps of Bianca, have thought there could no unhappiness enter into so beautiful a world. Why, oh, why is this budding season of life and love so transient—why is this rosy cloud of love that sheds such a glow over the morning of our days so prone to brew up into the whirlwind and the storm!

I was the first to awaken from this blissful delirium of the affections. I had gained Bianca's heart: what was I to do with it? I had no wealth nor prospects to entitle me to her hand. Was I to take advantage of her ignorance of the world, of her confiding affection, and draw her down to my own poverty? Was this requiting the hospitality of the Count?—was this requiting the love of Bianca?

Now first I began to feel that even successful love may have its bitterness. A corroding care gathered about my heart. I moved about the palace like a guilty being. I felt as if I had abused its hospitality—as if I were a thief within its walls. I could no longer look with unembarrassed mien in the countenance of the Count. I accused myself of perfidy to him, and I thought he read it in my looks, and began to distrust and despise me. His manner had always been ostentatious and condescending, it now appeared cold and haughty. Filippo, too, became reserved and distant; or at least I suspected him to be so. Heavens!—was this mere coinage of my brain: was I to become suspicious of all the world?—a poor surmising wretch; watching looks and gestures; and torturing myself with misconstructions. Or if true—was I to remain beneath a roof where I was merely tolerated, and linger there on sufferance? "This is not to be endured!" exclaimed I; "I will tear myself from this state of self abasement; I will break through this fascination and fly—Fly?—whither?—from the world?—for where is the world when I leave Bianca behind me?"

My spirit was naturally proud, and swelled within me at the idea of being looked upon with contumely. Many times I was on the point of declaring my family and rank, and asserting my equality, in the presence of Bianca, when I thought her relatives assumed an air of superiority. But the feeling was transient. I considered myself discarded and contemned by my family; and had solemnly vowed never to own relationship to them, until they themselves should claim it.

The struggle of my mind preyed upon my happiness and my health. It seemed as if the uncertainty of being loved would be less intolerable than thus to be assured of it, and yet not dare to enjoy the conviction. I was no longer the enraptured admirer of Bianca; I no longer hung in ecstasy on the tones of her voice, nor drank in with insatiate gaze the beauty of her countenance. Her very smiles ceased to delight me, for I felt culpable in having won them.

She could not but be sensible of the change in me, and inquired the cause with her usual frankness and simplicity. I could not evade the inquiry, for my heart was full to aching. I told her all the conflict of my soul; my devouring passion, my bitter self upbraiding. "Yes!" said I, "I am unworthy of you. I am an offcast from my family—a wanderer—a nameless, homeless wanderer, with nothing but poverty for my portion, and yet I have dared to love you—have dared to aspire to your love!"

My agitation moved her to tears; but she saw nothing in my situation so hopeless as I had depicted it. Brought up in a convent, she knew nothing of the world, its wants, its cares;—and, indeed, what woman is a worldly casuist in matters of the heart!—Nay, more—she kindled into a sweet enthusiasm when she spoke of my fortunes and myself. We had dwelt together on the works of the famous masters. I had related to her their histories; the high reputation, the influence, the magnificence to which they had attained;—the companions of princes, the favourites of kings, the pride and boast of nations. All this she applied to me. Her love saw nothing in their greatest productions that I was not able to achieve; and when I saw the lovely creature glow with fervor, and her whole countenance radiant with the visions of my glory, which seemed breaking upon her, I was snatched up for the moment into the heaven of her own imagination.

I am dwelling too long upon this part of my story; yet I cannot help Lingering over a period of my life, on which, with all its cares and conflicts, I look back with fondness; for as yet my soul was unstained by a crime. I do not know what might have been the result of this struggle between pride, delicacy, and passion, had I not read in a Neapolitan gazette an account of the sudden death of my brother. It was accompanied by an earnest inquiry for intelligence concerning me, and a prayer, should this notice meet my eye, that I would hasten to Naples, to comfort an infirm and afflicted father.

I was naturally of an affectionate disposition; but my brother had never been as a brother to me; I had long considered myself as disconnected from him, and his death caused me but little emotion. The thoughts of my father, infirm and suffering, touched me, however, to the quick; and when I thought of him, that lofty, magnificent being, now bowed down and desolate, and suing to me for comfort, all my resentment for past neglect was subdued, and a glow of filial affection was awakened within me.

The predominant feeling, however, that overpowered all others was transport at the sudden change in my whole fortunes. A home—a name—a rank—wealth awaited me; and love painted a still more rapturous prospect in the distance. I hastened to Bianca, and threw myself at her feet. "Oh, Bianca," exclaimed I, "at length I can claim you for my own. I am no longer a nameless adventurer, a neglected, rejected outcast. Look—read, behold the tidings that restore me to my name and to myself!"

I will not dwell on the scene that ensued. Bianca rejoiced in the reverse of my situation, because she saw it lightened my heart of a load of care; for her own part she had loved me for myself, and had never doubted that my own merits would command both fame and fortune.

I now felt all my native pride buoyant within me; I no longer walked with my eyes bent to the dust; hope elevated them to the skies; my soul was lit up with fresh fires, and beamed from my countenance.

I wished to impart the change in my circumstances to the Count; to let him know who and what I was, and to make formal proposals for the hand of Bianca; but the Count was absent on a distant estate. I opened my whole soul to Filippo. Now first I told him of my passion; of the doubts and fears that had distracted me, and of the tidings that had suddenly dispelled them. He overwhelmed me with congratulations and with the warmest expressions of sympathy. I embraced him in the fullness of my heart. I felt compunctious for having suspected him of coldness, and asked him forgiveness for having ever doubted his friendship.

Nothing is so warm, and enthusiastic as a sudden expansion of the heart between young men. Filippo entered into our concerns with the most eager interest. He was our confidant and counsellor. It was determined that I should hasten at once to Naples to re-establish myself in my father's affections and my paternal home, and the moment the reconciliation was effected and my father's consent insured, I should return and demand Bianca of the Count. Filippo engaged to secure his father's acquiescence; indeed, he undertook to watch over our interests, and was the channel through which we were to correspond.

My parting with Bianca was tender—delicious—agonizing. It was in a little pavilion of the garden which had been one of our favorite resorts. How often and often did I return to have one more adieu—to have her look once more on me in speechless emotion—to enjoy once more the rapturous sight of those tears streaming down her lovely cheeks—to seize once more on that delicate hand, the frankly accorded pledge of love, and cover it with tears and kisses! Heavens! There is a delight even in the parting agony of two lovers worth a thousand tame pleasures of the world. I have her at this moment before my eyes—at the window of the pavilion, putting aside the vines that clustered about the casement—her light form beaming forth in virgin white—her countenance all tears and smiles—sending a thousand and a thousand adieus after me, as, hesitating, in a delirium of fondness and agitation, I faltered my way down the avenue.

As the bark bore me out of the harbour of Genoa, how eagerly my eyes Stretched along the coast of Sestri, till it discerned the villa gleaming from among trees at the foot of the mountain. As long as day lasted, I gazed and gazed upon it, till it lessened and lessened to a mere white speck in the distance; and still my intense and fixed gaze discerned it, when all other objects of the coast had blended into indistinct confusion, or were lost in the evening gloom.

On arriving at Naples, I hastened to my paternal home. My heart yearned for the long-withheld blessing of a father's love. As I entered the proud portal of the ancestral palace, my emotions were so great that I could not speak. No one knew me. The servants gazed at me with curiosity and surprise. A few years of intellectual elevation and development had made a prodigious change in the poor fugitive stripling from the convent. Still that no one should know me in my rightful home was overpowering. I felt like the prodigal son returned. I was a stranger in the house of my father. I burst into tears, and wept aloud. When I made myself known, however, all was changed. I who had once been almost repulsed from its walls, and forced to fly as an exile, was welcomed back with acclamation, with servility. One of the servants hastened to prepare my father for my reception; my eagerness to receive the paternal embrace was so great that I could not await his return; but hurried after him.

What a spectacle met my eyes as I entered the chamber! My father, whom I had left in the pride of vigorous age, whose noble and majestic bearing had so awed my young imagination, was bowed down and withered into decrepitude. A paralysis had ravaged his stately form, and left it a shaking ruin. He sat propped up in his chair, with pale, relaxed visage and glassy, wandering eye. His intellects had evidently shared in the ravage of his frame. The servant was endeavouring to make him comprehend the visitor that was at hand. I tottered up to him and sunk at his feet. All his past coldness and neglect were forgotten in his present sufferings. I remembered only that he was my parent, and that I had deserted him. I clasped his knees; my voice was almost stifled with convulsive sobs. "Pardon—pardon—oh my father!" was all that I could utter. His apprehension seemed slowly to return to him. He gazed at me for some moments with a vague, inquiring look; a convulsive tremor quivered about his lips; he feebly extended a shaking hand, laid it upon my head, and burst into an infantine flow of tears.

From that moment he would scarcely spare me from his sight. I appeared the only object that his heart responded to in the world; all else was as a blank to him. He had almost lost the powers of speech, and the reasoning faculty seemed at an end. He was mute and passive; excepting that fits of childlike weeping would sometimes come over him without any immediate cause. If I left the room at any time, his eye was incessantly fixed on the door till my return, and on my entrance there was another gush of tears.

To talk with him of my concerns, in this ruined state of mind, would have been worse than useless; to have left him, for ever so short a time, would have been cruel, unnatural. Here then was a new trial for my affections. I wrote to Bianca an account of my return and of my actual situation; painting in colors vivid, for they were true, the torments I suffered at our being thus separated; for to the youthful lover every day of absence is an age of love lost. I enclosed the letter in one to Filippo, who was the channel of our correspondence. I received a reply from him full of friendship and sympathy; from Bianca full of assurances of affection and constancy.

Week after week, month after month elapsed, without making any change in my circumstances. The vital flame, which had seemed nearly extinct when first I met my father, kept fluttering on without any apparent diminution. I watched him constantly, faithfully— I had almost said patiently. I knew that his death alone would set me free; yet I never at any moment wished it. I felt too glad to be able to make any atonement for past disobedience; and, denied as I had been all endearments of relationship in my early days, my heart yearned towards a father, who, in his age and helplessness, had thrown himself entirely on me for comfort. My passion for Bianca gained daily more force from absence; by constant meditation it wore itself a deeper and deeper channel. I made no new friends nor acquaintances; sought none of the pleasures of Naples which my rank and fortune threw open to me. Mine was a heart that confined itself to few objects, but dwelt upon those with the intenser passion. To sit by my father, and administer to his wants, and to meditate on Bianca in the silence of his chamber, was my constant habit. Sometimes I amused myself with my pencil in portraying the image that was ever present to my imagination. I transferred to canvas every look and smile of hers that dwelt in my heart. I showed them to my father in hopes of awakening an interest in his bosom for the mere shadow of my love; but he was too far sunk in intellect to take any more than a child-like notice of them.

When I received a letter from Bianca it was a new source of solitary luxury. Her letters, it is true, were less and less frequent, but they were always full of assurances of unabated affection. They breathed not the frank and innocent warmth with which she expressed herself in conversation, but I accounted for it from the embarrassment which inexperienced minds have often to express themselves upon paper. Filippo assured me of her unaltered constancy. They both lamented in the strongest terms our continued separation, though they did justice to the filial feeling that kept me by my father's side.

Nearly eighteen months elapsed in this protracted exile. To me they were so many ages. Ardent and impetuous by nature, I scarcely know how I should have supported so long an absence, had I not felt assured that the faith of Bianca was equal to my own. At length my father died. Life went from him almost imperceptibly. I hung over him in mute affliction, and watched the expiring spasms of nature. His last faltering accents whispered repeatedly a blessing on me— alas! how has it been fulfilled!

When I had paid due honors to his remains, and laid them in the tomb of our ancestors, I arranged briefly my affairs; put them in a posture to be easily at my command from a distance, and embarked once more, with a bounding heart, for Genoa.

Our voyage was propitious, and oh! what was my rapture when first, in the dawn of morning, I saw the shadowy summits of the Apennines rising almost like clouds above the horizon. The sweet breath of summer just moved us over the long wavering billows that were rolling us on towards Genoa. By degrees the coast of Sestri rose like a sweet creation of enchantment from the silver bosom of the deep. I behold the line of villages and palaces studding its borders. My eye reverted to a well known point, and at length, from the confusion of distant objects, it singled out the villa which contained Bianca. It was a mere speck in the landscape, but glimmering from afar, the polar star of my heart.

Again I gazed at it for a livelong summer's day; but oh how different the emotions between departure and return. It now kept growing and growing, instead of lessening on my sight. My heart seemed to dilate with it. I looked at it through a telescope. I gradually defined one feature after another. The balconies of the central saloon where first I met Bianca beneath its roof; the terrace where we so often had passed the delightful summer evenings; the awning that shaded her chamber window—I almost fancied I saw her form beneath it. Could she but know her lover was in the bark whose white sail now gleamed on the sunny bosom of the sea! My fond impatience increased as we neared the coast. The ship seemed to lag lazily over the billows; I could almost have sprung into the sea and swam to the desired shore.

The shadows of evening gradually shrouded the scene, but the moon arose in all her fullness and beauty and shed the tender light so dear to lovers, over the romantic coast of Sestri. My whole soul was bathed in unutterable tenderness. I anticipated the heavenly evenings I should pass in wandering with Bianca by the light of that blessed moon.

It was late at night before we entered the harbour. As early next morning as I could get released from the formalities of landing I threw myself on horseback and hastened to the villa. As I galloped round the rocky promontory on which stands the Faro, and saw the coast of Sestri opening upon me, a thousand anxieties and doubts suddenly sprang up in my bosom. There is something fearful in returning to those we love, while yet uncertain what ills or changes absence may have effected. The turbulence of my agitation shook my very frame. I spurred my horse to redoubled speed; he was covered with foam when we both arrived panting at the gateway that opened to the grounds around the villa. I left my horse at a cottage and walked through the grounds, that I might regain tranquillity for the approaching interview. I chid myself for having suffered mere doubts and surmises thus suddenly to overcome me; but I was always prone to be carried away by these gusts of the feelings.

On entering the garden everything bore the same look as when I had left it; and this unchanged aspect of things reassured me. There were the alleys in which I had so often walked with Bianca; the same shades under which we had so often sat during the noontide. There were the same flowers of which she was fond; and which appeared still to be under the ministry of her hand. Everything around looked and breathed of Bianca; hope and joy flushed in my bosom at every step. I passed a little bower in which we had often sat and read together. A book and a glove lay on the bench. It was Bianca's glove; it was a volume of the Metestasio I had given her. The glove lay in my favorite passage. I clasped them to my heart. "All is safe!" exclaimed I, with rapture, "she loves me! she is still my own!"

I bounded lightly along the avenue down which I had faltered so slowly at my departure. I beheld her favorite pavilion which had witnessed our parting scene. The window was open, with the same vine clambering about it, precisely as when she waved and wept me an adieu. Oh! how transporting was the contrast in my situation.

As I passed near the pavilion, I heard the tones of a female voice. They thrilled through me with an appeal to my heart not to be mistaken. Before I could think, I *felt* they were Bianca's. For an instant I paused, overpowered with agitation. I feared to break in suddenly upon her. I softly ascended the steps of the pavilion. The door was open. I saw Bianca seated at a table; her back was towards me; she was warbling a soft melancholy air, and was occupied in drawing. A glance sufficed to show me that she was copying one of my own paintings. I gazed on her for a moment in a delicious tumult of emotions. She paused in her singing; a heavy sigh, almost a sob followed. I could no longer contain myself. "Bianca!" exclaimed I, in a half smothered voice. She started at the sound; brushed back the ringlets that hung clustering about her face; darted a glance at me; uttered a piercing shriek and would have fallen to the earth, had I not caught her in my arms.

"Bianca! my own Bianca!" exclaimed I, folding her to my bosom; my voice stifled in sobs of convulsive joy. She lay in my arms without sense or motion. Alarmed at the effects of my own precipitation, I scarce knew what to do. I tried by a thousand endearing words to call her back to consciousness. She slowly recovered, and half opening her eyes—"where am I?" murmured she faintly. "Here," exclaimed I, pressing her to my bosom. "Here! close to the heart that adores you; in the arms of your faithful Ottavio!"

"Oh no! no! no!" shrieked she, starting into sudden life and terror—"away! away! leave me! leave me!"

She tore herself from my arms; rushed to a corner of the saloon, and covered her face with her hands, as if the very sight of me were baleful. I was thunderstruck—I could not believe my senses. I followed her, trembling, confounded. I endeavored to take her hand, but she shrunk from my very touch with horror.

"Good heavens, Bianca," exclaimed I, "what is the meaning of this? Is this my reception after so long an absence? Is this the love you professed for me?"

At the mention of love, a shuddering ran through her. She turned to me a face wild with anguish. "No more of that! no more of that!" gasped she—"talk not to me of love—I—I—am married!"

I reeled as if I had received a mortal blow. A sickness struck to my very heart. I caught at a window frame for support. For a moment or two, everything was chaos around me. When I recovered, I beheld Bianca lying on a sofa; her face buried in a pillow, and sobbing convulsively. Indignation at her fickleness for a moment overpowered every other feeling.

"Faithless—perjured—" cried I, striding across the room. But another glance at that beautiful being in distress, checked all my wrath. Anger could not dwell together with her idea in my soul.

"Oh, Bianca," exclaimed I, in anguish, "could I have dreamt of this; could I have suspected you would have been false to me?"

She raised her face all streaming with tears, all disordered with emotion, and gave me one appealing look—"False to you!—they told me you were dead!"

"What," said I, "in spite of our constant correspondence?"

She gazed wildly at me—"correspondence!—what correspondence?"

"Have you not repeatedly received and replied to my letters?"

She clasped her hands with solemnity and fervor—"As I hope for mercy, never!"

A horrible surmise shot through my brain—"Who told you I was dead?"

"It was reported that the ship in which you embarked for Naples perished at sea."

"But who told you the report?"

She paused for an instant, and trembled—

"Filippo!"

"May the God of heaven curse him!" cried I, extending my clinched fists aloft.

"Oh do not curse him—do not curse him!" exclaimed she—"He is—he is—my husband!"

This was all that was wanting to unfold the perfidy that had been practised upon me. My blood boiled like liquid fire in my veins. I gasped with rage too great for utterance. I remained for a time bewildered by the whirl of horrible thoughts that rushed through my mind. The poor victim of deception before me thought it was with her I was incensed. She faintly murmured forth her exculpation. I will not dwell upon it. I saw in it more than she meant to reveal. I saw with a glance how both of us had been betrayed. "'Tis well!" muttered I to myself in smothered accents of concentrated fury. "He shall account to me for this!"

Bianca overheard me. New terror flashed in her countenance. "For mercy's sake do not meet him—say nothing of what has passed—for my sake say nothing to him—I only shall be the sufferer!"

A new suspicion darted across my mind—"what!" exclaimed I—"do you then *fear* him—is he *unkind* to you—tell me," reiterated I, grasping her hand and looking her eagerly in the face—"tell me—*dares* he to use you harshly!"

"No! no! no!" cried she faltering and embarrassed; but the glance at her face had told me volumes. I saw in her pallid and wasted features; in the prompt terror and subdued agony of her eye a whole history of a mind broken down by tyranny. Great God! and was this beauteous flower snatched from me to be thus trampled upon? The idea roused me to madness. I clinched my teeth and my hands; I foamed at the mouth; every passion seemed to have resolved itself into the fury that like a lava boiled within my heart. Bianca shrunk from me in speechless affright. As I strode by the window my eye darted down the alley. Fatal moment! I beheld Filippo at a distance! My brain was in a delirium—I sprang from the pavilion, and was before him with the quickness of lightning. He saw me as I came rushing upon him—he turned pale, looked wildly to right and left, as if he would have fled, and trembling drew his sword:—

"Wretch!" cried I, "well may you draw your weapon!"

I spoke not another word—I snatched forth a stiletto, put by the sword which trembled in his hand, and buried my poniard in his bosom. He fell with the blow, but my rage was unsated. I sprang upon him with the blood thirsty feeling of a tiger; redoubled my blows; mangled him in my frenzy, grasped him by the throat, until with reiterated wounds and strangling convulsions he expired in my grasp. I remained glaring on the countenance, horrible in death, that seemed to stare back with its protruded eyes upon me. Piercing shrieks roused me from my delirium. I looked round and beheld Bianca flying distractedly towards us. My brain whirled. I waited not to meet her, but fled from the scene of horror. I fled forth from the garden like another Cain, a hell within my bosom, and a curse upon my head. I fled without knowing whither—almost without knowing why— my only idea was to get farther and farther from the horrors I had left behind; as if I could throw space between myself and my conscience. I fled to the Apennines, and wandered for days and days among their savage heights. How I existed I cannot tell—what rocks and precipices I braved, and how I braved them, I know not. I kept on and on— trying to outtravel the curse that clung to me. Alas, the shrieks of Bianca rung for ever in my ear. The horrible countenance of my victim was for ever before my eyes. The blood of Filippo cried to me from the ground. Rocks, trees, and torrents all resounded with my crime.

Then it was I felt how much more insupportable is the anguish of remorse than every other mental pang. Oh! could I but have cast off this crime that festered in my heart; could I but have regained the innocence that reigned in my breast as I entered the garden at Sestri; could I but have restored my victim to life, I felt as if I could look on with transport even though Bianca were in his arms.

By degrees this frenzied fever of remorse settled into a permanent malady of the mind. Into one of the most horrible that ever poor wretch was cursed with. Wherever I went, the countenance of him I had slain appeared to follow me. Wherever I turned my head I beheld it behind me, hideous with the contortions of the dying moment. I have tried in every way to escape from this horrible phantom; but in vain. I know not whether it is an illusion of the mind, the consequence of my dismal education at the convent, or whether a phantom really sent by heaven to punish me; but there it ever is—at all times—in all places—nor has time nor habit had any effect in familiarizing me with its terrors. I have travelled from place to place, plunged into amusements—tried dissipation and distraction of every kind—all—all in vain.

I once had recourse to my pencil as a desperate experiment. I painted an exact resemblance of this phantom face. I placed it before me in hopes that by constantly contemplating the copy I might diminish the effect of the original. But I only doubled instead of diminishing the misery.

Such is the curse that has clung to my footsteps—that has made my life a burthen—but the thoughts of death, terrible. God knows what I have suffered. What days and days, and nights and nights, of sleepless torment. What a never-dying worm has preyed upon my heart; what an unquenchable fire has burned within my brain. He knows the wrongs that wrought upon my poor weak nature; that converted the tenderest of affections into the deadliest of fury. He knows best whether a frail erring creature has expiated by long-enduring torture and measureless remorse, the crime of a moment of madness. Often, often have I prostrated myself in the dust, and implored that he would give me a sign of his forgiveness, and let me die.—

Thus far had I written some time since. I had meant to leave this record of misery and crime with you, to be read when I should be no more. My prayer to heaven has at length been heard. You were witness to my emotions last evening at the performance of the Miserere; when the vaulted temple resounded with the words of atonement and redemption. I heard a voice speaking to me from the midst of the music; I heard it rising above the pealing of the organ and the voices of the choir; it spoke to me in tones of celestial melody; it promised mercy and forgiveness, but demanded from me full expiation. I go to make it. Tomorrow I shall be on my way to Genoa to surrender myself to justice. You who have pitied my sufferings; who have poured the balm of sympathy into my wounds, do not shrink from my memory with abhorrence now that you know my story. Recollect, when you read of my crime I shall have atoned for it with my blood!

* * *

When the Baronet had finished, there was an universal desire expressed to see the painting of this frightful visage. After much entreaty the Baronet consented, on condition that they should only visit it one by one. He called his housekeeper and gave her charge to conduct the gentlemen singly to the chamber. They all returned varying in their stories: some affected in one way, some in another; some more, some less; but all agreeing that there was a certain something about the painting that had a very odd effect upon the feelings.

I stood in a deep bow window with the Baronet, and could not help expressing my wonder. "After all," said I, "there are certain mysteries in our nature, certain inscrutable impulses and influences, that warrant one in being superstitious. Who can account for so many persons of different characters being thus strangely affected by a mere painting?"

"And especially when not one of them has seen it!" said the Baronet with a smile.

"How?" exclaimed I, "not seen it?"

"Not one of them?" replied he, laying his finger on his lips in sign of secrecy. "I saw that some of them were in a bantering vein, and I did not choose that the memento of the poor Italian should be made a jest of. So I gave the housekeeper a hint to show them all to a different chamber!"

* * *

Thus end the Stories of the Nervous Gentleman.

THE DEVIL AND TOM WALKER

A few miles from Boston, in Massachusetts, there is a deep inlet winding several miles into the interior of the country from Charles Bay, and terminating in a thickly-wooded swamp, or morass. On one side of this inlet is a beautiful dark grove; on the opposite side the land rises abruptly from the water's edge, into a high ridge on which grow a few scattered oaks of great age and immense size. It was under one of these gigantic trees, according to old stories, that Kidd the pirate buried his treasure. The inlet allowed a facility to bring the money in a boat secretly and at night to the very foot of the hill. The elevation of the place permitted a good look-out to be kept that no one was at hand, while the remarkable trees formed good landmarks by which the place might easily be found again. The old stories add, moreover, that the devil presided at the hiding of the money, and took it under his guardianship; but this, it is well-known, he always does with buried treasure, particularly when it has been ill gotten. Be that as it may, Kidd never returned to recover his wealth; being shortly after seized at Boston, sent out to England, and there hanged for a pirate.

About the year 1727, just at the time when earthquakes were prevalent in New England, and shook many tall sinners down upon their knees, there lived near this place a meagre miserly fellow of the name of Tom Walker. He had a wife as miserly as himself; they were so miserly that they even conspired to cheat each other. Whatever the woman could lay hands on she hid away; a hen could not cackle but she was on the alert to secure the new laid egg. Her husband was continually prying about to detect her secret hoards, and many and fierce were the conflicts that took place about what ought to have been common property. They lived in a forlorn-looking house, that stood alone and had an air of starvation. A few straggling savin trees, emblems of sterility, grew near it; no smoke ever curled from its chimney; no traveller stopped at its door. A miserable horse, whose ribs were as articulate as the bars of a gridiron, stalked about a field where a thin carpet of moss, scarcely covering the ragged beds of pudding stone, tantalized and balked his hunger; and sometimes he would lean his head over the fence, looked piteously at the passer-by, and seem to petition deliverance from this land of famine. The house and its inmates had altogether a bad name. Tom's wife was a tall termagant, fierce of temper, loud of tongue, and strong of arm. Her voice was often heard in wordy warfare with her husband; and his face sometimes showed signs that their conflicts were not confined to words. No one ventured, however, to interfere between them; the lonely wayfarer shrunk within himself at the horrid clamor and clapper clawing; eyed the den of discord askance, and hurried on his way, rejoicing, if a bachelor, in his celibacy.

One day that Tom Walker had been to a distant part of the neighbourhood, he took what he considered a short cut homewards through the swamp. Like most short cuts, it was an ill chosen route. The swamp was thickly grown with great gloomy pines and hemlocks, some of them ninety feet high; which made it dark at noon-day, and a retreat for all the owls of the neighbourhood. It was full of pits and quagmires, partly covered with weeds and mosses; where the green surface often betrayed the traveller into a gulf of black smothering mud; there were also dark and stagnant pools, the abodes of the tadpole, the bull frog, and the water snake, and where trunks of pines and hemlocks lay half drowned, half rotting, looking like alligators, sleeping in the mire.

Tom had long been picking his way cautiously through this treacherous forest; stepping from tuft to tuft of rushes and roots which afforded precarious footholds among deep sloughs; or pacing carefully, like a cat, among the prostrate trunks of trees; startled now and then by the sudden screaming of the bittern, or the quacking of a wild duck, rising on the wing from some solitary pool. At length he arrived at a piece of firm ground, which ran out like a peninsula into the deep bosom of the swamp. It had been one of the strongholds of the Indians during their wars with the first colonists. Here they had thrown up a kind of fort which they had looked upon as almost impregnable, and had used as a place of refuge for their squaws and children. Nothing remained of the Indian fort but a few embankments gradually sinking to the level of the surrounding earth, and already overgrown in part by oaks and other forest trees, the foliage of which formed a contrast to the dark pines and hemlocks of the swamp.

It was late in the dusk of evening that Tom Walker reached the old fort, and he paused there for a while to rest himself. Any one but he would have felt unwilling to linger in this lonely, melancholy place, for the common people had a bad opinion of it from the stories handed down from the time of the Indian wars; when it was asserted that the savages held incantations here and made sacrifices to the evil spirit. Tom Walker, however, was not a man to be troubled with any fears of the kind.

He reposed himself for some time on the trunk of a fallen hemlock, listening to the boding cry of the tree toad, and delving with his walking-staff into a mound of black mould at his feet. As he turned up the soil unconsciously, his staff struck against something hard. He raked it out of the vegetable mould, and lo! a cloven skull with an Indian tomahawk buried deep in it, lay before him. The rust on the weapon showed the time that had elapsed since this death blow had been given. It was a dreary memento of the fierce struggle that had taken place in this last foothold of the Indian warriors.

"Humph!" said Tom Walker, as he gave the skull a kick to shake the dirt from it.

"Let that skull alone!" said a gruff voice.

Tom lifted up his eyes and beheld a great black man, seated directly opposite him on the stump of a tree. He was exceedingly surprised, having neither seen nor heard any one approach, and he was still more perplexed on observing, as well as the gathering gloom would permit, that the stranger was neither negro nor Indian. It is true, he was dressed in a rude, half Indian garb, and had a red belt or sash swathed round his body, but his face was neither black nor copper color, but swarthy and dingy and begrimed with soot, as if he had been accustomed to toil among fires and forges. He had a shock of coarse black hair, that stood out from his head in all directions; and bore an axe on his shoulder.

He scowled for a moment at Tom with a pair of great red eyes.

"What are you doing in my grounds?" said the black man, with a hoarse growling voice.

"Your grounds?" said Tom, with a sneer; "no more your grounds than mine: they belong to Deacon Peabody."

"Deacon Peabody be d——d," said the stranger, "as I flatter myself he will be, if he does not look more to his own sins and less to his neighbour's. Look yonder, and see how Deacon Peabody is faring."

Tom looked in the direction that the stranger pointed, and beheld one of the great trees, fair and flourishing without, but rotten at the core, and saw that it had been nearly hewn through, so that the first high wind was likely to blow it down. On the bark of the tree was scored the name of Deacon Peabody. He now looked round and found most of the tall trees marked with the names of some great men of the colony, and all more or less scored by the axe. The one on which he had been seated, and which had evidently just been hewn down, bore the name of Crowninshield; and he recollected a mighty rich man of that name, who made a vulgar display of wealth, which it was whispered he had acquired by buccaneering.

"He's just ready for burning!" said the black man, with a growl of triumph. "You see I am likely to have a good stock of firewood for winter."

"But what right have you," said Tom, "to cut down Deacon Peabody's timber?"

"The right of prior claim," said the other. "This woodland belonged to me long before one of your white faced race put foot upon the soil."

"And pray, who are you, if I may be so bold?" said Tom.

"Oh, I go by various names. I am the Wild Huntsman in some countries; the Black Miner in others. In this neighbourhood I am known by the name of the Black Woodsman. I am he to whom the red men devoted this spot, and now and then roasted a white man by way of sweet smelling sacrifice. Since the red men have been exterminated by you white savages, I amuse myself by presiding at the persecutions of Quakers and Anabaptists; I am the great patron and prompter of slave dealers, and the grand master of the Salem witches."

"The upshot of all which is, that, if I mistake not," said Tom, sturdily, "you are he commonly called Old Scratch."

"The same at your service!" replied the black man, with a half civil nod.

Such was the opening of this interview, according to the old story, though it has almost too familiar an air to be credited. One would think that to meet with such a singular personage in this wild, lonely place, would have shaken any man's nerves; but Tom was a hard-minded fellow, not easily daunted, and he had lived so long with a termagant wife, that he did not even fear the devil.

It is said that after this commencement they had a long and earnest conversation together, as Tom returned homewards. The black man told him of great sums of money which had been buried by Kidd the pirate, under the oak trees on the high ridge not far from the morass. All these were under his command and protected by his power, so that none could find them but such as propitiated his favor. These he offered to place within Tom Walker's reach, having conceived an especial kindness for him: but they were to be had only on certain conditions. What these conditions were, may easily be surmised, though Tom never disclosed them publicly. They must have been very hard, for he required time to think of them, and he was not a man to stick at trifles where money was in view. When they had reached the edge of the swamp the stranger paused.

"What proof have I that all you have been telling me is true?" said Tom.

"There is my signature," said the black man, pressing his finger on Tom's forehead. So saying, he turned off among the thickets of the swamp, and seemed, as Tom said, to go down, down, down, into the earth, until nothing but his head and shoulders could be seen, and so on until he totally disappeared.

When Tom reached home he found the black print of a finger burnt, as it were, into his forehead, which nothing could obliterate.

The first news his wife had to tell him was the sudden death of Absalom Crowninshield, the rich buccaneer. It was announced in the papers with the usual flourish, that "a great man had fallen in Israel."

Tom recollected the tree which his black friend had just hewn down, and which was ready for burning. "Let the freebooter roast," said Tom, "who cares!" He now felt convinced that all he had heard and seen was no illusion.

He was not prone to let his wife into his confidence; but as this was an uneasy secret, he willingly shared it with her. All her avarice was awakened at the mention of hidden gold, and she urged her husband to comply with the black man's terms and secure what would make them wealthy for life. However Tom might have felt disposed to sell himself to the devil, he was determined not to do so to oblige his wife; so he flatly refused out of the mere spirit of contradiction. Many and bitter were the quarrels they had on the subject, but the more she talked the more resolute was Tom not to be damned to please her. At length she determined to drive the bargain on her own account, and if she succeeded, to keep all the gain to herself.

Being of the same fearless temper as her husband, she sat off for the old Indian fort towards the close of a summer's day. She was many hour's absent. When she came back she was reserved and sullen in her replies. She spoke something of a black man whom she had met about twilight, hewing at the root of a tall tree. He was sulky, however, and would not come to terms; she was to go again with a propitiatory offering, but what it was she forebore to say.

The next evening she set off again for the swamp, with her apron heavily laden. Tom waited and waited for her, but in vain: midnight came, but she did not make her appearance; morning, noon, night returned, but still she did not come. Tom now grew uneasy for her safety; especially as he found she had carried off in her apron the silver tea pot and spoons and every portable article of value. Another night elapsed, another morning came; but no wife. In a word, she was ever heard of more.

What was her real fate nobody knows, in consequence of so many pretending to know. It is one of those facts that have become confounded by a variety of historians. Some asserted that she lost her way among the tangled mazes of the swamp and sunk into some pit or slough; others, more uncharitable, hinted that she had eloped with the household booty, and made off to some other province; while others assert that the tempter had decoyed her into a dismal quagmire, on top of which her hat was found lying. In confirmation of this, it was said a great black man with an axe on his shoulder was seen late that very evening coming out of the swamp, carrying a bundle tied in a check apron, with an air of surly triumph.

The most current and probable story, however, observes that Tom Walker grew so anxious about the fate of his wife and his property that he sat out at length to seek them both at the Indian fort. During a long summer's afternoon he searched about the gloomy place, but no wife was to be seen. He called her name repeatedly, but she was no where to be heard. The bittern alone responded to his voice, as he flew screaming by; or the bull frog croaked dolefully from a neighbouring pool. At length, it is said, just in the brown hour of twilight, when the owls began to hoot and the bats to flit about, his attention was attracted by the clamor of carrion crows that were hovering about a cypress tree. He looked and beheld a bundle tied in a check apron and hanging in the branches of a tree;

with a great vulture perched hard by, as if keeping watch upon it. He leaped with joy, for he recognized his wife's apron, and supposed it to contain the household valuables.

"Let us get hold of the property," said he consolingly to himself, "and we will endeavor to do without the woman."

As he scrambled up the tree the vulture spread its wide wings, and sailed off screaming into the deep shadows of the forest. Tom seized the check apron, but, woful sight! found nothing but a heart and liver tied up in it.

Such, according to the most authentic old story, was all that was to be found of Tom's wife. She had probably attempted to deal with the black man as she had been accustomed to deal with her husband; but though a female scold is generally considered a match for the devil, yet in this instance she appears to have had the worst of it. She must have died game, however: from the part that remained unconquered. Indeed, it is said Tom noticed many prints of cloven feet deeply stamped about the tree, and several handfuls of hair that looked as if they had been plucked from the coarse black shock of the woodsman. Tom knew his wife's prowess by experience. He shrugged his shoulders as he looked at the signs of a fierce clapper-clawing. "Egad," said he to himself, "Old Scratch must have had a tough time of it!"

Tom consoled himself for the loss of his property by the loss of his wife; for he was a man of fortitude. He even felt something like gratitude towards the black woodsman, who he considered had done him a kindness. He sought, therefore, to cultivate a farther acquaintance with him, but for some time without success; the old black legs played shy, for whatever people may think, he is not always to be had for calling for; he knows how to play his cards when pretty sure of his game.

At length, it is said, when delay had whetted Tom's eagerness to the quick, and prepared him to agree to any thing rather than not gain the promised treasure, he met the black man one evening in his usual woodman dress, with his axe on his shoulder, sauntering along the edge of the swamp, and humming a tune. He affected to receive Tom's advance with great indifference, made brief replies, and went on humming his tune.

By degrees, however, Tom brought him to business, and they began to haggle about the terms on which the former was to have the pirate's treasure. There was one condition which need not be mentioned, being generally understood in all cases where the devil grants favors; but there were others about which, though of less importance, he was inflexibly obstinate. He insisted that the money found through his means should be employed in his service. He proposed, therefore, that Tom should employ it in the black traffic; that is to say, that he should fit out a slave ship. This, however, Tom resolutely refused; he was bad enough, in all conscience; but the devil himself could not tempt him to turn slave dealer.

Finding Tom so squeamish on this point, he did not insist upon it, but proposed instead that he should turn usurer; the devil being extremely anxious for the increase of usurers, looking upon them as his peculiar people.

To this no objections were made, for it was just to Tom's taste.

"You shall open a broker's shop in Boston next month," said the black man.

"I'll do it tomorrow, if you wish," said Tom Walker.

"You shall lend money at two per cent a month."

"Egad, I'll charge four!" replied Tom Walker.

"You shall extort bonds, foreclose mortgages, drive the merchant to bankruptcy—"

"I'll drive him to the d——l," cried Tom Walker, eagerly.

"You are the usurer for my money!" said the black legs, with delight. "When will you want the rhino?"

"This very night."

"Done!" said the devil.

"Done!" said Tom Walker.—So they shook hands and struck a bargain.

A few days' time saw Tom Walker seated behind his desk in a counting house in Boston. His reputation for a ready moneyed man, who would lend money out for a good consideration, soon spread abroad. Every body remembers the days of Governor Belcher, when money was particularly scarce. It was a time of paper credit. The country had been deluged with government bills; the famous Land Bank had been established; there had been a rage for speculating; the people had run mad with schemes for new settlements; for building cities in the wilderness; land jobbers went about with maps of grants, and townships, and Eldorados, lying nobody knew where, but which every body was ready to purchase. In a word, the great speculating fever which breaks out every now and then in the country, had raged to an alarming degree, and body was dreaming of making sudden fortunes from nothing. As usual, the fever had subsided; the dream had gone off, and the imaginary fortunes with it; the patients were left in doleful plight, and the whole country resounded with the consequent cry of "hard times."

At this propitious time of public distress did Tom Walker set up as a usurer in Boston. His door was soon thronged by customers. The needy and the adventurous; the gambling speculator; the dreaming land jobber; the thriftless tradesman; the merchant with cracked credit; in short, every one driven to raise money by desperate means and desperate sacrifices, hurried to Tom Walker.

Thus Tom was the universal friend of the needy, and he acted like a "friend in need"; that is to say, he always exacted good pay and good security. In proportion to the distress of the applicant was the hardness of his terms. He accumulated bonds and mortgages; gradually squeezed his customers closer and closer; and sent them, at length, dry as a sponge from his door.

In this way he made money hand over hand; became a rich and mighty man, and exalted his cocked hat upon 'change. He built himself, as usual, a vast house, out of ostentation; but left the greater part of it unfinished and unfurnished out of parsimony. He even set up a carriage in the fullness of his vain-glory, though he nearly starved the horses which drew it; and as the ungreased wheels groaned and screeched on the axle trees, you would have thought you heard the souls of the poor debtors he was squeezing.

As Tom waxed old, however, he grew thoughtful. Having secured the good things of this world, he began to feel anxious about those of the next. He thought with regret on the bargain he had made with his black friend, and set his wits to work to cheat him out of the conditions. He became, therefore, all of a sudden, a violent church goer. He prayed loudly and strenuously as if heaven were to be taken by force of lungs. Indeed, one might always tell when he had sinned most during the week, by the clamour of his Sunday devotion. The quiet Christians who had been modestly and steadfastly travelling Zion-ward, were struck with self reproach at seeing themselves so suddenly outstripped in their career by this new made convert. Tom was as rigid in religious, as in money matters; he was a stern supervisor and censurer of his neighbours, and seemed to think every sin entered up to their account became a credit on his own side of the page. He even talked of the expediency of reviving the persecution of Quakers and Anabaptists. In a word, Tom's zeal became as notorious as his riches.

Still, in spite of all this strenuous attention to forms, Tom had a lurking dread that the devil, after all, would have his due. That he might not be taken unawares, therefore, it is said he always carried a small Bible in his coat pocket. He had also a great folio Bible on his counting house desk, and would frequently be found reading it when people called on business; on such occasions he would lay his green spectacles on the book, to mark the place, while he turned round to drive some usurious bargain.

Some say that Tom grew a little crack brained in his old days, and that fancying his end approaching, he had his horse new shod, saddled and bridled, and buried with his feet uppermost; because he supposed that at the last day the world would be turned upside down; in which case he should find his horse standing ready for mounting, and he was determined at the worst to give his old friend a run for it. This, however, is probably a mere old wives' fable. If he really did take such a precaution it was totally superfluous; at least so says the authentic old legend, which closes his story in the following manner.

On one hot afternoon in the dog days, just as a terrible black thunder gust was coming up, Tom sat in his counting house in his white linen cap and India silk morning gown. He was on the point of foreclosing a mortgage, by which he would complete the ruin of an unlucky land speculator for whom he had professed the greatest friendship. The poor land jobber begged him to grant a few months' indulgence. Tom had grown testy and irritated and refused another day.

"My family will be ruined and brought upon the parish," said the land jobber.

"Charity begins at home," replied Tom, "I must take care of myself in these hard times."

"You have made so much money out of me," said the speculator.

Tom lost his patience and his piety—"The devil take me," said he, "if I have made a farthing!"

Just then there were three loud knocks at the street door. He stepped out to see who was there. A black man was holding a black horse which neighed and stamped with impatience.

"Tom, you're come for!" said the black fellow, gruffly. Tom shrunk back, but too late. He had left his little Bible at the bottom of his coat pocket, and his big Bible on the desk buried under the mortgage he was about to foreclose: never was sinner taken more unawares. The black man whisked him like a child astride the horse and away he galloped in the midst of a thunder storm. The clerks stuck their pens behind their ears and stared after him from the windows. Away went Tom Walker, dashing down the street; his white cap bobbing up and down; his morning gown fluttering in the wind, and his steed striking fire out of the pavement at every bound. When the clerks turned to look for the black man he had disappeared.

Tom Walker never returned to foreclose the mortgage. A countryman who lived on the borders of the swamp, reported that in the height of the thunder gust he had heard a great clattering of hoofs and a howling along the road, and that when he ran to the window he just caught sight of a figure, such as I have described, on a horse that galloped like mad across the fields, over the hills and down into the black hemlock swamp towards the old Indian fort; and that shortly after a thunder bolt fell in that direction which seemed to set the whole forest in a blaze.

The good people of Boston shook their heads and shrugged their shoulders, but had been so much accustomed to witches and goblins and tricks of the devil in all kinds of shapes from the first settlement of the colony, that they were not so much horror struck as might have been expected. Trustees were appointed to take charge of Tom's effects. There was nothing, however, to administer upon. On searching his coffers all his bonds and mortgages were found reduced to cinders. In place of gold and silver, his iron chest was filled with chips and shavings; two skeletons lay in his stable instead of his half starved horses, and the very next day his great house took fire and was burnt to the ground.

Such was the end of Tom Walker and his ill-gotten wealth. Let all griping money brokers lay this story to heart. The truth of it is not to be doubted. The very hole under the oak trees, from whence he dug Kidd's money, is to be seen to this day; and the neighbouring swamp and old Indian fort is often haunted in stormy nights by a figure on horseback, in a morning-gown and white cap, which is doubtless the troubled spirit of the usurer. In fact, the story has resolved itself into a proverb, and is the origin of that popular saying prevalent throughout New England, of "The Devil and Tom Walker."

WOLFERT WEBBER
OR, GOLDEN
DREAMS

In the year of grace one thousand seven hundred and—blank—
for I do not remember the precise date; however, it was somewhere in the early part of the last century, there lived in the
ancient city of the Manhattoes a worthy burgher, Wolfert Webber
by name. He was descended from old Cobus Webber of the Brille in
Holland, one of the original settlers, famous for introducing the
cultivation of cabbages, and who came over to the province during the
protectorship of Oloffe Van Kortlandt, otherwise called the Dreamer.

The field in which Cobus Webber first planted himself and his
cabbages had remained ever since in the family, who continued in
the same line of husbandry, with that praiseworthy perseverance
for which our Dutch burghers are noted. The whole family genius,
during several generations, was devoted to the study and development
of this one noble vegetable; and to this concentration of intellect may
doubtless be ascribed the prodigious size and renown to which the
Webber cabbages attained.

The Webber dynasty continued in uninterrupted succession; and
never did a line give more unquestionable proofs of legitimacy. The

eldest son succeeded to the looks, as well as the territory of his sire; and had the portraits of this line of tranquil potentates been taken, they would have presented a row of heads marvellously resembling in shape and magnitude the vegetables over which they reigned.

The seat of government continued unchanged in the family mansion:—a Dutch built house, with a front, or rather gable-end of yellow brick, tapering to a point, with the customary iron weathercock at the top. Every thing about the building bore the air of long-settled ease and security. Flights of martins peopled the little coops nailed against the walls, and swallows built their nests under the eaves; and every one knows that these house loving birds bring good luck to the dwelling where they take up their abode. In a bright sunny morning in early summer, it was delectable to hear their cheerful notes, as they sported about in the pure, sweet air, chirping forth, as it were, the greatness and prosperity of the Webbers.

Thus quietly and comfortably did this excellent family vegetate under the shade of a mighty button-wood tree, which by little and little grew so great as entirely to overshadow their palace. The city gradually spread its suburbs round their domain. Houses sprung up to interrupt their prospects. The rural lanes in the vicinity began to grow into the bustle and populousness of streets; in short, with all the habits of rustic life they began to find themselves the inhabitants of a city.

Still, however, they maintained their hereditary character, and hereditary possessions, with all the tenacity of petty German princes in the midst of the Empire. Wolfert was the last of the line, and succeeded to the patriarchal bench at the door, under the family tree, and swayed the sceptre of his fathers, a kind of rural potentate in the midst of a metropolis.

To share the cares and sweets of sovereignty, he had taken unto himself a help mate, one of that excellent kind called stirring women;

that is to say, she was one of those notable little housewives who are always busy when there is nothing to do. Her activity however, took one particular direction; her whole life seemed devoted to intense knitting; whether at home or abroad; walking or sitting, her needles were continually in motion, and it is even affirmed that by her unwearied industry she very nearly supplied her household with stockings throughout the year. This worthy couple were blessed with one daughter, who was brought up with great tenderness and care; uncommon pains had been taken with her education, so that she could stitch in every variety of way; make all kinds of pickles and preserves, and mark her own name on a sampler. The influence of her taste was seen also in the family garden, where the ornamental began to mingle with the useful; whole rows of fiery marigolds and splendid hollyhocks bordered the cabbage beds; and gigantic sunflowers lolled their broad, jolly faces over the fences, seeming to ogle most affectionately the passers by.

Thus reigned and vegetated Wolfert Webber over his paternal acres, peaceably and contentedly. Not but that, like all other sovereigns, he had his occasional cares and vexations. The growth of his native city sometimes caused him annoyance. His little territory gradually became hemmed in by streets and houses, which intercepted air and sunshine. He was now and then subject to the irruptions of the border population, that infest the streets of a metropolis, who would sometimes make midnight forays into his dominions, and carry off captive whole platoons of his noblest subjects. Vagrant swine would make a descent, too, now and then, when the gate was left open, and lay all waste before them; and mischievous urchins would often decapitate the illustrious sunflowers, the glory of the garden, as they lolled their heads so fondly over the walls. Still all these were petty grievances, which might now and then ruffle the surface of his mind, as a summer breeze will ruffle the surface of a mill pond; but they could not disturb the deep-seated quiet of his soul. He would seize a trusty staff, that stood behind the door, issue suddenly out, and anoint the back of the aggressor, whether pig or urchin, and then return within doors, marvellously refreshed and tranquillized.

The chief cause of anxiety to honest Wolfert, however, was the growing prosperity of the city. The expenses of living doubled and trebled; but he could not double and treble the magnitude of his cabbages; and the number of competitors prevented the increase of price; thus, therefore, while every one around him grew richer, Wolfert grew poorer, and he could not, for the life of him, perceive how the evil was to be remedied.

This growing care which increased from day to day, had its gradual effect upon our worthy burgher; insomuch, that it at length implanted two or three wrinkles on his brow; things unknown before in the family of the Webbers; and it seemed to pinch up the corners of his cocked hat into an expression of anxiety, totally opposite to the tranquil, broad brimmed, low crowned beavers of his illustrious progenitors.

Perhaps even this would not have materially disturbed the serenity of his mind had he had only himself and his wife to care for; but there was his daughter gradually growing to maturity; and all the world knows when daughters begin to ripen no fruit or flower requires so much looking after. I have no talent at describing female charms, else fain would I depict the progress of this little Dutch beauty. How her blue eyes grew deeper and deeper, and her cherry lips redder and redder; and how she ripened and ripened, and rounded and rounded in the opening breath of sixteen summers, until, in her seventeenth spring, she seemed ready to burst out of her bodice like a half-blown rosebud.

Ah, well-a-day! could I but show her as she was then, tricked out on a Sunday morning in the hereditary finery of the old Dutch clothes-press, of which her mother had confided to her the key. The wedding dress of her grandmother, modernized for use, with sundry ornaments, handed down as heirlooms in the family. Her pale brown hair smoothed with buttermilk in flat waving lines on each side of her fair forehead. The chain of yellow virgin gold, that encircled her neck; the little cross, that just rested at the entrance of a soft valley of happiness, as if it would sanctify the place. The—but pooh!—it is not for an old man like me to be prosing about female beauty: suffice it to say, Amy had attained her seventeenth year. Long since had her sampler exhibited hearts in couples desperately transfixed with arrows, and true lovers' knots worked in deep blue silk; and it was evident she began to languish for some more interesting occupation than the rearing of sunflowers or pickling of cucumbers.

At this critical period of female existence, when the heart within a damsel's bosom, like its emblem, the miniature which hangs without, is apt to be engrossed by a single image, a new visitor began to make his appearance under the roof of Wolfert Webber. This was Dirk Waldron, the only son of a poor widow, but who could boast of more fathers than any lad in the province; for his mother had had four husbands, and this only child, so that though born in her last wedlock, he might fairly claim to be the tardy fruit of a long course of cultivation. This son of four fathers united the merits and the vigor of his sires. If he had not a great family before him, he seemed likely to have a great one after him; for you had only to look at the fresh gamesome youth, to see that he was formed to be the founder of a mighty race.

This youngster gradually became an intimate visitor of the family. He talked little, but he sat long. He filled the father's pipe when it was empty, gathered up the mother's knitting-needle, or ball of worsted when it fell to the ground; stroked the sleek coat of the tortoise-shell cat, and replenished the teapot for the daughter from the bright copper kettle that sung before the fire. All these quiet little offices may seem of trifling import, but when true love is translated into Low Dutch, it is in this way that it eloquently expresses itself. They were not lost upon the Webber family. The winning youngster found marvellous favour in the eyes of the mother; the tortoise shell cat, albeit the most staid and demure of her kind, gave indubitable signs of approbation of his visits, the tea-kettle seemed to sing out a cheering note of welcome at his approach, and if the sly glances of the daughter might be rightly read, as she sat bridling and dimpling, and sewing by her mother's side, she was not a wit behind Dame Webber, or grimalkin, or the tea kettle in good will.

Wolfert alone saw nothing of what was going on. Profoundly wrapt up in meditation on the growth of the city and his cabbages, he sat looking in the fire, and puffing his pipe in silence. One night, however, as the gentle Amy, according to custom, lighted her lover to the outer door, and he, according to custom, took his parting salute, the smack resounded so vigorously through the long, silent entry as to startle even the dull ear of Wolfert. He was slowly roused to a new source of anxiety. It had never entered into his head, that this mere child, who, as it seemed but the other day, had been climbing about his knees, and playing with dolls and baby-houses, could all at once be thinking of love and matrimony. He rubbed his eyes, examined into the fact, and really found that while he had been dreaming of other matters, she had actually grown to be a woman, and what was more, had fallen in love. Here were new cares for poor Wolfert. He was a kind father, but he was a prudent man. The young man was a very stirring lad; but then he had neither money or land. Wolfert's ideas all ran in one channel, and he saw no alternative in case of a marriage, but to portion off the young couple with a corner of his cabbage garden, the whole of which was barely sufficient for the support of his family.

Like a prudent father, therefore, he determined to nip this passion in the bud, and forbade the youngster the house, though sorely did it go against his fatherly heart, and many a silent tear did it cause in the bright eye of his daughter. She showed herself, however, a pattern of filial piety and obedience. She never pouted and sulked; she never flew in the face of parental authority; she never fell into a passion, or fell into hysterics, as many romantic novel-read young ladies would do. Not she, indeed! She was none such heroical rebellious trumpery, I warrant ye. On the contrary, she acquiesced like an obedient daughter; shut the street door in her lover's face, and if ever she did grant him an interview, it was either out of the kitchen window, or over the garden fence.

Wolfert was deeply cogitating these things in his mind, and his brow wrinkled with unusual care, as he wended his way one Saturday afternoon to a rural inn, about two miles from the city. It was a favorite resort of the Dutch part of the community from being always held by a Dutch line of landlords, and retaining an air and relish of the good old times. It was a Dutch built house, that had probably been a country seat of some opulent burgher in the early time of the settlement. It stood near a point of land, called Corlears Hook, which stretches out into the Sound, and against which the tide, at its flux and reflux, sets with extraordinary rapidity. The venerable and somewhat crazy mansion was distinguished from afar, by a grove of elms and sycamores that seemed to wave a hospitable invitation, while a few weeping willows with their dank, drooping foliage, resembling falling waters, gave an idea of coolness, that rendered it an attractive spot during the heats of summer.

Here, therefore, as I said, resorted many of the old inhabitants of the Manhattoes, where, while some played at the shuffle board and quoits and ninepins, others smoked a deliberate pipe, and talked over public affairs.

It was on a blustering autumnal afternoon that Wolfert made his visit to the inn. The grove of elms and willows was stripped of its leaves, which whirled in rustling eddies about the fields. The ninepin alley was deserted, for the premature chilliness of the day had driven the company within doors. As it was Saturday afternoon, the habitual club was in session, composed principally of regular Dutch burghers, though mingled occasionally with persons of various, character and country, as is natural in a place of such motley population.

Beside the fire place, and in a huge leather bottomed armchair, sat the dictator of this little world, the venerable Rem, or, as it was pronounced, Ramm Rapelye. He was a man of Walloon race, and illustrious for the antiquity of his line, his great grandmother having been the first white child born in the province. But he was still more illustrious for his wealth and dignity: he had long filled the noble office of alderman, and was a man to whom the governor himself took off his hat. He had maintained possession of the leathern bottomed chair from time immemorial; and had gradually waxed in bulk as he sat in his seat of government, until in the course of years he filled its whole magnitude. His word was decisive with his subjects; for he was so rich a man, that he was never expected to support any opinion by argument. The landlord waited on him with peculiar officiousness; not that he paid better than his neighbours, but then the coin of a rich man seems always to be so much more acceptable. The landlord had always a pleasant word and a joke, to insinuate in the ear of the august Ramm. It is true, Ramm never laughed, and, indeed, maintained a mastiff-like gravity, and even surliness of aspect, yet he now and then rewarded mine host with a token of approbation; which, though nothing more nor less than a kind of grunt, yet delighted the landlord more than a broad laugh from a poorer man.

"This will be a rough night for the money diggers," said mine host, as a gust of wind howled round the house, and rattled at the windows.

"What, are they at their works again?" said an English half-pay captain, with one eye, who was a frequent attendant at the inn.

"Aye, are they," said the landlord, "and well may they be. They've had luck of late. They say a great pot of money has been dug up in the field, just behind Stuyvesant's orchard. Folks think it must have been buried there in old times by Peter Stuyvesant, the Dutch Governor."

"Fudge!" said the one-eyed man of war, as he added a small portion of water to a bottom of brandy.

"Well, you may believe, or not, as you please," said mine host, somewhat nettled; "but every body knows that the old governor buried a great deal of his money at the time of the Dutch troubles, when the English red coats seized on the province. They say, too, the old gentleman walks; aye, and in the very same dress that he wears in the picture which hangs up in the family house."

"Fudge!" said the half-pay officer.

"Fudge, if you please!—But didn't Corney Van Zandt see him at midnight, stalking about in the meadow with his wooden leg, and a drawn sword in his hand, that flashed like fire? And what can he be walking for, but because people have been troubling the place where he buried his money in old times?"

Here the landlord was interrupted by several guttural sounds from Ramm Rapelye, betokening that he was labouring with the unusual production of an idea. As he was too great a man to be slighted by a prudent publican, mine host respectfully paused until he should deliver himself. The corpulent frame of this mighty burgher now gave all the symptoms of a volcanic mountain on the point of an eruption. First, there was a certain heaving of the abdomen, not unlike an earthquake; then was emitted a cloud of tobacco smoke from that crater, his mouth; then there was a kind of rattle in the throat, as if the idea were working its way up through a region of phlegm; then there were several disjointed members of a sentence thrown out, ending in a cough; at length his voice forced its way in the slow, but absolute tone of a man who feels the weight of his purse, if not of his ideas; every portion of his speech being marked by a testy puff of tobacco smoke.

"Who talks of old Peter Stuyvesant's walking?—puff—Have people no respect for persons?—puff—puff—Peter Stuyvesant knew better what to do with his money than to bury it—puff—I know the Stuyvesant family—puff—every one of them—puff—not a more respectable family in the province—puff—old standers— puff—warm householders—puff—none of your upstarts—puff— puff—puff.—Don't talk to me of Peter Stuyvesant's walking—puff —puff—puff—puff."

Here the redoubtable Ramm contracted his brow, clasped up his mouth, till it wrinkled at each corner, and redoubled his smoking with such vehemence, that the cloudly volumes soon wreathed round his head, as the smoke envelopes the awful summit of Mount Etna.

A general silence followed the sudden rebuke of this very rich man. The subject, however, was too interesting to be readily abandoned. The conversation soon broke forth again from the lips of Peechy Prauw Van Hook, the chronicler of the club, one of those narrative old men who seem to grow incontinent of words, as they grow old, until their talk flows from them almost involuntarily.

Peechy, who could at any time tell as many stories in an evening as his hearers could digest in a month, now resumed the conversation, by affirming that, to his knowledge, money had at different times been dug up in various parts of the island. The lucky persons who had discovered them had always dreamt of them three times before-hand, and what was worthy of remark, these treasures had never been found but by some descendant of the good old Dutch families, which clearly proved that they had been buried by Dutchmen in the olden time.

"Fiddle stick with your Dutchmen!" cried the half-pay officer. "The Dutch had nothing to do with them. They were all buried by Kidd, the pirate, and his crew."

Here a key note was touched that roused the whole company. The name of Captain Kidd was like a talisman in those times, and was associated with a thousand marvellous stories.

The half-pay officer took the lead, and in the narrations fathered upon Kidd all the plunderings and exploits of Morgan, Blackbeard, and the whole list of bloody buccaneers.

The officer was a man of great weight among the peaceable members of the club, by reason of his military character, and of the gunpowder scenes which, by his own account, he had witnessed.

The golden stories of Kidd, however, were resolutely rivalled by the tales of Peechy Prauw, who, rather than suffer his Dutch progenitors to be eclipsed by a foreign freebooter, enriched every spot in the neighbourhood with the hidden wealth of Peter Stuyvesant and his contemporaries.

Not a word of this conversation was lost upon Wolfert Webber. He returned pensively home, full of magnificent ideas of buried riches. The soil of his native island seemed to be turned into gold-dust; and every field teemed with treasure. His head almost reeled at the thought how often he must have heedlessly rambled over places where countless sums lay, scarcely covered by the turf beneath his feet. His mind was in a vertigo with this whirl of new ideas. As he came in sight of the venerable mansion of his forefathers, and the little realm where the Webbers had so long and so contentedly flourished, his gorge rose at the narrowness of his destiny.

"Unlucky Wolfert!" exclaimed he, "others can go to bed and dream themselves into whole mines of wealth; they have but to seize a spade in the morning, and turn up doubloons like potatoes; but thou must dream of hardship, and rise to poverty—must dig thy field from year's end to year's end, and—and yet raise nothing but cabbages!"

Wolfert Webber went to bed with a heavy heart; and it was long before the golden visions that disturbed his brain, permitted him to sink into repose. The same visions, however, extended into his sleeping thoughts, and assumed a more definite form. He dreamt that he had discovered an immense treasure in the centre of his garden. At every stroke of the spade he laid bare a golden ingot; diamond crosses sparkled out of the dust; bags of money turned up their bellies, corpulent with pieces of eight, or venerable doubloons; and chests, wedged close with moidores, ducats, and pistareens, yawned before his ravished eyes, and vomited forth their glittering contents.

Wolfert awoke a poorer man than ever. He had no heart to go about his daily concerns, which appeared so paltry and profitless; but sat all day long in the chimney-corner, picturing to himself ingots and heaps of gold in the fire. The next night his dream was repeated. He was again in his garden, digging, and laying open stores of hidden wealth. There was something very singular in this repetition. He passed another day of reverie, and though it was cleaning-day, and the house, as usual in Dutch households, completely topsy turvy, yet he sat unmoved amidst the general uproar.

The third night he went to bed with a palpitating heart. He put on his red nightcap, wrong side outwards for good luck. It was deep midnight before his anxious mind could settle itself into sleep. Again the golden dream was repeated, and again he saw his garden teeming with ingots and money bags.

Wolfert rose the next morning in complete bewilderment. A dream three times repeated was never known to lie; and if so, his fortune was made.

In his agitation he put on his waistcoat with the hind part before, and this was a corroboration of good luck. He no longer doubted that a huge store of money lay buried somewhere in his cabbage field, coyly waiting to be sought for, and he half repined at having so long been scratching about the surface of the soil, instead of digging to the centre.

He took his seat at the breakfast-table full of these speculations; asked his daughter to put a lump of gold in to his tea, and on handing his wife a plate of slap jacks, begging her to help herself to a doubloon.

His grand care now was how to secure this immense treasure without it being known. Instead of working regularly in his grounds in the day-time, he now stole from his bed at night, and with spade and pickaxe, went to work to rip up and dig about his paternal acres, from one end to the other. In a little time the whole garden, which had presented such a goodly and regular appearance, with its phalanx of cabbages, like a vegetable army in battle array, was reduced to a scene of devastation, while the relentless Wolfert, with nightcap on head, and lantern and spade in hand, stalked through the slaughtered ranks, the destroying angel of his own vegetable world.

Every morning bore testimony to the ravages of the preceding night in cabbages of all ages and conditions, from the tender sprout to the full grown head, piteously rooted from their quiet beds like worthless weeds, and left to wither in the sunshine. In vain Wolfert's wife remonstrated; in vain his darling daughter wept over the destruction of some favourite marygold. "Thou shalt have gold of another guess sort," he would cry, chucking her under the chin; "thou shalt have a string of crooked ducats for thy wedding-necklace, my child." His family began really to fear that the poor man's wits were diseased. He muttered in his sleep at night of mines of wealth, of pearls and diamonds and bars of gold. In the day time he was moody and abstracted, and walked about as if in a trance. Dame Webber held frequent councils with all the old women of the neighbourhood, not omitting the parish dominie; scarce an hour in the day but a knot of them might be seen wagging their white caps together round her door, while the poor woman made some piteous recital. The daughter too was fain to seek for more frequent consolation from the stolen interviews of her favored swain Dirk Waldron. The delectable little Dutch songs with which she used to dulcify the house grew less and less frequent, and she would forget her sewing and look wistfully in her father's face as he sat pondering by the fire side. Wolfert caught her eye one day fixed on him thus anxiously, and for a moment was roused from his golden reveries—"Cheer up, my girl," said he, exultingly, "why dost thou droop?—thou shalt hold up thy head one day with the—and the Schenaerhorns, the Van Hornes, and the Van Dams—the patroon himself shall be glad to get thee for his son!"

Amy shook her head at this vain glorious boast, and was more than ever in doubt of the soundness of the good man's intellect.

In the mean time Wolfert went on digging, but the field was extensive, and as his dream had indicated no precise spot, he had to dig at random. The winter set in before one tenth of the scene of promise had been explored. The ground became too frozen and the nights too cold for the labours of the spade. No sooner, however, did the returning warmth of spring loosen the soil, and the small frogs begin to pipe in the meadows, but Wolfert resumed his labours with renovated zeal. Still, however, the hours of industry were reversed. Instead of working cheerily all day, planting and setting out his vegetables, he remained thoughtfully idle, until the shades of night summoned him to his secret labours. In this way he continued to dig from night to night, and week to week, and month to month, but not a stiver did he find. On the contrary, the more he digged the poorer he grew. The rich soil of his garden was digged away, and the sand and gravel from beneath were thrown to the surface, until the whole field presented an aspect of sandy barrenness.

In the mean time the seasons gradually rolled on. The little frogs that had piped in the meadows in early spring, croaked as bull-frogs in the brooks during the summer heats, and then sunk into silence. The peach tree budded, blossomed, and bore its fruit. The swallows and martins came, twittered about the roof, built their nests, reared their young, held their congress along the eaves, and then winged their flight in search of another spring. The caterpillar spun its winding sheet, dangled in it from the great buttonwood tree that shaded the house, turned into a moth, fluttered with the last sunshine of summer, and disappeared; and finally the leaves of the buttonwood tree turned yellow, then brown, then rustled one by one to the ground, and whirling about in little eddies of wind and dust, whispered that winter was at hand.

Wolfert gradually awoke from his dream of wealth as the year declined. He had reared no crop to supply the wants of his household during the sterility of winter. The season was long and severe, and for the first time the family was really straightened in its comforts. By degrees a revulsion of thought took place in Wolfert's mind, common to those whose golden dreams have been disturbed by pinching realities. The idea gradually stole upon him that he should come to want. He already considered himself one of the most unfortunate men in the province, having lost such an incalculable amount of undiscovered treasure, and now, when thousands of pounds had eluded his search, to be perplexed for shillings and pence was cruel in the extreme.

Haggard care gathered about his brow; he went about with a money-seeking air, his eyes bent downwards into the dust, and carrying his hands in his pockets, as men are apt to do when they have nothing else to put into them. He could not even pass the city almshouse without giving it a rueful glance, as if destined to be his future abode.

The strangeness of his conduct and of his looks occasioned much speculation and remark. For a long time he was suspected of being crazy, and then every body pitied him; at length it began to be suspected that he was poor, and then every body avoided him.

The rich old burghers of his acquaintance met him, outside of the door when he called, entertained him hospitably on the threshold, pressed him warmly by the hand on parting, shook their heads as he walked away, with the kind-hearted expression of "poor Wolfert," and turned a corner nimbly, if by chance they saw him approaching as they walked the streets. Even the barber and cobbler of the neighbourhood, and a tattered tailor in an alley hard by, three of the poorest and merriest rogues in the world, eyed him with that abundant sympathy which usually attends a lack of means, and there is not a doubt but their pockets would have been at his command, only that they happened to be empty.

Thus every body deserted the Webber mansion, as if poverty were contagious, like the plague; every body but honest Dirk Waldron, who still kept up his stolen visits to the daughter, and indeed seemed to wax more affectionate as the fortunes of his mistress were on the wane.

Many months had elapsed since Wolfert had frequented his old resort, the rural inn. He was taking a long lonely walk one Saturday afternoon, musing over his wants and disappointments, when his feet took instinctively their wonted direction, and on awaking out of a reverie, he found himself before the door of the inn. For some moments he hesitated whether to enter, but his heart yearned for companionship; and where can a ruined man find better companionship than at a tavern, where there is neither sober example nor sober advice to put him out of countenance?

Wolfert found several of the old frequenters of the tavern at their usual posts, and seated in their usual places; but one was missing, the great Ramm Rapelye, who for many years had filled the chair of state. His place was supplied by a stranger, who seemed, however, completely at home in the chair and the tavern. He was rather under-size, but deep-chested, square, and muscular. His broad shoulders, double joints, and bow-knees, gave tokens of prodigious strength. His face was dark and weather-beaten; a deep scar, as if from the slash of a cutlass, had almost divided his nose, and made a gash in his upper lip, through which his teeth shone like a bull-dog's. A mass of iron gray hair gave a grizzly finish to his hard favoured visage. His dress was of an amphibious character. He wore an old hat edged with tarnished lace, and cocked in martial style, on one side of his head; a rusty blue military coat with brass buttons, and a wide pair of short petticoat trousers, or rather breeches, for they were gathered up at the knees. He ordered every body about him with an authoritative air; talked in a brattling voice, that sounded like the crackling of thorns under a pot; damned the landlord and servants with perfect impunity, and was waited upon with greater obsequiousness than had ever been shown to the mighty Ramm himself.

Wolfert's curiosity was awakened to know who and what was this stranger who had thus usurped absolute sway in this ancient domain. He could get nothing, however, but vague information. Peechy Prauw took him aside, into a remote corner of the hall, and there in an under voice, and with great caution, imparted to him all that he knew on the subject. The inn had been aroused several months before, on a dark stormy night, by repeated long shouts, that seemed like the howlings of a wolf. They came from the water side; and at length were distinguished to be hailing the house in the seafaring manner. "House-a-hoy!" The landlord turned out with his head-waiter, tapster, hostler, and errand boy—that is to say with his old negro Cuff. On approaching the place from whence the voice proceeded, they found this amphibious-looking personage at the water's edge, quite alone, and seated on a great oaken sea-chest. How he came there, whether he had been set on shore from some boat, or had floated to land on his chest, nobody could tell, for he did not seem disposed to answer questions, and there was something in his looks and manners that put a stop to all questioning. Suffice it to say, he took possession of a corner room of the inn, to which his chest was removed with great difficulty. Here he had remained ever since, keeping about the inn and its vicinity. Sometimes, it is true, he disappeared for one, two, or three days at a time, going and returning without giving any notice or account of his movements. He always appeared to have plenty of money, though often of very strange, outlandish coinage; and he regularly paid his bill every evening before turning in.

He had fitted up his room to his own fancy, having slung a hammock from the ceiling instead of a bed, and decorated the walls with rusty pistols and cutlasses of foreign workmanship. A great part of his time was passed in this room, seated by the window, which commanded a wide view of the Sound, a short old fashioned pipe in his mouth, a glass of rum toddy at his elbow, and a pocket telescope in his hand, with which he reconnoitred every boat that moved upon the water. Large square rigged vessels seemed to excite but little attention; but the moment he descried any thing with a shoulder-of-mutton sail, or that a barge, or yawl, or jolly boat hove in sight, up went the telescope, and he examined it with the most scrupulous attention.

All this might have passed without much notice, for in those times the province was so much the resort of adventurers of all characters and climes that any oddity in dress or behavior attracted but little attention. But in a little while this strange sea monster, thus strangely cast up on dry land, began to encroach upon the long-established customs and customers of the place; to interfere in a dictatorial manner in the affairs of the ninepin alley and the bar room, until in the end he usurped an absolute command over the little inn. It was in vain to attempt to withstand his authority. He was not exactly quarrelsome, but boisterous and peremptory, like one accustomed to tyrannize on a quarter deck; and there was a dare devil air about every thing he said and did, that inspired a wariness in all bystanders. Even the half-pay officer, so long the hero of the club, was soon silenced by him; and the quiet burghers stared with wonder at seeing their inflammable man of war so readily and quietly extinguished.

And then the tales that he would tell were enough to make a peaceable man's hair stand on end. There was not a sea fight, or marauding or free-booting adventure that had happened within the last twenty years but he seemed perfectly versed in it. He delighted to talk of the exploits of the buccaneers in the West Indies and on the Spanish Main. How his eyes would glisten as he described the waylaying of treasure ships, the desperate fights, yard arm and yard arm—broadside and broadside—the boarding and capturing of large Spanish galleons! with what chuckling relish would he describe the descent upon some rich Spanish colony; the rifling of a church; the sacking of a convent! You would have thought you heard some gormandizer dilating upon the roasting a savory goose at Michaelmas as he described the roasting of some Spanish Don to make him discover his treasure—a detail given with a minuteness that made every rich old burgher present turn uncomfortably in his chair. All this would be told with infinite glee, as if he considered it an excellent joke; and then he would give such a tyrannical leer in the face of his next neighbour, that the poor man would be fain to laugh out of sheer faint heartedness. If any one, however, pretended to contradict him in any of his stories he was on fire in an instant. His very cocked hat assumed a momentary fierceness, and seemed to resent the contradiction.—"How the devil should you know as well as I! I tell you it was as I say!" and he would at the same time let slip a broadside of thundering oaths and tremendous sea phrases, such as had never been heard before within those peaceful walls.

Indeed, the worthy burghers began to surmise that he knew more of these stories than mere hearsay. Day after day their conjectures concerning him grew more and more wild and fearful. The strangeness of his manners, the mystery that surrounded him, all made him something incomprehensible in their eyes. He was a kind of monster of the deep to them—he was a merman—he was behemoth—he was leviathan—in short, they knew not what he was.

The domineering spirit of this boisterous sea urchin at length grew quite intolerable. He was no respecter of persons; he contradicted the richest burghers without hesitation; he took possession of the sacred elbow chair, which time out of mind had been the seat of sovereignty of the illustrious Ramm Rapelye. Nay, he even went so far in one of his rough jocular moods, as to slap that mighty burgher on the back, drink his toddy and wink in his face, a thing scarcely to be believed. From this time Ramm Rapelye appeared no more at the inn; his example was followed by several of the most eminent customers, who were too rich to tolerate being bullied out of their opinions, or being obliged to laugh at another man's jokes. The landlord was almost in despair, but he knew not how to get rid of this sea monster and his sea-chest, which seemed to have grown like fixtures, or excrescences on his establishment.

Such was the account whispered cautiously in Wolfert's ear, by the narrator, Peechy Prauw, as he held him by the button in a corner of the hall, casting a wary glance now and then towards the door of the bar-room, lest he should be overheard by the terrible hero of his tale.

Wolfert took his seat in a remote part of the room in silence; impressed with profound awe of this unknown, so versed in free-booting history. It was to him a wonderful instance of the revolutions of mighty empires, to find the venerable Ramm Rapelye thus ousted from the throne; a rugged tarpaulin dictating from his elbow chair, hectoring the patriarchs, and filling this tranquil little realm with brawl and bravado.

The stranger was on this evening in a more than usually communicative mood, and was narrating a number of astounding stories of plunderings and burnings upon the high seas. He dwelt upon them with peculiar relish, heightening the frightful particulars in proportion to their effect on his peaceful auditors. He gave a long swaggering detail of the capture of a Spanish merchantman. She was laying becalmed during a long summer's day, just off from an island which was one of the lurking places of the pirates. They had reconnoitred her with their spy glasses from the shore, and ascertained her character and force. At night a picked crew of daring fellows set off for her in a whale boat. They approached with muffled oars, as she lay rocking idly with the undulations of the sea and her sails flapping against the masts. They were close under her stern before the guard on deck was aware of their approach. The alarm was given; the pirates threw hand grenades on deck and sprang up the main chains sword in hand.

The crew flew to arms, but in great confusion some were shot down, others took refuge in the tops; others were driven overboard and drowned, while others fought hand to hand from the main deck to the quarter deck, disputing gallantly every inch of ground. There were three Spanish gentlemen on board with their ladies, who made the most desperate resistance; they defended the companion way, cut down several of their assailants, and fought like very devils, for they were maddened by the shrieks of the ladies from the cabin. One of the Dons was old and soon despatched. The other two kept their ground vigorously, even though the captain of the pirates was among their assailants. Just then there was a shout of victory from the main deck. "The ship is ours!" cried the pirates.

One of the Dons immediately dropped his sword and surrendered; the other, who was a hot-headed youngster, and just married, gave the captain a slash in the face that laid all open. The captain just made out to articulate the words "no quarter."

"And what did they do with their prisoners?" said Peechy Prauw, eagerly.

"Threw them all overboard!" said the merman.

A dead pause followed this reply. Peechy Prauw shrunk quietly back like a man who had unwarily stolen upon the lair of a sleeping lion. The honest burghers cast fearful glances at the deep scar slashed across the visage of the stranger, and moved their chairs a little farther off. The seaman, however, smoked on without moving a muscle, as though he either did not perceive or did not regard the unfavorable effect he had produced upon his hearers.

The half-pay officer was the first to break the silence; for he was continually tempted to make ineffectual head against this tyrant of the seas, and to regain his lost consequence in the eyes of his ancient companions. He now tried to match the gunpowder tales of the stranger by others equally tremendous. Kidd, as usual, was his hero, concerning whom he had picked up many of the floating traditions of the province. The seaman had always evinced a settled pique against the red-faced warrior. On this occasion he listened with peculiar impatience. He sat with one arm akimbo, the other elbow on a table, the hand holding on to the small pipe he was pettishly puffing; his legs crossed, drumming with one foot on the ground and casting every now and then the side glance of a basilisk at the prosing captain. At length the latter spoke of Kidd's having ascended the Hudson with some of his crew, to land his plunder in secrecy.

"Kidd up the Hudson!" burst forth the seaman, with a tremendous oath; "Kidd never was up the Hudson!"

"I tell you he was," said the other. "Aye, and they say he buried a quantity of treasure on the little flat that runs out into the river, called the Devil's Dans Kammer."

"The Devil's Dans Kammer in your teeth!" cried the seaman. "I tell you Kidd never was up the Hudson—what the plague do you know of Kidd and his haunts?"

"What do I know?" echoed the half-pay officer; "why, I was in London at the time of his trial, aye, and I had the pleasure of seeing him hanged at Execution Dock."

"Then, sir, let me tell you that you saw as pretty a fellow hanged as ever trod shoe leather. Aye!" putting his face nearer to that of the officer, "and there was many a coward looked on, that might much better have swung in his stead."

The half-pay officer was silenced; but the indignation thus pent up in his bosom glowed with intense vehemence in his single eye, which kindled like a coal.

Peechy Prauw, who never could remain silent, now took up the word, and in a pacifying tone observed that the gentleman certainly was in the right. Kidd never did bury money up the Hudson, nor indeed in any of those parts, though many affirm the fact. It was Bradish and others of the buccaneers who had buried money, some said in Turtle Bay, others on Long Island, others in the neighbourhood of Hell Gate. Indeed, added he, I recollect an adventure of Mud Sam, the negro fisherman, many years ago, which some think had something to do with the buccaneers. As we are all friends here, and as it will go no farther, I'll tell it to you.

"Upon a dark night many years ago, as Sam was returning from fishing in Hell Gate—"

Here the story was nipped in the bud by a sudden movement from the unknown, who, laying his iron fist on the table, knuckles downward, with a quiet force that indented the very boards, and looking grimly over his shoulder, with the grin of an angry bear. "Heark'ee, neighbour," said he, with significant nodding of the head, "you'd better let the buccaneers and their money alone—they're not for old men and old women to meddle with. They fought hard for their money, they gave body and soul for it, and wherever it lies buried, depend upon it he must have a tug with the devil who gets it."

This sudden explosion was succeeded by a blank silence throughout the room. Peechy Prauw shrunk within himself, and even the red-faced officer turned pale. Wolfert, who, from a dark corner of the room, had listened with intense eagerness to all this talk about buried treasure, looked with mingled awe and reverence on this bold buccaneer, for such he really suspected him to be. There was a chinking of gold and a sparkling of jewels in all his stories about the Spanish Main that gave a value to every period, and Wolfert would have given any thing for the rummaging of the ponderous sea-chest, which his imagination crammed full of golden chalices and crucifixes and jolly round bags of doubloons.

The dead stillness that had fallen upon the company was at length interrupted by the stranger, who pulled out a prodigious watch of curious and ancient workmanship, and which in Wolferts' eyes had a decidedly Spanish look. On touching a spring it struck ten o'clock; upon which the sailor called for his reckoning, and having paid it out of a handful of outlandish coin, he drank off the remainder of his beverage, and without taking leave of any one, rolled out of the room, muttering to himself as he stamped up stairs to his chamber.

It was some time before the company could recover from the silence into which they had been thrown. The very footsteps of the stranger, which were heard now and then as he traversed his chamber, inspired awe.

Still the conversation in which they had been engaged was too interesting not to be resumed. A heavy thunder-gust had gathered up unnoticed while they were lost in talk, and the torrents of rain that fell forbade all thoughts of setting off for home until the storm should subside. They drew nearer together, therefore, and entreated the worthy Peechy Prauw to continue the tale which had been so discourteously interrupted. He readily complied, whispering, however, in a tone scarcely above his breath, and drowned occasionally by the rolling of the thunder, and he would pause every now and then, and listen with evident awe, as he heard the heavy footsteps of the stranger pacing overhead.

The following is the purport of his story.

THE ADVENTURE OF
THE BLACK FISHERMAN

Every body knows Black Sam, the old negro fisherman, or, as he is commonly called, Mud Sam, who has fished about the Sound for the last twenty or thirty years. It is now many years since that Sam, who was then as active a young negro as any in the province, and worked on the farm of Killian Suydam on Long Island, having finished his work early, was fishing, one still summer evening, just about the neighbourhood of Hell Gate. He was in a light skiff, and being well acquainted with the currents and eddies, he had been able to shift his station with the shifting of the tide, from the Hen and Chickens to the Hog's back, and from the Hog's back to the Pot, and from the Pot to the Frying Pan; but in the eagerness of his sport Sam did not see that the tide was rapidly ebbing; until the roaring of the whirlpools and rapids warned him of his danger, and he had some difficulty in shooting his skiff from among the rocks and breakers, and getting to the point of Blackwell's Island. Here he cast anchor for some time, waiting the turn of the tide to enable him to return homewards. As the night set in it grew blustering and gusty. Dark clouds came bundling up in the west; and now and then a growl of thunder or a flash of lightning told that a summer storm was at hand. Sam pulled over, therefore, under the lee of Manhattan Island, and coasting along came to a snug nook, just under a steep beetling rock, where he fastened his skiff to the root of a tree that shot out from a cleft and spread its broad branches like a canopy over the water. The gust came scouring along; the wind threw up the river in white surges; the rain rattled among the leaves, the thunder bellowed worse than that which is now bellowing, the lightning seemed to lick up the surges of the stream; but Sam, snugly sheltered under rock and tree, lay crouched in his skiff, rocking upon the billows, until he fell asleep. When he awoke all was quiet. The gust had passed away, and only now and then a faint gleam of lightning in the east showed which way it had gone. The night was dark and moonless; and from the state of the tide Sam concluded it was near midnight. He was on the point of making loose his skiff to return homewards, when he saw a light gleaming along the water from a distance, which seemed rapidly approaching. As it drew near he perceived that it came from a lanthorn in the bow of a boat which was gliding along under shadow of the land. It pulled up in a small cove, close to where he was. A man jumped on shore, and searching about with the lanthorn exclaimed, "This is the place—here's the Iron ring." The boat was then made fast, and the man returning on board, assisted his comrades in conveying something heavy on shore. As the light gleamed among them, Sam saw that they were five stout, desperate-looking fellows, in red woollen caps, with a leader in a three-cornered hat, and that some of them were armed with dirks, or long knives, and pistols. They talked low to one another, and occasionally in some outlandish tongue which he could not understand.

On landing they made their way among the bushes, taking turns to relieve each other in lugging their burthen up the rocky bank. Sam's curiosity was now fully aroused, so leaving his skiff he clambered silently up the ridge that overlooked their path. They had stopped to rest for a moment, and the leader was looking about among the bushes with his lanthorn. "Have you brought the spades?" said one. "They are here," replied another, who had them on his shoulder. "We must dig deep, where there will be no risk of discovery," said a third.

A cold chill ran through Sam's veins. He fancied he saw before him a gang of murderers, about to bury their victim. His knees smote together. In his agitation he shook the branch of a tree with which he was supporting himself as he looked over the edge of the cliff.

"What's that?" cried one of the gang. "Some one stirs among the bushes!"

The lanthorn was held up in the direction of the noise. One of the red caps cocked a pistol, and pointed it towards the very lace where Sam was standing. He stood motionless—breathless; expecting the next moment to be his last. Fortunately, his dingy complexion was in his favor, and made no glare among the leaves.

"'Tis no one," said the man with the lanthorn. "What a plague! you would not fire off your pistol and alarm the country."

The pistol was uncocked; the burthen was resumed, and the party slowly toiled up the bank. Sam watched them as they went; the light sending back fitful gleams through the dripping bushes, and it was not till they were fairly out of sight that he ventured to draw breath freely. He now thought of getting back to his boat, and making his escape out of the reach of such dangerous neighbours; but curiosity was all-powerful with poor Sam. He hesitated and lingered and listened. By and bye he heard the strokes of spades.

"They are digging the grave!" said he to himself; the cold sweat started upon his forehead. Every stroke of a spade, as it sounded through the silent groves, went to his heart; it was evident there was as little noise made as possible; every thing had an air of mystery and secrecy. Sam had a great relish for the horrible,—a tale of murder was a treat for him; and he was a constant attendant at executions. He could not, therefore, resist an impulse, in spite of every danger, to steal nearer, and overlook the villains at their work. He crawled along cautiously, therefore, inch by inch; stepping with the utmost care among the dry leaves, lest their rustling should betray him. He came at length to where a steep rock intervened between him and the gang; he saw the light of their lanthorn shining up against the branches of the trees on the other side. Sam slowly and silently clambered up the surface of the rock, and raising his head above its naked edge, beheld the villains immediately below him, and so near that though he dreaded discovery, he dared not withdraw lest the least movement should be heard. In this way he remained, with his round black face peering over the edge of the rock, like the sun just emerging above the edge of the horizon, or the round cheeked moon on the dial of a clock.

The red caps had nearly finished their work; the grave was filled up, and they were carefully replacing the turf. This done, they scattered dry leaves over the place. "And now," said the leader, "I defy the devil himself to find it out."

"The murderers!" exclaimed Sam involuntarily.

The whole gang started, and looking up, beheld the round black head of Sam just above them. His white eyes strained half out of their orbits; his white teeth chattering, and his whole visage shining with cold perspiration.

"We're discovered!" cried one.

"Down with him!" cried another.

Sam heard the cocking of a pistol, but did not pause for the report. He scrambled over rock and stone, through bush and briar; rolled down banks like a hedgehog; scrambled up others like a catamount. In every direction he heard some one or other of the gang hemming him in. At length he reached the rocky ridge along the river; one of the red-caps was hard behind him. A steep rock like a wall rose directly in his way; it seemed to cut off all retreat, when he espied the strong cord-like branch of a grape vine reaching half way down it. He sprang at it with the force of a desperate man, seized it with both hands, and being young and agile, succeeded in swinging himself to the summit of the cliff. Here he stood in full relief against the sky, when the red-cap cocked his pistol and fired. The ball whistled by Sam's head. With the lucky thought of a man in an emergency, he uttered a yell, fell to the ground, and detached at the same time a fragment of the rock, which tumbled with a loud splash into the river.

"I've done his business," said the red-cap, to one or two of his comrades as they arrived panting. "He'll tell no tales, except to the fishes in the river."

His pursuers now turned off to meet their companions. Sam sliding silently down the surface of the rock, let himself quietly into his skiff, cast loose the fastening, and abandoned himself to the rapid current, which in that place runs like a mill stream, and soon swept him off from the neighbourhood. It was not, however, until he had drifted a great distance that he ventured to ply his oars; when he made his skiff dart like an arrow through the strait of Hell Gate, never heeding the danger of Pot, Frying-pan, or Hog's-back itself; nor did he feel himself thoroughly secure until safely nestled in bed in the cockloft of the ancient farm house of the Suydams.

Here the worthy Peechy paused to take breath and to take a sip of the gossip tankard that stood at his elbow. His auditors remained with open mouths and outstretched necks, gaping like a nest of swallows for an additional mouthful.

"And is that all?" exclaimed the half-pay officer.

"That's all that belongs to the story," said Peechy Prauw.

"And did Sam never find out what was buried by the red caps?" said Wolfert, eagerly; whose mind was haunted by nothing but ingots and doubloons.

"Not that I know of; he had no time to spare from his work; and to tell the truth, he did not like to run the risk of another race among the rocks. Besides, how should he recollect the spot where the grave had been digged? every thing would look different by daylight. And then, where was the use of looking for a dead body, when there was no chance of hanging the murderers?"

"Aye, but are you sure it was a dead body they buried?" said Wolfert.

"To be sure," cried Peechy Prauw, exultingly. "Does it not haunt in the neighbourhood to this very day?"

"Haunts!" exclaimed several of the party, opening their eyes still wider and edging their chairs still closer.

"Aye, haunts," repeated Peechy; "has none of you heard of father red cap that haunts the old burnt farm house in the woods, on the border of the Sound, near Hell Gate?"

"Oh, to be sure, I've heard tell of something of the kind, but then I took it for some old wives' fable."

"Old wives' fable or not," said Peechy Prauw, "that farmhouse stands hard by the very spot. It's been unoccupied time out of mind, and stands in a wild, lonely part of the coast; but those who fish in the neighbourhood have often heard strange noises there; and lights have been seen about the wood at night; and an old fellow in a red cap has been seen at the windows more than once, which people take to be the ghost of the body that was buried there. Once upon a time three soldiers took shelter in the building for the night, and rummaged it from top to bottom, when they found old father red cap astride of a cider barrel in the cellar, with a jug in one hand and a goblet in the other. He offered them a drink out of his goblet, but just as one of the soldiers was putting it to his mouth—Whew! a flash of fire blazed through the cellar, blinded every mother's son of them for several minutes, and when they recovered their eye sight, jug, goblet, and red cap had vanished, and nothing but the empty cider-barrel remained."

Here the half-pay officer, who was growing very muzzy and sleepy, and nodding over his liquor, with half-extinguished eye, suddenly gleamed up like an expiring rushlight.

"That's all humbug!" said he, as Peechy finished his last story.

"Well, I don't vouch for the truth of it myself," said Peechy Prauw, "though all the world knows that there's something strange about the house and grounds; but as to the story of Mud Sam, I believe it just as well as if it had happened to myself."

The deep interest taken in this conversation by the company, had made them unconscious of the uproar that prevailed abroad, among the elements, when suddenly they were all electrified by a tremendous clap of thunder. A lumbering crash followed instantaneously that made the building shake to its foundation. All started from their seats, imagining it the shock of an earthquake, or that old father red cap was coming among them in all his terrors. They listened for a moment, but only heard the rain pelting against the windows, and the wind howling among the trees. The explosion was soon explained by the apparition of an old negro's bald head thrust in at the door, his white goggle eyes contrasting with his jetty poll, which was wet with rain and shone like a bottle. In a jargon but half intelligible he announced that the kitchen chimney had been struck with lightning.

A sullen pause of the storm, which now rose and sunk in gusts, produced a momentary stillness. In this interval the report of a musket was heard, and a long shout, almost like a yell, resounded from the shore. Every one crowded to the window; another musket shot was heard, and another long shout, that mingled wildly with a rising blast of wind. It seemed as if the cry came up from the bosom of the waters; for though incessant flashes of lightning spread a light about the shore, no one was to be seen.

Suddenly the window of the room overhead was opened, and a loud halloo uttered by the mysterious stranger. Several hailings passed from one party to the other, but in a language which none of the company in the bar-room could understand; and presently they heard the window closed, and a great noise overhead as if all the furniture were pulled and hauled about the room. The negro servant was summoned, and shortly after was seen assisting the veteran to lug the ponderous sea-chest down stairs.

The landlord was in amazement. "What, you are not going on the water in such a storm?"

"Storm!" said the other, scornfully, "do you call such a sputter of weather a storm?"

"You'll get drenched to the skin—You'll catch your death!" said Peechy Prauw, affectionately.

"Thunder and lightning!" exclaimed the merman, "don't preach about weather to a man that has cruised in whirlwinds and tornadoes."

The obsequious Peechy was again struck dumb. The voice from the water was again heard in a tone of impatience; the bystanders stared with redoubled awe at this man of storms, which seemed to have come up out of the deep and to be called back to it again. As, with the assistance of the negro, he slowly bore his ponderous sea-chest towards the shore, they eyed it with a superstitious feeling; half doubting whether he were not really about to embark upon it, and launch forth upon the wild waves. They followed him at a distance with a lanthorn.

"Douse the light!" roared the hoarse voice from the water. "No one wants light here!"

"Thunder and lightning!" exclaimed the veteran; "back to the house with you!"

Wolfert and his companions shrunk back is dismay. Still their curiosity would not allow them entirely to withdraw. A long sheet of lightning now flickered across the waves, and discovered a boat, filled with men, just under a rocky point, rising and sinking with the heavy surges, and swashing the water at every heave. It was with difficulty held to the rocks by a boat hook, for the current rushed furiously round the point. The veteran hoisted one end of the lumbering sea chest on the gunwale of the boat; he seized the handle at the other end to lift it in, when the motion propelled the boat from the shore; the chest slipped off from the gunwale, sunk into the waves, and pulled the veteran headlong after it. A loud shriek was uttered by all on shore, and a volley of execrations by those on board; but boat and man were hurried away by the rushing swiftness of the tide. A pitchy darkness succeeded; Wolfert Webber indeed fancied that he distinguished a cry for help, and that he beheld the drowning man beckoning for assistance; but when the lightning again gleamed along the water all was drear and void. Neither man nor boat was to be seen; nothing but the dashing and weltering of the waves as they hurried past.

The company returned to the tavern, for they could not leave it before the storm should subside. They resumed their seats and gazed on each other with dismay. The whole transaction had not occupied five minutes and not a dozen words had been spoken. When they looked at the oaken chair they could scarcely realize the fact that the strange being who had so lately tenanted it, full of life and Herculean vigor, should already be a corpse. There was the very glass he had just drunk from; there lay the ashes from the pipe which he had smoked as it were with his last breath. As the worthy burghers pondered on these things, they felt a terrible conviction of the uncertainty of human existence, and each felt as if the ground on which he stood was rendered less stable by this awful example.

As, however, the most of the company were possessed of that valuable philosophy which enables a man to bear up with fortitude against the misfortunes of his neighbours, they soon managed to console themselves for the tragic end of the veteran. The landlord was happy that the poor dear man had paid his reckoning before he went.

"He came in a storm, and he went in a storm; he came in the night, and he went in the night; he came nobody knows from whence, and he has gone nobody knows where. For aught I know he has gone to sea once more on his chest and may land to bother some people on the other side of the world! Though it's a thousand pities," added the landlord, "if he has gone to Davy Jones' locker, that he had not left his own locker behind him."

"His locker! St. Nicholas preserve us!" said Peechy Prauw. "I'd not have had that sea chest in the house for any money; I'll warrant he'd come racketing after it at nights, and making a haunted house of the inn. And as to his going to sea on his chest, I recollect what happened to Skipper Onderdonk's ship on his voyage from Amsterdam.

"The boatswain died during a storm, so they wrapped him up in a sheet, and put him in his own sea-chest, and threw him overboard; but they neglected in their hurry-skurry to say prayers over him—and the storm raged and roared louder than ever, and they saw the dead man seated in his chest, with his shroud for a sail, coming hard after the ship; and the sea breaking before him in great sprays like fire, and there they kept scudding day after day and night after night, expecting every moment to go to wreck; and every night they saw the dead boatswain in his sea chest trying to get up with them, and they heard his whistle above the blasts of wind, and he seemed to send great seas mountain high after them, that would have swamped the ship if they had not put up the dead lights. And so it went on till they lost sight of him in the fogs of Newfoundland, and supposed he had veered ship and stood for Dead Man's Isle. So much for burying a man at sea without saying prayers over him."

The thundergust which had hitherto detained the company was now at an end. The cuckoo clock in the hall struck midnight; every one pressed to depart, for seldom was such a late hour trespassed on by these quiet burghers. As they sallied forth they found the heavens once more serene. The storm which had lately obscured them had rolled aways and lay piled up in fleecy masses on the horizon, lighted up by the bright crescent of the moon, which looked like a silver lamp hung up in a palace of clouds.

The dismal occurrence of the night, and the dismal narrations they had made, had left a superstitious feeling in every mind. They cast a fearful glance at the spot where the buccaneer had disappeared, almost expecting to see him sailing on his chest in the cool moonshine. The trembling rays glittered along the waters, but all was placid; and the current dimpled over the spot where he had gone down. The party huddled together in a little crowd as they repaired homewards; particularly when they passed a lonely field where a man had been murdered; and he who had farthest to go and had to complete his journey alone, though a veteran sexton, and accustomed, one would think to ghosts and goblins, yet went a long way round, rather than pass by his own church yard.

Wolfert Webber had now carried home a fresh stock of stories and notions to ruminate upon. His mind was all of a whirl with these freebooting tales; and then these accounts of pots of money and Spanish treasures, buried here and there and every where about the rocks and bays of this wild shore, made him almost dizzy.

"Blessed St. Nicholas!" ejaculated he, half aloud, "is it not possible to come upon one of these golden hoards, and so make one's self rich in a twinkling. How hard that I must go on, delving and delving, day in and day out, merely to make a morsel of bread, when one lucky stroke of a spade might enable me to ride in my carriage for the rest of my life!"

As he turned over in his thoughts all that he had been told of the singular adventure of the black fisherman, his imagination gave a totally different complexion to the tale. He saw in the gang of red caps nothing but a crew of pirates burying their spoils, and his cupidity was once more awakened by the possibility of at length getting on the traces of some of this lurking wealth. Indeed, his infected fancy tinged every thing with gold. He felt like the greedy inhabitant of Bagdad, when his eye had been greased with the magic ointment of the dervise, that gave him to see all the treasures of the earth. Caskets of buried jewels, chests of ingots, bags of outlandish coins, seemed to court him from their concealments, and supplicate him to relieve them from their untimely graves.

On making private inquiries about the grounds said to be haunted by father red cap, he was more and more confirmed in his surmise. He learned that the place had several times been visited by experienced money diggers, who had heard Black Sam's story, though none of them had met with success. On the contrary, they had always been dogged with ill luck of some kind or other, in consequence, as Wolfert concluded, of their not going to work at the proper time, and with the proper ceremonials. The last attempt had been made by Cobus Quackenbos, who dug for a whole night and met with incredible difficulty, for as fast as he threw one shovel full of earth out of the hole, two were thrown in by invisible hands. He succeeded so far, however, as to uncover an iron chest, when there was a terrible roaring, and ramping, and raging of uncouth figures about the hole, and at length a shower of blows, dealt by invisible cudgels, that fairly belaboured him off the forbidden ground. This Cobus Quackenbos had declared on his death-bed, so that there could not be any doubt of it. He was a man that had devoted many years of his life to money-digging, and it was thought would have ultimately succeeded, had he not died suddenly of a brain fever in the alms-house.

Wolfert Webber was now in a worry of trepidation and impatience; fearful lest some rival adventurer should get a scent of the buried gold. He determined privately to seek out the negro fisherman and get him to serve as guide to the place where he had witnessed the mysterious scene of interment. Sam was easily found; for he was one of those old habitual beings that live about a neighbourhood until they wear themselves a place in the public mind, and become, in a manner, public characters. There was not an unlucky urchin about the town that did not know Mud Sam the fisherman, and think that he had a right to play his tricks upon the old negro. Sam was an amphibious kind of animal, something more of a fish than a man; he had led the life of an otter for more than half a century, about the shores of the bay, and the fishing grounds of the Sound. He passed the greater part of his time on and in the water, particularly about Hell Gate; and might have been taken, in bad weather, for one of the hobgoblins that used to haunt that strait. There would he be seen, at all times, and in all weathers; sometimes in his skiff, anchored among the eddies, or prowling, like a shark about some wreck, where the fish are supposed to be most abundant. Sometimes seated on a rock from hour to hour, looming through mist and drizzle, like a solitary heron watching for its prey. He was well acquainted with every hole and corner of the Sound; from the Wallabout to Hell Gate, and from Hell Gate even unto the Devil's Stepping Stones; and it was even affirmed that he knew all the fish in the river by their christian names.

Wolfert found him at his cabin, which was not much larger than a tolerable dog-house. It was rudely constructed of fragments of wrecks and drift wood, and built on the rocky shore, at the foot of the old fort, just about what at present forms the point of the Battery. A "most ancient and fish-like smell" pervaded the place. Oars, paddles, and fishing rods were leaning against the wall of the fort; a net was spread on the sands to dry; a skiff was drawn up on the beach, and at the door of his cabin lay Mud Sam himself, indulging in a true negro's luxury—sleeping in the sunshine.

Many years had passed away since the time of Sam's youthful adventure, and the snows of many a winter had grizzled the knotty wool upon his head. He perfectly recollected the circumstances, however, for he had often been called upon to relate them, though in his version of the story he differed in many points from Peechy Prauw; as is not unfrequently the case with authentic historians. As to the subsequent researches of money-diggers, Sam knew nothing about them; they were matters quite out of his line; neither did the cautious Wolfert care to disturb his thoughts on that point. His only wish was to secure the old fisherman as a pilot to the spot, and this was readily effected. The long time that had intervened since his nocturnal adventure had effaced all Sam's awe of the place, and the promise of a trifling reward roused him at once from his sleep and his sunshine.

The tide was adverse to making the expedition by water, and Wolfert was too impatient to get to the land of promise, to wait for its turning; they set off, therefore, by land. A walk of four or five miles brought them to the edge of a wood, which at that time covered the greater part of the eastern side of the island. It was just beyond the pleasant region of Bloomen-dael. Here they struck into a long lane, straggling among trees and bushes, very much overgrown with weeds and mullein stalks as if but seldom used, and so completely overshadowed as to enjoy but a kind of twilight. Wild vines entangled the trees and flaunted in their faces; brambles and briars caught their clothes as they passed; the garter snake glided across their path; the spotted toad hopped and waddled before them, and the restless cat-bird mewed at them from every thicket. Had Wolfert Webber been deeply read in romantic legend he might have fancied himself entering upon forbidden, enchanted ground; or that these were some of the guardians set to keep a watch upon buried treasure. As it was, the loneliness of the place, and the wild stories connected with it, had their effect upon his mind.

On reaching the lower end of the lane they found themselves near the shore of the Sound, in a kind of amphitheatre, surrounded by forest tree. The area had once been a grass plot, but was now shagged with briars and rank weeds. At one end, and just on the river bank, was a ruined building, little better than a heap of rubbish, with a stack of chimneys rising like a solitary tower out of the centre. The current of the Sound rushed along just below it, with wildly grown trees drooping their branches into its waves.

Wolfert had not a doubt that this was the haunted house of father red cap, and called to mind the story of Peechy Prauw. The evening was approaching, and the light falling dubiously among these places, gave a melancholy tone to the scene, well calculated to foster any lurking feeling of awe or superstition. The night-hawk, wheeling about in the highest regions of the air, emitted his peevish, boding cry. The woodpecker gave a lonely tap now and then on some hollow tree, and the fire bird, as he streamed by them with his deep red plumage.

They now came to an enclosure that had once been a garden. It extended along the foot of a rocky ridge, but was little better than a wilderness of weeds, with here and there a matted rose-bush, or a peach or plum tree grown wild and ragged, and covered with moss. At the lower end of the garden they passed a kind of vault in the side of the bank, facing the water. It had the look of a root house. The door, though decayed, was still strong, and appeared to have been recently patched up. Wolfert pushed it open. It gave a harsh grating upon its hinges, and striking against something like a box, a rattling sound ensued, and a skull rolled on the floor. Wolfert drew back shuddering, but was reassured on being informed by Sam that this was a family vault belonging to one of the old Dutch families that owned this estate; an assertion which was corroborated by the sight of coffins of various sizes piled within. Sam had been familiar with all these scenes when a boy, and now knew that he could not be far from the place of which they were in quest.

They now made their way to the water's edge, scrambling along ledges of rocks, and having often to hold by shrubs and grape vines to avoid slipping into the deep and hurried stream. At length they came to a small cove, or rather indent of the shore. It was protected by steep rocks and overshadowed by a thick copse of oaks and chestnuts, so as to be sheltered and almost concealed. The beach sloped gradually within the cove, but the current swept deep and black and rapid along its jutting points. Sam paused; raised his remnant of a hat, and scratched his grizzled poll for a moment, as he regarded this nook: then suddenly clapping his hands, he stepped exultingly forward, and pointing to a large iron ring, stapled firmly in the rock, just where a broad shelve of stone furnished a commodious landing-place. It was the very spot where the red-caps had landed. Years had changed the more perishable features of the scene; but rock and iron yield slowly to the influence of time. On looking more narrowly, Wolfert remarked three crosses cut in the rock just above the ring, which had no doubt some mysterious signification. Old Sam now readily recognized the overhanging rock under which his skiff had been sheltered during the thundergust. To follow up the course which the midnight gang had taken, however, was a harder task. His mind had been so much taken up on that eventful occasion by the persons of the drama, as to pay but little attention to the scenes; and places looked different by night and day. After wandering about for some time, however, they came to an opening among the trees which Sam thought resembled the place. There was a ledge of rock of moderate height like a wall on one side, which Sam thought might be the very ridge from which he overlooked the diggers. Wolfert examined it narrowly, and at length described three crosses similar to those above the iron ring, cut deeply into the face of the rock, but nearly obliterated by the moss that had grown on them. His heart leaped with joy, for he doubted not but they were the private marks of the buccaneers, to denote the places where their treasure lay buried. All now that remained was to ascertain the precise spot; for otherwise he might dig at random without coming upon the spoil, and he has already had enough of such profitless labour. Here, however, Sam was perfectly at a loss, and, indeed, perplexed him by a variety of opinions; for his recollections were all confused. Sometimes he declared it must have been at the foot of a mulberry tree hard by; then it was just beside a great white stone; then it must have been under a small green knoll, a short distance from the ledge of rock: until at length Wolfert became as bewildered as himself.

The shadows of evening were now spreading themselves over the woods, and rock and tree began to mingle together. It was evidently too late to attempt anything farther at present; and, indeed, Wolfert had come unprepared with implements to prosecute his researches. Satisfied, therefore, with having ascertained the place, he took note of all its landmarks, that he might recognize it again, and set out on his return homeward, resolved to prosecute this golden enterprise without delay.

The leading anxiety which had hitherto absorbed every feeling being now in some measure appeased, fancy began to wander, and to conjure up a thousand shapes and chimeras as he returned through this haunted region. Pirates hanging in chains seemed to swing on every tree, and he almost expected to see some Spanish Don, with his throat cut from ear to ear, rising slowly out of the ground, and shaking the ghost of a money bag.

Their way back lay through the desolate garden, and Wolfert's nerves had arrived at so sensitive a state that the flitting of a bird, the rustling of a leaf, or the falling of a nut was enough to startle him. As they entered the confines of the garden, they caught sight of a figure at a distance advancing slowly up one of the walks and bending under the weight of a burthen. They paused and regarded him attentively. He wore what appeared to be a woollen cap, and still more alarming, of a most sanguinary red. The figure moved slowly on, ascended the bank, and stopped at the very door of the sepulchral vault. Just before entering he looked around. What was the horror of Wolfert when he recognized the grizzly visage of the drowned buccaneer. He uttered an ejaculation of horror. The figure slowly raised his iron fist and shook it with a terrible menace. Wolfert did not pause to see more, but hurried off as fast as his legs could carry him, nor was Sam slow in following at his heels, having all his ancient terrors revived. Away, then, did they scramble, through bush and brake, horribly frightened at every bramble that tagged at their skirts, nor did they pause to breathe, until they had blundered their way through this perilous wood and had fairly reached the high road to the city.

Several days elapsed before Wolfert could summon courage enough to prosecute the enterprise, so much had he been dismayed by the apparition, whether living dead, of the grizzly buccaneer. In the mean time, what a conflict of mind did he suffer! He neglected all his concerns, was moody and restless all day, lost his appetite; wandered in his thoughts and words, and committed a thousand blunders. His rest was broken; and when he fell asleep, the nightmare, in shape of a huge money bag, sat squatted upon his breast. He babbled about incalculable sums; fancied himself engaged in money digging; threw the bed-clothes right and left, in the idea that he was shovelling among the dirt, groped under the bed in quest of the treasure, and lugged forth, as he supposed, an inestimable pot of gold.

Dame Webber and her daughter were in despair at what they conceived a returning touch of insanity. There are two family oracles, one or other of which Dutch housewives consult in all cases of great doubt and perplexity: the dominie and the doctor. In the present instance they repaired to the doctor. There was at that time a little, dark, mouldy man of medicine famous among the old wives of the Manhattoes for his skill not only in the healing art, but in all matters of strange and mysterious nature. His name was Dr. Knipperhausen, but he was more commonly known by the appellation of the High

German doctor. To him did the poor women repair for counsel and assistance touching the mental vagaries of Wolfert Webber.

They found the doctor seated in his little study, clad in his dark camblet robe of knowledge, with his black velvet cap, after the manner of Boorhaave, Van Helmont, and other medical sages: a pair of green spectacles set in black horn upon his clubbed nose, and poring over a German folio that seemed to reflect back the darkness of his physiognomy. The doctor listened to their statement of the symptoms of Wolfert's malady with profound attention; but when they came to mention his raving about buried money, the little man pricked up his ears. Alas, poor women! they little knew the aid they had called in.

Dr. Knipperhausen had been half his life engaged in seeking the short cuts to fortune, in quest of which so many a long lifetime is wasted. He had passed some years of his youth in the Harz mountains of Germany, and had derived much valuable instruction from the miners, touching the mode of seeking treasure buried in the earth. He had prosecuted his studies also under a travelling sage who united all the mysteries of medicine with magic and legerdemain. His mind, therefore, had become stored with all kinds of mystic lore: he had dabbled a little in astrology, alchemy, and divination; knew how to detect stolen money, and to tell where springs of water lay hidden; in a word, by the dark nature of his knowledge he had acquired the name of the High German doctor, which is pretty nearly equivalent to that of necromancer. The doctor had often heard rumours of treasure being buried in various parts of the island, and had long been anxious to get on the traces of it. No sooner were Wolfert's waking and sleeping vagaries confided to him, than he beheld in them the confirmed symptoms of a case of money digging, and lost no time in probing it to the bottom. Wolfert had long been sorely depressed in mind by the golden secret, and as a family physician is a kind of father confessor, he was glad of the opportunity of unburthening himself. So far from curing, the doctor caught the malady from his patient. The circumstances unfolded to him awakened all his cupidity; he had not a doubt of money being buried somewhere in the neighbourhood of the mysterious crosses, and offered to join Wolfert in the search. He informed him that much secrecy and caution must be observed in enterprises of the kind; that money is only to be digged for at night; with certain forms and ceremonies; the burning of drugs; the repeating of mystic words, and above all, that the seekers must be provided with a divining rod, which had the wonderful property of pointing to the very spot on the surface of the earth under which treasure lay hidden. As the doctor had given much of his mind to these matters, he charged himself with all the necessary preparations, and, as the quarter of the moon was propitious, he undertook to have the divining rod ready by a certain night.

Wolfert's heart leaped with joy at having met with so learned and able a coadjutor. Every thing went on secretly, but swimmingly. The doctor had many consultations with his patient, and the good women of the household lauded the comforting effect of his visits. In the mean time, the wonderful divining rod, that great key to nature's secrets, was duly prepared. The doctor had thumbed over all his books of knowledge for the occasion; and Mud Sam was engaged to take them in his skiff to the scene of enterprise; to work with spade and pickaxe in unearthing the treasure; and to freight his bark with the weighty spoils they were certain of finding.

At length the appointed night arrived for this perilous undertaking. Before Wolfert left his home he counselled his wife and daughter to go to bed, and feel no alarm if he should not return during the night. Like reasonable women, on being told not to feel alarm, they fell immediately into a panic. They saw at once by his manner that something unusual was in agitation; all their fears about the unsettled state of his mind were roused with tenfold force: they hung about him entreating him not to expose himself to the night air, but all in vain. When Wolfert was once mounted on his hobby, it was no easy matter to get him out of the saddle. It was a clear starlight night, when he issued out of the portal of the Webber palace. He wore a large napped hat tied under the chin with a handkerchief of his daughter's, to secure him from the night damp, while Dame Webber threw her long red cloak about his shoulders, and fastened it round his neck.

The doctor had been no less carefully armed and accoutred by his housekeeper, the vigilant Frau Ilsy, and sallied forth in his camblet robe by way of surtout; his black velvet cap under his cocked hat, a thick clasped book under his arm, a basket of drugs and dried herbs in one hand, and in the other the miraculous rod of divination.

The great church clock struck ten as Wolfert and the doctor passed by the church yard, and the watchman bawled in hoarse voice a long and doleful "All's well!" A deep sleep had already fallen upon this primitive little burgh; nothing disturbed this awful silence, excepting now and then the bark of some profligate night-walking dog, or the serenade of some romantic cat. It is true, Wolfert fancied more than once that he heard the sound of a stealthy footfall at a distance behind them; but it might have been merely the echo of their own steps echoing along the quiet streets. He thought also at one time that he saw a tall figure skulking after them—stopping when they stopped, and moving on as they proceeded; but the dim and uncertain lamp light threw such vague gleams and shadows, that this might all have been mere fancy.

They found the negro fisherman waiting for them, smoking his pipe in the stern of his skiff, which was moored just in front of his little cabin. A pickaxe and spade were lying in the bottom of the boat, with a dark lanthorn, and a stone jug of good Dutch courage, in which honest Sam no doubt, put even more faith than Dr. Knipperhausen in his drugs.

Thus then did these three worthies embark in their cockleshell of a skiff upon this nocturnal expedition, with a wisdom and valor equalled only by the three wise men of Gotham, who went to sea in a bowl. The tide was rising and running rapidly up the Sound. The current bore them along, almost without the aid of an oar. The profile of the town lay all in shadow. Here and there a light feebly glimmered from some sick chamber, or from the cabin window of some vessel at anchor in the stream. Not a cloud obscured the deep starry firmament, the lights of which wavered on the surface of the placid river; and a shooting meteor, streaking its pale course in the very direction they were taking, was interpreted by the doctor into a most propitious omen.

In a little while they glided by the point of Corlears' Hook with the rural inn which had been the scene of such night adventures. The family had retired to rest, and the house was dark and still. Wolfert felt a chill pass over him as they passed the point where the buccaneer had disappeared. He pointed it out to Dr. Knipperhausen. While regarding it, they thought they saw a boat actually lurking at the very place; but the shore cast such a shadow over the border of the water that they could discern nothing distinctly. They had not proceeded far when they heard the low sounds of distant oars, as if cautiously pulled. Sam plied his oars with redoubled vigor, and knowing all the eddies and currents of the stream, soon left their followers, if such they were, far astern. In a little while they stretched across Turtle Bay and Kip's Bay, then shrouded themselves in the deep shadows of the Manhattan shore, and glided swiftly along, secure from observation.

At length Sam shot his skiff into a little cove, darkly embowered by trees, and made it fast to the well known iron ring. They now landed, and lighting the lanthorn, gathered their various implements and proceeded slowly through the bushes. Every sound startled them, even that of their footsteps among the dry leaves; and the hooting of a screech owl, from the shattered chimney of father red cap's ruin, made their blood run cold.

In spite of all Wolfert's caution in taking note of the landmarks, it was some time before they could find the open place among the trees, where the treasure was supposed to be buried. At length they came to the ledge of rock; and on examining its surface by the aid of the lanthorn, Wolfert recognized the three mystic crosses. Their hearts beat quick, for the momentous trial was at hand that was to determine their hopes.

The lanthorn was now held by Wolfert Webber, while the doctor produced the divining rod. It was a forked twig, one end of which was grasped firmly in each hand, while the centre, forming the stem, pointed perpendicularly upwards. The doctor moved this wand about, within a certain distance of the earth, from place to place, but for some time without any effect, while Wolfert kept the light of the lanthorn turned full upon it, and watched it with the most breathless interest. At length the rod began slowly to turn. The doctor grasped it with greater earnestness, his hand trembling with the agitation of his mind. The wand continued slowly to turn, until at length the stem had reversed its position, and pointed perpendicularly downward; and remained pointing to one spot as fixedly as the needle to the pole.

"This is the spot!" said the doctor in an almost inaudible tone.

Wolfert's heart was in his throat.

"Shall I dig?" said Sam, grasping the spade.

"*Pots tousends,* no!" replied the little doctor, hastily. He now ordered his companions to keep close by him and to maintain the most inflexible silence. That certain precautions must be taken, and ceremonies used to prevent the evil spirits which keep about buried treasure from doing them any harm. The doctor then drew a circle round the place, enough to include the whole party. He next gathered dry twigs and leaves, and made a fire, upon which he threw certain drugs and dried herbs which he had brought in his basket. A thick smoke rose, diffusing a potent odor, savoring marvellously of brimstone and assafoetida, which, however grateful it might be to the olfactory nerves of spirits, nearly strangled poor Wolfert, and produced a fit of coughing and wheezing that made the whole grove resound. Doctor Knipperhausen then unclasped the volume which he had brought under his arm, which was printed in red and black characters in German text. While Wolfert held the lanthorn, the doctor, by the aid of his spectacles, read off several forms of conjuration in Latin and German. He then ordered Sam to seize the pick-axe and proceed to work. The close-bound soil gave obstinate signs of not having been disturbed for many a year. After having picked his way through the surface, Sam came to a bed of sand and gravel, which he threw briskly to right and left with the spade.

"Hark!" said Wolfert, who fancied he heard a trampling among the dry leaves, and a rustling through the bushes. Sam paused for a moment, and they listened.—No footstep was near. The bat flitted about them in silence; a bird roused from its nest by the light which glared up among the trees, flew circling about the flame. In the profound stillness of the woodland they could distinguish the current rippling along the rocky shore, and the distant murmuring and roaring of Hell Gate.

Sam continued his labours, and had already digged a considerable hole. The doctor stood on the edge, reading formulae every now and then from the black letter volume, or throwing more drugs and herbs upon the fire; while Wolfert bent anxiously over the pit, watching every stroke of the spade. Any one witnessing the scene thus strangely lighted up by fire, lanthorn, and the reflection of Wolfert's red mantle, might have mistaken the little doctor for some foul magician, busied in his incantations, and the grizzled-headed Sam as some swart goblin, obedient to his commands.

At length the spade of the fisherman struck upon something that sounded hollow. The sound vibrated to Wolfert's heart. He struck his spade again.

"'Tis a chest," said Sam.

"Full of gold, I'll warrant it!" cried Wolfert, clasping his hands with rapture.

Scarcely had he uttered the words when a sound from overhead caught his ear. He cast up his eyes, and lo! by the expiring light of the fire he beheld, just over the disk of the rock, what appeared to be the grim visage of the drowned buccaneer, grinning hideously down upon him.

Wolfert gave a loud cry and let fall the lanthorn. His panic communicated itself to his companions. The negro leaped out of the hole, the doctor dropped his book and basket and began to pray in German. All was horror and confusion. The fire was scattered about, the lanthorn extinguished. In their hurry skurry they ran against and confounded one another. They fancied a legion of hobgoblins let loose upon them, and that they saw by the fitful gleams of the scattered embers, strange figures in red caps gibbering and ramping around them. The doctor ran one way, Mud Sam another, and Wolfert made for the water side. As he plunged struggling onwards through bush and brake, he heard the tread of some one in pursuit. He scrambled frantically forward. The footsteps gained upon him. He felt himself grasped by his cloak, when suddenly his pursuer was attacked in turn: a fierce fight and struggle ensued—a pistol was discharged that lit up rock and bush for a period, and showed two figures grappling together—all was then darker than ever. The contest continued—the combatants clenched each other, and panted and groaned, and rolled among the rocks. There was snarling and growling as of a cur, mingled with curses in which Wolfert fancied he could recognize the voice of the buccaneer. He would fain have fled, but he was on the brink of a precipice and could go no farther.

Again the parties were on their feet; again there was a tugging and struggling, as if strength alone could decide the combat, until one was precipitated from the brow of the cliff and sent headlong into the deep stream that whirled below. Wolfert heard the plunge, and a kind of strangling bubbling murmur, but the darkness of the night hid every thing from view, and the swiftness of the current swept every thing instantly out of hearing. One of the combatants was disposed of, but whether friend or foe Wolfert could not tell, nor whether they might not both be foes. He heard the survivor approach and his terror revived. He saw, where the profile of the rocks rose against the horizon, a human form advancing. He could not be mistaken: it must be the buccaneer. Whither should he fly! a precipice was on one side; a murderer on the other. The enemy approached: he was close at hand. Wolfert attempted to let himself down the face of the cliff. His cloak caught in a thorn that grew on the edge. He was jerked from off his feet and held dangling in the air, half choked by the string with which his careful wife had fastened the garment round his neck. Wolfert thought his last moment had arrived; already had he committed his soul to

St. Nicholas, when the string broke and he tumbled down the bank, bumping from rock to rock and bush to bush, and leaving the red cloak fluttering like a bloody banner in the air.

It was a long while before Wolfert came to himself. When he opened his eyes the ruddy streaks of the morning were already shooting up the sky. He found himself lying in the bottom of a boat, grievously battered. He attempted to sit up but was too sore and stiff to move. A voice requested him in friendly accents to lie still. He turned his eyes toward the speaker: it was Dirk Waldron. He had dogged the party, at the earnest request of Dame Webber and her daughter, who, with the laudable curiosity of their sex, had pried into the secret consultations of Wolfert and the doctor. Dirk had been completely distanced in following the light skiff of the fisherman, and had just come in time to rescue the poor money-digger from his pursuer.

Thus ended this perilous enterprise. The doctor and Mud Sam severally found their way back to the Manhattoes, each having some dreadful tale of peril to relate. As to poor Wolfert, instead of returning in triumph, laden with bags of gold, he was borne home on a shutter, followed by a rabble route of curious urchins. His wife and daughter saw the dismal pageant from a distance, and alarmed the neighbourhood with their cries: they thought the poor man had suddenly settled the great debt of nature in one of his wayward moods. Finding him, however, still living, they had him conveyed speedily to bed, and a jury of old matrons of the neighbourhood assembled to determine how he should be doctored. The whole town was in a buzz with the story of the money-diggers. Many repaired to the scene of the previous night's adventures: but though they found the very place of the digging, they discovered nothing that compensated for their trouble. Some say they found the fragments of an oaken chest and an iron pot lid, which savored strongly of hidden money; and that in the old family vault there were traces of holes and boxes, but this is all very dubious.

In fact, the secret of all this story has never to this day been discovered: whether any treasure was ever actually buried at that place, whether, if so, it was carried off at night by those who had buried it; or whether it still remains there under the guardianship of gnomes and spirits until it shall be properly sought for, is all matter of conjecture. For my part I incline to the latter opinion; and make no doubt that great sums lie buried, both there and in many other parts of this island and its neighbourhood, ever since the times of the buccaneers and the Dutch colonists; and I would earnestly recommend the search after them to such of my fellow citizens as are not engaged in any other speculations.

There were many conjectures formed, also, as to who and what was the strange man of the seas who had domineered over the little fraternity at Corlears Hook for a time; disappeared so strangely, and reappeared so fearfully. Some supposed him a smuggler stationed at that place to assist his comrades in landing their goods among the rocky coves of the island. Others that he was a buccaneer; one of the ancient comrades either of Kidd or Bradish, returned to convey away treasures formerly hidden in the vicinity. The only circumstance that throws any thing like a vague light over this mysterious matter is a report that prevailed of a strange foreign built shallop, with the look of a piccaroon, having been seen hovering about the Sound for several days without landing or reporting herself, though boats were seen going to and from her at night: and that she was seen standing out of the mouth of the harbour, in the gray of the dawn after the catastrophe of the money-diggers.

I must not omit to mention another report, also, which I confess is rather apocryphal, of the buccaneer, who was supposed to have been drowned, being seen before day break, with a lanthorn in his hand, seated astride his great sea-chest and sailing through Hell Gate, which just then began to roar and bellow with redoubled fury.

While all the gossip world was thus filled with talk and rumour, poor Wolfert lay sick and sorrowful in his bed, bruised in body and sorely beaten down in mind. His wife and daughter did all they could to bind up his wounds both corporal and spiritual. The good old dame never stirred from his bedside, where she sat knitting from morning till night; while his daughter busied herself about him with the fondest care. Nor did they lack assistance from abroad. Whatever may be said of the desertions of friends in distress, they had no complaint of the kind to make. Not an old wife of the neighbourhood but abandoned her work to crowd to the mansion of Wolfert Webber, inquire after his health and the particulars of his story. Not one came, moreover, without her little pipkin of pennyroyal, sage, balm, or other herb tea, delighted at an opportunity of signalizing her kindness and her doctorship. What drenchings did not the poor Wolfert undergo, and all in vain. It was a moving sight to behold him wasting away day by day; growing thinner and thinner and ghastlier and ghastlier, and staring with rueful visage from under an old patchwork counterpane upon the jury of matrons kindly assembled to sigh and groan and look unhappy around him.

Dirk Waldron was the only being that seemed to shed a ray of sunshine into this house of mourning. He came in with cheery look and manly spirit, and tried to reanimate the expiring heart of the poor money digger, but it was all in vain. Wolfert was completely done over. If any thing was wanting to complete his despair, it was a notice served upon him in the midst of his distress, that the corporation were about to run a new street through the very centre of his cabbage garden. He saw nothing before him but poverty and ruin; his last reliance, the garden of his forefathers, was to be laid waste, and what then was to become of his poor wife and child?

His eyes filled with tears as they followed the dutiful Amy out of the room one morning. Dirk Waldron was seated beside him; Wolfert grasped his hand, pointed after his daughter, and for the first time since his illness broke the silence he had maintained.

"I am going!" said he, shaking his head feebly, "and when I am gone—my poor daughter—"

"Leave her to me, father!" said Dirk, manfully—"I'll take care of her!"

Wolfert looked up in the face of the cheery, strapping youngster, and saw there was none better able to take care of a woman.

"Enough," said he, "she is yours!—and now fetch me a lawyer—let me make my will and die."

The lawyer was brought—a dapper, bustling, round-headed little man, Roorback (or Rollebuck, as it was pronounced) by name. At the sight of him the women broke into loud lamentations, for they looked upon the signing of a will as the signing of a death warrant. Wolfert made a feeble motion for them to be silent. Poor Amy buried her face and her grief in the bed-curtain. Dame Webber resumed her knitting to hide her distress, which betrayed itself, however, in a pellucid tear, that trickled silently down and hung at the end of her peaked nose; while the cat, the only unconcerned member of the family, played with the good dame's ball of worsted, as it rolled about the floor.

Wolfert lay on his back, his nightcap drawn over his forehead; his eyes closed; his whole visage the picture of death. He begged the lawyer to be brief, for he felt his end approaching, and that he had no time to lose. The lawyer nibbed his pen, spread out his paper, and prepared to write.

"I give and bequeath," said Wolfert, faintly, "my small farm—"

"What—all!" exclaimed the lawyer.

Wolfert half opened his eyes and looked upon the lawyer.

"Yes—all" said he.

"What! all that great patch of land with cabbages and sunflowers, which the corporation is just going to run a main street through?"

"The same," said Wolfert, with a heavy sigh and sinking back upon his pillow.

"I wish him joy that inherits it!" said the little lawyer, chuckling and rubbing his hands involuntarily.

"What do you mean?" said Wolfert, again opening his eyes.

"That he'll be one of the richest men in the place!" cried little Rollebuck.

The expiring Wolfert seemed to step back from the threshold of existence: his eyes again lighted up; he raised himself in his bed, shoved back his red worsted nightcap, and stared broadly at the lawyer.

"You don't say so!" exclaimed he.

"Faith, but I do!" rejoined the other. "Why, when that great field and that piece of meadow come to be laid out in streets, and cut up into snug building lots—why, whoever owns them need not pull off his hat to the patroon!"

"Say you so?" cried Wolfert, half thrusting one leg out of bed, "why, then I think I'll not make my will yet!"

To the surprise of everybody the dying man actually recovered. The vital spark which had glimmered faintly in the socket, received fresh fuel from the oil of gladness, which the little lawyer poured into his soul. It once more burnt up into a flame.

Give physic to the heart, ye who would revive the body of a spirit-broken man! In a few days Wolfert left his room; in a few days more his table was covered with deeds, plans of streets and building lots. Little

Rollebuck was constantly with him, his right-hand man and adviser, and instead of making his will, assisted in the more agreeable task of making his fortune. In fact, Wolfert Webber was one of those worthy Dutch burghers of the Manhattoes whose fortunes have been made, in a manner, in spite of themselves; who have tenaciously held on to their hereditary acres, raising turnips and cabbages about the skirts of the city, hardly able to make both ends meet, until the corporation has cruelly driven streets through their abodes, and they have suddenly awakened out of a lethargy, and, to their astonishment, found themselves rich men.

Before many months had elapsed a great bustling street passed through the very centre of the Webber garden, just where Wolfert had dreamed of finding a treasure. His golden dream was accomplished; he did indeed find an unlooked-for source of wealth; for, when his paternal lands were distributed into building lots, and rented out to safe tenants, instead of producing a paltry crop of cabbages, they returned him an abundant crop of rents; insomuch that on quarter day, it was a goodly sight to see his tenants rapping at his door, from morning to night, each with a little round bellied bag of money, the golden produce of the soil.

The ancient mansion of his forefathers was still kept up, but instead of being a little yellow fronted Dutch house in a garden, it now stood boldly in the midst of a street, the grand house of the neighbourhood; for Wolfert enlarged it with a wing on each side, and a cupola or tea room on top, where he might climb up and smoke his pipe in hot weather; and in the course of time the whole mansion was overrun by the chubby-faced progeny of Amy Webber and Dirk Waldron.

As Wolfert waxed old and rich and corpulent, he also set up a great gingerbread coloured carriage drawn by a pair of black Flanders mares with tails that swept the ground; and to commemorate the origin of his greatness he had for a crest a fullblown cabbage painted on the pannels, with the pithy motto *Alles Kopf*: that is to say, ALL HEAD; meaning thereby that he had risen by sheer head work.

To fill the measure of his greatness, in the fullness of time the renowned Ramm Rapelye slept with his fathers, and Wolfert Webber succeeded to the leathern bottomed arm chair in the inn parlor at Corlears Hook; where he long reigned greatly honored and respected, insomuch that he was never known to tell a story without its being believed, nor to utter a joke without its being laughed at.

GUESTS FROM GIBBET ISLAND

Whoever has visited the ancient and renowned village of Communipaw may have noticed an old stone building, of most ruinous and sinister appearance. The doors and window shutters are ready to drop from their hinges; old clothes are stuffed in the broken panes of glass, while legions of half starved dogs prowl about the premises, and rush out and bark at every passer by; for your beggarly house in a village is most apt to swarm with profligate and ill conditioned dogs. What adds to the sinister appearance of this mansion is a tall frame in front, not a little resembling a gallows, and which looks as if waiting to accommodate some of the inhabitants with a well-merited airing. It is not a gallows, however, but an ancient sign post; for this dwelling, in the golden days of Communipaw, was one of the most orderly and peaceful of village taverns, where all the public affairs of Communipaw were talked and smoked over. In fact, it was in this very building that Oloffe the Dreamer, and his companions, concerted that great voyage of discovery and colonization, in which they explored Buttermilk Channel, were nearly shipwrecked in the strait of Hell Gate, and finally landed on the Island of Manhattan, and founded the great city of New Amsterdam.

Even after the province had been cruelly wrested from the sway of their High Mightinesses, by the combined forces of the British and Yankees, this tavern continued its ancient loyalty. It is true, the head of the Prince of Orange disappeared from the sign; a strange bird being painted over it, with the explanatory legend of "DIE WILDE GANS," or The Wild Goose; but this all the world knew to be a sly riddle of the landlord, the worthy Teunis Van Gieson, a knowing man in a small way, who laid his finger beside his nose and winked, when any one studied the signification of his sign, and observed that his goose was hatching, but would join the flock whenever they flew over the water; an enigma which was the perpetual recreation and delight of the loyal but fat headed burghers of Communipaw.

Under the sway of this patriotic, though discreet and quiet publican, the tavern continued to flourish in primeval tranquillity, and was the resort of all true hearted Nederlanders, from all parts of Pavonia; who met here quietly and secretly, to smoke and drink the downfall of Briton and Yankee, and success to Admiral Van Tromp.

The only drawback on the comfort of the establishment was a nephew of mine host, a sister's son, Yan Yost Vanderscamp by name, and a real scamp by nature. This unlucky whipster showed an early propensity to mischief, which he gratified in a small way, by playing tricks upon the frequenters of the Wild Goose,—putting gunpowder in their pipes, or squibs in their pockets, and astonishing them with an explosion, while they sat nodding round the fire place in the bar room; and if perchance a worthy burgher from some distant part of Pavonia lingered until dark over his potation, it was odds but that young Vanderscamp would slip a briar under his horse's tail, as he mounted, and send him clattering along the road, in neck-or-nothing style, to the infinite astonishment and discomfiture of the rider.

It may be wondered at, that mine host of the Wild Goose did not turn such a graceless varlet out of doors; but Teunis Van Gieson was an easy tempered man, and, having no child of his own, looked upon his nephew with almost parental indulgence. His patience and good nature were doomed to be tried by another inmate of his mansion. This was a cross grained curmudgeon of a negro, named Pluto, who was a kind of enigma in Communipaw. Where he came from, nobody knew. He was found one morning, after a storm, cast like a sea monster on the strand, in front of the Wild Goose, and lay there, more dead than alive. The neighbours gathered round, and speculated on this production of the deep; whether it were fish or flesh, or a compound of both, commonly yclept a merman. The kind hearted Teunis Van Gieson, seeing that he wore the human form, took him into his house, and warmed him into life. By degrees, he showed signs of intelligence, and even uttered sounds very much like language, but which no one in Communipaw could understand. Some thought him a negro just from Guinea, who had either fallen overboard, or escaped from a slave ship. Nothing, however, could ever draw from him any account of his origin. When questioned on the subject, he merely pointed to Gibbet Island, a small rocky islet, which lies in the open bay, just opposite to Communipaw, as if that were his native place, though every body knew it had never been inhabited.

In the process of time, he acquired something of the Dutch language, that is to say, he learnt all its vocabulary of oaths and maledictions, with just words sufficient to string them together. "*Donder en blicksem!*" (thunder and lightning,) was the gentlest of his ejaculations. For years he kept about the Wild Goose, more like one of those familiar spirits, or household goblins, that we read of, than like a human being. He acknowledged allegiance to no one, but performed various domestic offices, when it suited his humor; waiting occasionally on the guests; grooming the horses, cutting wood, drawing water; and all this without being ordered. Lay any command on him, and the stubborn sea urchin was sure to rebel. He was never so much at home, however, as when on the water, plying about in skiff or canoe, entirely alone, fishing, crabbing, or grabbing for oysters, and would bring home quantities for the larder of the Wild Goose, which he would throw down at the kitchen door, with a growl. No wind nor weather deterred him from launching forth on his favorite element: indeed, the wilder the weather, the more he seemed to enjoy it. If a storm was brewing, he was sure to put off from shore; and would be seen far out in the bay, his light skiff dancing like a feather on the waves, when sea and sky were all in a turmoil, and the stoutest ships were fain to lower their sails. Sometimes, on such occasions, he would be absent for days together. How he weathered the tempest, and how and where he subsisted, no one could divine, nor did any one venture to ask, for all had an almost superstitious awe of him. Some of the Communipaw oystermen declared that they had more than once seen him suddenly disappear, canoe and all, as if they plunged beneath the waves, and after a while come up again, in quite a different part of the bay; whence they concluded that he could live under water like that notable species of wild duck, commonly called the hell diver. All began to consider him in the light of a foul-weather bird, like the Mother Carey's chicken, or stormy petrel; and whenever they saw him putting far out in his skiff, in cloudy weather, made up their minds for a storm.

The only being for whom he seemed to have any liking, was Yan Yost Vanderscamp, and him he liked for his very wickedness. He in a manner took the boy under his tutelage, prompted him to all kinds of mischief, aided him in every wild, harum scarum freak, until the lad became the complete scapegrace of the village; a pest to his uncle, and to every one else. Nor were his pranks confined to the land; he soon learned to accompany old Pluto on the water. Together these worthies would cruise about the broad bay, and all the neighbouring straits and rivers; poking around in skiffs and canoes; robbing the set nets of the fishermen; landing on remote coasts, and laying waste orchards and water-melon patches; in short, carrying on a complete system of piracy, on a small scale. Piloted by Pluto, the youthful Vanderscamp soon became acquainted with all the bays, rivers, creeks, and inlets of the watery world around him; could navigate from the Hook to Spiting-devil on the darkest night, and learned to set even the terrors of Hell Gate at defiance.

At length negro and boy suddenly disappeared, and days and weeks elapsed, but without tidings of them. Some said they must have run away and gone to sea; others jocosely hinted, that old Pluto, being no other than his namesake in disguise, had spirited away the boy to the nether regions. All, however, agreed in one thing, that the village was well rid of them.

In the process of time, the good Teunis Van Gieson slept with his fathers, and the tavern remained shut up, waiting for a claimant, for the next heir was Yan Yost Vanderscamp, and he had not been heard of for years. At length, one day, a boat was seen pulling for the shore, from a long, black, rakish looking schooner, that lay at anchor in the bay. The boat's crew seemed worthy of the craft from which they debarked. Never had such a set of noisy, roistering, swaggering varlets landed in peaceful Communipaw. They were outlandish in garb and demeanor, and were headed by a rough, burly, bully ruffian, with fiery whiskers, a copper nose, a scar across his face, and a great Flaunderish beaver slouched on one side of his head, in whom, to their dismay, the quiet inhabitants were made to recognize their early pest, Yan Yost Vanderscamp. The rear of this hopeful gang was brought up by old Pluto, who had lost an eye, grown grizzly headed, and looked more like a devil than ever. Vanderscamp renewed his acquaintance with the old burghers, much against their will, and in a manner not at all to their taste. He slapped them familiarly on the back, gave them an iron grip of the hand, and was hail fellow well met. According to his own account, he had been all the world over; had made money by bags full; had ships in every sea, and now meant to turn the Wild Goose into a country seat, where he and his comrades, all rich merchants from foreign parts, might enjoy themselves in the interval of their voyages.

Sure enough, in a little while there was a complete metamorphose of the Wild Goose. From being a quiet, peaceful Dutch public house, it became a most riotous, uproarious private dwelling; a complete rendezvous for boisterous men of the seas, who came here to have what they called a "blow out" on dry land, and might be seen at all hours, lounging about the door, or lolling out of the windows; swearing among themselves, and cracking rough jokes on every passer by. The house was fitted up, too, in so strange a manner: hammocks slung to the walls, instead of bedsteads; odd kinds of furniture, of foreign fashion; bamboo couches, Spanish chairs; pistols, cutlasses, and blunderbusses, suspended on every peg; silver crucifixes on the mantel-pieces, silver candle-sticks and porringers on the tables, contrasting oddly with the pewter and Delf ware of the original establishment. And then the strange amusements of these sea-monsters! Pitching Spanish dollars, instead of quoits; firing blunderbusses out of the window; shooting at a mark, or at any unhappy dog, or cat, or pig, or barn-door fowl, that might happen to come within reach.

The only being who seemed to relish their rough waggery, was old Pluto; and yet he led but a dog's life of it; for they practised all kinds of manual jokes upon him; kicked him about like a foot ball; shook him by his grizzly mop of wool, and never spoke to him without coupling a curse by way of adjective to his name, and consigning him to the infernal regions. The old fellow, however, seemed to like them the better, the more they cursed him, though his utmost expression of pleasure never amounted to more than the growl of a petted bear, when his ears are rubbed.

Old Pluto was the ministering spirit at the orgies of the Wild Goose; and such orgies as took place there! Such drinking, singing, whooping, swearing; with an occasional interlude of quarrelling and fighting. The noisier grew the revel, the more old Pluto plied the potations, until the guests would become frantic in their merriment, smashing every thing to pieces, and throwing the house out of the windows. Sometimes, after a drinking bout, they sallied forth and scoured the village, to the dismay of the worthy burghers, who gathered their women within doors, and would have shut up the house. Vanderscamp, however, was not to be rebuffed. He insisted on renewing acquaintance with his old neighbours, and on introducing his friends, the merchants, to their families; swore he was on the look-out for a wife, and meant, before he stopped, to find husbands for all their daughters. So, will-ye, nill-ye, sociable he was; swaggered about their best parlors, with his hat on one side of his head; sat on the good wife's nicely-waxed mahogany table, kicking his heels against the carved and polished legs; kissed and tousled the young *vrows*; and, if they frowned and pouted, gave them a gold rosary, or a sparkling cross, to put them in good humor again.

Sometimes nothing would satisfy him, but he must have some of his old neighbours to dinner at the Wild Goose. There was no refusing him, for he had got the complete upper hand of the community, and the peaceful burghers all stood in awe of him. But what a time would the quiet, worthy men have, among these rake-hells, who would delight to astound them with the most extravagant gunpowder tales, embroidered with all kinds of foreign oaths; clink the can with them; pledge them in deep potations; bawl drinking songs in their ears; and occasionally fire pistols over their heads, or under the table, and then laugh in their faces, and ask them how they liked the smell of gunpowder.

Thus was the little village of Communipaw for a time like the unfortunate wight possessed with devils; until Vanderscamp and his brother merchants would sail on another trading voyage, when the Wild Goose would be shut up, and every thing relapse into quiet, only to be disturbed by his next visitation.

The mystery of all these proceedings gradually dawned upon the tardy intellects of Communipaw. These were the times of the notorious Captain Kidd, when the American harbors were the resorts of piratical adventurers of all kinds, who, under pretext of mercantile voyages, scoured the West Indies, made plundering descents upon the Spanish Main, visited even the remote Indian Seas, and then came to dispose of their booty, have their revels, and fit out new expeditions, in the English colonies.

Vanderscamp had served in this hopeful school, and having risen to importance among the buccaneers, had pitched upon his native village and early home, as a quiet, out of the way, unsuspected place, where he and his comrades, while anchored at New York, might have their feasts, and concert their plans, without molestation.

At length the attention of the British government was called to these piratical enterprises, that were becoming so frequent and outrageous. Vigorous measures were taken to check and punish them. Several of the most noted freebooters were caught and executed, and three of Vanderscamp's chosen comrades, the most riotous swash bucklers of the Wild Goose, were hanged in chains on Gibbet Island, in full sight of their favorite resort. As to Vanderscamp himself, he and his man Pluto again disappeared, and it was hoped by the people of Communipaw that he had fallen in some foreign brawl, or been swung on some foreign gallows.

For a time, therefore, the tranquillity of the village was restored; the worthy Dutchmen once more smoked their pipes in peace, eying, with peculiar complacency, their old pests and terrors, the pirates, dangling and drying in the sun, on Gibbet Island.

This perfect calm was doomed at length to be ruffled. The fiery persecution of the pirates gradually subsided. Justice was satisfied with the examples that had been made, and there was no more talk of Kidd, and the other heroes of like kidney. On a calm summer evening, a boat, somewhat heavily laden, was seen pulling into Communipaw. What was the surprise and disquiet of the inhabitants, to see Yan Yost Vanderscamp seated at the helm, and his man Pluto tugging at the oars! Vanderscamp, however, was apparently an altered man. He brought home with him a wife, who seemed to be a shrew, and to have the upper hand of him. He no longer was the swaggering, bully ruffian, but affected the regular merchant, and talked of retiring from business, and settling down quietly, to pass the rest of his days in his native place.

The Wild Goose mansion was again opened, but with diminished splendor, and no riot. It is true, Vanderscamp had frequent nautical visitors, and the sound of revelry was occasionally overheard in his house; but every thing seemed to be done under the rose; and old Pluto was the only servant that officiated at these orgies. The visitors, indeed, were by no means of the turbulent stamp of their predecessors; but quiet, mysterious traders, full of nods, and winks, and hieroglyphic signs, with whom, to use their cant phrase, "everything was smug." Their ships came to anchor at night in the lower bay; and, on a private signal, Vanderscamp would launch his boat, and accompanied solely by his man Pluto, would make them mysterious visits. Sometimes boats pulled in at night, in front of the Wild Goose, and various articles of merchandise were landed in the dark, and spirited away, nobody knew whither. One of the more curious of the inhabitants kept watch, and caught a glimpse of the features of some of these night visitors, by the casual glance of a lantern, and declared that he recognized more than one of the freebooting frequenters of the Wild Goose, in former times; from whence he concluded that Vanderscamp was at his old game, and that this mysterious merchandise was nothing more nor less than piratical plunder. The more charitable opinion, however, was, that Vanderscamp and his comrades, having been driven from their old line of business, by the "oppressions of government," had resorted to smuggling to make both ends meet.

Be that as it may: I come now to the extraordinary fact, which is the butt-end of this story. It happened late one night, that Yan Yost Vanderscamp was returning across the broad bay, in his light skiff, rowed by his man Pluto. He had been carousing on board of a vessel, newly arrived, and was somewhat obfuscated in intellect, by the liquor he had imbibed. It was a still, sultry night; a heavy mass of lurid clouds was rising in the west, with the low muttering of distant thunder. Vanderscamp called on Pluto to pull lustily, that they might get home before the gathering storm. The old negro made no reply, but shaped his course so as to skirt the rocky shores of Gibbet Island. A faint creaking overhead caused Vanderscamp to cast up his eyes, when, to his horror, he beheld the bodies of his three pot companions and brothers in iniquity dangling in the moonlight, their rags fluttering, and their chains creaking, as they were slowly swung backward and forward by the rising breeze.

"What do you mean, you blockhead!" cried Vanderscamp, "by pulling so close to the island?"

"I thought you'd be glad to see your old friends once more," growled the negro; "you were never afraid of a living man, what do you fear from the dead?"

"Who's afraid?" hiccupped Vanderscamp, partly heated by liquor, partly nettled by the jeer of the negro; "who's afraid! Hang me, but I would be glad to see them once more, alive or dead, at the Wild Goose. Come, my lads in the wind!" continued he, taking a draught, and flourishing the bottle above his head, "here's fair weather to you in the other world; and if you should be walking the rounds tonight, odds fish! but I'll be happy if you will drop in to supper."

A dismal creaking was the only reply. The wind blew loud and shrill, and as it whistled round the gallows, and among the bones, sounded as if there were laughing and gibbering in the air. Old Pluto chuckled to himself, and now pulled for home. The storm burst over the voyagers, while they were yet far from shore. The rain fell in torrents, the thunder crashed and pealed, and the lightning kept up an incessant blaze. It was stark midnight, before they landed at Communipaw.

Dripping and shivering, Vanderscamp crawled homeward. He was completely sobered by the storm; the water soaked from without, having diluted and cooled the liquor within. Arrived at the Wild Goose, he knocked timidly and dubiously at the door, for he dreaded the reception he was to experience from his wife. He had reason to do so. She met him at the threshold, in a precious ill humour.

"Is this a time," said she, "to keep people out of their beds, and to bring home company, to turn the house upside down?"

"Company?" said Vanderscamp, meekly; "I have brought no company with me, wife."

"No, indeed! they have got here before you, but by your invitation; and blessed looking company they are, truly!"

Vanderscamp's knees smote together. "For the love of heaven, where are they, wife?"

"Where?—why, in the blue-room, up stairs, making themselves as much at home as if the house were their own."

Vanderscamp made a desperate effort, scrambled up to the room, and threw open the door. Sure enough, there at a table, on which burned a light as blue as brimstone, sat the three guests from Gibbet Island, with halters round their necks, and bobbing their cups together, as if they were hob or nobbing, and trolling the old Dutch freebooter's glee, since translated into English:

> "For three merry lads be we,
>   And three merry lads be we;
>   I on the land, and thou on the sand,
>   And Jack on the gallows tree."

Vanderscamp saw and heard no more. Starting back with horror, he missed his footing on the landing place, and fell from the top of the stairs to the bottom. He was taken up speechless, and, either from the fall or the fright, was buried in the yard of the little Dutch church at Bergen, on the following Sunday.

From that day forward, the fate of the Wild Goose was sealed. It was pronounced a *haunted house*, and avoided accordingly. No one inhabited it but Vanderscamp's shrew of a widow, and old Pluto, and they were considered but little better than its hobgoblin visitors. Pluto grew more and more haggard and morose, and looked more like an imp of darkness than a human being. He spoke to no one, but went about muttering to himself; or, as some hinted, talking with the devil, who, though unseen, was ever at his elbow. Now and then he was seen pulling about the bay alone, in his skiff, in dark weather, or at the approach of night-fall; nobody could tell why, unless on an errand to invite more guests from the gallows. Indeed it was affirmed that the Wild Goose still continued to be a house of entertainment for such guests, and that on stormy nights, the blue chamber was occasionally illuminated, and sounds of diabolical merriment were overheard, mingling with the howling of the tempest. Some treated these as idle stories, until on one such night, it was about the time of the equinox, there was a horrible uproar in the Wild Goose, that could not be mistaken. It was not so much the sound of revelry, however, as strife, with two or three piercing shrieks, that pervaded every part of the village. Nevertheless, no one thought of hastening to the spot. On the contrary, the honest burghers of Communipaw drew their night caps over their ears, and buried their heads under the bed-clothes, at the thoughts of Vanderscamp and his gallows companions.

The next morning, some of the bolder and more curious undertook to reconnoitre. All was quiet and lifeless at the Wild Goose. The door yawned wide open, and had evidently been open all night, for the storm had beaten into the house. Gathering more courage from the silence and apparent desertion, they gradually ventured over the threshold. The house had indeed the air of having been possessed by devils. Every thing was topsy-turvy; trunks had been broken open, and chests of drawers and corner cupboards turned inside out, as in a time of general sack and pillage; but the most woful sight was the widow of Yan Yost Vanderscamp, extended a corpse on the floor of the blue-chamber, with the marks of a deadly gripe on the wind pipe.

All now was conjecture and dismay at Communipaw; and the disappearance of old Pluto, who was no where to be found, gave rise to all kinds of wild surmises. Some suggested that the negro had betrayed the house to some of Vanderscamp's buccaneering associates, and that they had decamped together with the booty; others surmised that the negro was nothing more nor less than a devil incarnate, who had now accomplished his ends, and made off with his dues.

Events, however, vindicated the negro from this last imputation. His skiff was picked up, drifting about the bay, bottom upward, as if wrecked in a tempest; and his body was found, shortly afterward, by some Communipaw fishermen, stranded among the rocks of Gibbet Island, near the foot of the pirates' gallows. The fishermen shook their heads, and observed that old Pluto had ventured once too often to invite Guests from Gibbet Island.

LEGEND OF THE TWO DISCREET STATUES

There lived once in a waste apartment of the Alhambra, a merry little fellow, named Lope Sanchez, who worked in the gardens, and was as brisk and blithe as a grasshopper, singing all day long. He was the life and soul of the fortress; when his work was over, he would sit on one of the stone benches of the esplanade, strum his guitar, and sing long ditties about the Cid, and Bernardo del Carpio, and Fernando del Pulgar, and other Spanish heroes, for the amusement of the old soldiers of the fortress, or would strike up a merrier tune, and set the girls dancing boleros and fandangos.

Like most little men, Lope Sanchez had a strapping buxom dame for a wife, who could almost have put him in her pocket; but he lacked the usual poor man's lot—instead of ten children he had but one. This was a little black eyed girl about twelve years of age, named Sanchica, who was as merry as himself, and the delight of his heart. She played about him as he worked in the gardens, danced to his guitar as he sat in the shade, and ran as wild as a young fawn about the groves and alleys and ruined halls of the Alhambra.

It was now the eve of the blessed St. John, and the holiday-loving gossips of the Alhambra, men, women, and children, went up at night to the mountain of the sun, which rises above the Generalife, to keep their midsummer vigil on its level summit. It was a bright moonlight night, and all the mountains were gray and silvery, and the city, with its domes and spires, lay in shadows below, and the Vega was like a fairy land, with haunted streams gleaming among its dusky groves. On the highest part of the mountain they lit up a bonfire, according to an old custom of the country handed down from the Moors. The inhabitants of the surrounding country were keeping a similar vigil, and bonfires, here and there in the Vega, and along the folds of the mountains, blazed up palely in the moonlight.

The evening was gaily passed in dancing to the guitar of Lope Sanchez, who was never so joyous as when on a holiday revel of the kind. While the dance was going on, the little Sanchica with some of her playmates sported among the ruins of an old Moorish fort that crowns the mountain, when, in gathering pebbles in the fosse, she found a small hand curiously carved of jet, the fingers closed, and the thumb firmly clasped upon them. Overjoyed with her good fortune, she ran to her mother with her prize. It immediately became a subject of sage speculation, and was eyed by some with superstitious distrust. "Throw it away," said one; "it's Moorish—depend upon it, there's mischief and witchcraft in it." "By no means," said another; "you may sell it for something to the jewellers of the Zacatin." In the midst of this discussion an old tawny soldier drew near, who had served in Africa, and was as swarthy as a Moor. He examined the hand with a knowing look. "I have seen things of this kind," said he, "among the Moors of Barbary. It is a great virtue to guard against the evil eye, and all kinds of spells and enchantments. I give you joy, friend Lope, this bodes good luck to your child."

Upon hearing this, the wife of Lope Sanchez tied the little hand of jet to a riband, and hung it round the neck of her daughter.

The sight of this talisman called up all the favourite superstitions about the Moors. The dance was neglected, and they sat in groups on the ground, telling old legendary tales handed down from their ancestors. Some of their stories turned upon the wonders of the very mountain upon which they were seated, which is a famous hobgoblin region. One ancient crone gave a long account of the subterranean palace in the bowels of that mountain where Boabdil and all his Moslem court are said to remain enchanted. "Among yonder ruins," said she, pointing to some crumbling walls and mounds of earth on a distant part of the mountain, "there is a deep black pit that goes down, down into the very heart of the mountain. For all the money in Granada I would not look down into it. Once upon a time a poor man of the Alhambra, who tended goats upon this mountain, scrambled down into that pit after a kid that had fallen in. He came out again all wild and staring, and told such things of what he had seen, that every one thought his brain was turned. He raved for a day or two about the hobgoblin Moors that had pursued him in the cavern, and could hardly be persuaded to drive his goats up again to the mountain. He did so at last, but, poor man, he never came down again. The neighbours found his goats browsing about the Moorish ruins, and his hat and mantle lying near the mouth of the pit, but he was never more heard of."

The little Sanchica listened with breathless attention to this story. She was of a curious nature, and felt immediately a great hankering to peep into this dangerous pit. Stealing away from her companions she sought the distant ruins, and after groping for some time among them came to a small hollow, or basin, near the brow of the mountain, where it swept steeply down into the valley of the Darro. In the centre of this basin yawned the mouth of the pit. Sanchica ventured to the verge, and peeped in. All was as black as pitch, and gave an idea of immeasurable depth. Her blood ran cold; she drew back, then peeped in again, then would have run away, then took another peep—the very horror of the thing was delightful to her. At length she rolled a large stone, and pushed it over the brink. For some time it fell in silence; then struck some rocky projection with a violent crash, then rebounded from side to side, rumbling and tumbling, with a noise like thunder, then made a final splash into water, far, far below—and all was again silent.

The silence, however, did not long continue. It seemed as if something had been awakened within this dreary abyss. A murmuring sound gradually rose out of the pit like the hum and buzz of a beehive. It grew louder and louder; there was the confusion of voices as of a distant multitude, together with the faint din of arms, clash of cymbals and clangor of trumpets, as if some army were marshalling for battle in the very bowels of the mountain.

The child drew off with silent awe, and hastened back to the place where she had left her parents and their companions. All were gone. The bonfire was expiring, and its last wreath of smoke curling up in the moonshine. The distant fires that had blazed along the mountains and in the Vega were all extinguished, and every thing seemed to have sunk to repose. Sanchica called her parents and some of her companions by name, but received no reply. She ran down the side of the mountain, and by the gardens of the Generalife, until she arrived in the alley of trees leading to the Alhambra, when she seated herself on a bench of a woody recess to recover breath. The bell from the watch tower of the Alhambra tolled midnight. There was a deep tranquillity as if all nature slept, excepting the low tinkling sound of an unseen stream that ran under the covert of the bushes. The breathing sweetness of the atmosphere was lulling her to sleep, when her eye was caught by something glittering at a distance, and to her surprise she beheld a long cavalcade of Moorish warriors pouring down the mountain side and along the leafy avenues. Some were armed with lances and shields, others with scimitars and battle axes, and with polished cuirasses that flashed in the moonbeams. Their horses pranced proudly and champed upon their bits, but their tramp caused no more sound than if they had been shod with felt, and the riders were all as pale as death. Among them rode a beautiful lady, with a crowned head and long golden locks entwined with pearls. The housings of her palfrey were of crimson velvet embroidered with gold, and swept the earth; but she rode all disconsolate, with eyes ever fixed upon the ground.

Then succeeded a train of courtiers magnificently arrayed in robes and turbans of divers colours, and amidst them, on a cream coloured charger, rode King Boabdil el Chico, in a royal mantle covered with jewels, and a crown sparkling with diamonds. The little Sanchica knew him by his yellow beard, and his resemblance to his portrait, which she had often seen in the picture gallery of the Generalife. She gazed in wonder and admiration at this royal pageant, as it passed glistening among the trees; but though she knew these monarchs and courtiers and warriors, so pale and silent, were out of the common course of nature, and things of magic and enchantment, yet she looked on with a bold heart, such courage did she derive from the mystic talisman of the hand, which was suspended about her neck.

The cavalcade having passed by, she rose and followed. It continued on to the great Gate of Justice, which stood wide open; the old invalid sentinels on duty lay on the stone benches of the barbican, buried in profound and apparently charmed sleep, and the phantom pageant swept noiselessly by them with flaunting banner and triumphant state. Sanchica would have followed; but to her surprise she beheld an opening in the earth, within the barbican, leading down beneath the foundations of the tower. She entered for a little distance, and was encouraged to proceed by finding steps rudely hewn in the rock, and a vaulted passage here and there lit up by a silver lamp, which, while it gave light, diffused likewise a grateful fragrance. Venturing on, she came at last to a great hall, wrought out of the heart of the mountain, magnificently furnished in the Moorish style, and lighted up by silver and crystal lamps. Here, on an ottoman, sat an old man in Moorish dress, with a long white beard, nodding and dozing, with a staff in his hand, which seemed ever to be slipping from his grasp; while at a little distance sat a beautiful lady, in ancient Spanish dress, with a coronet all sparkling with diamonds, and her hair entwined with pearls, who was softly playing on a silver lyre. The little Sanchica now recollected a story she had heard among the old people of the Alhambra, concerning a Gothic princess confined in the centre of the mountain by an old Arabian magician, whom she kept bound up in magic sleep by the power of music.

The lady paused with surprise at seeing a mortal in that enchanted hall. "Is it the eve of the blessed St. John?" said she.

"It is," replied Sanchica.

"Then for one night the magic charm is suspended. Come hither, child, and fear not. I am a Christian like thyself, though bound here by enchantment. Touch my fetters with the talisman that hangs about thy neck, and for this night I shall be free."

So saying, she opened her robes and displayed a broad golden band round her waist, and a golden chain that fastened her to the ground. The child hesitated not to apply the little hand of jet to the golden band, and immediately the chain fell to the earth. At the sound the old man woke and began to rub his eyes; but the lady ran her fingers over the chords of the lyre, and again he fell into a slumber and began to nod, and his staff to falter in his hand. "Now," said the lady, "touch his staff with the talismanic hand of jet." The child did so, and it fell from his grasp, and he sank in a deep sleep on the ottoman. The lady gently laid the silver lyre on the ottoman, leaning it against the head of the sleeping magician; then touching the chords until they vibrated in his ear—"O potent spirit of harmony," said she, "continue thus to hold his senses in thraldom till the return of day. Now follow me, my child," continued she, "and thou shalt behold the Alhambra as it was in the days of its glory, for thou hast a magic talisman that reveals all enchantments." Sanchica followed the lady in silence. They passed up through the entrance of the cavern into the barbican of the Gate of Justice, and thence to the Plaza de los Algibes, or esplanade within the fortress. This was all filled with Moorish soldiery, horse and foot, marshalled in squadrons, with banners displayed. There were royal guards also at the portal, and rows of African blacks with drawn cimeters. No one spoke a word, and Sanchica passed on fearlessly after her conductor. Her astonishment increased on entering the royal palace, in which she had been reared. The broad moonshine lit up all the halls and courts and gardens almost as brightly as if it were day, but revealed a far different scene from that to which she was accustomed. The walls of the apartments were no longer stained and rent by time. Instead of cobwebs, they were now hung with rich silks of Damascus, and the gildings and arabesque paintings were restored to their original brilliancy and freshness. The halls, no longer naked and unfurnished, were set out with divans and ottomans of the rarest stuffs, embroidered with pearls and studded with precious gems, and all the fountains in the courts and gardens were playing.

The kitchens were again in full operation; cooks were busy preparing shadowy dishes, and roasting and boiling the phantoms of pullets and partridges; servants were hurrying to and fro with silver dishes heaped up with dainties, and arranging a delicious banquet. The Court of Lions was thronged with guards, and courtiers, and alfaquis, as in the old times of the Moors; and at the upper end, in the saloon of judgment, sat Boabdil on his throne, surrounded by his court, and swaying a shadowy sceptre for the night. Notwithstanding all this throng and seeming bustle, not a voice nor a footstep was to be heard; nothing interrupted the midnight silence but the splashing of the fountains. The little Sanchica followed her conductress in mute amazement about the palace, until they came to a portal opening to the vaulted passages beneath the great Tower of Comares. On each side of the portal sat the figure of a nymph, wrought out of alabaster. Their heads were turned aside, and their regards fixed upon the same spot within the vault. The enchanted lady paused, and beckoned the child to her.

"Here," said she, "is a great secret, which I will reveal to thee in reward for thy faith and courage. These discreet statues watch over a treasure hidden in old times by a Moorish king. Tell thy father to search the spot on which their eyes are fixed, and he will find what will make him richer than any man in Granada. Thy innocent hands alone, however, gifted as thou art also with the talisman, can remove the treasure. Bid thy father use it discreetly, and devote a part of it to the performance of daily masses for my deliverance from this unholy enchantment."

When the lady had spoken these words, she led the child onward to the little garden of Lindaraxa, which is hard by the vault of the statues. The moon trembled upon the waters of the solitary fountain in the centre of the garden, and shed a tender light upon the orange and citron trees. The beautiful lady plucked a branch of myrtle and wreathed it round the head of the child. "Let this be a memento," said she, "of what I have revealed to thee, and a testimonial of its truth. My hour is come; I must return to the enchanted hall; follow me not, lest evil befal thee—farewell. Remember what I have said, and have masses performed for my deliverance." So saying, the lady entered a dark passage leading beneath the Tower of Comares, and was no longer seen.

The faint crowing of a cock was now heard from the cottages below the Alhambra, in the valley of the Darro, and a pale streak of light began to appear above the eastern mountains. A slight wind arose, there was a sound like the rustling of dry leaves through the courts and corridors, and door after door shut to with a jarring sound.

Sanchica returned to the scenes she had so lately beheld thronged with the shadowy multitude, but Boabdil and his phantom court were gone. The moon shone into empty halls and galleries stripped of their transient splendor, stained and dilapidated by time, and hung with cobwebs. The bat flitted about in the uncertain light, and the frog croaked from the fish pond.

Sanchica now made the best of her way to a remote staircase that led up to the humble apartment occupied by her family. The door as usual was open, for Lope Sanchez was too poor to need bolt or bar; she crept quietly to her pallet, and, putting the myrtle wreath beneath her pillow, soon fell asleep.

In the morning she related all that had befallen her to her father. Lope Sanchez, however, treated the whole as a mere dream, and laughed at the child for her credulity. He went forth to his customary labours in the garden, but had not been there long when his little daughter came running to him almost breathless. "Father! father!" cried she, "behold the myrtle wreath which the Moorish lady bound round my head."

Lope Sanchez gazed with astonishment, for the stalk of the myrtle was of pure gold, and every leaf was a sparkling emerald! Being not much accustomed to precious stones, he was ignorant of the real value of the wreath, but he saw enough to convince him that it was something more substantial than the stuff of which dreams are generally made, and that at any rate the child had dreamt to some purpose. His first care was to enjoin the most absolute secrecy upon his daughter; in this respect, however, he was secure, for she had discretion far beyond her years or sex. He then repaired to the vault, where stood the statues of the two alabaster nymphs. He remarked that their heads were turned from the portal, and that the regards of each were fixed upon the same point in the interior of the building. Lope Sanchez could not but admire this most discreet contrivance for guarding a secret. He drew a line from the eyes of the statues to the point of regard, made a private mark on the wall, and then retired.

All day, however, the mind of Lope Sanchez was distracted with a thousand cares. He could not help hovering within distant view of the two statues, and became nervous from the dread that the golden secret might be discovered. Every footstep that approached the place made him tremble. He would have given any thing could he but have turned the heads of the statues, forgetting that they had looked precisely in the same direction for some hundreds of years, without any person being the wiser.

"A plague upon them!" he would say to himself, "they'll betray all; did ever mortal hear of such a mode of guarding a secret?" Then on hearing any one advance, he would steal off, as though his very lurking near the place would awaken suspicion. Then he would return cautiously, and peep from a distance to see if every thing was secure, but the sight of the statues would again call forth his indignation. "Aye, there they stand," would he say, "always looking, and looking, and looking, just where they should not. Confound them! they are just like all their sex; if they have not tongues to tattle with, they'll be sure to do it with their eyes."

At length, to his relief, the long anxious day drew to a close. The sound of footsteps was no longer heard in the echoing halls of the Alhambra; the last stranger passed the threshold, the great portal was barred and bolted, and the bat and the frog and the hooting owl gradually resumed their nightly vocations in the deserted palace.

Lope Sanchez waited, however, until the night was far advanced before he ventured with his little daughter to the hall of the two nymphs. He found them looking as knowingly and mysteriously as ever at the secret place of deposit. "By your leaves, gentle ladies," thought Lope Sanchez, as he passed between them, "I will relieve you from this charge that must have set so heavy in your minds for the last two or three centuries." He accordingly went to work at the part of the wall which he had marked, and in a little while laid open a concealed recess, in which stood two great jars of porcelain. He attempted to draw them forth, but they were immovable, until touched by the innocent hand of his little daughter. With her aid he dislodged them from their niche, and found, to his great joy, that they were filled with pieces of Moorish gold, mingled with jewels and precious stones. Before daylight he managed to convey them to his chamber, and left the two guardian statues with their eyes still fixed on the vacant wall.

Lope Sanchez had thus on a sudden become a rich man; but riches, as usual, brought a world of cares to which he had hitherto been a stranger. How was he to convey away his wealth with safety? How was he even to enter upon the enjoyment of it without awakening suspicion? Now, too, for the first time in his life the dread of robbers entered into his mind. He looked with terror at the insecurity of his habitation, and went to work to barricade the doors and windows; yet after all his precautions he could not sleep soundly. His usual gaiety was at an end, he had no longer a joke or a song for his neighbours, and, in short, became the most miserable animal in the Alhambra. His old comrades remarked this alteration, pitied him heartily, and began to desert him; thinking he must be falling into want, and in danger of looking to them for assistance. Little did they suspect that his only calamity was riches.

The wife of Lope Sanchez shared his anxiety, but then she had ghostly comfort. We ought before this to have mentioned that Lope, being rather a light inconsiderate little man, his wife was accustomed, in all grave matters, to seek the counsel and ministry of her confessor Fray Simon, a sturdy, broad shouldered, blue bearded, bullet headed friar of the neighbouring convent of San Francisco, who was in fact the spiritual comforter of half the good wives of the neighborhood. He was moreover in great esteem among divers sisterhoods of nuns; who requited him for his ghostly services by frequent presents of those little dainties and knick-knacks manufactured in convents, such as delicate confections, sweet biscuits, and bottles of spiced cordials, found to be marvellous restoratives after fasts and vigils.

Fray Simon thrived in the exercise of his functions. His oily skin glistened in the sunshine as he toiled up the hill of the Alhambra on a sultry day. Yet notwithstanding his sleek condition, the knotted rope round his waist showed the austerity of his self discipline; the multitude doffed their caps to him as a mirror of piety, and even the dogs scented the odor of sanctity that exhaled from his garments, and howled from their kennels as he passed.

Such was Fray Simon, the spiritual counsellor of the comely wife of Lope Sanchez; and as the father confessor is the domestic confidant of women in humble life in Spain, he was soon acquainted, in great secrecy, with the story of the hidden treasure.

The friar opened his eyes and mouth and crossed himself a dozen times at the news. After a moment's pause, "Daughter of my soul!" said he, "know that thy husband has committed a double sin—a sin against both state and church! The treasure he hath thus seized upon for himself, being found in the royal domains, belongs of course to the crown; but being infidel wealth, rescued as it were from the very fangs of Satan, should be devoted to the church. Still, however, the matter may be accommodated. Bring hither thy myrtle wreath."

When the good father beheld it, his eyes twinkled more than ever with admiration of the size and beauty of the emeralds. "This," said he, "being the first fruits of this discovery, should be dedicated to pious purposes. I will hang it up as a votive offering before the image of San Francisco in our chapel, and will earnestly pray to him, this very night, that your husband be permitted to remain in quiet possession of your wealth."

The good dame was delighted to make her peace with heaven at so cheap a rate, and the friar putting the wreath under his mantle, departed with saintly steps toward his convent.

When Lope Sanchez came home, his wife told him what had passed. He was excessively provoked, for he lacked his wife's devotion, and had for some time groaned in secret at the domestic visitations of the friar. "Woman," said he, "what hast thou done? thou hast put every thing at hazard by thy tattling."

"What!" cried the good woman, "would you forbid my disburdening my conscience to my confessor?"

"No, wife! confess as many of your own sins as you please; but as to this money—digging, it is a sin of my own, and my conscience is very easy under the weight of it."

There was no use, however, in complaining; the secret was told, and, like water spilled on the sand, was not again to be gathered. Their only chance was, that the friar would be discreet.

The next day, while Lope Sanchez was abroad there was a humble knocking at the door, and Fray Simon entered with meek and demure countenance.

"Daughter," said he, "I have earnestly prayed to San Francisco, and he has heard my prayer. In the dead of the night the saint appeared to me in a dream, but with a frowning aspect. 'Why,' said he, 'dost thou pray to me to dispense with this treasure of the Gentiles, when thou seest the poverty of my chapel? Go to the house of Lope Sanchez, crave in my name a portion of the Moorish gold, to furnish two candlesticks for the main altar, and let him possess the residue in peace.' "

When the good woman heard of this vision, she crossed herself with awe, and going to the secret place where Lope had hid the treasure, she filled a great leathern purse with pieces of Moorish gold, and gave it to the friar. The pious monk bestowed upon her, in return, benedictions enough, if paid by Heaven to enrich her race to the latest posterity; then slipping the purse into the sleeve of his habit, he folded his hands upon his breast, and departed with an air of humble thankfulness.

When Lope Sanchez heard of this second donation to the church, he had well nigh lost his senses. "Unfortunate man," cried he, "what will become of me? I shall be robbed by piece-meal; I shall be ruined and brought to beggary!"

It was with the utmost difficulty that his wife could pacify him, by reminding him of the countless wealth that yet remained, and how considerate it was for San Francisco to rest contented with so small a portion.

Unluckily, Fray Simon had a number of poor relations to be provided for, not to mention some half—dozen sturdy bullet headed orphan children, and destitute foundlings that he had taken under his care. He repeated his visits, therefore, from day to day, with solicitations on behalf of Saint Dominick, Saint Andrew, Saint James, until poor Lope was driven to despair, and found that unless he got out of the reach of this holy friar, he should have to make peace offerings to every saint in the calendar. He determined, therefore, to pack up his remaining wealth, beat a secret retreat in the night, and make off to another part of the kingdom.

Full of his project, he bought a stout mule for the purpose, and tethered it in a gloomy vault underneath the Tower of the Seven Floors; the very place whence the Belludo, or goblin horse, is said to issue forth at midnight, and scour the streets of Granada, pursued by a pack of hell hounds. Lope Sanchez had little faith in the story, but availed himself of the dread occasioned by it, knowing that no one would be likely to pry into the subterranean stable of the phantom steed. He sent off his family in the course of the day with orders to wait for him at a distant village of the Vega. As the night advanced, he conveyed his treasure to the vault under the tower, and having loaded his mule, he led it forth, and cautiously descended the dusky avenue.

Honest Lope had taken his measures with the utmost secrecy, imparting them to no one but the faithful wife of his bosom. By some miraculous revelation, however, they became known to Fray Simon. The zealous friar beheld these infidel treasures on the point of slipping for ever out of his grasp, and determined to have one more dash at them for the benefit of the church and San Francisco. Accordingly, when the bells had rung for animas, and all the Alhambra was quiet, he stole out of his convent, and descending through the Gate of Justice, concealed himself among the thickets of roses and laurels that border the great avenue. Here he remained, counting the quarters of hours as they were sounded on the bell of the watch-tower, and listening to the dreary hootings of owls, and the distant barking of dogs from the gipsy caverns.

At length he heard the tramp of hoofs, and, through the gloom of the overshadowing trees, imperfectly beheld a steed descending the avenue. The sturdy friar chuckled at the idea of the knowing turn he was about to serve honest Lope.

Tucking up the skirts of his habit, and wriggling like a cat watching a mouse, he waited until his prey was directly before him, when darting forth from his leafy covert, and putting one hand on the shoulder and the other on the crupper, he made a vault that would not have disgraced the most experienced master of equitation, and alighted well-forked astride the steed. "Ah ha!" said the sturdy friar, "we shall now see who best understands the game." He had scarce uttered the words when the mule began to kick, and rear, and plunge, and then set off full speed down the hill. The friar attempted to check him, but in vain. He bounded from rock to rock, and bush to bush; the friar's habit was torn to ribbons and fluttered in the wind, his shaven poll received many a hard knock from the branches of the trees, and many a scratch from the brambles. To add to his terror and distress, he found a pack of seven hounds in full cry at his heels, and perceived, too late, that he was actually mounted upon the terrible Belludo!

Away then they went, according to the ancient phrase, "pull devil, pull friar," down the great avenue, across the Plaza Nueva, along the

Zacatin, around the Vivarrambla—never did huntsman and hound make a more furious run, or more infernal uproar. In vain did the friar invoke every saint in the calendar, and the holy Virgin into the bargain; every time he mentioned a name of the kind it was like a fresh application of the spur, and made the Belludo bound as high as a house. Through the remainder of the night was the unlucky Fray Simon carried hither and thither, and whither he would not, until every bone in his body ached, and he suffered a loss of leather too grievous to be mentioned. At length the crowing of a cock gave the signal of returning day. At the sound the goblin steed wheeled about, and galloped back for his tower. Again he scoured the Vivarrambla, the Zacatin, the Plaza Nueva, and the avenue of fountains, the seven dogs yelling, and barking, and leaping up, and snapping at the heels of the terrified friar. The first streak of day had just appeared as they reached the tower; here the goblin steed kicked up his heels, sent the friar a somerset through the air, plunged into the dark vault followed by the infernal pack, and a profound silence succeeded to the late deafening clamor.

Was ever so diabolical a trick played off upon a holy friar? A peasant going to his labors at early dawn found the unfortunate Fray Simon lying under a fig tree at the foot of the tower, but so bruised and bedevilled that he could neither speak nor move. He was conveyed with all care and tenderness to his cell, and the story went that he had been waylaid and maltreated by robbers. A day or two elapsed before he recovered the use of his limbs; he consoled himself, in the meantime, with the thoughts that though the mule with the treasure had escaped him, he had previously had some rare pickings at the infidel spoils. His first care on being able to use his limbs, was to search beneath his pallet, where he had secreted the myrtle wreath and the leathern pouches of gold extracted from the piety of Dame Sanchez. What was his dismay at finding the wreath, in effect, but a withered branch of myrtle, and the leathern pouches filled with sand and gravel!

Fray Simon, with all his chagrin, had the discretion to hold his tongue, for to betray the secret might draw on him the ridicule of the public, and the punishment of his superior: it was not until many years afterwards, on his death—bed, that he revealed to his confessor his nocturnal ride on the Belludo.

Nothing was heard of Lope Sanchez for a long time after his disappearance from the Alhambra. His memory was always cherished as that of a merry companion, though it was feared, from the care and melancholy observed in his conduct shortly before his mysterious departure, that poverty and distress had driven him to some extremity. Some years afterwards one of his old companions, an invalid soldier, being at Malaga, was knocked down and nearly run over by a coach and six. The carriage stopped; an old gentleman magnificently dressed, with a bag wig and sword, stepped out to assist the poor invalid. What was the astonishment of the latter to behold in this grand cavalier his old friend Lope Sanchez, who was actually celebrating the marriage of his daughter Sanchica with one of the first grandees in the land.

The carriage contained the bridal party. There was Dame Sanchez, now grown as round as a barrel, and dressed out with feathers and jewels, and necklaces of pearls, and necklaces of diamonds, and rings on every finger, altogether a finery of apparel that had not been seen since the days of Queen Sheba. The little Sanchica had now grown to be a woman, and for grace and beauty might have been mistaken for a duchess, if not a princess outright. The bridegroom sat beside her—rather a withered spindle shanked little man, but this only proved him to be of the true blue blood, a legitimate Spanish grandee being rarely above three cubits in stature. The match had been of the mother's making.

Riches had not spoiled the heart of honest Lope. He kept his old comrade with him for several days; feasted him like a king, took him to plays and bullfights, and at length sent him away rejoicing, with a big bag of money for himself, and another to be distributed among his ancient messmates of the Alhambra.

Lope always gave out that a rich brother had died in America and left him heir to a copper mine; but the shrewd gossips of the Alhambra insist that his wealth was all derived from his having discovered the secret guarded by the two marble nymphs of the Alhambra. It is remarked that these very discreet statues continue, even unto the present day, with their eyes fixed most significantly on the same part of the wall; which leads many to suppose there is still some hidden treasure remaining there well worthy the attention of the enterprising traveller. Though others, and particularly all female visitors, regard them with great complacency as lasting monuments of the fact that women can keep a secret.

THE GRAND PRIOR
OF MINORCA

A VERITABLE GHOST STORY

*"Keep my wits, heaven! They say spirits appear
To melancholy minds, and the graves open!"*

——*FLETCHER*

A bout the middle of the last century, while the Knights of Saint John of Jerusalem still maintained something of their ancient state and sway in the Island of Malta, a tragical event took place there, which is the groundwork of the following narrative.

It may be as well to premise, that at the time we are treating of, the order of Saint John of Jerusalem, grown excessively wealthy, had degenerated from its originally devout and warlike character. Instead of being a hardy body of "monk-knights," sworn soldiers of the cross, fighting the Paynim in the Holy Land, or scouring the Mediterranean, and scourging the Barbary coasts with their galleys, or feeding the poor, and attending upon the sick at their hospitals, they led a life of luxury and libertinism, and were to be found in the most voluptuous courts of Europe. The order, in fact, had become a mode of providing for the needy branches of the Catholic aristocracy of Europe. "A commandery," we are told, was a splendid provision for a younger brother; and men of rank, however dissolute, provided they belonged to the highest aristocracy, became Knights of Malta, just as they did bishops, or colonels of regiments, or court chamberlains. After a brief Residence at Malta, the knights passed the rest of their time in their own countries, or only made a visit now and then to the island. While there, having but little military duty to perform, they beguiled their idleness by paying attentions to the fair.

There was one circle of society, however, into which they could not obtain currency. This was composed of a few families of the old Maltese nobility, natives of the island. These families, not being permitted to enroll any of their members in the order, affected to hold no intercourse with its chevaliers; admitting none into their exclusive coteries but the Grand Master, whom they acknowledged as their sovereign, and the members of the chapter which composed his council.

To indemnify themselves for this exclusion, the chevaliers carried their gallantries into the next class of society, composed of those who held civil, administrative, and judicial situations. The ladies of this class were called *honorate*, or honorables, to distinguish them from the inferior orders; and among them were many of superior grace, beauty, and fascination.

Even in this more hospitable class, the chevaliers were not all equally favored. Those of Germany had the decided preference, owing to their fair and fresh complexions, and the kindliness of their manners: next to these came the Spanish cavaliers, on account of their profound and courteous devotion, and most discreet secrecy. Singular as it may seem, the chevaliers of France fared the worst. The Maltese ladies dreaded their volatility, and their proneness to boast of their amours, and shunned all entanglement with them. They were forced, therefore, to content themselves with conquests among females of the lower orders. They revenged themselves, after the gay French manner, by making the "honorate" the objects of all kinds of jests and mystifications; by prying into their tender affairs with the more favored chevaliers, and making them the theme of song and epigram.

About this time, a French vessel arrived at Malta, bringing out a distinguished personage of the order of Saint John of Jerusalem, the Commander de Foulquerre, who came to solicit the post of commander-in-chief of the galleys. He was descended from an old and warrior line of French nobility, his ancestors having long been seneschals of Poitou, and claiming descent from the first counts of Angouleme.

The arrival of the commander caused a little uneasiness among the peaceably inclined, for he bore the character, in the island, of being fiery, arrogant, and quarrelsome. He had already been three times at Malta, and on each visit had signalized himself by some rash and deadly affray.

As he was now thirty-five years of age, however, it was hoped that time might have taken off the fiery edge of his spirit, and that he might prove more quiet and sedate than formerly. The commander set up an establishment befitting his rank and pretensions; for he arrogated to himself an importance greater even than that of the Grand Master. His house immediately became the rallying place of all the young French chevaliers. They informed him of all the slights they had experienced or imagined, and indulged their petulant and satirical vein at the expense of the *honorate* and their admirers. The chevaliers of other nations soon found the topics and tone of conversation at the commander's irksome and offensive, and gradually ceased to visit there. The commander remained the head of a national *clique*, who looked up to him as their model. If he was not as boisterous and quarrelsome as formerly, he had become haughty and overbearing. He was fond of talking over his past affairs of punctilio and bloody duel. When walking the streets, he was generally attended by a ruffling train of young French cavaliers, who caught his own air of assumption and bravado. These he would conduct to the scenes of his deadly encounters, point out the very spot where each fatal lunge had been given, and dwell vaingloriously on every particular.

Under his tuition, the young French chevaliers began to add bluster and arrogance to their former petulance and levity; they fired up on the most trivial occasions, particularly with those who had been most successful with the fair; and would put on the most intolerable drawcansir airs. The other chevaliers conducted themselves with all possible forbearance and reserve; but they saw it would be impossible to keep on long, in this manner, without coming to an open rupture.

Among the Spanish cavaliers was one named Don Luis de Lima Vasconcellos. He was distantly related to the Grand Master; and had been enrolled at an early age among his pages, but had been rapidly promoted by him, until, at the age of twenty-six, he had been given the richest Spanish commandery in the order. He had, moreover, been fortunate with the fair, with one of whom, the most beautiful *honorata* of Malta, he had long maintained the most tender correspondence.

The character, rank, and connexions of Don Luis put him on a par with the imperious Commander de Foulquerre, and pointed him out as a leader and champion to his countrymen. The Spanish chevaliers repaired to him, therefore, in a body; represented all the grievances they had sustained, and the evils they apprehended, and urged him to use his influence with the commander and his adherents to put a stop to the growing abuses.

Don Luis was gratified by this mark of confidence and esteem on the part of his countrymen, and promised to have an interview with the Commander de Foulquerre on the subject. He resolved to conduct himself with the utmost caution and delicacy on the occasion; to represent to the commander the evil consequences which might result from the inconsiderate conduct of the young French chevaliers, and to entreat him to exert the great influence he so deservedly possessed over them, to restrain their excesses. Don Luis was aware, however, of the peril that attended any interview of the kind with this imperious and fractious man, and apprehended, however it might commence, that it would terminate in a duel. Still, it was an affair of honor, in which Castilian dignity was concerned; beside, he had a lurking disgust at the overbearing manners of De Foulquerre, and perhaps had been somewhat offended by certain intrusive attentions which he had presumed to pay to the beautiful *honorata*.

It was now Holy Week; a time too sacred for worldly feuds and passions, especially in a community under the dominion of a religious order; it was agreed, therefore, that the dangerous interview in question should not take place until after the Easter holidays. It is probable, from subsequent circumstances, that the Commander de Foulquerre had some information of this arrangement among the Spanish chevaliers, and was determined to be beforehand, and to mortify the pride of their champion, who was thus preparing to read him a lecture. He chose Good Friday for his purpose. On this sacred day, it is customary in Catholic countries to make a tour of all the churches, offering up prayers in each. In every Catholic Church, as is well known, there is a vessel of holy water near the door. In this, every one, on entering, dips his fingers, and makes therewith the sign of the cross on his forehead and breast. An office of gallantry, among the young Spaniards, is to stand near the door, dip their hands in the holy vessel, and extend them courteously and respectfully to any lady of their acquaintance who may enter; who thus receives the sacred water at second hand, on the tips of her fingers, and proceeds to cross herself, with all due decorum. The Spaniards, who are the most jealous of lovers, are impatient when this piece of devotional gallantry is proffered to the object of their affections by any other hand: on Good Friday, therefore, when a lady makes a tour of the churches, it is the usage among them for the inamorato to follow her from church to church, so as to present her the holy water at the door of each; thus testifying his own devotion, and at the same time preventing the officious services of a rival.

On the day in question, Don Luis followed the beautiful *honorata*, to whom, as has already been observed, he had long been devoted. At the very first church she visited, the Commander de Foulquerre was stationed at the portal, with several of the young French chevaliers about him. Before Don Luis could offer her the holy water, he was anticipated by the commander, who thrust himself between them, and, while he performed the gallant office to the lady, rudely turned his back upon her admirer, and trod upon his feet. The insult was enjoyed by the young Frenchmen who were present: it was too deep and grave to be forgiven by Spanish pride; and at once put an end to all Don Luis' plans of caution and forbearance. He repressed his passion for the moment, however, and waited until all the parties left the church; then, accosting the commander with an air of coolness and unconcern, he inquired after his health, and asked to what church he proposed making his second visit. "To the Magisterial Church of Saint John." Don Luis offered to conduct him thither, by the shortest route. His offer was accepted, apparently without suspicion, and they proceeded together. After walking some distance, they entered a long, narrow lane, without door or window opening upon it, called the "Strada Stretta," or narrow street. It was a street in which duels were tacitly permitted, or connived at, in Malta, and were suffered to pass as accidental encounters. Every where else they were prohibited. This restriction had been instituted to diminish the number of duels, formerly so frequent in Malta. As a farther precaution to render these encounters less fatal, it was an offence, punishable with death, for any one to enter this street armed with either poniard or pistol. It was a lonely, dismal street, just wide enough for two men to stand upon their guard, and cross their swords; few persons ever traversed it, unless with some sinister design; and on any preconcerted *duello*, the seconds posted themselves at each end, to stop all passengers, and prevent interruption.

In the present instance, the parties had scarce entered the street, when Don Luis drew his sword, and called upon the commander to defend himself.

De Foulquerre was evidently taken by surprise: he drew back, and attempted to expostulate; but Don Luis persisted in defying him to the combat.

After a second or two, he likewise drew his sword, but immediately lowered the point.

"Good Friday!" ejaculated he, shaking his head: "one word with you; it is full six years since I have been in a confessional: I am shocked at the state of my conscience; but within three days—that is to say, on Monday next—"

Don Luis would listen to nothing. Though naturally of a peaceable disposition, he had been stung to fury, and people of that character, when once incensed, are deaf to reason. He compelled the commander to put himself on his guard. The latter, though a man accustomed to brawl in battle, was singularly dismayed. Terror was visible in all his features. He placed himself with his back to the wall, and the weapons were crossed. The contest was brief and fatal. At the very first thrust, the sword of Don Luis passed through the body of his antagonist. The commander staggered to the wall, and leaned against it.

"On Good Friday!" ejaculated he again, with a failing voice, and despairing accents. "Heaven pardon you!" added he; "take my sword to Têtefoulques, and have a hundred masses performed in the chapel of the castle, for the repose of my soul!" With these words he expired.

The fury of Don Luis was at an end. He stood aghast, gazing at the bleeding body of the commander. He called to mind the prayer of the deceased for three days' respite, to make his peace with heaven; he had refused it; had sent him to the grave, with all his sins upon his head! His conscience smote him to the core; he gathered up the sword of the commander, which he had been enjoined to take to Têtefoulques, and hurried from the fatal Strada Stretta.

The duel of course made a great noise in Malta, but had no injurious effect upon the worldly fortunes of Don Luis. He made a full declaration of the whole matter, before the proper authorities; the Chapter of the Order considered it one of those casual encounters of the Strada Stretta, which were mourned over, but tolerated; the public, by whom the late commander had been generally detested, declared that he had deserved his fate. It was but three days after the event, that Don Luis was advanced to one of the highest dignities of the Order, being invested by the Grand Master with the priorship of the kingdom of Minorca.

From that time forward, however, the whole character and conduct of Don Luis underwent a change. He became a prey to a dark melancholy, which nothing could assuage. The most austere piety, the severest penances, had no effect in allaying the horror which preyed upon his mind. He was absent for a long time from Malta; having gone, it was said, on remote pilgrimages: when he returned, he was more haggard than ever. There seemed something mysterious and inexplicable in this disorder of his mind. The following is the revelation made by himself, of the horrible visions, or chimeras, by which he was haunted:

"When I had made my declaration before the Chapter," said he, "and my provocations were publicly known, I had made my peace with man; but it was not so with God, nor with my confessor, nor with my own conscience. My act was doubly criminal, from the day on which it was committed, and from my refusal to a delay of three days, for the victim of my resentment to receive the sacraments. His despairing ejaculation, 'Good Friday! Good Friday!' continually rang in my ears. 'Why did I not grant the respite!' cried I to myself; 'was it not enough to kill the body, but must I seek to kill the soul!'

"On the night of the following Friday, I started suddenly from my sleep. An unaccountable horror was upon me. I looked wildly around. It seemed as if I were not in my apartment, nor in my bed, but in the fatal Strada Stretta, lying on the pavement. I again saw the commander leaning against the wall; I again heard his dying words: 'Take my sword to Têtefoulques, and have a hundred masses performed in the chapel of the castle, for the repose of my soul!'

"On the following night, I caused one of my servants to sleep in the same room with me. I saw and heard nothing, either on that night, or any of the nights following, until the next Friday; when I had again the same vision, with this difference, that my valet seemed to be lying at some distance from me on the pavement of the Strada Stretta. The vision continued to be repeated on every Friday night, the commander always appearing in the same manner, and uttering the same words: 'Take my sword to Têtefoulques, and have a hundred masses performed in the chapel of the castle for the repose of my soul!' On questioning my servant on the subject, he stated, that on these occasions he dreamed that he was lying in a very narrow street, but he neither saw nor heard any thing of the commander.

"I knew nothing of this Têtefoulques, whither the defunct was so urgent I should carry his sword. I made inquiries, therefore, concerning it among the French chevaliers. They informed me that it was an old castle, situated about four leagues from Poitiers, in the midst of a forest. It had been built in old times, several centuries since, by Foulques Taillefer, (or Fulke Hackiron,) a redoubtable, hard-fighting Count of Angouleme, who gave it to an illegitimate son, afterward created Grand Seneschal of Poitou, which son became the pro genitor of the Foulquerres of Têtefoulques, hereditary Seneschals of Poitou. They farther informed me, that strange stories were told of this old castle, in the surrounding country, and that it contained many curious reliques. Among these, were the arms of Foulques Taillefer, together with all those of the warriors he had slain; and that it was an immemorial usage with the Foulquerres to have the weapons deposited there which they had wielded either in war or in single combat. This, then, was the reason of the dying injunction of the commander respecting his sword. I carried this weapon with me, wherever I went, but still I neglected to comply with his request.

"The visions still continued to harass me with undiminished horror. I repaired to Rome, where I confessed myself to the Grand Cardinal penitentiary, and informed him of the terrors with which I was haunted. He promised me absolution, after I should have performed certain acts of penance, the principal of which was, to execute the dying request of the commander, by carrying the sword to Têtefoulques, and having the hundred masses performed in the chapel of the castle for the repose of his soul.

"I set out for France as speedily as possible, and made no delay in my journey. On arriving at Poitiers, I found that the tidings of the death of the commander had reached there, but had caused no more affliction than among the people of Malta. Leaving my equipage in the town, I put on the garb of a pilgrim, and taking a guide, set out on foot for Têtefoulques. Indeed the roads in this part of the country were impracticable for carriages.

"I found the castle of Têtefoulques a grand but gloomy and dilapidated pile. All the gates were closed, and there reigned over the whole place an air of almost savage loneliness and desertion. I had understood that its only inhabitant were the concierge, or warder, and a kind of hermit who had charge of the chapel. After ringing for some time at the gate, I at length succeeded in bringing forth the warder, who bowed with reverence to my pilgrim's garb. I begged him to conduct me to the chapel, that being the end of my pilgrimage. We found the hermit there, chanting the funeral service; a dismal sound to one who came to perform a penance for the death of a member of the family. When he had ceased to chant, I informed him that I came to accomplish an obligation of conscience, and that I wished him to perform a hundred masses for the repose of the soul of the commander. He replied that, not being in orders, he was not authorized to perform mass, but that he would willingly undertake to see that my debt of conscience was discharged. I laid my offering on the altar, and would have placed the sword of the commander there, likewise. 'Hold!' said the hermit, with a melancholy shake of the head, 'this is no place for so deadly a weapon, that has so often been bathed in Christian blood. Take it to the armory; you will find there trophies enough of like character. It is a place into which I never enter.'

"The warder here took up the theme abandoned by the peaceful man of God. He assured me that I would see in the armory the swords of all the warrior race of Foulquerres, together with those of the enemies over whom they had triumphed. This, he observed, had been a usage kept up since the time of Mellusine, and of her husband, Geoffrey à la Grand-dent, or Geoffrey with the Great-tooth.

"I followed the gossiping warder to the armory. It was a great dusty hall, hung round with Gothic-looking portraits, of a stark line of warriors, each with his weapon, and the weapons of those he had slain in battle, hung beside his picture. The most conspicuous portrait was that of Foulques Taillefer (Fulke Hack-iron), Count of Angouleme, and founder of the castle. He was represented at full-length, armed cap-a-pie, and grasping a huge buckler, on which were emblazoned three lions passant. The figure was so striking, that it seemed ready to start from the canvas: and I observed beneath this picture, a trophy composed of many weapons, proofs of the numerous triumphs of this hard-fighting old cavalier. Beside the weapons connected with the portraits, there were swords of all shapes, sizes, and centuries, hung round the hall; with piles of armor, placed as it were in effigy.

"On each side of an immense chimney, were suspended the portraits of the first seneschal of Poitou (the illegitimate son of Foulques Taillefer) and his wife Isabella de Lusignan; the progenitors of the grim race of Foulquerres that frowned around. They had the look of being perfect likenesses; and as I gazed on them, I fancied I could trace in their antiquated features some family resemblance to their unfortunate descendant, whom I had slain! This was a dismal neighbourhood, yet the armory was the only part of the castle that had a habitable air; so I asked the warder whether he could not make a fire, and give me something for supper there, and prepare me a bed in one corner.

" 'A fire and a supper you shall have, and that cheerfully, most worthy pilgrim,' said he; 'but as to a bed, I advise you to come and sleep in my chamber.'

" 'Why so?' inquired I; 'why shall I not sleep in this hall?'

" 'I have my reasons; I will make a bed for you close to mine.'

"I made no objections, for I recollected that it was Friday, and I dreaded the return of my vision. He brought in billets of wood, kindled a fire in the great overhanging chimney, and then went forth to prepare my supper. I drew a heavy chair before the fire, and seating myself in it, gazed musingly round upon the portraits of the Foulquerres, and the antiquated armor and weapons, the mementos of many a bloody deed. As the day declined, the smoky draperies of the hall gradually became confounded with the dark ground of the paintings, and the lurid gleams from the chimney only enabled me to see visages staring at me from the gathering darkness. All this was dismal in the extreme, and somewhat appalling; perhaps it was the state of my conscience that rendered me peculiarly sensitive, and prone to fearful imaginings.

"At length the warder brought in my supper. It consisted of a dish of trout, and some crawfish taken in the fosse of the castle. He procured also a bottle of wine, which he informed me was wine of Poitou. I requested him to invite the hermit to join me in my repast; but the holy man sent back word that he allowed himself nothing but roots and herbs, cooked with water. I took my meal, therefore, alone, but prolonged it as much as possible, and sought to cheer my drooping spirits by the wine of Poitou, which I found very tolerable.

"When supper was over, I prepared for my evening devotions. I have always been very punctual in reciting my breviary; it is the prescribed and bounden duty of all chevaliers of the religious orders; and I can answer for it, is faithfully performed by those of Spain.

I accordingly drew forth from my pocket a small missal and a rosary, and told the warder he need only designate to me the way to his chamber, where I could come and rejoin him, when I had finished my prayers.

"He accordingly pointed out a winding stair-case, opening from the hall. 'You will descend this stair case,' said he, 'until you come to the fourth landing-place, where you enter a vaulted passage, terminated by an arcade, with a statue of the blessed Jeanne of France; you cannot help finding my room, the door of which I will leave open; it is the sixth door from the landing place. I advise you not to remain in this hall after midnight. Before that hour, you will hear the hermit ring the bell, in going the rounds of the corridors. Do not linger here after that signal.'

"The warder retired, and I commenced my devotions. I continued at them earnestly; pausing from time to time to put wood upon the fire. I did not dare to look much around me, for I felt myself becoming a prey to fearful fancies. The pictures appeared to become animated. If I regarded one attentively, for any length of time, it seemed to move the eyes and lips. Above all, the portraits of the Grand Seneschal and his lady, which hung on each side of the great chimney, the progenitors of the Foulquerres of Têtefoulque, regarded me, I thought, with angry and baleful eyes: I even fancied they exchanged significant glances with each other. Just then a terrible blast of wind shook all the casements, and, rushing through the hall, made a fearful rattling and clashing among the armor. To my startled fancy, it seemed something supernatural.

"At length I heard the bell of the hermit, and hastened to quit the hall. Taking a solitary light, which stood on the supper table, I descended the winding stair case; but before I had reached the vaulted passage leading to the statue of the blessed Jeanne of France, a blast of wind extinguished my taper. I hastily remounted the stairs, to light it again at the chimney; but judge of my feelings, when, on arriving at the entrance to the armory, I beheld the Seneschal and his lady, who had descended from their frames, and seated themselves on each side of the fire place!

" 'Madam, my love,' said the Seneschal, with great formality, and in antiquated phrase, 'what think you of the presumption of this Castilian, who comes to harbor himself and make wassail in this our castle, after having slain our descendant, the commander, and that without granting him time for confession?'

" 'Truly, my lord,' answered the female spectre, with no less state-liness of manner, and with great asperity of tone; 'truly, my lord, I opine that this Castilian did a grievous wrong in this encounter; and he should never be suffered to depart hence, without your throwing him the gauntlet.' I paused to hear no more, but rushed again down-stairs, to seek the chamber of the warder. It was impossible to find it in the darkness, and in the perturbation of my mind. After an hour and a half of fruitless search, and mortal horror and anxieties, I endeavored to persuade myself that the day was about to break, and listened impatiently for the crowing of the cock; for I thought if I could hear his cheerful note, I should be reassured; catching, in the disordered state of my nerves, at the popular notion that ghosts never appear after the first crowing of the cock.

"At length I rallied myself, and endeavored to shake off the vague terrors which haunted me. I tried to persuade myself that the two figures which I had seemed to see and hear, had existed only in my troubled imagination. I still had the end of the candle in my hand, and determined to make another effort to relight it, and find my way to bed; for I was ready to sink with fatigue. I accordingly sprang up the stair case, three steps at a time, stopped at the door of the armory, and peeped cautiously in. The two Gothic figures were no longer in the chimney corners, but I neglected to notice whether they had reascended to their frames. I entered, and made desperately for the fire place, but scarce had I advanced three strides, when Messire Foulques Taillefer stood before me, in the centre of the hall, armed cap-a-pie, and standing in guard, with the point of his sword silently presented to me. I would have retreated to the stair-case, but the door of it was occupied by the phantom figure of an esquire, who rudely flung a gauntlet in my face. Driven to fury, I snatched down a sword from the wall: by chance, it was that of the commander which I had placed there. I rushed upon my fantastic adversary, and seemed to pierce him through and through; but at the same time I felt as if something pierced my heart, burning like a red-hot iron. My blood inundated the hall, and I fell senseless.

"When I recovered consciousness, it was broad day, and I found myself in a small chamber, attended by the warder and the hermit. The former told me that on the previous night, he had awakened long after the midnight hour, and perceiving that I had not come to his chamber, he had furnished himself with a vase of holy water, and set out to seek me. He found me stretched senseless on the pavement of the armory, and bore me to this room. I spoke of my wound, and of the quantity of blood that I had lost. He shook his head, and knew nothing about it; and to my surprise, on examination, I found myself perfectly sound and unharmed. The wound and blood, therefore, had been all delusion. Neither the warder nor the hermit put any questions to me, but advised me to leave the castle as soon as possible. I lost no time in complying with their counsel, and felt my heart relieved from an oppressive weight, as I left the gloomy and fate bound battlements of Têtefoulques behind me.

"I arrived at Bayonne, on my way to Spain, on the following Friday. At midnight I was startled from my sleep, as I had formerly been; but it was no longer by the vision of the dying commander. It was old Foulques Taillefer who stood before me, armed cap-a-pie, and presenting the point of his sword. I made the sign of the cross, and the spectre vanished, but I received the same red hot thrust in the heart which I had felt in the armory, and I seemed to be bathed in blood. I would have called out, or have arisen from my bed and gone in quest of succor, but I could neither speak nor stir. This agony endured until the crowing of the cock, when I fell asleep again; but the next day I was ill, and in a most pitiable state. I have continued to be harassed by the same vision every Friday night; no acts of penitence and devotion have been able to relieve me from it; and it is only a lingering hope in divine mercy, that sustains me, and enables me to support so lamentable a visitation."

* * *

The Grand Prior of Minorca wasted gradually away under this constant remorse of conscience, and this horrible incubus. He died some time after having revealed the preceding particulars of his case, evidently the victim of a diseased imagination.

The above relation has been rendered, in many parts literally, from the French memoir, in which it is given as a true story: if so, it is one of those instances in which truth is more romantic than fiction.

DON JUAN: A SPECTRAL RESEARCH

"I have heard of spirits walking with aërial bodies,
and have been wondered at by others; but I must only
wonder at myself, for, if they be not mad, I'me come to
my own buriall."

SHIRLEY'S *"WITTY FAIRIE ONE"*

Everybody has heard of the fate of Don Juan, the famous libertine of Seville, who, for his sins against the fair sex and other minor peccadilloes, was hurried away to the infernal regions. His story has been illustrated in play, in pantomime, and farce, on every stage in Christendom, until at length it has been rendered the theme of the opera of operas, and embalmed to endless duration in the glorious music of Mozart. I well recollect the effect of this story upon my feelings in my boyish days, though represented in grotesque pantomime; the awe with which I contemplated the monumental statue on horseback of the murdered commander, gleaming by pale moonlight in the convent cemetery; how my heart quaked as he bowed his marble head, and accepted the impious invitation of

Don Juan; how each footfall of the statue smote upon my heart, as I heard it approach, step by step, through the echoing corridor, and beheld it enter, and advance, a moving figure of stone, to the supper-table! But then the convivial scene in the charnel house, where Don Juan returned the visit of the statue, was offered a banquet of skulls and bones, and on refusing to partake, was hurled into a yawning gulf under a tremendous shower of fire! These were accumulated horrors enough to shake the nerves of the most pantomime loving school boy. Many have supposed the story of Don Juan a mere fable. I myself thought so once; but "seeing is believing." I have since beheld the very scene where it took place, and now to indulge any doubt on the subject, would be preposterous.

I was one night perambulating the streets of Seville, in company with a Spanish friend, a curious investigator of the popular traditions and other good-for-nothing lore of the city, and who was kind enough to imagine he had met, in me, with a congenial spirit. In the course of our rambles, we were passing by a heavy dark gateway, opening into the court yard of a convent, when he laid his hand upon my arm: "Stop!" said he; " this is the convent of San Francisco; there is a story connected with it, which I am sure must be known to you. You cannot but have heard of Don Juan and the marble statue."

"Undoubtedly," replied I; "it has been familiar to me from childhood."

"Well, then, it was in the cemetery of this very convent that the events took place."

"Why, you do not mean to say that the story is founded on fact?"

"Undoubtedly it is. The circumstances of the case are said to have occurred during the reign of Alfonso XI. Don Juan was of the noble family of Tenorio, one of the most illustrious houses of Andalusia. His father, Don Diego Tenorio, was a favorite of the ting, and his family ranked among the *veintecuatros,* or magistrates, of the city. Presuming on his high descent and powerful connections, Don Juan set no bounds to his excesses; no female, high or low, was sacred from his pursuit; and he soon became the scandal of Seville. One of his most daring outrages was, to penetrate by night into the palace of Don Gonzalo de Ulloa, Commander of the Order of Calatrava, and attempt to carry off his daughter. The household was alarmed; a scuffle in the dark took place; Don Juan escaped, but the unfortunate commander was found weltering in his blood, and expired without being able to name his murderer. Suspicions attached to Don Juan; he did not stop to meet the investigations of justice and the vengeance of the powerful family of Ulloa, but fled from Seville, and took refuge with his uncle, Don Pedro Tenorio, at that time ambassador at the court of Naples. Here he remained until the agitation occasioned by the murder of Don Gonzalo had time to subside; and the scandal which the affair might cause to both the families of Ulloa and Tenorio had induced them to hush it up. Don Juan, however, continued his libertine career at Naples, until at length his excesses forfeited the protection of his uncle the ambassador, and obliged him again to flee. He had made his way back to Seville, trusting that his past misdeeds were forgotten, or rather trusting to his dare-devil spirit and the power of his family, to carry him through all difficulties.

"It was shortly after his return, and while in the height of his arrogance, that on visiting this very convent of Francisco, he beheld on a monument the equestrian statue of the murdered commander, who had been buried within the walls of this sacred edifice, where the family of Ulloa had a chapel. It was on this occasion that Don Juan, in a moment of impious levity, invited the statue to the banquet, the awful catastrophe of which has given such celebrity to his story."

"And pray how much of this story," said I, "is believed in Seville ?"

"The whole of it by the populace, with whom it has been a favorite tradition since time immemorial, and who crowd to the theatres to see it represented in dramas written long since by Tyrso de Molina, and another of our popular writers. Many in our higher ranks also, accustomed from childhood to this story, would feel somewhat indignant at hearing it treated with contempt. An attempt has been made to explain the whole, by asserting that, to put an end to the extravagances of Don Juan, and to pacify the family of Ulloa, without exposing the delinquent to the degrading penalties of justice, he was decoyed into this convent under false pretext, and either plunged into a perpetual dungeon, or privately hurried out of existence ; while the story of the statue was circulated by the monks, to account for his sudden disappearance. The populace, however, are not to be cajoled out of a ghost story by any of these plausible explanations; and the marble statue still strides the stage, and Don Juan is still plunged into the infernal regions, as an awful warning to all rake helly youngsters, in like case offending."

While my companion was relating these anecdotes, we had traversed the exterior court yard of the convent, and made our way into a great interior court, partly surrounded by cloisters and dormitories, partly by chapels, and having a large fountain in the centre. The pile had evidently once been extensive and magnificent; but it was for the greater part in ruins. By the light of the stars, and of twinkling lamps placed here and there in the chapels and corridors, I could see that many of the columns and arches were broken; the walls were rent and riven; while burnt beams and rafters showed the destructive effects of fire. The whole place had a desolate air; the night breeze rustled through grass and weeds flaunting out of the crevices of the walls, or from the shattered columns; the bat flitted about the vaulted passages, and the owl hooted from the ruined belfry. Never was any scene more completely fitted for a ghost-story.

While I was indulging in picturings of the fancy, proper to such a place, the deep chant of the monks from the convent church came swelling upon the ear. "It is the vesper service," said my companion; "follow me."

Leading the way across the court of the cloisters, and through one or two ruined passages, he reached the portal of the church, and pushing open a wicket, cut in the folding-doors, we found ourselves in the deep arched vestibule of the sacred edifice. To our left was the choir, forming one end of the church, and having a low vaulted coiling, which gave it the look of a cavern. About this were ranged the monks, seated on stools, and chanting from immense books placed on music stands, and having the notes scored in such gigantic characters as to be legible from every part of the choir. A few lights on these music stands dimly illumined the. choir, gleamed on the shaven heads of the monks, and threw their shadows on the walls. They were gross, blue-bearded, bullet-headed men, with bass voices, of deep metallic tone, that reverberated out of the cavernous choir.

To our right extended the great body of the church. It was spacious and lofty; some of the side chapels had gilded grates, and were decorated with images and paintings, representing the sufferings of our Saviour. Aloft was a great painting by Murillo, but too much in the dark to be distinguished. The gloom of the whole church was but faintly relieved by the reflected light from the choir, and the glimmering here and there of a votive lamp before the shrine of the saint.

As my eye roamed about the shadowy pile, it was struck with the dimly seen figure of a man on horseback, near a distant altar. I touched my companion, and pointed to it: "The spectre statue!" said I.

"No," replied he ; "it is the statue of the blessed St. Iago; the statue of the commander was in the cemetery of the convent, and was destroyed at the time of the conflagration. But," added he, "as I see you take a proper interest in these kind of stories, come with me to the other end of the church, where our whisperings will not disturb these holy fathers at their devotions, and I will tell you another story that has been current for some generations in our city, by which you will find that Don Juan is not the only libertine that has been the object of supernatural castigation in Seville."

I accordingly followed him with noiseless tread to the farther part of the church, where we took our seats on the steps of an altar opposite to the suspicious-looking figure on horseback, and there, in a low mysterious voice, he related to me the following narrative:—

* * *

"There was once in Seville a gay young fellow, Don Manuel de Manara by name, who, having come to a great estate by the death of his father, gave the reins to his passions, and plunged into all kinds of dissipation. Like Don Juan, whom he seemed to have taken for a model, he became famous for his enterprises among the fair sex, and was the cause of doors being barred and windows grated with more than usual strictness. All in vain. No balcony was too high for him to scale : no bolt nor bar was proof against his efforts; and his very name was a word of terror to all the jealous husbands and cautious fathers of Seville. His exploits extended to country as well as city; and in the village dependent on his castle scarce a rural beauty was safe from his arts and enterprises.

"As she was one day ranging the streets of Seville, with several of his dissolute companions, he beheld a procession, about to enter the gate of a convent. In the centre was a young female, arrayed in the dress of a bride; it was a novice, who, having accomplished her year of probation, was about to take the black veil, and consecrate herself to heaven. The companions of Don Manuel drew back, out of respect to the sacred pageant; but he pressed forward, with his usual impetuosity, to gain a near view of the novice. He almost jostled her, in passing through the portal of the church, when, on her turning round, he beheld the countenance of a beautiful village girl, who had been the object of his ardent pursuit, but who had been spirited secretly out of his reach by her relatives. She recognized him at the same moment, and fainted, but was borne within the grate of the chapel. It was supposed the agitation of the ceremony and the heat of the throng had overcome her. After some time, the curtain which hung within the grate was drawn up: there stood the novice, pale and trembling, surrounded by the abbess and the nuns. The ceremony proceeded; the crown of flowers was taken from her head, she was shorn of her silken tresses, received the black veil, and went passively through the remainder of the ceremony.

"Don Manuel de Manara, on the contrary, was roused to fury at the sight of this sacrifice. His passion, which had almost faded away in the absence of the object, now glowed with tenfold ardor, being inflamed by the difficulties placed in his way, and piqued by the measures which had been taken to defeat him. Never had the object of his pursuit appeared so lovely and desirable as when within the grate of the convent; and he swore to have her, in defiance of heaven and earth. By dint of bribing a female servant of the convent, he contrived to convey letters to her, pleading his passion in the most eloquent and seductive terms. How successful they were, is only matter of conjecture; certain it is, he undertook one night to scale the garden-wall of the convent, either to carry off the nun, or gain admission to her cell. Just as he was mounting the wall, he was suddenly plucked back, and a stranger, muffled in a cloak, stood before him.

" 'Rash man, forbear!' cried he: 'is it not enough to have violated all human ties ? Wouldst thou steal a bride from heaven!'

"The sword of Don Manuel had been drawn on the instant, and, furious at this interruption, he passed it through the body of the stranger, who fell dead at his feet. Hearing approaching footsteps, he fled the fatal spot, and mounting his horse, which was at hand, retreated to his estate in the country, at no great distance from Seville. Here he remained throughout the next day, full of horror and remorse, dreading lest he should be known as the murderer of the deceased, and fearing each moment the arrival of the officers of justice.

"The day passed, however, without molestation; and, as the evening advanced, unable any longer to endure this state of uncertainty and apprehension, he ventured back to Seville. Irresistibly his footsteps took the direction of the convent, but he paused and hovered at a distance from the scene of blood. Several persons were gathered round the place, one of whom was busy nailing something against the convent-wall. After a while they dispersed, and one passed near to Don Manuel. The latter addressed him, with hesitating voice.

" 'Señor,' said he, 'may I ask the reason of yonder throng?'

" 'A cavalier,' replied the other, 'has been murdered.'

" 'Murdered!' echoed Don Manuel; 'and can you tell me his name?'

" 'Don Manuel de Manara,' replied the stranger, and passed on.

"Don Manuel was startled at this mention of his own name, especially when applied to the murdered man. He ventured, when it was entirely deserted, to approach the fatal spot. A small cross had been nailed against the wall, as is customary in Spain, to mark the place where a murder has been committed; and just below it he read, by the twinkling light of a lamp: 'Here was murdered Don Manuel de Manara. Pray to God for his soul!'

"Still more confounded and perplexed by this inscription, he wandered about the streets until the night was far advanced, and all was still and lonely. As he entered the principal square, the light of torches suddenly broke on him, and he beheld a grand funeral procession moving across it. There was a great train of priests, and many persons of dignified appearance, in ancient Spanish dresses, attending as mourners, none of whom he knew. Accosting a servant who followed in the train, he demanded the name of the defunct.

" 'Don Manuel de Manara,' was the reply; and it went cold to his heart. He looked, and indeed beheld the armorial bearings of his family emblazoned on the funeral escutcheons. Yet not one of his family was to be seen among the mourners. The mystery was more and more incomprehensible.

"He followed the procession as it moved on to the cathedral. The bier was deposited before the high altar; the funeral service was commenced, and the grand organ began to peal through the vaulted aisles.

"Again the youth ventured to question this awful pageant. 'Father,' said he, with trembling voice, to one of the priests, 'who is this you are about to inter?'

" 'Don Manuel de Manara!' replied the priest.

" 'Father,' cried Don Manuel, impatiently, "you are deceived. This is some imposture. Know that Don Manuel de Manara is alive and well, and now stands before you. *I* am Don Manuel de Manara!"

" 'Avaunt, rash youth!' cried the priest, 'know that Don Manuel de Manara is dead!—is dead!—is dead!—and we are all souls from purgatory, his deceased relatives and ancestors, and others that have been aided by masses from his family, who are permitted to come here and pray for the repose of his soul!'

"Don Manuel cast round a fearful glance upon the assemblage in antiquated Spanish garbs, and recognized in their pale and ghastly countenances the portraits of many an ancestor that hung in the family picture gallery. He now lost all self command, rushed up to the bier, and beheld the counterpart of himself, but in the fixed and livid lineaments of death. Just at that moment the whole choir burst forth with a '*Requiescat in pace,*' that shook the vaults of the cathedral. Don Manuel sank senseless on the pavement. He was found there early the next morning by the sacristan, and conveyed to his home. When sufficiently recovered, he sent for a friar, and made a full confession of all that had happened.

" 'My son,' said the friar, 'all this is a miracle and a mystery intended for thy conversion and salvation. The corpse thou hast seen was a token that thou hadst died to sin and the world; take warning by it, and henceforth live to righteousness and heaven!'

"Don Manuel did take warning by it. Guided by the counsels of the worthy friar, he disposed of all his temporal affairs; dedicated the greater part of his wealth to pious uses, especially to the performance of masses for souls in purgatory; and finally, entering a convent, became one of the most zealous and exemplary monks in Seville."

* * *

While my companion was relating this story, my eyes wandered, from time to time, about the dusky church. Methought the burly countenances of the monks in the distant choir assumed a pallid, ghastly hue, and their deep metallic voices a sepulchral sound. By the time the story was ended, they had ended their chant; and, extinguishing their lights, glided, one by one, like shadows, through a small door in the side of the choir. A deeper gloom prevailed over the church; the figure opposite me on horseback grew more and more spectral; and I almost expected to see it bow its head.

"It is time to be off," said my companion, "unless we intend to sup with the statue."

"I have no relish for such fare nor such company," replied I; and following my companion, we groped our way through the mouldering cloisters. As we passed by the ruined cemetery, keeping up a casual conversation, by way of dispelling the loneliness of the scene, I called to mind the words of the poet:—

> "The tombs
> And monumental caves of death look cold,
> And shoot a dullness to my trembling heart!
> Give me thy hand, and let me hear thy voice;
> Nay, speak—and let me hear thy voice;
> Mine own affrights me with its echoes."

There wanted nothing but the marble statue of the commander, striding along the echoing cloisters, to complete the haunted scene.

Since that time, I never fail to attend the theatre whenever the story of Don Juan is represented, whether in pantomime or opera. In the sepulchral scene, I feel myself quite at home; and when the statue makes his appearance, I greet him as an old acquaintance. When the audience applaud, I look round upon them with a degree of compassion. "Poor souls!" I say to myself, "they think they are pleased; they think they enjoy this piece, and yet they consider the whole as a fiction! How much more would they enjoy it, if, like me, they knew it to be true—*and had seen the very place!*"

LEGEND OF THE ENGULPHED CONVENT

At the dark and melancholy period when Don Roderick the Goth and his chivalry were overthrown on the banks of the Guadalete, and all Spain was overrun by the Moors, great was the devastation of churches and convents throughout that pious kingdom. The miraculous fate of one of those holy piles is thus recorded in one of the authentic legends of those days.

On the summit of a hill, not very distant from the capital city of Toledo, stood an ancient convent and chapel, dedicated to the invocation of Saint Benedict, and inhabited by a sisterhood of Benedictine nuns. This holy asylum was confined to females of noble lineage. The younger sisters of the highest families were here given in religious marriage to their Saviour, in order that the portions of their elder sisters might be increased, and they enabled to make suitable matches on earth, or that the family wealth might go undivided to elder brothers, and the dignity of their ancient houses be protected from decay. The convent was renowned, therefore, for enshrining within its walls a sisterhood of the purest blood, the most immaculate virtue, and most resplendent beauty, of all Gothic Spain.

When the Moors overran the kingdom, there was nothing that more excited their hostility than these virgin asylums. The very sight of a convent-spire was sufficient to set their Moslem blood in a foment, and they sacked it with as fierce a zeal as though the sacking of a nunnery were a sure passport to Elysium.

Tidings of such outrages committed in various parts of the kingdom reached this noble sanctuary and filled it with dismay. The danger came nearer and nearer; the infidel hosts were spreading all over the country; Toledo itself was captured; there was no flying from the convent, and no security within its walls.

In the midst of this agitation, the alarm was given one day that a great band of Saracens were spurring across the plain. In an instant the whole convent was a scene of confusion. Some of the nuns wrung their fair hands at the windows; others waved their veils and uttered shrieks from the tops of the towers, vainly hoping to draw relief from a country over-run by the foe. The sight of these innocent doves thus fluttering about their dovecot, but increased the zealot fury of the whiskered Moors. They thundered at the portal, and at every blow the ponderous gates trembled on their hinges.

The nuns now crowded round the abbess. They had been accustomed to look up to her as all powerful, and they now implored her protection. The mother abbess looked with a rueful eye upon the treasures of beauty and vestal virtue exposed to such imminent peril. Alas! how was she to protect them from the spoiler! She had, it is true, experienced many signal interpositions of providence in her individual favor. Her early days had been passed amid the temptations of a court, where her virtue had been purified by repeated trials, from none of which had she escaped but by a miracle. But were miracles never to cease? Could she hope that the marvellous protection shown to herself would be extended to a whole sisterhood? There was no other resource. The Moors were at the threshold; a few moments more and the convent would be at their mercy. Summoning her nuns to follow her, she hurried into the chapel; and throwing herself on her knees before the image of the blessed Mary, "Oh, holy Lady!" exclaimed she, "oh, most pure and immaculate of virgins! thou seest our extremity. The ravager is at the gate, and there is none on earth to help us! Look down with pity, and grant that the earth may gape and swallow us rather than that our cloister vows should suffer violation!"

The Moors redoubled their assault upon the portal; the gates gave way, with a tremendous crash; a savage yell of exultation arose; when of a sudden the earth yawned; down sank the convent, with its cloisters, its dormitories, and all its nuns. The chapel tower was the last that sank, the bell ringing forth a peal of triumph in the very teeth of the infidels.

* * *

Forty years had passed and gone, since the period of this miracle. The subjugation of Spain was complete. The Moors lorded it over city and country; and such of the Christian population as remained, and were permitted to exercise their religion, did it in humble resignation to the Moslem sway.

At this time, a Christian cavalier, of Cordova, hearing that a patriotic band of his countrymen had raised the standard of the cross in the mountains of the Asturias, resolved to join them, and unite in breaking the yoke of bondage. Secretly arming himself, and caparisoning his steed, he set forth from Cordova, and pursued his course by unfrequented mule paths, and along the dry channels made by winter torrents. His spirit burned with indignation, whenever, on commanding a view over a long sweeping plain, he beheld the mosque swelling in the distance, and the Arab horsemen careering about, as if the rightful lords of the soil. Many a deep-drawn sigh, and heavy groan, also, did the good cavalier utter, on passing the ruins of churches and convents desolated by the conquerors.

It was on a sultry midsummer evening, that this wandering cavalier, in skirting a hill thickly covered with forest, heard the faint tones of a vesper bell sounding melodiously in the air, and seeming to come from the summit of the hill. The cavalier crossed himself with wonder, at this unwonted and Christian sound. He supposed it to proceed from one of those humble chapels and hermitages permitted to exist through the indulgence of the Moslem conquerors. Turning his steed up a narrow path of the forest, he sought this sanctuary, in hopes of finding a hospitable shelter for the night. As he advanced, the trees threw a deep gloom around him, and the bat flitted across his path. The bell ceased to toll, and all was silence.

Presently a choir of female voices came stealing sweetly through the forest, chanting the evening service, to the solemn accompaniment of an organ. The heart of the good cavalier melted at the sound, for it recalled the happier days of his country. Urging forward his weary steed, he at length arrived at a broad grassy area, on the summit of the hill, surrounded by the forest. Here the melodious voices rose in full chorus, like the swelling of the breeze; but whence they came, he could not tell. Sometimes they were before, sometimes behind him; sometimes in the air, sometimes as if from within the bosom of the earth. At length they died away, and a holy stillness settled on the place.

The cavalier gazed around with bewildered eye. There was neither chapel nor convent, nor humble hermitage, to be seen; nothing but a moss grown stone pinnacle, rising out of the centre of the area, surmounted by a cross. The greensward around appeared to have been sacred from the tread of man or beast, and the surrounding trees bent toward the cross, as if in adoration.

The cavalier felt a sensation of holy awe. He alighted and tethered his steed on the skirts of the forest, where he might crop the tender herbage; then approaching the cross, he knelt and poured forth his evening prayers before this relic of the Christian days of Spain. His orisons being concluded, he laid himself down at the foot of the pinnacle, and reclining his head against one of its stones, fell into a deep sleep.

About midnight, he was awakened by the tolling of a bell, and found himself lying before the gate of an ancient convent. A train of nuns passed by, each bearing a taper. The cavalier rose and followed them into the chapel; in the centre of which was a bier, on which lay the corpse of an aged nun. The organ performed a solemn requiem: the nuns joining in chorus. When the funeral service was finished, a melodious voice chanted, *"Requiescat in pace!"*—"May she rest in peace!" The lights immediately vanished; the whole passed away as a dream; and the cavalier found himself at the foot of the cross, and beheld, by the faint rays of the rising moon, his steed quietly grazing near him.

When the day dawned, the cavalier descended the hill, and following the course of a small brook, came to a cave, at the entrance of which was seated an ancient man, clad in hermit's garb, with rosary and cross, and a beard that descended to his girdle. He was one of those holy anchorites permitted by the Moors to live unmolested in dens and caves, and humble hermitages, and even to practise the rites of their religion. The cavalier checked his horse, and dismounting, knelt and craved a benediction. He then related all that had befallen him in the night, and besought the hermit to explain the mystery.

"What thou hast heard and seen, my son," replied the other, "is but type and shadow of the woes of Spain."

He then related the foregoing story of the miraculous deliverance of the convent.

"Forty years," added the holy man, "have elapsed since this event, yet the bells of that sacred edifice are still heard, from time to time, sounding from under ground, together with the pealing of the organ, and the chanting of the choir. The Moors avoid this neighbourhood, as haunted ground, and the whole place, asthou mayest perceive, has become covered with a thick and lonely forest."

The cavalier listened with wonder to the story of this engulphed convent, as related by the holy man. For three days and nights did they keep vigils beside the cross; but nothing more was to be seen of nun or convent. It is supposed that, forty years having elapsed, the natural lives of all the nuns were finished, and that the cavalier had beheld the obsequies of the last of the sisterhood. Certain it is, that from that time, bell, and organ, and choral chant have never more been heard.

The mouldering pinnacle, surmounted by the cross, still remains an object of pious pilgrimage. Some say that it anciently stood in front of the convent, but others assert that it was the spire of the sacred edifice, and that, when the main body of the building sank, this remained above ground, like the top-mast of some tall ship that has foundered. These pious believers maintain, that the convent is miraculously preserved entire in the centre of the mountain, where, if proper excavations were made, it would be found, with all its treasures, and monuments, and shrines, and reliques, and the tombs of its virgin nuns.

Should any one doubt the truth of this marvellous interposition of the Virgin, to protect the vestal purity of her votaries, let him read the excellent work entitled "España Triumphante," written by Padre Fray Antonio de Sancta Maria, a bare foot friar of the Carmelite order, and he will doubt no longer.

THE ENCHANTED ISLAND

Break, Phantsie, from thy cave of cloud,
And wave thy purple wings,
Now all thy figures are allowed,
And various shapes of things.
Create of airy forms a stream;
It must have blood and nought of phlegm;
And though it be a walking dream,
Yet let it like an odor rise
To all the senses here,
And fall like sleep upon their eyes,
Or music on their ear.

—*BEN JOHNSON*

"There are more things in heaven and earth than are dreamed of in our philosophy," and among these may be placed that marvel and mystery of the seas, the island of St. Brandan. Every school-boy can enumerate and call by name the Canaries, the Fortunate Islands of the ancients; which, according to some ingenious speculative minds, are mere wrecks and remnants of the vast island of Atalantis, mentioned by Plato, as having been swallowed up by the ocean. Whoever has read the history of those isles, will remember the wonders told of another island, still more beautiful, seen occasionally from their shores, stretching away in the clear bright west, with long shadowy promontories, and high, sun-gilt peaks. Numerous expeditions, both in ancient and modern days, have launched forth from the Canaries in quest of that island; but, on their approach, mountain and promontory have gradually faded away, until nothing has remained but the blue sky above, and the deep blue water below. Hence it was termed by the geographers of old, Aprositus, or the Inaccessible; while modern navigators have called its very existence in question, pronouncing it a mere optical illusion, like the Fata Morgana of the Straits of Messina; or classing it with those unsubstantial regions known to mariners as Cape Flyaway, and the Coast of Cloud Land.

Let not permit, however, the doubts of the worldly wise sceptics of modern days rob us of all the glorious realms owned by happy credulity in days of yore. Be assured, O reader of easy faith!—thou for whom I delight to labour—be assured, that such an island does actually exist, and has, from time to time, been revealed to the gaze, and trodden by the feet, of favored mortals. Nay, though doubted by historians and philosophers, its existence is fully attested by the poets, who, being an inspired race, and gifted with a kind of second sight, can see into the mysteries of nature, hidden from the eyes of ordinary mortals. To this gifted race it has ever been a region of fancy and romance, teeming with all kinds of wonders. Here once bloomed, and perhaps still blooms, the famous garden of the Hesperides, with its golden fruit. Here, too, was the enchanted garden of Armida, in which that sorceress held the Christian paladin, Rinaldo, in delicious but inglorious thraldom; as is set forth in the immortal lay of Tasso. It was on this island, also, that Sycorax, the witch, held sway, when the good Prospero, and his infant daughter Miranda, were wafted to its shores. The isle was then

—"full of noises,
Sounds, and sweet airs, that give delight, and hurt not."

Who does not know the tale, as told in the magic page of Shakspeare?

In fact, the island appears to have been, at different times, under the sway of different powers, genii of earth, and air, and ocean; who made it their shadowy abode; or rather, it is the retiring place of old worn-out deities and dynasties, that once ruled the poetic world, but are now nearly shorn of all their attributes. Here Neptune and Amphitrite hold a diminished court, like sovereigns in exile. Their ocean chariot lies bottom upward, in a cave of the island, almost a perfect wreck, while their pursy Tritons and haggard Nereids bask listlessly, like seals about the rocks. Sometimes they assume a shadow of their ancient pomp, and glide in state about the glassy sea; while the crew of some tall Indiaman, that lies becalmed with flapping sails, hear with astonishment the mellow note of the Triton's shell swelling upon the ear, as the invisible pageant sweeps by. Sometimes the quondam monarch of the ocean is permitted to make himself visible to mortal eyes, visiting the ships that cross the line, to exact a tribute from new comers; the only remnant of his ancient rule, and that, alas! performed with tattered state, and tarnished splendour.

On the shores of this wondrous island, the mighty kraken heaves his bulk, and wallows many a rood; here, too, the sea serpent lies coiled up, during the intervals of his much contested revelations to the eyes of true believers; and here it is said, even the Flying Dutchman finds a port and casts his anchor, and furls his shadowy sail, and takes a short repose from his eternal wanderings.

Here all the treasures lost in the deep are safely garnered. The caverns of the shores are piled with golden ingots, hexes of pearls, rich bales of oriental silks; and their deep recesses sparkle with diamonds, or flame with carbuncles. Here, in deep bays and harbors, lies many a spell bound ship, long given up as lost by the ruined merchant. Here, too, its crew, long bewailed as swallowed up in ocean, lie sleeping in mossy grottoes, from age to age, or wander about enchanted shores and groves, in pleasing oblivion of all things.

Such are some of the marvels related of this island, and which may serve to throw some light on the following legend, of unquestionable truth, which I recommend to the entire belief of the reader.

* * *

THE ADELANTADO OF THE SEVEN CITIES
A Legend of St. Brandan

In the early part of the fifteenth century, when Prince Henry of Portugal, of worthy memory, was pushing the career of discovery along the western coast of Africa, and the world was resounding with reports of golden regions on the main land, and new found islands in the ocean, there arrived at Lisbon an old bewildered pilot of the seas, who had been driven by tempests, he knew not whither, and who raved about an island far in the deep, on which he had landed, and which he had found peopled with Christians, and adorned with noble cities.

The inhabitants, he said, gathered round, and regarded him with surprise, having never before been visited by a ship. They told him they were descendants of a band of Christians, who fled from Spain when that country was conquered by the Moslems. They were

curious about the state of their fatherland, and grieved to hear that
the Moslems still held possession of the kingdom of Granada. They
would have taken the old navigator to church, to convince him of
their orthodoxy; but, either through lack of devotion, or lack of faith
in their words, he declined their invitation, and preferred to return
on board of his ship. He was properly punished. A furious storm
arose, drove him from his anchorage, hurried him out to sea, and he
saw no more of the unknown island.

This strange story caused great marvel in Lisbon and elsewhere.
Those versed in history, remembered to have read, in an ancient
chronicle, that, at the time of the conquest of Spain, in the eighth
century, when the blessed cross was cast down, and the crescent
erected in its place, and when Christian churches were turned into
Moslem mosques, seven bishops, at the head of seven bands of pious
exiles, had fled from the peninsula, and embarked in quest of some
ocean island, or distant land, where they might found seven Christian
cities, and enjoy their faith unmolested.

The fate of these pious saints errant had hitherto remained a
mystery, and their story had faded from memory; the report of the old
tempest tossed pilot, however, revived this long forgotten theme; and
it was determined by the pious and enthusiastic, that the island thus
accidentally discovered, was the identical place of refuge, whither the
wandering bishops had been guided by a protecting Providence, and
where they had folded their flocks.

This most excitable of worlds has always some darling object of
chimerical enterprise: the "Island of the Seven Cities" now awakened
as much interest and longing among zealous Christians, as has the
renowned city of Timbuctoo among adventurous travellers, or the
North-east Passage among hardy navigators; and it was a frequent
prayer of the devout, that these scattered and lost portions of the

Christian family might be discovered, and reunited to the great body of Christendom.

No one, however, entered into the matter with half the zeal of Don Fernando de Ulmo, a young cavalier of high standing in the Portuguese court, and of most sanguine and romantic temperament. He had recently come to his estate, and had run the round of all kinds of pleasures and excitements, when this new theme of popular talk and wonder presented itself. The Island of the Seven Cities became now the constant subject of his thoughts by day and his dreams by night; it even rivalled his passion for a beautiful girl, one of the greatest belles of Lisbon, to whom he was betrothed. At length his imagination became so inflamed on the subject, that he determined to fit out an expedition, at his own expense, and set sail in quest of this sainted island. It could not be a cruise of any great extent; for according to the calculations of the tempest-tossed pilot, it must be somewhere in the latitude of the Canaries; which at that time, when the new world was as yet undiscovered, formed the frontier of ocean enterprise. Don Fernando applied to the crown for countenance and protection. As he was a favorite at court, the usual patronage was readily extended to him; that is to say, he received a commission from the king, Don Ioam II, constituting him Adelantado, or military governor, of any country he might discover, with the single proviso, that he should bear all the expenses of the discovery and pay a tenth of the profits to the crown.

Don Fernando now set to work in the true spirit of a projector. He sold acre after acre of solid land, and invested the proceeds in ships, guns, ammunition, and sea-stores. Even his old family mansion in Lisbon was mortgaged without scruple, for he looked forward to a palace in one of the Seven Cities of which he was to be Adelantado. This was the age of nautical romance, when the thoughts of all

speculative dreamers were turned to the ocean. The scheme of Don
Fernando, therefore, drew adventurers of every kind. The merchant
promised himself new marts of opulent traffic; the soldier hoped to
sack and plunder some one or other of those Seven Cities; even the fat
monk shook off the sleep and sloth of the cloister, to join in a crusade
which promised such increase to the possessions of the church.

One person alone regarded the whole project with sovereign
contempt and growling hostility. This was Don Ramiro Alvarez,
the father of the beautiful Serafina, to whom Don Fernando was
betrothed. He was one of those perverse, matter of fact old men who
are prone to oppose every thing speculative and romantic. He had no
faith in the Island of the Seven Cities; regarded the projected cruise
as a crack brained freak; looked with angry eye and internal heart-
burning on the conduct of his intended son in law, chaffering away
solid lands for lands in the moon, and scoffingly dubbed him
Adelantado of Lubberland. In fact, he had never really relished the
intended match, to which his consent had been slowly extorted by
the tears and entreaties of his daughter. It is true he could have no
reasonable objections to the youth, for Don Fernando was the very
flower of Portuguese chivalry. No one could excel him at the tilting
match, or the riding at the ring; none was more bold and dexterous in
the bullfight; none composed more gallant madrigals in praise of his
lady's charms, or sang them with sweeter tones to the accompaniment
of her guitar; nor could any one handle the castanets and dance the
bolero with more captivating grace. All these admirable qualities and
endowments, however, though they had been sufficient to win the
heart of Serafina, were nothing in the eyes of her unreasonable father.
O Cupid, god of Love! why will fathers always be so unreasonable!

The engagement to Serafina had threatened at first to throw an
obstacle in the way of the expedition of Don Fernando, and for a

time perplexed him in the extreme. He was passionately attached to the young lady; but he was also passionately bent on this romantic enterprise. How should he reconcile the two passionate inclinations? A simple and obvious arrangement at length presented itself: marry Serafina, enjoy a portion of the honeymoon at once, and defer the rest until his return from the discovery of the Seven Cities!

He hastened to make known this most excellent arrangement to Don Ramiro, when the long smothered wrath of the old cavalier burst forth in a storm about his ears. He reproached him with being the dupe of wandering vagabonds and wild schemers, and of squandering all his real possessions in pursuit of empty bubbles. Don Fernando was too sanguine a projector, and too young a man, to listen tamely to such language. He acted with what is technically called "becoming spirit." A high quarrel ensued; Don Ramiro pronounced him a mad man, and forbade all farther intercourse with his daughter, until he should give proof of returning sanity by abandoning this mad cap enterprise; while Don Fernando flung out of the house, more bent than ever on the expedition, from the idea of triumphing over the incredulity of the grey beard when he should return successful.

Don Ramiro repaired to his daughter's chamber the moment the youth had departed. He represented to her the sanguine, unsteady character of her lover and the chimerical nature of his schemes; showed her the propriety of suspending all intercourse with him until he should recover from his present hallucination; folded her to his bosom with parental fondness, kissed the tear that stole down her cheek, and, as he left the chamber, gently locked the door; for although he was a fond father, and had a high opinion of the submissive temper of his child, he had a still higher opinion of the conservative virtues of lock and key. Whether the damsel had been in any wise shaken in her faith as to the schemes of her lover, and the existence of the Island of the Seven Cities, by the sage representations of her father, tradition does not say; but it is certain that she became a firm believer the moment she heard him turn the key in the lock.

Notwithstanding the interdict of Don Ramiro, therefore, and his shrewd precautions, the intercourse of the lovers continued, although clandestinely. Don Fernando toiled all day, hurrying forward his nautical enterprise, while at night he would repair, beneath the grated balcony of his mistress, to carry on at equal pace the no less interesting enterprise of the heart. At length the preparations for the expedition were completed. Two gallant caravels lay anchored in the Tagus, ready to sail with the morning dawn; while late at night, by the pale light of a waning moon, Don Fernando sought the stately mansion of Alvarez to take a last farewell of Serafina. The customary signal of a few low touches of a guitar brought her to the balcony. She was sad at heart and full of gloomy forebodings; but her lover strove to impart to her his own buoyant hope and youthful confidence. "A few short months," said he, "and I shall return in triumph. Thy father will then blush at his incredulity, and will once more welcome me to his house, when I cross its threshold a wealthy suitor and Adelantado of the Seven Cities."

The beautiful Serafina shook her head mournfully. It was not on those points that she felt doubt or dismay. She believed most implicitly in the Island of the Seven Cities, and trusted devoutly in the success of the enterprise; but she had heard of the inconstancy of the seas, and the inconstancy of those who roam them. Now, let the truth be spoken, Don Fernando, if he had any fault in the world, it was that he was a little too inflammable; that is to say, a little too subject to take fire from the sparkle of every bright eye: he had been somewhat of a rover among the sex on shore, what might he not be on sea? Might he not meet with other loves in foreign ports? Might he not behold some peerless beauty in one or other of those seven cities, who might efface the image of Serafina from his thoughts?

At length she ventured to hint her doubts; but Don Fernando spurned at the very idea. Never could his heart be false to Serafina! Never could another be captivating in his eyes!—never—never! Repeatedly did he bend his knee, and smite his breast, and call upon the silver moon to witness the sincerity of his vows. But might not Serafina, herself, be forgetful of her plighted faith? Might not some wealthier rival present, while he was tossing on the sea, and, backed by the authority of her father, win the treasure of her hand?

Alas, how little did he know Serafina's heart! The more her father should oppose, the more would she be fixed in her faith. Though years should pass before his return, he would find her true to her vows. Even should the salt seas swallow him up, (and her eyes streamed with salt tears at the very thought,) never would she be the wife of another—never—never! She raised her beautiful white arms between the iron bars of the balcony, and invoked the moon as a testimonial of her faith.

Thus, according to immemorial usage, the lovers parted, with many a vow of eternal constancy. But will they keep those vows? Perish the doubt! Have they not called the constant moon to witness?

With the morning dawn the caravels dropped down the Tagus and put to sea. They steered for the Canaries, in those days the regions of nautical romance. Scarcely had they reached those latitudes, when a violent tempest arose. Don Fernando soon lost sight of the accompanying caravel, and was driven out of all reckoning by the fury of the storm. For several weary days and nights he was tossed to and fro, at the mercy of the elements, expecting each moment to be swallowed up. At length, one day toward evening, the storm subsided; the clouds cleared up, as though a veil had suddenly been withdrawn from the face of heaven, and the setting sun shone gloriously upon a fair and mountainous island, that seemed close at hand. The tempest-tossed mariners rubbed their eyes, and gazed almost incredulously upon this land, that had emerged so suddenly from the murky gloom; yet there it lay, spread out in lovely landscapes; enlivened by villages, and towers, and spires, while the late stormy sea rolled in peaceful billows to its shores. About a league from the sea, on the banks of a river, stood a noble city, with lofty walls and towers, and a protecting castle. Don Fernando anchored off the mouth of the river, which appeared to form a spacious harbor. In a little while a barge was seen issuing from the river. It was evidently a barge of ceremony, for it was richly though quaintly carved and gilt, and decorated with a silken awning and fluttering streamers, while a banner, bearing the sacred emblem of the cross, floated to the breeze. The barge advanced slowly, impelled by sixteen oars, painted of a bright crimson. The oarsmen were uncouth, or rather antique, in their garb, and kept stroke to the regular cadence of an old Spanish ditty. Beneath the awning sat a cavalier, in a rich though old-fashioned doublet, with an enormous sombrero and feather.

When the barge reached the caravel, the cavalier stepped on board. He was tall and gaunt, with a long, Spanish visage, and lack-lustre eyes, and an air of lofty and somewhat pompous gravity. His mustaches were curled up to his ears, his beard was forked and precise; he wore gauntlets that reached to his elbows, and a Toledo blade that strutted out behind, while, in front, its huge basket-hilt might have served for a porringer.

Thrusting out a long spindle leg, and taking off his sombrero with a grave and stately sweep, he saluted Don Fernando by name, and welcomed him, in old Castilian language, and in the style of old Castilian courtesy.

Don Fernando was startled at hearing himself accosted by name, by an utter stranger, in a strange land. As soon as he could recover from his surprise, he inquired what land it was at which he had arrived.

"The Island of the Seven Cities!"

Could this be true? Had he indeed been thus tempest driven upon the very land of which he was in quest? It was even so. The other caravel, from which he had been separated in the storm, had made a neighbouring port of the island, and announced the tidings of this expedition, which came to restore the country to the great community of Christendom. The whole island, he was told, was given up to rejoicings on the happy event; and they only awaited his arrival to acknowledge allegiance to the crown of Portugal, and hail him as Adelantado of the Seven Cities. A grand fête was to be solemnized that very night in the palace of the Alcayde or governor of the city; who, on beholding the most opportune arrival of the caravel, had despatched his grand chamberlain, in his barge of state, to conduct the future Adelantado to the ceremony.

Don Fernando could scarcely believe but that this was all a dream. He fixed a scrutinizing gaze upon the grand chamberlain, who, having delivered his message, stood in buckram dignity, drawn up to his full stature, curling his whiskers, stroking his beard, and looking down upon him with inexpressible loftiness through his lack lustre eyes. There was no doubting the word of so grave and ceremonious a hidalgo.

Don Fernando now arrayed himself in gala attire. He would have launched his boat, and gone on shore with his own men, but he was informed the barge of state was expressly provided for his accommodation, and, after the fête, would bring him back to his ship; in which, on the following day, he might enter the harbor in befitting style. He accordingly stepped into the barge, and took his seat beneath the awning. The grand chamberlain seated himself on the cushion opposite. The rowers bent to their oars, and renewed their mournful old ditty, and the gorgeous, but unwieldy barge moved slowly and solemnly through the water.

The night closed in, before they entered the river. They swept along, past rock and promontory, each guarded by its tower. The sentinels at every post challenged them as they passed by.

"Who goes there?"

"The Adelantado of the Seven Cities."

"He is welcome. Pass on."

On entering the harbor, they rowed close along an armed galley, of the most ancient form. Soldiers with cross bows were stationed on the deck.

"Who goes there?" was again demanded.

"The Adelantado of the Seven Cities."

"He is welcome. Pass on."

They landed at a broad flight of stone steps, leading up, between two massive towers, to the water-gate of the city, at which they knocked for admission. A sentinel, in an ancient steel casque, looked over the wall. "Who is there?"

"The Adelantado of the Seven Cities."

The gate swung slowly open, grating upon its rusty hinges. They entered between two rows of iron-clad warriors, in battered armour, with cross-bows, battle-axes, and ancient maces, and with faces as old fashioned and rusty as their armour. They saluted Don Fernando in military style, but with perfect silence, as he passed between their ranks. The city was illuminated, but in such manner as to give a more shadowy and solemn effect to its old time architecture. There were bonfires in the principal streets, with groups about them in such old fashioned garbs, that they looked like the fantastic figures that roam the streets in carnival time. Even the stately dames who gazed from the balconies, which they had hung with antique tapestry, looked more like effigies dressed up for a quaint mummery, than like ladies in their fashionable attire. Every thing, in short, bore the stamp of former ages, as if the world had suddenly rolled back a few centuries. Nor was this to be wondered at. Had not the Island of the Seven Cities been for several hundred years cut off from all communication with the rest of the world, and was it not natural that the inhabitants should retain many of the modes and customs brought here by their ancestors?

One thing certainly they had conserved; the old-fashioned Spanish gravity and stateliness. Though this was a time of public rejoicing, and though Don Fernando was the object of their gratulations, every thing was conducted with the most solemn ceremony, and wherever he appeared, instead of acclamations, he was received with profound silence, and the most formal reverences and swayings of their sombreros.

Arrived at the palace of the Alcayde, the usual ceremonial was repeated. The chamberlain knocked for admission.

"Who is there?" demanded the porter.

"The Adelantado of the Seven Cities."

"He is welcome. Pass on."

The grand portal was thrown open. The chamberlain led the way up a vast but heavily moulded marble stair case, and so through one of those interminable suites of apartments, that are the pride of Spanish palaces. All were furnished in a style of obsolete magnificence. As they passed through the chambers, the title of Don Fernando was forwarded on by servants stationed at every door; and every where produced the most profound reverences and courtesies. At length they reached a magnificent saloon, blazing with tapers, in which the Alcayde, and the principal dignitaries of the city, were waiting to receive their illustrious guest. The grand chamberlain presented Don Fernando in due form, and falling back among the other officers of the household, stood as usual curling his whiskers and stroking his forked beard.

Don Fernando was received by the Alcayde and the other dignitaries with the same stately and formal courtesy that he had every where remarked. In fact, there was so much form and ceremonial, that it seemed difficult to get at any thing social or substantial. Nothing but bows, and compliments, and old-fashioned courtesies. The Alcayde and his courtiers resembled, in face and form, those quaint worthies to be seen in the pictures of old illuminated manuscripts; while the cavaliers and dames who thronged the saloon, might have beep taken for the antique figures of gobelin tapestry suddenly vivified and put in motion.

The banquet, which had been kept back until the arrival of Don Fernando, was now announced; and such a feast! such unknown dishes and obsolete dainties; with the peacock, that bird of state and ceremony, served up in full plumage, in a golden dish, at the head of the table. And then, as Don Fernando cast his eyes over the glittering board, what a vista of odd heads and head dresses, of formal bearded dignitaries, and stately dames, with castellated locks and towering plumes!

As fate would have it, on the other side of Don Fernando, was seated the daughter of the Alcayde. She was arrayed, it is true, in a dress that might have been worn before the flood; but then, she had a melting black Andalusian eye, that was perfectly irresistible. Her voice, too, her manner, her movements, all smacked of Andalusia, and showed how female fascination may be transmitted from age to age, and clime to clime, without ever losing its power, or going out of fashion. Those who know the witchery of the sex, in that most amorous region of old Spain, may judge what must have been the fascination to which Don Fernando was exposed, when seated beside one of the most captivating of its descendants. He was, as has already been hinted, of an inflammable temperament; with a heart ready to get in a light blaze at every instant. And then he had been so wearied by pompous, tedious old cavaliers, with their formal bows and speeches; is it to be wondered at that he turned with delight to the Alcayde's daughter, all smiles, and dimples, and melting looks, and melting accents? Beside, for I wish to give him every excuse in my power, he was in a particularly excitable mood, from the novelty of the scene before him, and his head was almost turned with this sudden and complete realization of all his hopes and fancies; and then, in the flurry of the moment, he had taken frequent draughts at the wine cup, presented him at every instant by officious pages, and all the world knows the effect of such draughts in giving potency to female charms. In a word, there is no concealing the matter, the banquet was not half over, before Don Fernando was making love, outright, to the Alcayde's daughter. It was his cold habitude, contracted long before his matrimonial engagement. The young lady hung her head coyly; her eye rested upon a ruby heart, sparkling in a ring on the hand of Don Fernando, a parting gage of love from Serafina. A blush crimsoned her very temples. She darted a glance of doubt at the ring, and then at Don Fernando. He read her doubt, and in the giddy intoxication of the moment, drew off the pledge of his affianced bride, and slipped it on the finger of the Alcayde's daughter.

At this moment the banquet broke up. The chamberlain with his lofty demeanor, and his lack lustre eyes, stood before him, and announced that the barge was waiting to conduct him back to the caravel. Don Fernando took a formal leave of the Alcayde and his dignitaries, and a tender farewell of the Alcayde's daughter, with a promise to throw himself at her feet on the following day. He was rowed back to his vessel in the same slow and stately manner, to the cadence of the same mournful old ditty. He retired to his cabin, his brain whirling with all that he had seen, and his heart now and then giving him a twinge as he recollected his temporary infidelity to the beautiful Serafina. He flung himself on his bed, and soon fell into a feverish sleep. His dreams were wild and incoherent. How long he slept he knew not, but when he awoke he found himself in a strange cabin, with persons around him of whom he had no knowledge. He rubbed his eyes to ascertain whether he were really awake. In reply to his inquiries, he was informed that he was on board of a Portuguese ship, bound to Lisbon; having been taken senseless from a wreck drifting about the ocean.

Don Fernando was confounded and perplexed. He retraced every thing distinctly that had happened to him in the Island of the Seven Cities, and until he had retired to rest on board of the caravel. Had his vessel been driven from her anchors, and wrecked during his sleep? The people about him could give him no information on the subject. He talked to them of the Island of the Seven Cities, and of all that had befallen him there. They regarded his words as the ravings of delirium, and in their honest solicitude, administered such rough remedies, that he was fain to drop the subject, and observe a cautious taciturnity.

At length they arrived in the Tagus, and anchored before the famous city of Lisbon. Don Fernando sprang joyfully on shore, and hastened to his ancestral mansion. To his surprise, it was inhabited by strangers; and when he asked about his family, no one could give him any information concerning them.

He now sought the mansion of Don Ramiro, for the temporary flame kindled by the bright eyes of the Alcayde's daughter had long since burnt itself out, and his genuine passion for Serafina had revived with all its fervor. He approached the balcony, beneath which he had so often serenaded her. Did his eyes deceive him? No! There was Serafina herself at the balcony. An exclamation of rapture burst from him, as he raised his arms toward her. She cast upon him a look of indignation, and hastily retiring, closed the casement. Could she have heard of his flirtation with the Alcayde's daughter? He would soon dispel every doubt of his constancy. The door was open. He rushed up stairs, and entering the room, threw himself at her feet. She shrank back with affright, and took refuge in the arms of a youthful cavalier.

"What mean you, Sir," cried the latter, "by this intrusion?"

"What right have you," replied Don Fernando, "to ask the question?"

"The right of an affianced suitor!"

Don Fernando started, and turned pale. "Oh, Serafina! Serafina!" cried he in a tone of agony, "is this thy plighted constancy?"

"Serafina?—what mean you by Serafina? If it be this young lady you intend, her name is Maria."

"Is not this Serafina Alvarez, and is not that her portrait?" cried Don Fernando, pointing to a picture of his mistress.

"Holy Virgin!" cried the young lady; "he is talking of my great-grandmother!"

An explanation ensued, if that could be called an explanation, which plunged the unfortunate Fernando into tenfold perplexity. If he might believe his eyes, he saw before him his beloved Serafina; if he might believe his ears, it was merely her hereditary form and features, perpetuated in the person of her great-granddaughter.

His brain began to spin. He sought the office of the Minister of Marine, and made a report of his expedition, and of the Island of the Seven Cities, which he had so fortunately discovered. No body knew any thing of such an expedition, or such an island. He declared that he had undertaken the enterprise under a formal contract with

the crown, and had received a regular commission, constituting him
Adelantado. This must be matter of record, and he insisted loudly,
that the books of the department should be consulted. The wordy
strife at length attracted the attention of an old, grey headed clerk,
who sat perched on a high stool, at a high desk, with iron rimmed
spectacles on the top of a thin, pinched nose, copying records into an
enormous folio. He had wintered and summered in the department
for a great part of a century, until he had almost grown to be a piece
of the desk at which he sat; his memory was a mere index of official
facts and documents, and his brain was little better than red tape
and parchment. After peering down for a time from his lofty perch,
and ascertaining the matter in controversy, he put his pen behind
his ear, and descended. He remembered to have heard something
from his predecessor about an expedition of the kind in question, but
then it had sailed during the reign of Don Ioam II, and he had been
dead at least a hundred years. To put the matter beyond dispute,
however, the archives of the Torve do Tombo, that sepulchre of old
Portuguese documents, were diligently searched, and a record was
found of a contract between the crown and one Fernando de Ulmo,
for the discovery of the Island of the Seven Cities, and of a commission
secured to him as Adelantado of the country he might discover.

"There!" cried Don Fernando, triumphantly, "there you have proof,
before your own eyes, of what I have said. I am the Fernando de Ulmo
specified in that record. I have discovered the Island of the Seven
Cities, and am entitled to be Adelantado, according to contract."

The story of Don Fernando had certainly, what is pronounced
the best of historical foundation, documentary evidence; but when
a man, in the bloom of youth, talked of events that had taken place
above a century previously, as having happened to himself, it is no
wonder that he was set down for a mad man.

The old clerk looked at him from above and below his spectacles, shrugged his shoulders, stroked his chin, reascended his lofty stool, took the pen from behind his ears, and resumed his daily and eternal task, copying records into the fiftieth volume of a series of gigantic folios. The other clerks winked at each other shrewdly, and dispersed to their several places, and poor Don Fernando, thus left to himself, flung out of the office, almost driven wild by these repeated perplexities.

In the confusion of his mind, he instinctively repaired to the mansion of Alvarez, but it was barred against him. To break the delusion under which the youth apparently laboured, and to convince him that the Serafina about whom he raved was really dead, he was conducted to her tomb. There she lay, a stately matron, cut out in alabaster; and there lay her husband beside her; a portly cavalier, in armor; and there knelt, on each side, the effigies of a numerous progeny, proving that she had been a fruitful vine. Even the very monument gave proof of the lapse of time, for the hands of her husband, which were folded as if in prayer, had lost their fingers, and the face of the once lovely Serafina was noseless.

Don Fernando felt a transient glow of indignation at beholding this monumental proof of the inconstancy of his mistress; but who could expect a mistress to remain constant during a whole century of absence? And what right had he to rail about constancy, after what had passed between him and the Alcayde's daughter? The unfortunate cavalier performed one pious act of tender devotion; he had the alabaster nose of Serafina restored by a skilful statuary, and then tore himself from the tomb.

He could now no longer doubt the fact that, somehow or other, he had skipped over a whole century, during the night he had spent at the Island of the Seven Cities; and he was now as complete a stranger in his native city, as if he had never been there. A thousand times did he wish himself back to that wonderful island, with its antiquated banquet halls, where he had been so courteously received; and now that the once young and beautiful Serafina was nothing but a great-grandmother in marble, with generations of descendants, a thousand times would he recall the melting black eyes of the Alcayde's daughter, who doubtless, like himself, was still flourishing in fresh juvenility, and breathe a secret wish that he were seated by her side.

He would at once have set on foot another expedition, at his own expense, to cruise in search of the sainted island, but his means were exhausted. He endeavored to rouse others to the enterprise, setting forth the certainty of profitable results, of which his own experience furnished such unquestionable proof. Alas! no one would give faith to his tale; but looked upon it as the feverish dream of a shipwrecked man. He persisted in his efforts; holding forth in all places and all companies, until he became an object of jest and jeer to the light-minded, who mistook his earnest enthusiasm for a proof of insanity; and the very children in the streets bantered him with the title of "The Adelantado of the Seven Cities."

Finding all his efforts in vain, in his native city of Lisbon, he took shipping for the Canaries, as being nearer the latitude of his former cruise, and inhabited by people given to nautical adventure. Here he found ready listeners to his story; for the old pilots and mariners of those parts were notorious island hunters and devout believers in all the wonders of the seas. Indeed, one and all treated his adventure as a common occurrence, and turning to each other, with a sagacious nod of the head, observed, "He has been at the Island of St. Brandan."

They then went on to inform him of that great marvel and enigma of the ocean; of its repeated appearance to the inhabitants of their islands; and of the many but ineffectual expeditions that had been made in search of it. They took him to a promontory of the island of Palma, from whence the shadowy St. Brandan had oftenest been descried, and they pointed out the very tract in the west where its mountains had been seen.

Don Fernando listened with rapt attention. He had no longer a doubt that this mysterious and fugacious island must be the same with that of the Seven Cities; and that there must be some supernatural influence connected with it, that had operated upon himself, and made the events of a night occupy the space of a century.

He endeavored, but in vain, to rouse the islanders to another attempt at discovery; they had given up the phantom island as indeed inaccessible. Fernando, however, was not to be discouraged. The idea wore itself deeper and deeper in his mind, until it became the engrossing subject of his thoughts and object of his being. Every morning he would repair to the promontory of Palma, and sit there throughout the live-long day, in hopes of seeing the fairy mountains of St. Brandan peering above the horizon; every evening he returned to his home, a disappointed man, but ready to resume his post on the following morning.

His assiduity was all in vain. He grew grey in his ineffectual attempt; and was at length found dead at his post. His grave is still shown in the island of Palma, and a cross is erected on the spot where he used to sit and look out upon the sea, in hopes of the reappearance of the enchanted island.